'A dark-dazzling archive of enchantments, pursuit, and desire' Eley Williams

'This is the most adventurous, stylistically magnificent thing I've read for years. Nobody does fantasy like Zoe Gilbert' Natasha Pulley

'A deeply lyrical, century-spanning polyphony of voices; a dazzling new take on an ancient myth, reminding us of the wildness within. I adored it' Kerry Andrew

'*Mischief Acts* is brimming with magic – full of wild hunts, river spirits and revelry. The story of Herne, like the forest itself, transforms, entangles and enchants' Lucy Wood

'Superb. A work of shimmering allure. By turns beguiling and mercurial, Gilbert takes British folklore to new heights' Irenosen Okojie

BY THE SAME AUTHOR

Folk

ZOE GILBERT'S debut novel *Folk* was shortlisted for the Dylan Thomas Prize and named an *Observer* Book of the Year. *Folk* was also adapted for BBC Radio 4 and is the basis for a forthcoming song cycle. She is the winner of the Costa Short Story Award 2014, and her work has appeared in anthologies and journals in the UK and internationally. She is a Senior Visiting Fellow at the university of Suffolk English department, and is the co-founder of London Lit Lab, where she teaches and mentors writers. Zoe Gilbert lives on the coast in Kent.

zoegilbert.com
@mindandlanguage

MISCHIEF ACTS

ZOE GILBERT

BLOOMSBURY PUBLISHING
LONDON • OXFORD • NEW YORK • NEW DELHI • SYDNEY

BLOOMSBURY PUBLISHING
Bloomsbury Publishing Plc
50 Bedford Square, London, WC1B 3DP, UK
29 Earlsfort Terrace, Dublin 2, Ireland

BLOOMSBURY, BLOOMSBURY PUBLISHING and
the Bloomsbury Circus logo are trademarks of
Bloomsbury Publishing Plc

First published in Great Britain 2022
This edition published 2023

A catalogue record for this book is
available from the British Library

ISBN: PB: 978-1-5266-2879-4; EBOOK: 978-1-5266-2881-7;
EPDF: 978-1-5266-4540-1

2 4 6 8 10 9 7 5 3

Typeset by Marsha Swan (www.iota-books.ie)
Printed and bound in Great Britain by CPI Group (UK) Ltd,
Croydon CR0 4YY

To find out more about our authors and books visit
www.bloomsbury.com and sign up for our newsletters

For Richard, Finn and Max, boys in the wood

CONTENTS

PART II: DISENCHANTMENT

PART III: RE-ENCHANTMENT

Stray-singer, long have you lacked these songs. Learn them again, understand them, and do some good.

INTRODUCTION

Our memories, and therefore our sense of self, are rooted in time and space. The narratives we spin from these memories determine our identities, the folklore of our selves. We are mutable: we become, respond and transform. The same is true of myth.

The episodes related below reveal the trials and triumphs of one myth through time and ever-shifting space. We follow Herne the Hunter, whose time began (in one version of his myth, at least) around the fourteenth century, and whose space was the Great North Wood, a forest that covered a swathe of what became South London. As we will see, it was not just his physical environs that changed: a wood neglected, broken up by Enclosure Acts, eventually shrunk down to scraps of park and railway verges. Herne the Hunter's cultural context has been just as volatile.

Before magical thinking was pitted against scientific rationalism, there was plenty of room for a rascally psychopomp like Herne. Enchantment was not, back then, a dubious state of mind relegated to dreamers and readers of fairy tales. But the Enlightenment awaited, and the scientific and industrial revolutions awoke us to new comforts, both cerebral and practical. Everything could be known by calculation, it turned out; and anything that could not was devoid of meaning. Some, following Max Weber, have called our progress from magical thinking to materialism and scientific advancement the 'disenchantment of the world'. As Keats had it, such philosophy will 'unweave a rainbow'. Myth faced a rough ride.

Organised religion, not much more compatible with science, was no help to a myth such as Herne the Hunter either. For Herne embodies a kind of mischief that fails to count as 'good' in a traditional sense. Mischief used to have a nastier meaning: malevolent harm, even wickedness. Obviously, this was ungodly, and soon forbidden. But the meaning has mellowed through time, so that while the mischief-maker now may well be reckless, roguish, irresponsible to the point of causing harm, they may also be merry, passionate, full of glee. Still more full-blooded than 'antics', mischief might be seen as a particularly risky way of letting off steam – in fact, the riskiness feels essential. To bend or break the rules, to transgress social expectations, can be enjoyable, but it can also allow us to test ourselves, to find the edge and balance there, thrilling to be alive. There remains ambivalence about this kind of mischief. Consider once more the woods, Herne's dominion and the space beyond civilisation, a danger zone where we can shake off the rules, carouse and fight and fuck. We leave the imprints of illicit fires, graffiti, tyre marks and detritus. These are not always welcome, but they are signs of life. Mischief has always been made in the wood.

Herne has contended with many changes: his shrinking Great North Wood, a swiftly mutating culture, time that seems to fly ever faster through new and better ways to live. His identity, his existence, might have been in jeopardy, had he not a multitude of counterparts, whose guises he might revive and borrow. Poke around in western and eastern Europe, Scandinavia and beyond, and you will find them. Herne's tangled thread snags on such woodland tricksters as Puck, Robin Goodfellow, even Robin Hood. It binds him to every tale of the Wild Hunt and its throng of leaders, from Odin to Holda, Gwyn ap Nudd and even Frau Gaude. His thread is spun from the fibres of so many horned gods – Cernunnos, Pan and Dionysus – and loops right through the Horned God archetype of Jungian psychology. He is tied to the chthonic wild man, the Green Man, Oberon and more nefarious forest spirits such as the Erl-king. He is stitched into the chequered cloth of Harlequin; he patterns King Herla's finery.

Sometimes the names themselves give away the overlapping identities: Herne, Hellekin, Harlequin, Erl-king. Sometimes it is the horns these counterparts wear; their hunting habits; their tendencies to usher away the dead or to usher in trouble. While each of their individual narratives has been embroidered by places and zeitgeists, their connecting thread always leads us into, and through, the forest. If Herne can alter almost everything about himself, as he remakes himself through time, one aspect remains: he is never indoors. He is charging around, stealing, tricking, seducing, magicking, and it's in the wood that he's up to no good.

In the twenty-first century, as we settled into the age of technology, the disenchantment of the world was already old news. Calls rang out for re-enchantment. They were concurrent with calls for rewilding – a return to respect, if not reverence, for nature. This was no coincidence. We might expect a myth such as Herne the Hunter, so inextricably bound to the forest, to take advantage of this turn. Wildness is more than nature run riot. Like enchantment, it is a state of mind, and one that allows, even begets, mischief.

Professor Lizbet Gore
Trevone College, 2021

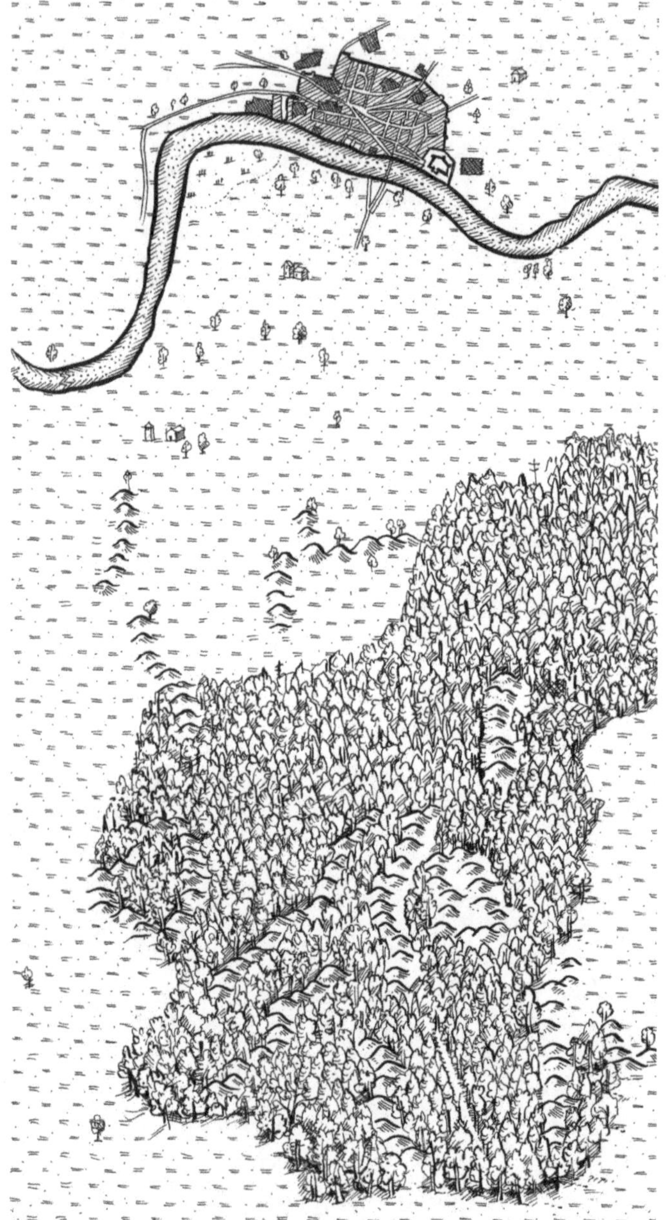

PART I
ENCHANTMENT

MOSS SONG

Many-seasoned, green spur,
Shaded-wood grows.
Golden head, rufous beard,
Whip fork shows.

Summer moss
Between your toes.

Starry earth, woodsy silk,
Luminous grows.
Bright green cave, green pocket,
Pointed spear goes.

Blue dew moss
Between your toes.

Tongue-leaved copper, rugged collar,
Dapple-mouthed crows.

Foxtail-feather, rusty swan-neck,
Crookneck nodding grows.

Green yoke moss
Between your toes.

Starry hoar, glittering wood,
Black tufted shows.
Archangelic, slender silver,
Heart-leaved spear knows.

Carrion moss
Between your toes.

H. B.

1

HERNE THE HUNTER
1392

Charm: If a hanged man swinging from a tree I see, this is the song to bring him down and have him speak to me.

As in a dream, he woke.
He told us this. It was as if he dreamed.
A kind of fever, it seemed, a terror –
Or a chill delight, to watch, as we did, the great white
 stag, silver in that magic hour –
The hour before night –
To watch it leap, almost fly, a great horned angel,
A demon, becoming, the dreadful churn of hooves as
 it charged –
Charged our king.
Why was our king not on horseback?
He had slipped down to rest, to cool his heated thighs.
He had seen our man, before the rest of us, and wished
 to greet him.

Dickie, the kind king, friend to all, had seen our man, his favourite hunter,
Prized most of all, Herne the head hunter,
Whose absence that day had put us in gleeful mood.
For Dickie might have eyes for us, with Herne left at home.
He might see us, nimble, swift,
Ruthless, full of grace, in the hunt,
Without the shadow of Herne casting us all into the dark.
He was not such a fine hunter.
But fine in Dickie's eyes.
And Dickie King. A king is sacred.
Perhaps the stag knew this, horned angel, then demon,
A silver charge across that leafy space, brown and gold in sideways dropping sun that made us squint,
Made us see but not see,
Dickie raise a great, powerful arm,
In greeting to Herne, who was suddenly upon us, having snuck out to the wood.
In greeting to the stag, which was suddenly upon him, having leapt from the wood.
We saw, but did not see,
Herne's leap.
Like a dark stag,
A shadow stag,
Betwixt –
Betwixt king and crown of antlers.
A crown not meant for our kind king.
Meant for Herne.

An act of brave self-sacrifice.
An act. He would be most beloved, not just as hunter,
but as saviour.
Cunning martyr.
As if we all dreamt it, standing with our eyes wide open,
Herne took the blow.
A sickening tear of cloth and flesh,
Leather hanging loose, and innard,
The stag rearing, turning, a miracle of strength,
rebuked,
And soon only a trail of silver,
Like smoke, gone through the trees.
Did Herne cry out, when he fell?
We heard and did not hear.
For it was Dickie's shout, that rang out:
Beloved Herne!
All our stomachs turned at the one torn, and spilling,
now, on the ground at the king's feet.
As he bent close, breath steaming,
It mingled with the steam of Herne, that rose up,
Almost as if his soul –
Some of the men sped after the stag, headlong,
Heads bent as they went under branches.
And while Herne gasped,
And Dickie gaped,
Breathing one another's steam,
We heard the shouts, in the wood,
And we heard the hoot, the shriek.
He's ours, they called.
We'd missed it. The chance of victory.

The chance to take Herne's place, that was.
For we saw how he was fading,
His fingers all mired in the purple-brown that spilled,
And the king's open mouth.
That was when Bearman came.
Bearman, whose magic sours the wood.
Bearman, whose sour countenance pleases no man.
No reason why a sorcerer should be near a hunt,
But here he came, from among the trees, his eyes as wild as his mount's.
The scene before him as if on a stage,
A stricken king, his finest hunter laid out,
Almost gone,
Honour and horror all in the air.
Bearman rode near and bent to Dickie's ear.
A strange look came upon the king's face.
He could not grow more pale, then, for he was white as the stag already,
And he nodded, and gazed at Bearman with awe.
With fear.
This is our king. If it was fear, it was not for long.
Lift him, he ordered us, and pointed.
From my cloak, we made a kind of sling.
It had been a fine cloak, sacrificed. We lifted Herne in,
Without even a groan, for he knew not what we did, nor any of the world around him now.
One at head, one at foot, we carried him, following Bearman.
The light was sluggish by then. Dusk was nearly upon us,
So the gleam of the stag where it lay stood out against the greying leaves.

That splendid cloak, we then must tear and use to bind Herne's middle,
To stop the spillage.
A foul job, but we were as if in a dream, in the darkening wood,
Which was quiet, as if it honoured the king's grief.
Yet he did not hang his head.
His look was wild, as if the hunt were on and he sighted his prey, seeing that he might win it.
He was watching Bearman,
Who stood at the stag's head,
Small beside that beast.
Angel.
Demon.
Bearman raised an axe,
Swung it down without a sound,
Except the crack, the crunch,
As he hacked the antlers off.
Did the king not want that fine head for his hall?
Revenge for his favourite hunter, dead.
He only nodded, with that fevered look, then, *stand back*, he said,
As Bearman dragged the antlers, one by one.
He laid them beside Herne.
Not beside, but at his head.
It was hard not to see, in the mind's eye –
What might be. It was hard to believe we did not dream.
Dickie, our stricken king, muttered at Herne's feet.
A prayer?
The wood darkened yet.

It was hard to see what Bearman did, his hands working fast. Lifting Herne at the neck, binding,
Drawing the antlers in close and tight,
Winding, some tattered stuff,
Not rope, not cloth,
So that Herne's head grew, his brow dark and deep,
The king muttering.
Bearman paused to swig from a flask which he then held high.
Offering it to the king, we thought,
But no. Bearman poured from the flask some black water.
It splashed on the antlers, the only things that showed white now in the gloom.
Then he poured again,
Into Herne's mouth,
Into his own,
And with his swallow made a choking noise,
We thought.
But no.
It was Herne who choked.
The king stumbled back.
He rested one heavy palm on my shoulder. I felt the hard grip, and his noble weight as he leaned.
Herne grimaced.
Herne opened his eyes.

Where was Bearman, then?
For it was the king who went to Herne, reached to clasp.

It's me, Dickie, he said.
My Herne, you live.

When Herne walked, he swayed a little. Groggy,
But it was the weight he carried,
Those horns.
Like a walking tree, he seemed, swaying in a light wind,
Nearly twice the height of our king, now.
A spiked man.
A man-stag.
You'll get used to it, Dickie said. He put an arm about Herne's shoulders,
Who had my cloak still bound about his middle,
Who had the king's eye,
His love,
Who glanced back at us,
And smiled.
Or seemed to. There was little light to see as the king led us, careful of low branches, out of the wood.
It is as if I dream, Herne said. He raised a hand, to touch –
To touch his new crown. But Dickie, kind king, took that hand in his own,
And on his own weary feet, all the way without a mount,
He led Herne home.

*

Get used to it? We did,
And we did not. But a king is sacred, so we kept our smirks to ourselves.
We spoke to Herne, when it was called for, as if he was just as before.
And in a way, he was. Still the king's favourite hunter,
The best hunter, in Dickie's eyes,
But more precious, now.
And more dangerous.
He knocked lit candles from their sconces.
Ripped a gauzy hanging from its pole.
The ladies ogled. One, a flimsy maiden, swooned upon a stone floor.
I saw the bruise, blue, nasty. But Herne laughed.
Oh, he was in fine spirits, those first few days.
The ladies giggled, became flighty, noisy.
We heard the patter of their hurrying feet, whispers, squeals.
We heard worse.
The moans of that flimsy maiden when Herne took her to his room.
The scrape of antler on stone above his bed.
The marks are still there.
Did the king hear?
Most likely.
Most likely he was pleased. He hid his own queen in the royal bed for hours on end,
And ravenous, feasted on venison.
Every day, venison,
And jug upon jug of wine.

It was, those first few days, a very festival.
Herne hailed.
Herne toasted.
Ladies wide-eyed,
Or narrow-eyed, at the flimsy maiden bouncing in
Herne's lap.
But meat stays good to eat only a few days.
The rest of the stag was salted and packed for the winter,
And the king declared himself hungry again.
Not for meat, or his queen, but for the hunt.

We did wonder, how Herne would fare.
Not swaying any more, but still, weighed down,
And almost twice the height he was before.

When the day came, the clouds hung low.
Would he catch those spikes in them, become tangled
as in cobweb?
A childish jest, among many.
Yes, but we wondered, for he was, now,
Unwieldy.

We all set out, with the ladies waving, blowing kisses,
All eyes on Herne,
And most of all, the king's.

*

Herne's skill lay in tracking,
In trapping by sly manoeuvre.

He had, perhaps, a hound's scent,
A hare's keen ear,
For he had seemed, in his prime, to see right through both broad oak and undergrowth to his quarry.
He had always been sure.
That sullen day, he rode ahead, so high on his horse he was like a god of the forest.
Not for long.
Though long and cruel that morning felt, as we followed him now this way, now that.
By noon, the horses hung their heads.
Dickie's cheer grew false, then fell away.
We saw how he gazed at Herne in angst,
A spurned lover, almost.
He was our king. Kind Dickie, hiding his temper,
While Herne grew first bewildered, then ashamed,
And soon after that, full of wrath.
We stood in a great clearing, then, Herne turning in our midst,
Eyeing each of us as we backed away.
We each shook our heads.
We'd seen no stag, either.
No hind, no boar, no slinking wolf.
But we were not leading.
We were not the king's darling,
As it were,
We were not horned men, given the strength of that beast in order to live again.
For this is surely what had befallen Herne.
Some magick in Bearman's tattered binding.

He fell, he rose.
We'd seen it.
And now, back in the wood, shadowless under that
heavy cloud,
He fell again.
Not to the ground, this time,
But we did see, there was no doubting it,
Dickie's great arm raised,
The noble hand pointing Herne towards home,
And to go alone.
John will lead now, he said.

*

Boar, roasting. Stuffed with apples and juniper,
That perfume filled the passages, the courtyard,
It filled our mouths and the mouths of the quiet ladies,
All waiting,
All gathering, very late, in the hall, at the king's pleasure,
To eat, to drink.
We were not merry.
Though some secret smile seemed to catch amongst the
men as the king stood, wiping his full and shining lips,
Glancing to his left, at Herne's empty chair.
I learned, this day, he said.
He paused to drink.
*That high skill is a gift from God. And one he can take
away*.
He drank again, a deep draught.
God did not make man with horns. He tried a laugh.

A lady tittered.
He has punished us. I humbly offer Him my apology.
He bent low,
But only briefly, for then he raised his cup.
The role of royal huntsman, leader of our troop, I offer,
He grinned,
To John.
We roared, as required.
But it was a low roar, a rumble of thunder.
We clashed cups and drank.
The candles in their high black sconces flickered,
And the flimsy maiden, shivering, fled the room.
Did she go to speak with Herne? Or did she already know,
What we found out, next morning?

We ourselves did not see –
Though it was hard not to, in the mind's eye –
The antlers reaching from the tree,
The Great Oak, shrouded in mist, that chill evening,
The antlers reaching through the mist,
And from the Great Oak's broadest branch,
Herne, hanging.
Herne, hanged.

*

A week passed.
The king was hungry.
John, solemn in his new part,

In his new cloak, stitched with a motif of antlers,
Led the first hunt. We passed the Great Oak in silence.
In silence, we returned,
John red-faced,
The king white,
The strained white of fury.

Curlitt was next to lead the hunt.
Ormandon was next.
Robert was –
No better.
Kind Dickie was kind no longer.
We heard,
And we did not hear,
The queen's wails in the royal chamber,
The whispers amongst the ladies where they hid,
Refusing to consort,
For they believed,
Truly,
It was a curse.

Bearman broke the silence first.
Coming from where, we knew not,
For he had kept himself hidden, tucked away with
his magick,
Out of the king's accusing sight.
He slipped into the courtyard –
It was a moonless night –
And gathered about him John, Curlitt, Ormandon,
Robert.

We saw,
And did not see, it being a moonless, thick-dark night,
Their shaking heads,
As he said, *You all must act. Herne was too strong. He has shared his curse.*
But this magick was down to you, they hissed. *We only wished to take our turn, at leading the hunt.*
His laugh was a raven's,
Black.
You will all take a turn, yes, you will take turn upon turn, through the forest, following Herne.
Herne is dead, they said.
Bearman stepped closer to them, said, *It is the only way.*
We hurried away then,
Wanting no part in these dark doings,
Wanting the curse to spread no further.
But we had wished it, too.
We both had wished it.
We had longed for a hunt that would show us truly. Nimble, swift,
Ruthless, full of grace, in the hunt.
We had wished for bad luck,
For Herne,
For a fall. But not –
We thought of the tattered stuff that Bearman wound about Herne's head.
We thought of the collar of hanging cord Herne wound about his neck.
We began to run, as far from the courtyard –
Out, past the kitchen to the hovels,

There to hide, in shame.
To tell ourselves we had not heard a word, that night.
Bearman was waiting.
You too, he said. The raven laugh. *If you wish to hunt again.*
The stables, both of you.
We walked, his cold hands to the backs of our necks.
His cold fingers sending ice down to our hearts.
We roused the horses.
We roused the hounds.
All our beasts were horribly ready, raring, despite the hour,
Mouths frothing, feet pawing.
But all the men, dour.
John, Curlitt, Ormandon, Robert and the rest.
Curlitt snarled. Robert turned his back,
When Bearman swung the stable door wide.
The Great Oak, he said. *Or forever be made fools before your king.*
John's horse reared up. *For my skill*, he cried, *and so be it.*
The hounds led the way, into the night.

*

As if in a nightmare, Herne stood.
He filled the wood with a kind of glamour,
Made his own moon, to light that demon crown of his,
To light the length of rope that trailed still, from his neck.
The hounds huddled down. Herne crooned to them,

To our mounts,
And to us, in our nightmare, said –
In a hoarse whisper that deafened,
A whisper that filled with dread –
The hunt is on.
All night, we would ride.
All beasts, we would find and slaughter.
We would trample the plantings,
Slash the saplings,
Stamp down hedges and break the runnel's bridges.
We would wreck the king's wood.
Wreck ourselves.

Herne, the king's angel of the hunt, now demon.
Herne. Antlered, magicked from the Great Oak,
Dead and risen, dead and risen once more.
It was Robert who spoke.
Friend, he said. *This is Bearman's curse. Let us take it up with him. May you rest –*
We heard the raven's caw, in the Great Oak's branches.
We heard Herne's laugh, too long, too cold.
The hunt is on, he said.
And so it was.

*

Hag-ridden, we are.
Haggard.
We stand before you, kind king,
And you see our despair,

Our regret.
You see the mingled blood on our hands, our own and the blood of beasts.
Beasts we have been,
We admit,
We regret.
Kind king, friend to all, we had no choice.
For fervently, we wish to serve you,
And how do we serve you?
With our skill in the hunt.
And with our skill, restored, we throw ourselves upon your mercy.
We beg to be used in pursuit of stag, or hind, or boar,
Or slinking wolf.
We beg to be forgiven, for the damage done,
The plantings trampled,
The saplings slashed,
The hedges stamped,
And runnel bridges broken.
For the heap of bodies,
Beast bodies,
Here beneath the Great Oak.
We beseech you, do not –
We ask you, kind Dickie, sacred king, do not –
We beg for our lives.
Here hang John, and Curlitt, and Ormandon, and Robert.
Here also hanged was Herne.
Five men, fine hunters.
Herne finest of all.

We cannot match them, true.
But we have given our true account, and hidden
nothing.
Bearman hides yet, deep in his magick.
It is his confession you deserve.
Our envy was small. It moved us to no more than gossip.
But who offered magick?
Who bound Herne's head and made a god of him?
A monster?
Who summoned all your men, on a moonless night,
and wrought this ruin?
Spare us, kind Dickie.
Not the rope.
Angel, Dickie.
Demon king.

WHO LEADS THE WILD HUNT

a clapping rhyme

Who leads the Wild Hunt?

Ask the girls.

Is it
Holda?
Holle?
Berchta?
Frik?

Ride, and ride on.

Then is it
Wild Baba?
Hecate?
Frau Gaude?
Berchtli?

Ride, and ride on.

Then is it
Freya?
Diana?
Guro Rysserova?

Ride, and ride on forever. Go!

Who leads the Wild Hunt?

Ask the boys.

Is it
Herla?
Hellekin?
Odin?
Cain?

Ride, and ride on.

Then is it
Dando?
Annwn?
Old Nick?
Old Crockern?

Ride, and ride on.

Then is it
Derk with his little dogs?
Gait with his little dogs?
Henske with his little dogs?
Derk with his bear?

Ride, and ride on.

Then is it
Wild Edric?
Hereward the Wake?
St Guthlac?
Theodric the Great?

Ride, and ride on.

Then is it
King Arthur?
Manannan?
Gwyn ap Nudd?
Gwydion?

Ride, and ride on.

Then is it
The Devil?

Ride, and ride on forever,
Or you'll turn to dust!

Anon

2

OVERHEARD IN A GREENWOOD
1451

Charm: I know a song to stay your foes by making blunt their blades, and they shall not hurt you.

These days, it is not so curious to find, at a crossroads in the eastern reaches of the Great North Wood, a large cage hanging from an old oak tree. And in that cage, on this autumnal dawn, standing and watching the world go by, a woman. She is old, too; scrawny in parts and plump in others. There is something of the rat about her, with her ragged brown dress, her whiskery hair and long front teeth, which show because she is smiling. But this sight is curious enough for Jay, the young girl passing on the north–south path with her father, to dawdle, stare and drift to a halt.

The old woman's tongue pokes from her mouth. 'Not long now,' she says.

Jay scowls. She can smell urine, and the must of ancient bones.

'You'll come back and see.'

The girl's father has turned, and he reaches to grab her by the wrist. 'Mad as a basket of eels, that one,' he snarls. 'Come away.' He spits at the cage.

'What's she done wrong?' Jay asks. She is watching the woman, who caught the gob of spit in her palm and is now adding her own, swiftly stirring with her thumb.

'Just look at her, child. Wrong all over.'

As Jay's father drags her away, the gobbet comes flying and slaps the back of his neck.

'I'll give you wrong,' the old woman calls. 'May your hair all grow inwards.' She catches the girl's eye and winks.

As they hurry off along the path, Jay's father is already scratching at the back of his head.

In this part of the Great North Wood, up on the high ridge that runs along its eastern flank, the sun rises early. At the crossroads, where trees are sparse around the Great Oak, the old woman leans inside her cage and basks in the first low rays. It is her third morning, dangling there, and there is no denying the weakness in her limbs, the dryness in her throat. The birds are singing up a racket. A few rabbits dash about. A trickle of smoke drifts from a charcoal burner's kiln somewhere nearby.

It is not long before Jay returns. A little out of breath, she pants, 'Did you curse him?'

'If he thinks I did,' says the old woman. She is sitting with her back to the sun. They size each other up.

'What did you do? To end up in there.'

'Pleased to meet you, too.'

The girl squints in the sunlight. 'I'm Jay.'

'Well, if you'll fetch me some embers from that charcoal burner yonder, Jay, I'll tell you.'

'I've nothing to give him in return.'

'Tell him they're for Goody Bearman. Now be off.'

When the girl returns with the embers, the old woman is snoring softly. Jay sets about gathering twigs and stones to build a small fire – for what else could the embers be for – and it is soon spitting and crackling near the cage. She creeps close enough to prod the old woman's rump, but does not want to touch. 'Goody Bearman,' she shouts.

'Call me Agnes,' comes the grumbling reply.

Jay points at the fire. 'You owe me,' she says.

'Look at that.' The old woman struggles to her feet. The cage swings and groans. 'Think you can keep it going?'

'I'm supposed to be setting snares.'

'Jay, you're a useful thing. So, I don't mind telling you that I got up to a bit of mischief.'

'But why are you here? In there.' The girl reaches and gives the cage a little push. They both look up at the broad branch it hangs from, which is striped with use.

'Do you know, before this eyesore got rigged up, what made those marks upon the bough?'

'Was it you, Goody Bearman?'

'I said, call me Agnes. This is the very tree where Herne the Hunter hanged himself.' Her sigh is long.

Jay wrinkles her nose at the waft of ancient breath. 'Who's that?'

'Has your father taught you nothing? He's the leader of the Wild Hunt.' Agnes smiles, with pride, or memory.

But the girl shakes her head. 'No. The leader of the Wild Hunt is King Herla.'

'That's a nonsense story.' Agnes gives her a sharp look. 'I should know, if anyone does.'

'Why?' The girl sidles round the cage, closer, but Agnes is looking over her head, peering into the trees beyond the crossroads.

'It's not far, down the hill from here, to the Effra. Go and fetch me water, and I'll tell you how I know.'

'But I've no pot.'

'Well, I'll talk no more then. I'm parched through and through.' Agnes makes a loud croaking sound and slumps against the side of the cage.

'I'll be in trouble with my father.'

The croak turns to a hoarse laugh. 'You and me both.'

The shadow of the Great Oak shrinks, inch by inch. Dew mists up and away. Beneath the oak's frilly canopy, the cage is in shade by the time the girl returns, clanking an iron pot of river water. The little fire she set has dwindled to an ashy patch, and while the old woman dozes Jay darts about, finding sticks to build it up. She is placing large stones around the new licks of flame when Agnes speaks.

'I hope you said thanks for that.'

'I only borrowed it,' says Jay, not turning from her work.

'Not for the pot. For Effra's waters. You're a useful thing, but short of manners.'

'You're not so parched you can't tattle at me.'

When the fire is good enough to heat the pot, the girl stretches herself out on the dry ground and stares up at the cage. She can see the old woman's blotched calves, the blackened soles of her feet. 'My father's seen the Wild Hunt,' she says. 'He told me it's King Herla. He showed me the cave where the elf-king lives.'

Agnes rubs her head, and whiskery hairs float down. 'I suppose he told you that King Herla went to the elf-king's wedding feast in there. And the elf-king gave him parting gifts of hunting gear, everything from arrows to slathering hounds.'

'The cave is down by the spring,' says Jay. 'I touched the stone.'

'Aren't you a bold one. I suppose he told you the elf-king placed a hound in King Herla's lap, and told him and his men not to dismount until the hound had jumped down. A likely story.'

'He did say that. But then a hundred years had passed.'

'You're jumping ahead.' Agnes sniffs. 'So, off King Herla went, laden, and in the forest he greeted a charcoal burner. But the charcoal man didn't recognise him. He said there used to be a King Herla, two hundred years ago, but nobody knew what became of him.'

'You mean one hundred.'

'And that was when one of Herla's men got down from his horse, in his bewilderment. And I suppose your father told you what happened next.'

'When he touched the ground, the man turned to dust.'

'That's how the story goes. A curse. An unlikely one, if you ask me,' says Agnes.

The pot is beginning to steam.

'I bet you can't do a curse that strong,' says Jay, rolling on to her front. 'Is that why you're in there?'

'We all turn to dust in the end. Herla and all his furious men could have just taken a deep breath, jumped down from their horses and got it over with. It makes no sense to me that instead they'd go hurtling around on horseback, forever. And anyway, it's not true.'

'You're not going to tell me what you did, are you?'

Agnes runs her bony fingers along the cage. 'I'm aching all over. If you fetch me a herb to steep in that water, I'll tell you the whole truth.'

Jay jumps up. 'My father cuts willow bark, to help an ache.'

'Never mind that. I want something stronger.' Agnes's hand trembles as she points south along the ridge. 'Follow the path until it runs downhill. Look for a crowd of birch trees, and beyond them, a brackish pond. Pick the plant with the purple flowers like little hoods. I want it roots and all. As much as you can carry.'

'Is that heart's-ease?'

'Of a sort.'

'And then you'll tell?'

Agnes nods and slumps back down. 'No nibbling,' she calls, as Jay runs away along the path.

The clearing around the crossroads is quiet. The air is still, and nobody passes the Great Oak on their way through the wood. You might almost think it was under a spell, on this warm autumn afternoon. Wasps saunter between ivy flowers.

Hoverflies laze in a crowd above Agnes's head. A boar snuffling acorns nearby is startled away by the thumps of Jay's feet as she returns with her bundle of flowers. Her mouth is stained blue. She has been eating blackberries.

She wakes the old woman by thrusting a fistful of squashed fruit between the bars. 'Agnes? Aren't you hungry?'

The old woman's nose twitches. She opens one eye. 'You're a useful thing, but tactless,' she says, and knocks the fruit away. It falls to the ground and rolls, picking up dust.

'Who's short of manners now?' says Jay, but she lets Agnes reach through the bars to touch her shoulder.

Agnes eyes the wilting flowers. 'Whole lot, in the pot, and stew it up awhile.'

Once the fire is rekindled, Jay dangles a handful of roots over the pot. 'In they go,' she calls, 'if you tell what you did.' She grins at Agnes, who pokes out her grey tongue and shifts her rump around, as if getting comfortable, which she cannot be.

'It was my fault,' she says, and pauses to nod at the pot. Jay lowers the roots closer. 'Yes, it was all my fault, what happened to Herne the Hunter. You see, we were lovers.'

Jay drops in the roots. 'You? But you're old.'

'I am so very old. But once I was as young and lithe and pretty as a lily. And Herne was strong and handsome and fearless.'

Jay rolls her eyes. She picks up a handful of stalks with their purple flowers and tosses them into the water, pulling a face at the stink that drifts up.

'Shove it all in. Nothing like it for tired old bones. Now, listen. Herne was the best of the lot when it came to hunting. It was his great passion. He lived to ride with the hounds, cared for nothing so much as the chase, the kill. But it also made him the king's favourite, the envy of all. And to keep a king's favour, you have to be loyal above all else. That's how Herne came a cropper.'

'You said it was your fault,' says Jay, pushing more stalks into the pot.

'I'm coming to that. So, when they were all out hunting, and a stag lunged at the king, it was poor Herne who had to throw himself in its way. He was as good as dead. But as luck would have it, a sorcerer came riding along, and saved his life. Only he saved it by fixing the stag's horns on to Herne's head.'

Jay glares at her. 'You said the curse on King Herla was unlikely. That's no better.'

Agnes goes on. 'Things got worse. Because after that, Herne found he was useless at hunting. The sorcerer had given him his life back, but stolen his skill in return. No more royal favour for Herne. He was a laughing stock.' She sniffs the bitter steam and licks her lips. 'No tasting, now,' she warns. 'It's all for me.'

'You're welcome to it,' says Jay, grimacing.

'Herne was furious. He had lost all he cared most about: the hunt, the king's favour, his standing. He was beloved, but by me only, and that was not enough. So, he hanged himself. From this tree. And I might have done the same, if he hadn't come back.'

Jay sees the sorrow pass over Agnes's face, just for a moment, before she gives a gleeful smile. 'You mean he wasn't dead that time, either?'

'Oh, he died. In his old form. But now he was far more powerful. He was a dream and a nightmare, and a better hunter than ever. He commanded his own hunting party from among the king's men, and against their will they gathered around the wraith Herne, here at the Great Oak, ready to follow him through the night. The glorious Wild Hunt. And they still come, ever seeking souls to join them. As your father ought to know. King Herla, indeed.'

'I don't see why it was your fault,' says Jay.

'You're too young. You've yet to be troubled by love. You've yet to trouble your father with it.'

Jay, reminded that she is playing truant, glances around the clearing in fear.

'He won't come here,' says Agnes. She gazes into the plume of steam that rises and ebbs between them. 'It was my fault because my father found out, that I loved Herne. He couldn't stand it. He said Herne was wayward and foxy and rascally and wild, and he was right. That was why I loved him, and why I do still. So, my father played a great trick.'

'How?'

'He was the sorcerer. Ranulf Bearman.'

Jay's eyes widen. 'But he did it. The horns. It was his fault. If any of it's true,' she adds, and edges further away from the acrid steam.

'My father was an ass. Much like yours. He couldn't stand mischief, especially if it was joyous.' Agnes hauls herself to her feet and rests her head against the cage. 'How's that liquor looking?'

'That's what you said, before. You got caught making mischief. But you're not in that cage because you loved Herne. That must have been a hundred years ago.' Jay skulks towards the cage, and looks up into Agnes's face. 'This is all a trick, too. You've done something so bad that you can't admit it.'

'Maybe I have,' says Agnes. 'Maybe I'll tell you.'

Jay gives a vexed groan. 'Please?'

'You're wearing me out. How about you sneak a rabbit out of one of your father's snares for an old woman's supper?'

'I'll get in trouble.'

'We already are, the both of us.'

'I'll come back tomorrow instead.'

'And leave me hungry? Besides, I won't be here tomorrow.'

The sun has dropped behind the trees, and a sharp breeze twitches the leaves of the Great Oak. Two foxes trot along the path and pause to sniff at the cooling pot of steepwater. They take no notice of Agnes, who is curled in the cage with her feet tucked under her tattered dress, dreaming. The first bat of the evening flits past just as Jay returns with a rabbit over her shoulder and a clutch of green sticks. She tends the fire once more, then sits down to skin the rabbit. Agnes barely stirs.

'Yes,' says Jay, 'I'm a useful thing.' She tugs out the last leg and throws the pelt to the ground. Then she busies herself with the green sticks and soon has the meat over the flames. 'And not a word of thanks for it.' She points to the pot. 'Aren't you going to drink that?'

Agnes has not bothered to sit up. 'The smell of that rabbit will do to wet my tongue for now,' she murmurs.

Jay goes to the cage, reaches through the bars and gingerly rubs Agnes's knee. The old woman does not even open one eye. 'There'll be meat soon,' Jay says. 'Though I'll be paying for it when my father finds out.'

She stands by the cage for a long time, with her hand resting on the old woman's knee, while the rabbit roasts, and the fire smoke goes up, and dusk comes down like a black spell.

When there is only firelight to see by, Agnes lifts her head. Her eyes glint with reflected flames. 'I think it's time for that brew. And then you should go home. You said yourself you'd be in trouble. Bring me that pot.' She drags herself to her knees and pokes her bony arms out through the bars.

'About time,' says Jay, hurrying the pot into the old woman's hands. Agnes struggles to hold it up, so Jay tips it to the old woman's lips as she presses her face between the bars and slurps, dribbling bluish water down her chin. When she has drunk, and all that is left in the pot is a soft slime of stalks and roots, she reels backwards, her eyes rolling white and her mouth sucking in air. Her legs begin to judder and she wipes clumsily at her brow.

Jay drops the pot. She is trembling. 'That wasn't heart's-ease, was it?'

'Wolfsbane. Not so sure of your woodland cures after all.' Agnes coughs and gulps, pressing her palms to her belly. 'Enough to fell ten men, you got. Good girl.'

'I only wanted to know what you did, to be put in the cage.' Jay stumbles back, towards the fire. 'I was helping you.'

'Oh, I stole a cheese.' Agnes's face is crumpled up, but she manages a sort of smile. 'I have a passion for it. But all you've done is brought me freedom. He'll be here soon. He'll come to catch my soul, right out of my last breath.'

Jay stares down at the blackening carcass on the fire. 'My father—'

'He'll never know. If you're going to stay and eat that rabbit, tuck yourself away quick. In that bracken over there. Have a chew and see Herne the Hunter for yourself. I dare you.' The old woman's words are overtaken by wheezes, and she curls up into a brown ball. 'Not long now,' she croaks.

But Jay can already hear the ground beginning to rumble, every roosting bird shrieking upwards out of the trees as a thundering gallop crashes along the ridge.

'Bit of mischief,' Agnes cries. 'It's good for the soul.'

As Jay runs and hurls herself into the bracken patch, a horn sounds close to the crossroads. A hundred hounds bay in response, and a thousand trees creak with fear. The clearing around the Great Oak flickers, first with firelight and then with the chill blue light of ghostly manes and trampling hooves. Jay hides her head in her hands, so she only hears the echoing crow of Herne the Hunter, as wayward and foxy and rascally and wild as ever he was, riding headlong through the clearing and then sweeping away into the night, leaving the cage swinging behind him, empty and silent as an unfilled grave.

LULLABY FOR FUNGI

Rowan crown, hare's ear,
Panthercap, smoky cavalier.

Thistle rust, livid pinkgill,
Tongues of fire, destroying angel.

What ails thee, little sweet?

Pale stagshorn, birch bark stripper,
Horn of plenty, the pretender.

Leaf brain, crystal brain,
Jack o' lantern, vampire's bane.

Hush now, forbear to weep.

Scaly tooth, tiger's eye,
Toothed disco, sweet poisonpie.

Velvet shank, Rosy spike,
Burning beacon, swarming spire.

Little one, oh won't you sleep?

Alder tongue, twisted deceiver,
Green earth tongue, clouded cavalier.

Darkfoot greyling, beechwood sickener,
Bearded dapperling, herald of winter.

Be still my babe, let slumber creep.

Green-spored dapperling, greenfoot tooth,
Wood woollyfoot, devil's tooth.

Weathered earthstar,
Elegant earthstar,
Tiny earthstar,
Crowned earthstar.

Sleep now, little one, sleep.

R. G. Fellow

3

VENERY
1500

Charm: I might bewitch a woman's heart with this song, though she be artful, I will sing her thoughts towards me.

Effra, drowsy, night-chilled, twisting herself from sleep in the early dawn.

Effra, silty, still clogged with waterweed but awake, listening. A primaeval silence, in the Great North Wood. Deer slumber nearby: dappled dreams. The birds are not yet poised for the first pearlised ray of enchanted morning.

Effra, resolute, focused, browsing now in the clear-headed quiet, choosing her day's study. She has been sluggish. She seems to have dreamed away these last few hundred years. This she regrets. All the waters of the world; river, spring, stream, well, lake, sound, sea, marsh. All her long life to learn them. And she has, if she is honest, merely dabbled.

Effra dowses, then, tracing the world's water for the morning's subject – one she will give the full flow of her concentration. She must be scholarly, for she is only a tributary, here in the wood. She will never preside over solemn glacier, polyglot delta or chromatic waterfall. But she will know them, distantly, for they are all her ancestors and her descendants, her proud grandmothers and her intrepid broods. A family tree of waters and those who dwell in them. It is her duty to know all.

She chooses, for this soft, breezing day, the lakes of a faraway continent. Their colours are of robins' eggs, bluebell haze, opal sky. Their milky opacity admits no reflections, but the birds that scoot nearby are fairy creatures in toy hues. Effra tries not to notice the pleasure of becoming absorbed, her mind flowing clear, these images cast bright as fish within it. She tries, simply, to learn.

Around her, the wood wakes. Dawn in the enchanted forest is both chaotic and harmonic. Beneath the arpeggios of blackbirds and other phonic warm-ups in the canopy, anemones blink open, and paths snake into place. Ablutions must be made: skin freshened, tresses arranged, horns buffed, beards fluffed. There is dawdling in the glades, by the stream and along the ridge, in the flattering leaf-filtered light. There is hope: for love, sorrow, joy or tragedy. There is the promise of fulfilment in the green, silky air. And above all, there is gossip.

Effra, intent, is absorbing all she can about her far-off cousins. Alkalinity, temperature range, beneficial properties, common visitors, preferred appearance, disposition, associated legends both inaccurate and accurate. She wills herself on, steels herself against distraction. She is saving up the questions she most desires to answer, in the hope this will keep her engaged, concentrating. Agua Azul: she loves the name, the laziness of that 'g' barely enunciated, as if the hard rock of the word has been smoothed by the curl of the water.

I saw him.

She saw him. She saw him. She saw him.

Who?

Oh, didn't you see? I saw him. Me! Me.

Effra incants, Agua Azul, Agua Azul, a spell for her attention.

She saw him.

She saw him.

Who?

It echoes, but is not an echo. It is the dryads, beginning their gossip earlier than usual. Effra had counted on another quiet hour. The message flits from tree to tree, fast as an errant wren. The pitch of their clamour rises. Effra busies herself in thoughts of Agua Azul, strange and beautiful cousin, rich in calcium, sodium; soft to the finger dipped.

We saw him.

But I felt him. He leaned here, against my trunk. No, he did, he did.

Was he hot?

Damp?

Strong?

Did you feel his beating heart?

There is a localised blizzard of giggles. Small cries, some envious, some cynical.

I heard his breath, loud as a horse, warm through my branches.

Oh delicious! Warm through your branches.

Her branches, warm, warmed by him.

A mistral of dryad sighs drifts through the wood.

No, no. He rode. That was his horse's breath you felt.

The breath of his horse! Driven so hard through the night.

There ring out squeals of delight, and triumphant disgust.

Effra rolls her eyes, and then her long body, wriggling downstream a little. The dryads – air-headed, sappy things – might sing this empty chorus all morning. She feels, deep in the ground, the plangent grumble of the trees. A resigned chestnut. A weary oak. As weary as she is of the dryads' shrill sharing. She will not listen.

Does anyone know who he is?

Where he is?

I want to feel that warm breath.

That was his horse. I want to feel his heart beating against my trunk.

Does anyone know?

I know he rode so hard he skinned a hornbeam root, up on the ridge.

Indignant interest spices the pause.

Darlings, we must rally.

Is she well? Does she hurt?

Send word!

Off they flit, in a flurry of concerned cooing.

Just a scratch, thinks Effra. Just you wait, until there's a proper storm. None of them remembers anything much longer than a night and a day, or they are so easily distracted that it appears that way. Effra, on the other hand, is becoming learned – a word redolent of respected oaks, of scholars enchanted by their books of wisdom. The opposite of this sweet-sly twaddle polluting the morning wood. She closes her eyes. Back to Agua Azul, to research microclimate, invertebrates present, magical properties, ritual uses.

Ah, me! Oh, my!

A dryad nearby is snivelling. She embellishes with wails and sobs, louder and louder. They are rarely original.

Why, oh why? And today, of all days.

Then, there is a hopeful silence.

Effra tries not to listen. She knows this trick. She can't resist counting; it does not take long.

What is it? What ails?

We're here for you, let us soothe?

More silence. Then a small sniff, a whisper.

It really hurts.

As the elaborate ballet of performed sympathy, disguised envy and competitive rallying begins, Effra eels upstream again to take a look. It's true, the dryad's tender sweet chestnut tree has a low branch torn away. If you believe dryads, then it would, indeed, sting. The others are bringing consoling gifts – peonies, ribbons, a collared dove; Effra has no idea where they get them from – and tut, or frown, or weep over the broken bough.

Effra spies, sarcastically, waiting out the hubbub.

The dryad is grave, but Effra can see the glints of pleasure in her eyes: to be the very centre of all gossip and care for a while. Her pink little mouth twitches. Surrounded by her array of bestowed fripperies, flora and fauna, she bites her lip.

I have something to tell you. The rider who did this, I saw him. And he had terrible, angry eyes, and an angry horse, and he was horribly strong and fast. But the thing I saw, and I can't forget, is that he had antlers upon his head.

There is a brief hush, beneath the sweet chestnut.

Were they – tied on?

A kind of – hat?

The dryad shakes her head, pale hair sliding over her slender shoulders.

They were rooted there. As if they grew on him, just like a stag. Oh, they were tall!

She shudders. The two dryads nearest drape their arms limply about her.

A stag-headed man. This is new. Effra tracks the flickers of interest, an adder tongue slithering through the group. Low-lashed glances; locks twisted on fingers; secret assessments; comparisons of pulchritude. For all their sweet appearance, none are sugar plums.

The dryad of the broken chestnut lets drop a few tears. The others ignore the tiny reddish shoots that furl up from the ground where they fall.

We must be vigilant.

Effra notes the green thread of arousal in the voice.

We must help and heal.

There are nods, straightenings of supple spines. The speaker grasps the wounded dryad's wrist and holds her arm aloft. The dryad winces.

Everyone, we will bring comfrey, heart's-ease, horsetail and marigold.

A murmur spreads: the promise of a day ostentatiously gathering flowers, and with perfect justification. The hum is rising, faux-modest smiles springing, when there is a pitiful wail from up the slope. Another dryad, hurrying towards them.

My neighbour, a young linden! Barely a span wide.

She is in the middle of the gathering now, pausing. For effect, Effra thinks.

Knocked sideways, leaning, her bark split.

Little cries silver the air.

Where?

Poor thing.

Poor darling.

The dryad points, her eyes wide, her mouth anguished.

I'll lead you.

And at a dainty dash, they are all flooding away, up the hill. To get a good look. Only the injured one is left beneath her chestnut tree. She is forlorn, until they are out of sight. Then – Effra notes with relish – furious. She stamps her small foot, mashing one of her own new shoots into the ground.

Effra sighs, a stream of tart bubbles. She has failed, again, to resist the wood's melodrama. A horned man. She should not be tantalised, but she is. She indulges the image: dark furred head, tensile antlers gleaming amidst the night's foliage. A headlong ride, tearing the trees, churning the earth. But she felt no shudders through the ground, last night, while she lay still, suspended in her stream. Effra does not sleep, exactly, though she dreams.

The chestnut dryad tuts, flexing her wrist. With a self-righteous sniff, she climbs up – they are all so very nimble – and settles herself in a crook, there to gaze and drape, a lissom garland for a splendid tree.

Effra prefers the trees, for company, to their decorative dwellers. It is a kind of uncelebrated joke of the forest: that the dryads are so preoccupied with their own chatter, their own sylph selves, that they have never noticed the talk amongst their hosts. Effra, earthbound but itinerant, can tap down, tune in. There are roots that share her bed, and her banks. She can press a shell ear, rest her head, and hear, then, slow but sure: the sonorous harmonics of the grown trees; the ticklish percussion of mycorrhizal static. So much more pleasant than the reedy voices of the dryads. The trees are pragmatic, practical. They know of the night's destruction, and are passing succour, and nourishment, to the victims. They act without fuss. Though all the trees love the dryads, their weird daughters, there is no hope of being heard by them. No point in even shaking their heads, and groaning. Instead, they do what counts.

Through the underwater root nearest, Effra understands the extent of the horned man's rampage. Even she winces a little. Saplings trampled, bark slashed. A stand of silver birches hacked at shoulder height. There are dead and dying.

In an enchanted forest, death is met with dignity, if it comes at all. Trees look after their elderly. They know that time bestows wisdom, and centuries especially. There is no wisdom, and no dignity, in this wanton slaying. What kind of man, or beast, has done it? Trees are rarely vengeful, but perhaps this will have hurt enough. Effra can hear, in the Delphic chords that thrum through the root, notes of pain. A calm ache. Almost a soothing sound. It fills her with pity.

While they mend as best they can, while they minister to their dear ones, she will find this antler-toting fool. She will warn him off, or calm him down. She has never done it, but *in extremis*, Effra has the power to drown.

*

Enchantment is not in and of itself old-fashioned. It may change its form. It can, like all eternal concepts, respond to the zeitgeist. England flickers in the dawning light of the Renaissance, and the forest is remade in the *modi antichi*, a self-conscious paean to the fantasies of classical antiquity. And while a charcoal burner, deep in the Great North Wood, may never see a dryad, here they are, in a lacquered overlay of artistic fancy.

There is room for all in the enchanted forest. But there are also rules – not written, but in the architecture of the enchanted imagination. We might disdain this imagination, finding it lacks our own principles of liberty, equality. We dare say the enchanted forest in which Effra now hunts the horseman (he is also a hunter, but she does not know that yet) is an old-fashioned one, by our current measures. Though, as you will have noted, some things never change.

Nevertheless, this enchanted forest, with its minstrel birds, its nymphs, its wakeful paths and merciful trees, is one that does not welcome lone, malevolent riders. It permits their existence; this is, perhaps, the weakness of enchantment. But they are not listed in the catalogue of mischief that the enchanted forest tolerates. We will not enumerate those forms of mischief here, for you may be offended, or alarmed. But you know the ribald reputation of fauns, the nefarious status of goblins, sorcerers and crones, lustful dragons and jealous sprites. Herne the Hunter, alas, is made of rougher stuff than these romantic confections. Naturally, he is riled by the invasion, this new veneer of artful beauty, this *sfumato chiaroscuro*, which leaves his own myth in the shade.

There is always gossip, in the forest: seduction, trickery, imprisonment, impersonation, and so much involuntary metamorphosis. One becomes accustomed. So it is for Effra. It is only natural that she would be charmed by the evidence of something new, something anarchic. Who doesn't love a rebel?

*

Effra meanders, her favourite mode. She makes use of every waterway to range through as much of the wood as she can. The ridge is impossible, of course. But when it rains, she will wait for the scent of this man to trickle down and meet her. On her rounds, she pauses at elder roots and dabbling willow fronds, to hear the trees' ponderous concerti. She maps the damage wrought, until she has in her mind the path taken by the marauder. It is a purposeless one – or rather, its only purpose seems to have been to wound. There is no logic to it, that she can make out. It does not take him from here to there, or show any pattern.

Rebel.

The trail peters out amongst a patch of shredded marsh grass before an open sward. Effra can go no further. She sits in the small, muddy pond, absent-mindedly smearing the sediment over her shins, her knees, her thighs. River goddesses have skin like weathered silk, and it takes upkeep. What will she do when she finds him? Scold, explain the unwritten rules. Threaten him? Perhaps try to understand first; let sympathy take its chance.

She pokes more mud between her toes, considering. Her kindness might be all that's needed, to bring forth confession, tears even, reconciliation to the forest's proper ways. Effra pictures him, his large eyes pleading forgiveness, his antler tips pinking with remorse. She goes on with her bath, spreading mud up over her hips, across her belly, around her breasts, savouring the daydream, Agua Azul and her earnest education forgotten. *I was angry, I was stupid, I should never have* … the antlered man is whispering, his chest rising and falling, while Effra nods, solemn, full of mercy. She swirls mud over her shoulders and down her rounded arms as she imagines them reaching out, embracing, the beast tamed. She has succumbed to the nectar-sweetened narrative of the dryads. She has heard their innocent fantasies too often, but even as she acknowledges this, she does not resist the pleasure it gives her.

The mud is cool on her water-smoothed skin. She lies back in the shallow pond, letting its minerals seep into her, letting the enchanted afternoon lull her, as it lulls everything. Wood pigeons purr, soft as the dreams of lion cubs, while the shriller birds save their voices for the pandemoniac evensong. A tremble of deer crosses the open sward and dapples dutifully in the falling, then failing, sunlight. The dryads, if they are in the nearby trees at all, lie quiet in their branches, not a loud sigh let fall among them. Effra snoozes, in her element, dreaming lion cubs, dreaming antlers, a hunt with no kill, a wild, ecstatic chase.

She is woken by the scurry of small hooves, the panicked deer swarming towards the pond, leaping over her and vanishing between the trees. They leave a trace of fear in the air. Effra sits up and listens. Dusk hovers low, piebald with pink cloud. The birds are hesitant, offering a tuning note here and there, unsure what tone to set. Something has unsettled this reach of the forest. There is a tinkle, a sequinned shiver, from the trees that flank the darkening sward. It is a familiar sound, for they are often practising: the flirtation laugh of a dryad. She strains to hear more, in vain. There is only a murmur, a vibration of throat low beside the dryad's descant.

Effra presses her ear to earth, hoping the trees are watchful too, and she might eavesdrop. But they are busy with more diverting matters: the night's forecast, the viability of the tiny new saplings that sprang from the chestnut nymph's tears that morning. At a soaring whinny, she jerks fully upright. It is followed by a squeal from the dryad, of delight, or dread; possibly both. After a suspended moment of silence, a great ash-coloured horse breaks from the line of trees and turns to pelt away down the long strip of grassland. On its back, a dryad, silk hair flying, arms clung tight around the waist of a man who is dark and furred and proud as a prince, a crown of antlers upon his head.

The horse pounds along the treeline, swift and thunderous, then turns with a horrible rear of its muzzle to gallop headlong towards Effra. The dryad is hidden now by the bulk of the man, who goads his mount forward, his face contorted. It is not a grin, not a grimace, but a rictus of obsession, the eyes with a focus, an intent she cannot read. Does he see her, sitting mud-smeared in the pond? He doesn't show it, wheeling the horse about so that turf flicks into the air, and they hurtle away once more. Three turns about the sward this rider takes, with the dryad rippling behind him, a silver flag through the twilight. The birds have fled elsewhere, following the deer. There is only the drumbeat of hooves, the snort and whinny of the riders.

Show-off, Effra thinks. Even a faun can impress a tree nymph, and they have the legs of a goat. Yet she is a little enthralled by those horns, shocking but natural, greying in the crepuscular half-light. Still, she ought to halt this circus. The interloper must heed the rules, or else find another forest to torment.

Effra rises up to her full height. Standing does not come easily to her; she is almost always recumbent, travelling eel-wise, held by her water or propped in a couch of reeds. Upright, Effra is taller than all mortal men – nearly as tall as a man on horseback. Effra is painted from head to toe in dark grey mud. Effra steps from the pond.

She cannot stay out of the water long: it is her element. But the mud, and her determination, will give her long enough. The horse turns at the far end of the sward and this time slows as it comes closer. She feels the blood heat of it, lung breath, hide sweat. She clenches her elongated muscles, in thighs, buttocks, in extensile back. His pale eyes are level with hers. His grey crown soars above them.

'Get down,' she says to the dryad who peers round at his elbow, flushed, her small white knees pressed either side of his flanks, her white forearms branching across his belly. He grasps the dryad's hands, catching her in place. 'She might not know what you wreaked in this wood last night, but I do. Many do. And it will not— we can't have you tearing up the forest for no reason.'

He looks at her, almost as if he does not hear her at all, or as if her voice is no more than a dull bird's, piping from a bush somewhere, unseen.

'Who are you, and where do you come from?' She is formal, sharp. She tries to harden her shoulders, not to droop.

'He's Herne,' the dryad simpers.

The antlers, she notices, are jewelled with tiny droplets, as if they perspire. The effect is sensual. They seem to invite a tongue: salt lick.

'Herne,' she says. Not a flicker from him. 'Ride more carefully, or ride here not at all. This is not the only forest. But this one has its ways. It has an order.'

It is the horse that snorts and shakes its head, but it is as if the man does it. His eyes sneer. His bristled chin juts. Then with one hand he swings the dryad out by her arm and drops her to the ground. She rubs her elbow but gazes up at him. With the same hand he points behind, towards the trees, and with a sweet sigh off the dryad trots, home to her bower.

Effra raises an eyebrow. 'Don't feel too pleased with yourself,' she says, but she can already hear tomorrow's morning chorus, this delectable gossip spinning the dryads into a frenzy of hair-braiding, tree-tidying and laugh-practising. *I will ride with him! Me. Me!* 'They'll jump on anything. You are—'

But Herne interrupts. His voice is not what she expected. It is rasping, muted. 'My pleasure is in the hunt,' he says.

'Is that what you do? Then you lack skill.'

That rictus look again. He does not deign even to defend himself. He does not care.

'Take your pleasure elsewhere.' Effra's muscles twinge with the pond's gravity. She turns and steps slowly, controlled as if she danced, until she can wade. She has dropped to her knees in the water when she feels the hand scooping up her hair, letting it fall, knuckles brushing her spine.

'My pleasure is in the hunt,' he says again.

*

What does it mean, to be enchanted? It is more than the mere delight of being *enchanté* to meet you. It is to be enthralled, mesmerised, pixilated, daft. *Chanter* means 'to sing', and this is at the heart of the enchanted forest – a place that is in itself a song, sung in so many languages, by so many minds, by gods, mortals, and everything in between.

To enchant is also to incant. Utterance has its powers, and Herne's words, repeated, are incantatory.

What is it, for Effra to be enchanted? She is a river song, sung. When Herne chants, he sings.

When Herne hunts, he grins.

*

Effra, hearing his words, feeling his knuckles, pauses only as an eel poised for flight. Then she plunges, and limbs grown heavy with air are freed by water, they are water, and Effra races, corkscrewing, undulating, pouring through the waterways of the Great North Wood, as intrinsic to her as her veins. Behind, Herne leaps and splashes, from bank to stream bed and back again, navigating, calculating, keeping the quarry in sight. Effra does not look. She senses him as she ripples and dives. They are a double wave, running into deeper waters. They grow in power, their cold blood rich with exertion.

Effra races, but not too fast. There are limits, to the forest, to the web of watery paths, to a man's prowess. Antlers are heavy, and she is almost weightless. But the hunter himself is enchanted. She can hear the pleasure he takes in those springing bounds from bank to bank, in the thrash of his thighs when he wades through the streams with her. She can hear it in the breaths that bark from him, hard yet controlled, a body that knows its might.

She leads him downstream, to where the flow is widest, deepest, where the banks become root-knotted walls, and there are hangings of velvet moss. The chase has washed the mud from her skin and she glows all the colours of her vespertine element, ivy dark and copper tinted. Three stars are out, but their light does not reach down here. There is only the haze that hangs always in the enchanted forest in the hours after sundown, for which we have no name now it is lost. It is like side-lit dust motes, or powdered sugar blown and swirling in the air.

Through this haze, pale antlers glow. Their reflection quivers in the water's eye. While Herne is here, river-bound, the wood may rest, unperturbed, unscarred.

Effra lets her hair float up towards his hands.

Water. Air. Water. Air. Effra turns with Herne from roar of breath to stream of bubbles and back again. Their joint strength keeps them bound, grip sliding: antler; throat; hip; hand. Where Herne tugs her, she follows. Where she rolls him, he falls. Beneath the curtains of moss they collide and collapse together, both furious, both triumphant, both coercive. The chase has vitalised Herne, and Effra is fierce in the water. Their incantation of one another goes on until the forest's haze has dissolved entirely and they catch themselves, suddenly moonlit, brazen.

Effra wriggles away and presses herself for a moment against the smooth stones of the river bottom. Herne's face appears above her, swaying in the water as he looks down at her. She reaches for a branch of his crown, to pull herself up, but he jerks aside and when she rises he is standing, antlers dripping, turned towards the shadows of the trees.

'Rest with me,' she says, and curls about his legs. He whistles. She laughs, and dips her head down between his thighs, rubbing her cheek up over his buttocks, then his back. It is then she sees what he sees: the dark outline of his horse as it walks towards them. It does not come close but waits a little way off, discreet beneath a hornbeam.

'Rest,' she repeats, sliding round to face him.

He gathers her hair in one hand. 'My pleasure is in the chase,' he says.

Before she can rise to her feet, and take hold of that obscene crown of his, he has let go her hair and is pulling himself, root by root, up the bank. He is striding to his horse, he is up on its back, and he is gone.

Effra, wide awake, makes a whirlpool of her chosen pond, urging up silt, turning her water thick and black. She does not need to lean her ear to the willow roots to know that Herne rides slipshod through the forest, cutting his own haphazard line while the enchanted paths sleep. Insolent vandal, maiming, killing. What pleasure can there be in it? His sprees buy him no status. They will make an outlaw of him. There will be resistance, surely – if not among the dryads. Effra circles faster, trying not to think of the morning to come, the morning after, her own possible place in the gossamer web of gossip that they will spin out. They forget so fast, she reminds herself. Besides, she was valiant. She meant to spare the wood another night of carnage. They need not know there was pleasure in that. The pleasure was not only hers.

Rebel.

No: brute.

Condemn him. Effra: hypocrite.

Study will distract her, absorption in her family's captivating diversity. Agua Azul, beautiful turquoise cousin. Taker of unsuitable lovers? Even suitable ones. Suitors. Effra has been courted, in her endless time. Knights, trying for something to brag about. The more outrageous fauns trying their luck. A naiad, once, in thrall to Effra's goddess standing, and she was lovely, though worshipful. One thing Herne certainly was not.

But the smallest hours are no time for study. It is not her fault that her mind wanders. The clarity of daylight, the disorganised joy of the enchanted dawn, is what she needs. A fresh, unsilted pond.

Effra bides, sullen, still tingling a little. Rebel. Brute.

*

The enchanted forest harbours many horned beasts. Fauns and their related fey, the odd troll damp in his cave, unicorns of course, and splendid white stags. (No jackalopes – American inventions that only nod to enchantment, though their time may yet come.) But Herne, once the finest hunter, now stag-headed, both dead and blazing with life, is unique among them. Arrogant Herne is an archetype. If the enchanted forest survives his nightly ruination, Effra will one day be able to study this, too. Herne, the horned god, is multiple. He is double, triple, he is all. Herne is King Herla, Erl-king, Woden. He is Harlequin, Hairy Man, chthonic wild man. He is leader of the Wild Hunt, he is psychopomp: dream, nightmare; kind, clever, lethal.

Effra has Herne's fate, his deeds, his destruction, his chance of redemption, more in her power than she knows.

Herne, the king's favourite disgraced, then ousted from his post, now sees his wild hunting grounds metamorphosed. He is all vengeance, and he doesn't know what's good for him.

*

Effra, night-chilled, forcing her mind to focus in the early dawn. She is not drowsy – far from it. A head start, is her plan: to be deep in her study before the birds wake and summon the forest's smirks and suppositions.

Effra, silty and a little sore, perusing the map that is the world in her watery veins. She will choose somewhere closer, more comparable, more sister than cousin. A sylvan tributary; a source among the root tangle of an English wood.

Effra, hope-hearted, settling with quiet delight on a fellow enchanted forest, not far north of the Thames. It is threaded with exuberantly winding streams, striped with merry brooks. My kindred, Effra thinks. She will learn of their clay, their spring heights and summer diminutions, their minerals, their lore, their lovers.

Effra has found Ching, tributary of the River Lea, and with sisterly devotion is cataloguing her weed types and dependent wildlife, when the birds begin their serenade of the morning's first beam of sunlight. Throats open in tree and bush, on stumps amid dewy grasses, and with blithe disregard for their fellow virtuosi, the birds are soon muddling the air with a clash of toccata, scherzo, aria and fugue.

She rode.

With him, on his horse's back.

At his back.

The dryads' tone is uncertain, a show of concern tinged with envy, and deep thrill.

She lives by the pasture.

Up and down they rode.

Not for long.

For hours! She pressed against him.

Oh!

Don't listen. They obsess and then they forget. Effra sinks deeper, into her insulating mud.

Not for long. He left her.

For another?

Their murmurs are of speculation. Which dryad won him? Who will tell? They have forgotten yesterday's outrage, Effra thinks. Love, the illusory promise of it, this ludicrous yearning for romance, has obliterated such recently wounded friends. There is nothing so fickle, so self-absorbed, as a dryad.

But gossip is gossip, and now the news is at full flow. Tales of the night's casualties fly from tree to tree, from glade to grove. The dryads flit, unable – unwilling – to settle: he is hero, he is threat, he is heart-throb, he is Death. Trees have been twisted and hang, unsteady, by a single root. Briars have been torn and wound about, strangling themselves. A hazel has been nearly flattened, her thin stems akimbo, sap leaking.

The dryads vacillate between hope and dread. While the trees make slow repairs, their nymphs splinter into hurrying groups. They collect flowers indiscriminately – foxglove, stitchwort, lily of the valley – but still pause where a puddle of lemon sunlight falls to shake out their locks, self-conscious, aglow. Their chatter swarms in the air, infuriating, contradictory.

Effra lies low. Let them quibble and wonder, feeble-minded vanities. But there is one here, poking half-heartedly at the violets on Effra's banks. She keeps peering down, frowning as much as a dryad can ever frown, as if trying to read the water. Effra glares, and turns the surface messy with ripples. Still, the pale shape of the dryad hovers. Another appears beside her.

Is she there?

It looks so cold. So murky.

Naiads aren't like us.

Will you recognise her?

Cruel naiad.

Wicked.

Thief.

Effra, minor goddess, stifles the urge to rise up and pull rank. Perhaps they seek an actual naiad. She might let their waspish accusations fall elsewhere, then defend her junior, summon a maternal rage, quash the rumour and send it spinning away from her. They would forget.

But it is Herne she wishes to blame, not her kind. Implacable, he is the cruel one. The thief. If he goes on with these nocturnal performances, the dryads will be reminded each night, they will surrender to his new pattern. Every dawn will herald its own hunt – for ghoulish news, dashed limbs and lovelorn nymphs: bleak, or besotted, or both.

Which is she?

Effra, wrathful, breaks through her ripples and rises, until water laps at her hips. The dryads cringe, but they are curious. Such dark, springing hair, such marsh scent and kingfisher gleams she has. They speak before she does.

Oh. Not her.

She is so …

Large.

Their dimpled chins tilt, true coquettes, their eyes darting for witnesses.

Effra, wily, lifts her arms. She has the victorious shoulders of a swimmer, the heavy grace of an eel out of water.

'Girls,' she says. 'Do you think, if you cavort with this man, you will be admired? Revered?'

The dryads smirk, but only briefly.

'You will have the envy of your friends, for a moment. You will have knowledge, of a bully, a marauder. But do you think it will do you good?' Effra sweeps her shining hands through the air, letting fall a silver helix of droplets. 'The forest will soon hate him, for he hurts it. And the forest does not only belong to us. It belongs to kings, princes, knights: honourable men, who prize only pure nymphs. What will they do, when they find you have been sullied by this intruder, who disorders their garden with such zeal? They will not caress you, or make queens of you. Yours will be a full and permanent disgrace.'

The dryads are staring at her. Do they understand, or even hear?

'Disgrace!' she repeats, in a cry that empties her divine lungs. The willows quiver. The stream around her hips swirls and foams. 'Girls, when dusk comes, tuck your feet up high in your trees. Turn your faces from the last of the light. Be silent, and still, let him ride by. He will tire. Do not give him even your breath. Hate him secretly, and do not speak of him by day. We'll be rid of him.'

The dryads share a conferring glance.

Queens.

Us.

But those antlers …

'They'll leave their mark,' Effra snaps, 'if they don't run you through. But you have the power to make him nothing. Irrelevant. Impotent. You must shun him in all your talk. No gossip. Do you understand?'

They both bite their lips. They plushly pout.

No gossip.

Ignore him.

And kings will love us?

'Yes,' Effra sighs, dropping her hands, sinking a little back into her ebbing flow. 'More or less.'

But they linger still, as if mulling this deal, as cobbled and mendacious as it is.

We don't see why you should get to—

And we don't get to—

Effra, cunning, has saved a trick for this eventuality. The dryads have never seen it before, kept as it is for dire threats. 'Look what he has done to me,' she says, her voice becoming a screech and then a burbling hiss as Effra turns, in one great scale-studded writhe, into a river serpent. She drops with a wet explosion into the water and boils there, flicking her ugly tail, darting her long, striped neck as if in agony.

The dryads scream, of course they scream, all the way back to their trees and long enough to bring their coterie hastening, posies in hands.

It will do, she thinks. It is new enough that it might make gossip for two more days. But she needs a plan. And she has inspired herself, with her rare metamorphosis. Not to turn her serpentine coils on Herne, but to turn downstream, with Herne in heated, lustful pursuit, and lead him, ecstatic in the chase, all the way to the Thames. There to present him, breathless and proud, to Isis and her riverine beasts. To dob him in, and let her senior mete out the punishment.

It will be a humiliation, a relinquishing of authority. But it buys her – well, who can say what permutations of limb and tongue might be required, to tempt him on his way.

Effra lumbers downstream, turns behind a curtain of moss and shakes off her scales, shakes out her hair once more. Then, her study abandoned and Ching forgotten, she lets the soft currents lull her until the wood and its thousand busy voices fade to a faint hum. Effra does not sleep, though she dreams.

*

Can Herne be disenchanted? A prolonged dip in the majestic Thames, at the mercy of her tides, her ever-widening banks and charismatic currents, might do it. But he is of a piece with enchantment itself.

This particular enchanted forest, in all its dazzle and panache, cannot last. Not long now, and those naughty nymphs will droop and fade. Their fauns and other frisky colleagues will be but a twinkle in nostalgia's eye. And how will Herne have his fun, then? The forest of our imaginations will be a dimmer place, overshadowed by fear, unlit by that elusive evening light whose name is lost to time. It will appeal to the smarting Herne, whose antlers will trail a scent of goddess lust, whose muscles will ache with an anger that can last centuries, but who, despite his fall, cannot countenance disenchantment.

Herne, our horned god, our psychopomp, is no fair-weather friend. Like Effra, Herne does not sleep; his dreams are ever wild and ever ours.

*

Effra, rousing, smiles to herself. She is not a goddess for nothing, even if a minor one. Herne will be shunned, Herne will be ousted. Even if Isis leaves him intact, he will take his attention-seeking antlers elsewhere. She has dreamt of him, memories made in mud, and seen the need in his ungulate eyes. The boy too early crowned, monstered by his own patron. An ego that will be easy to drown.

The enchanted evening is tender. As she patrols the forest's waterways, she sees dryads draped in their boughs early, like convalescing princesses. They have appealed to the fauns, who preen among the roots below, leaning on elbows, mischief at bay while they enjoy the honour of their guard posts. Harmony, and goodwill. The wood dressed in its best, rising above the scoundrel trespasser.

Effra dawdles in that enchanted evening haze that hangs, like earthbound starshine amongst the trunks, in the glades and groves, until night claims her time. It is beautiful. It is flattering, to enchanted skin like weathered silk, should a goddess recline casually against her stream banks, agleam. The trees are quiet, their rhizomes offering but a low crackle, major chords of relative content.

Effra, alert, protective, aroused by the success of her gambit, forgives herself her serpent trick and pretends to loll. Herne will come. She will be waiting.

It does not take long. As the last whispers of the twilight's haze vanish, before moonlight can nudge through the still canopy, the rhythm of riding hooves is in the earth. The tremor draws along the ridge, skirts the empty sward. It finds and follows the stream bank. Effra's water ripples in the dark.

The thrum peters out. A head is close by hers, a gleam of moonlit crown reflected, a mouth at her ear.

'My pleasure is in the hunt,' he says.

Effra dives.

A WASSAIL

Wassail, wassail, all over the town!
Our toast it is white, and our ale it is brown,
Our bowl it is made of the white maple tree;
With the wassailing bowl we'll drink to thee.

So here is to Cherry and to his right cheek,
Pray God send our master a good piece of beef,
And a good piece of beef that may we all see;
With the wassailing bowl we'll drink to thee.

And here is to Dobbin and to his right eye,
Pray God send our master a good Christmas pie,
And a good Christmas pie that may we all see;
With our wassailing bowl we'll drink to thee.

So here is to Broad May and to her broad horn,
May God send our master a good crop of corn,
And a good crop of corn that may we all see;

With the wassailing bowl we'll drink to thee.

And here is to Fillpail and to her left ear,
Pray God send our master a happy New Year,
And a happy New Year as e'er he did see;
With our wassailing bowl we'll drink to thee.

And here is to Colly and to her long tail,
Pray God send our master he never may fail
A bowl of strong beer; I pray you draw near,
And our jolly wassail it's then you shall hear.

Come, butler, come fill us a bowl of the best,
Then we hope that your soul in heaven may rest;
But if you do draw us a bowl of the small,
Then down shall go butler, bowl and all.

Then here's to the maid in the lily-white smock,
Who tripped to the door and slipped back the lock!
Who tripped to the door and pulled back the pin,
For to let these jolly wassailers in.

Anon

4

LORD OF MISRULE
1606

Charm: When hatred runs high amongst heroes, I may soothe it with this song.

Being a *True Protestant*, and a man of good Fayth and Standing, & being neverthelesse accus'd of Debauch, Injury & being partie to *Witchcraft*, I, Robert Burrman, give here a *True Relation* of all that befell me and my neighbours of Dulwich on *Christmas laste*.

With this Account will I shew that, if Bad Deedes have been done, Blame should fall neither upon me nor upon our great Gentleman *Master Alleyne*, who did requeste our Revels and give money for the sayme.

The *Lord of Misrule* being this year chosen by a method of Chance, & therefore *Undetermin'd* by M. Alleyne & his good family, a Stranger, one *Master Herne*, did perswade us that he should take up the role. This Account being *Honest* in recall and True in evrie detail, hereby will I shew that M.

Herne did himself bring about such *Debauch* & *Injurie* as I be accus'd of. And if *Witchcraft* be withal here perceiv'd, may *M. Herne* be found and punish'd as the *Perpetrator* thereof.

ST NICHOLAS'S DAY

It being a chill day and the village beset by blizzards, M. Alleyne did invite to his owne House all who would make his propos'd *Christmas Revells*. The Companie being gath-er'd in his fine drawing room, they did make a Straynge Sight. Standing there on M. Alleyne's rich red carpet, & sittinge on his plush couches by a greate Fire, I counted all the farm-hands, servants & humbler toilers of the Parish. These being Pertinent to my Accounte, I here note that among them stood *Master Pollen, M. Burly, M. Truelove,* & withall *Captain Ferver* & the *Rev. Neice*. Not all those presente were known to me, I having come only a year since to Dulwych.

Punch being serv'd from a great silver'd dish, only the Rev. Neice & I did refuse it, shewing our standing as *Good Protestants*. Neice did declayre to me then, in hush'd voice, his wish that *Puritan Reform* be gently urg'd in the Parish, & that while Christmass be kept, it was our *Dutie* to see that matters become not Bawdy.

The men about us slerping their cups dry, M. Alleyne did ding the Punchbowl with the ladle to call for attention. Though he prance no longer on the *Theatre Boardes* of London, still he is a Commanding Man, broad & faire & generous of laughter, with large, gesturing handes. Swinging these towards the door, he gave a whistle. Thereupon was carried into the room a *Bulging Cake*. This sette upon the table, M. Alleyne did wink at severall who stood about there & began his *Addresse*.

'This is a Tradition, in the Alleyne family of olde,' said he. 'And for this, my familly's first Christmas at Dulwiche Manor, I intend a *Revivall*.' He did take up a great knife & began to cut into the Cake. 'We will have our Twelve Days' *Madness*, and all will be deduc'd by our own *Lord of Misrule*.' Cutting still, with his other greate hand he held aloft a piece of the *Black Cake*. 'My Father would call our Christmas Lord the *Bean-Kinge*,' he said. 'Whosoever discovers a bean in his share, will be *Bean-King*, and Lord of this year's Misrule!'

The Assemblie crowding fast about the Cake, all pieces were swiftly taken up. I did resolve that, should I find the portentous *Bean*, my Rule would foremoste meet the Approvall of Rev. Neice, & be bothe *Moderate & Modest*. The others cramm'd their mouths, but fearing for my laste good toothe, I did crumble the Cake in my fist. Young Pollen, chewing beside me, gave a Start & grasp'd at his throate. His eyes bulg'd. Fearing he had swallow'd the famous *Bean*, I whack'd him hard on his back & in the Tumult of his coughing fit I did not spie the *Stranger* who edg'd thro' the munching horde and took the last small lumpe of Cake.

I did wonder, then, to hear this Stranger, being one *M. Herne*, shout 'I am the *Bean-King*!' Turning to looke, I did wonder all the more to perceive that this fellowe wore upon his crowne a *Headdress of Horns*. The syght did so vex me that I only star'd as others cheer'd & shooke of his hand. The whole Companie grew merrie, except Pollen who, ceasing to cough, shew'd me in his palm a mush of cake, and lying therein a *Shiny Red Bean*.

M. Alleyne, clapping his great handes, his actor's voice booming, did declayre, 'We have our *Lord of Misrule*, and an apt one withal, being already in Fancifulle Costume,' & he did toast *M. Herne* and request his Counsel henceforth, on all matters of the *Greate Revels*.

There follow'd much prattling among the fellowes & votes put forth for *Games & Disports* & the Dressing of Houses about the village in Winter Greenerie. I staid sitting quiet by the great fire, wherein Pollen threw his handfull of mush & the secrette *Beane*. Some moments later, above the clamoure in the room, there issued from the hearth a loud *Crack*, and Sparkes of green flew from the fire.

'A Gunpowder Plotte,' shouted M. Truelove, whereat all roar'd in great merrimente.

M. Herne took occasione to jump upon a chaise, so that the Antlers he wore loom'd above us. 'We shall have *Fireworks*,' said he. 'We shall have Feasts & Festivall & the most *Wanton* of Games.'

Nodding beside him, M. Alleyn did add, 'There must be Mumming, and a *Fine Play* for Twelfth Night, that all the village will come to see.'

'What play will it be?' *M. Herne* ask'd the crowde. Names of divers being call'd out, M. Truelove bellow'd loude, 'A Midsomer Night's Dream,' & forthwith Pollen began braying like an ass & calling, 'Let me be Bottom!'

''Tis not the season,' M. Alleyn said, & laugh'd heartily. 'Though the Scenes do take place in a *Woode*, which is most suited to Dulwich & the Forest hereabout. What other *Woodland Tale* myght we play?'

The Companie mumbling, uncertain, M. Alleyn look'd to *M. Herne* atop his chaise. He did not seem to mind the

Durty Bootes that stamp'd upon his fyne velvet there. 'Why, we might play your Namesake, *Herne the Hunter*,' cried he. 'And we shall have the Woods for our backdrop. Your fine *Headdresse* will be our Prop.'

M. Herne, appearing mighty pleas'd with this Suggestion, did bend to murmur in M. Alleyn's ear. The Gentleman grinn'd & said to all: 'A fine idea. Herne here asks if M. Henslowe & I might supplie a *Beaste* for the Hunting Scene, from our own *Beargarden* in the City. And so it shall be.'

Looking about me, I perceiv'd that the Rev. Neice did frowne & shayke his head. At many a meeting of our *Puritan Friends* had he condemn'd the *Beargarden* as the Worste of the Theatres, whereat much Gambling & even Fighting went on over the faytes of the Beastes baited there. I did bite my tongue, resolving to address M. Allene on this matter another day soone.

Long did the discourse continue amongst the thronge there, as they plann'd the Play & the Mumming & much other *Disport*. I did observe how, under *M. Herne's Misrule*, the humble fellowes grew *Rowdie* & their ideas Wild. Neverthelesse, M. Alleyn nodded and smil'd at all, declaring ours would be the finest *Twelve Days' Madness* in the Kingdom.

Pollen making merrie with the others, I did not mention the secrette of the *Second Bean*. This I now regrette, for as my Account will shew, *M. Herne* did lead Good Men into *Foul Ways*, & myself powerless to halt such Revells as were approv'd by our Upstanding Gentleman Alleyne. Dwelling not more than a yeare in that Parish myself, I had not before met *M. Herne*. Had I knowne he was a *Stranger* to all present, I would have taken occasione to challenge him. It is true that he held sway in that roome at the Great House, & all men did warme to him so that he seemd *Frend* to all. The *Devil* always goes in Disguise.

The Fortnight til *Christmas* saw a Frenzie of preparations. Looking out from my windowe I saw men hurrying hither & thither, carrying armfulls of *Greenerie* from the wood & tacking such to house fronts, & bearing back to the wood hay bayles, tools & many divers Props besides. Each evening the Companie gather'd at the Inn with their *Lord of Misrule*, there to plotte & have great Discourse on the matter of Games, Songs, Parades & Pageants, Hunting Parties, Bell-ringing, Wassails, Guises & Feastes.

Often spying M. Alleyne as he saunter'd to meet them, I did followe. In this I had no great content, the Inn being one of freely flowing Ale & *Bawdy Repute*. But I tooke it upon myself to provide there the *Voice of Moderaytion*, & to keep *M. Herne* from leading the flocke too far astray. Always he did persist in wearing his *Crowne of Antlers*, & sincerely thought himselfe not foolish but handsome. He smil'd & laugh'd with all the Assemblie and took occasione to bring even meek M. Pollen into any discourse. The men prais'd & follow'd him & were stirr'd by his Words & *Extravagances* in their plans.

One nyght, *M. Herne* having all cups fill'd once more with *Wine*, excepting my own (I tooke only ale), he ask'd what Games the men would play at Christmas, that the servants of the *Lorde of Misrule* might gather any bittes & pieces needed.

'Snap Dragon,' call'd out Pollen, & all did agree.

'We will want *Brandie*, then,' said *M. Herne*, nodding to M. Burly that he must tayke note, he being the nomminated Master for this taske. 'And raisins, too. What else by way of Games?'

Fox in thy Hole, King Arthur, Mumblety-Peg being all suggested, alongside Quoits, Skittles and Dice, I bethought myself to warn M. Alleyne that he ought not to encourage *Gambling* in his house, for always does this accompanie such Pastimes. I nudg'd closer to him in the crowde & did tappe his shoulder, at which moment *M. Herne* bellow'd, 'And what about *Mould-My-Cockle-Bread*?' As all roar'd and jeer'd in Approvall, & M. Alleyn along with them, *M. Herne* did stare directly at me, and did winke and shake his reare end most lasciviouslie.

I confess I durst not show any *Goode Puritan Morals* just then, lest the others take agaynst me. I should have been more bolde. For it was in this *Insidious Manner*, beginning as it did with Suggestions for Indecente Gaymes, that *M. Herne* brought Good Men to *Debauchery*.

For the most parte, then, I thought but to Observe and Monitor, and onlie to speake up if matters should get out of hand. I saw that, despite his Standing, M. Alleyne truly wish'd an exceedingly *Merrie Christmastide* for all at Dulwich. If he had only chosen me, or M. Pollen, as *Beane-King*, we should have had it.

Come *Christmas Eve*, the Village, the Church & M. Allyne's greate Manor House did shine with a *Thousand Candles*, and along the streete evry wall spread with Hollie and Ivy

& all manner of greene branches cutte from the wood hereabout. It was a cheering syght. Walking with Rev. Neice, who wanted help acrosse the icy ground, we both were warm'd by such a glow, and without the need of *Punch*. I do recall Rev. Neice, his knees cracking & his voyce frail such was his age, turn to me and pronounce it the moste *Decorated* he had seen the Parish in many a year. 'I hope, onlie,' he went on, 'that this *Excesse* is restricted to Decoration, & the burning of candles, & the Kinde Folk of Dulwyche will see out a gay *Twelve Dayes* with no Harm done.'

'You think of *M. Herne*,' I hinted. Neice nodded, & clutch'd my arm tighter as we trod through depe snow.

'An Uncannie Hold, he has, over those fellowes. He bespeakes Mischief. Do you know, I have never seen him come to the Church?'

The image rising in my mynd of *M. Herne* taking a pew, those *Hornes* atop his head, did mayke me shudder. This I took as a *Sign*. 'There is indeed some thing *Unholy* about the man,' said I.

'Keepe your eyes sharp & your Wittes about you, Robert,' was Neice's wise Instruction. We were glad both to reach the Church then, where God myght protect us from *Evill*.

All the above I set down to shew that, if I am at fault, it is in failing to follow an Instinct allready alive in those of Dulwych whose *Puritan Souls* did recoil at *M. Herne* & his Influence. What followes now is a *True Relation* of our Twelvetide at Dulwich, excepting those dayes when events did kepe me from Festivities, those Events standing themselves as Evidence of *Malice & Misdeede* on the part of *M. Herne*.

CHRISTMAS DAY

All the Poor of the Parish being invited, we did gather once more at the Greate House of M. Alleyne, that Famouse Gentleman & unfortunate *Benefactor* to our *Lord of Misrule*. Evry room within was scented with Oranges & Swete Spice, and litte with great fires and many candles, so that at first we gap'd and were quiet.

M. Alleyne and his Good Wife shook evry hand & plac'd thererin an orange stucke with cloves. His children sang a Carol, bolde before the great store of Companie, and this gentle Merriment did restore my *Faith* and convince me all woulde be calm awhile. Perhaps onlie the Grandeur of the House cow'd us, for as soon as we sat to table and the Ale was pass'd along and about, all began to babble.

Watching M. Alleyn as he gazed happily upon the Gathering, I saw he wisht us only *Goode* & I did take a cup of hot ale, swete with sugar and cinammon, & did bless our Hoste. Then echo'd in the room the Beate of a Drum, loud & moste *Ceremonious*. M. Alleyne rais'd his cup, & whether Solemn or in Mockery I could not tell, cry'd, 'To our *Lord of Misrule*, the Marvellous, the Mischievous, the Miscreante, *Monsieur Herne*!'

At which there enter'd the room a gaggle of men, amonge them M. Truelove & M. Burly, bearing *M. Herne* aloft on their shoulders, he all bedeck'd in ivy & *Mad Drapery* & upon his face a grin like a Satyr. Stucke about his ludicrous Horn Headdress were candles, the wax dripping and myngling with the *Mistletow* there twin'd about. His beard, too, was greene, as if his chin sprouted not hair but Moss. He sat at the *Head* of the long table, where M. Allene should have bene. Plates being then brought, pil'd with a Plenitude of beef, woodcocke, pork, goose, and a hundred venison pasties, the Companie did fall upon them with Greedie hands.

Sumptuous as was this Repast, I could not tayke my eyes from *M. Herne*. Thus did I see how he gaz'd at all presente as if they sat at his own table, & he *King* among them. I did not like it.

The meate being savourie and well season'd, all drank of much Ale, and men & women both did growe exceedingly *Merrie*. I do now suspect that the spices and sugar therein hid a lacing of *Brandie*, a sly addition by *M. Herne* himselfe, who did many tymes urge more Drink upon the companie. Soone there roll'd about the rugs oranges, goblettes and Men withal. From beneathe the greate table rang squeals & laughter, and my shoe was tugg'd from my foote more than once. The *Tumult* swelling, it was onlie when *M. Herne* bang'd loud & hard upon his Drummes that the Companie could be brought to their senses and led to the greate hall. Reliev'd at first, I soon perceiv'd that here were laid out many Gaymes & more jugges of Wine & Ale. And soon began such *Disorder*, the men and women being already quite beside themselves, I can hardlie describe it all. Find belowe a Summarie of the most notable *Misdeeds & Excesses* of this Bedevill'd afternoone.

i) The bowle of *Brandy* well aflame for the game of Snap Dragon, and both M. Burly & M. Truelove snatching therefrom the swollen raisin with greate zeal & much howling, I did espie *M. Herne* leading Capt. Ferver there to tayke his turne. The Capt. being now elderly and not at all quicke in hand or foot, & fair *Drunk* besides, I did feare for his safetie. Hurrying to intervene, I reach'd the burning *Brandie Bowl* just as Capt. Ferver reach'd for a bobbing raisin. I cry'd out in warning, at which Capt. Ferver did pause to gayze up at me, and the *Flayme* catching his sleeve made fast work of running up to his elbowe. Ferver wail'd like a childe, and at *M. Herne's* cry of 'Quick! Water!' M. Truelove did upturn the Brandy Bowl over Ferver's fiery arme, so feeding the flame that pass'd now across his *Cheste*. It was our Gentleman M. Alleyn who quench'd him, bearing from I saw not where a thicke Rug, which he wrapped about the quailing Ferver til *Smoke* rose from him as from a damp'd candle. Thus did *M. Herne's* Mischief cause *Injurie* to a poor old man.

ii) *M. Herne* began to processe about the hall, declayring that, should any man or woman find themselves o'ershadow'd by his mistletoe-stucke *Horns*, they must give one another a Kiss, & the Ladie must kiss *M. Herne* withall. This bringing about a *Skirmish*, as the men dash'd to lurk by their chosen Amours, I found myself quite trapp'd, refusing to run immodestlie as did the others, so that finally I stoode between the hearth & the maid Rachel, being the Younge Sister of M. Pollen. *M. Herne*, perceiving this, approach'd with much *Devillish* Glee, & sidl'd between us, shayking his foolish *Hornes*. I saw that Rachel blush'd red as a holly berrie when *M. Herne* kiss'd her unbidden, & he pushing her forthwith towards me, she did seem to quake. 'Another kiss, for the Maiden?' urg'd *M. Herne*, at which poor Rachel, frighted by his *Power*, did burste into a flood of tears & run to her brother who, *Mistayking* the culprit, did glare at me. Thus did *M. Herne* encourage the *Intimidaytion* of young Ladies and cause much *Upsette* amongst them.

iii) Amidst the many Games of cards, as well as quoits, skittles, & other raucous sports play'd all aboute the hall, I did perceive many *Wagers* being plac'd. Regretting the love of *Gambling* amongst my frends & neighbours, and wishing to quell it for the sayke of their pryde & enjoyment, I sought out M. Alleyn and made what I thought a wise *Proposall.* Since all who had dutifully kiss'd beneath *M. Herne's* begreen'd Antlers had pluck'd therefrom a *Berry* of Mistletow, why did not the players use these tokens in their Wagers, in place of coins? M. Alleyne, finding this a fine & *Festive* idea, did summon *M. Herne.* 'Since he is *Lorde of Misrule*,' he told me, 'he must propose it, not I.' So, I watch'd as they exchang'd a few words, & then to my content did *M. Herne* smite his drumme & declayre that *Mistletoe Berrys* should count for wagers in all games henceforth. Whereupon he shook his *Head* moste violently, so that all the remaining Berries fell from their stalkes & roll'd hither and thither. Then *M. Herne* smote his Drumme once more, shouting, 'And all Berrys brought to me come the Strike of Midnight shall be exchang'd without prejudice for a *True Pearl*!' In Horror did I look on as the Throng in that hall fell upon one another and upon the floor, scrabbling & scratching for Mistletow Berries as if they had already been magick'd into precious *Pearls*. In the *Fray* I saw that M. Truelove punch'd M. Burly, & elsewhere was much hair pull'd & clothing torne, the companie reduc'd to greedie dogs. One amongst the brawl crying, 'There be Misseltoe in the trees!' severall there did disentangle themselves & *Stampede* towards the doors that open'd to M. Alleyne's gardens, & were soon seen making attemptes on the greate *Linden Trees* that growe there. While most fell back & did moan & tumble on the ground, M. Truelove prov'd himselfe nimble and rose some *Fifteen Feet* thro' the branches, onlie to fynd himself there lodg'd, and Unable to descend. He was sav'd with the help of a Ladder, & return'd to the hall with much *Mirth* and a ball of *Mistletoe* as big as a barrel. Thus did *M. Herne* bring about *Brawling*, Greed & renew'd *Gambling* besydes.

iv) Alarm'd by these deprav'd doings, spurr'd by the glaring Rev. Neice, and likely embolden'd by such accidental consumption of *Brandied Ale* as had been forc'd upon me by *M. Herne*, I did resolve to bring a halt to his reign of *Debaucherie & Disorder*, once & for all. Again did I seek out M. Allene, & tho' the way be hamper'd by pelted skittles, spilt goblets & staggering *Drunkards*, I brought him to M. Pollen. Being at that moment engag'd in a game of Quoits, & a little more sober than his opponents, I waited til his turne be over, then took him by the shoulder &

shew'd him to M. Alleyn. '*M. Herne* play'd a *Trick*,' said I. 'Pollen is our true *Bean-King*. I saw with my owne eyes the red *Beane* in his share of the cake.' But M. Pollen shooke his head. 'You are mistaken,' he said. 'It was a *Cherry*, which I did not like to eat, for Mother told me that cherries bring on the Gout.' I perceiv'd that this was an *Excuse*, for he redden'd. But M. Allene, seeing in this an Occasione for *Sport*, did take Pollen's hand & raise it high in the air. M. Allyne being so tall, this near lifted Pollen's Feet from the floor. 'We have a *Challenger*,' roar'd M. Alleyn. 'A *Usurper* to our *Lord of Misrule*!' 'Then I do call for a Duel,' said *M. Herne*, appearing sudden at Pollen's side. All about us cheer'd & swung their cups, splashing Ale upon M. Pollen, whose red cheeks turn'd then quite pale. 'Swords, or Bows?' asked *M. Herne*. The crowde then chanting, some for *Swordes*, others for *Bows*, Pollen tooke fright at the *Clamour*, & twisting his hand from M. Alleyne's grasp, made a Sprint for the dores to the *Garden*. *M. Herne* pursued him, the chanting Horde at his heels. As we came out into the cold nyght air, all heard a Crack, follow'd by a *Splashe*, and then a gurgling Yell from Pollen. Thus did *M. Herne's* rash conduct drive poor Pollen to fall into M. Alleyn's *Pond*, & thereafter to catch Cold & be kept abed the fulle duration of *Twelvetide*.

These number but a few of *M. Herne's Misdemeanours* on Christmas Day. I need not descrybe the Vulgar Dancing, the unseemly performance of *Mould-My-Cockle-Bread*, & the lewde Mirth resulting therefrom, nor the cruder Games of kissing & chasing *M. Herne* devis'd as the nighte went on. There are many witnesses to this *Devilry*, tho the cunning of M. Herne in adding Brandie to the ale has no doubt ensur'd that few recall it with the *Clarity* shewn in my own Accounte, & indeede may misremember & fynd Fault where none is deserv'd.

ST STEPHEN'S DAY

My *Dutie* to watch over the poor people of our Parish being establish'd, I took occasione on St Stephen's Day to pursue *M. Herne* & his merrie band into the Wood. This day had he chosen for a *Squirrel Hunt*, a Custom amonge the youngsters of Dulwyche, and with much banging and shouting did the small Hunstsmen process allong the streete. It being sunshine, the Frost glitter'd all about and the Squirrels raced amongst the bare branches. Hanging back from the laste of the Boys, I observ'd *M. Herne* as he led all to a Clearing, and there did hand out *Bows & Arrowes*. These were not the toy kind, but properly fletch'd & with *Pointed* Tippes. The Youngsters did delyghte in this & forthwith were chasing thro the Trees, M. Herne at their head. His *Headdress* of *Antlers* bobbing high beneathe the branches, I did easily followe, & the boys making such a Din, hollowing & hitting trunks with their Stickes, the squirrels thereabout soon fled deeper into the Woode.

Fearing that some boy may mistakenly pierce another with his *Arrow*, I kept close by, treading quietlie as I was able lest my unexpected presence alarme them. So swift was their *Chayse*, & their course helter skelter thro the tangle of Trees and Bushes, I struggl'd in my persuit, being unus'd to such Exertion. The boys scattering, I hasten'd after a few who ran together, the ground growing boggy & rutted beneathe the Frost & the trees more densely growing. I was some way behynd them when I stumbl'd and tripp'd over an obscur'd *Tree Roote*.

Hearing the boys pause in their *Chase*, I staid still in the clump of Hollie & Bramble into which I had fallen, tho it did prickle me sorely.

'What's that?' call'd one.

'Some big *Beaste*,' said another.

Then their cries rang out, 'Mister *Herne*, Mister *Herne*!'

Hearing his Approche, I shrank deeper into my thorny bed.

'I dare say you have disturb'd a *Boar*,' said he. Methought I heard a note of *Humor* in his voyce. But the boys gasp'd. 'Well? What shall we do?' ask'd *M. Herne*.

'Give chase!' cry'd the boys, and with much Hollering & *Whooping* did they sprint towards my Hiding Place.

As I have alreadie here mention'd, they bore *Bowes & Arrows* meant for True Huntsmen. Fearing for my own *Fleshe* then, I began to blunder away, steering my course through the undergrowthe & Uphill withal, the Effort of which did tyre my legs & weaken my Heart. Whether my dun-colour'd clothing were the Cause, or my hasty *Flight* through bramble & bracken, the boys did not realyse their Mistake but continued their *Pursuit*, being goaded all the whyle by *M. Herne*. It was perhaps Excitemente that blinded them to my human form, or perhaps the *Confusion* of branches & ivie that kept them trampling after me, shouting 'Stick the *Boare*!'

Already exhausted, I felte one *Arrow* swish past my head. Then another, & feeling a *Paine* in my left shoulder, I cry'd out & fell, my face press'd to the grounde. Upon their reaching me, I did hear that both *M. Herne* & the hunting boys all laugh'd.

'It is but a grayze,' said *M. Herne*, and with his Rough Hands did he roll me over & wave in my face the offending *Arrowe*. Not heeding my *Distresse*, he turn'd to the boys. 'And what shall we do with our Quarry?' he ask'd, grinning all the while.

'With a Boare, you should tayke him home & *Roast* him,' said one.

'He is the Huntsman's Bountie,' agreed *M. Herne*. 'And this one will feed a *Hundred*.'

'We'll have goode crackling off him, that's for sure,' said another, & all laugh'd once more, til Teares came to their eyes.

More boys gathering from the wood about, a great Discourse was had on how best to *Carrie*, *Cooke* & *Serve* me, just as if I understoode not a word. When I try'd to sit up, *M. Herne* push'd my shoulder back to earthe & did hold me there with his Muddied Heele. 'A sturdie branch. Nay, a *Trunk*,' he order'd, & the boys did sette about bending & breaking a coppiced Hazell.

'This is not seemly,' I declayr'd. 'It will be reported to M. Allene & will see the End of your *Misrule*, which has been only *Deleterious* & *Injurious* to our parish.'

But pulling a length of rope from his coate, *M. Herne* began to force my hands & feete into Cruel *Knottes* & these he did bynd to the Hazel Branch, so that I was trounced and truss'd. Believing my *Humiliation* to be compleat, I did tolerate the boys to dance aboute me, chanting & crowing, before I requested that *M. Herne* untether me.

It is with Regrette that I now report how *M. Herne* pretended he did not hear me, & instead went on with his Game, instructing the boys how to lifte & bear the weight of the Hazel Branch, that their *Boar* may be presented at the next Feaste.

In this way was I carried, dizzy with swinging and oft bruised against the frost-harden'd *Ground*, back to the village. There was I hoisted along the Streete, witness'd by all my neighbours, who stood at their windowes with their hands over their mouths.

Thus did *M. Herne* incyte not only Disrespecte amongst the youth of Dulwych for their Elders, but furthermore urg'd them to *Mocke & Humilliate* a Good and Humble man for no more reason than to diverte themselves. For such *Abuse* of my person & standing, and the Abuse of young boy's *Moralls*, I do condemn him, & beseech thee to do the sayme.

CHILDERMAS &C.

After the *Ignominie & Insult* of St Stephen's Day, I bethought me to rest at home awhile, & be forgotten by the *Lorde of Misrule* & his disciples. I admit that my directe attempts at preserving the Safety, Goodwill & *Moral Souls* of my fellowe parishioners had been a Failure thus far. And so, while nursing my sore wrists & ankles, which were strip'd red raw by *M. Herne's* malicious *Ropes*, I did devyse an improv'd

Method by which to subdue his Revells, & restore Peace & *Order* to Dulwiche's *Twelvetide*.

I began by seeking out *M. Herne's* Abode. For tho' I had not seene him before St Nicholas's Daye, he must live neare-by, to be invited by M. Alleyn to the Manor. In vayne did I search, waiting til *Darke* to stride by the Houses not familiar to me, & peere in at their lit windowes. I did not approve of my own Furtive Method, but felt it *Necessarie*. In this manner did I survey the whole Village, my hunte taking me even to the *Outermoste Cottages*, & those almost enclos'd by the Greate Wood.

It was at one suche house, layte of an evening, that I did spie a *Behorn'd Headdress* that hung from a chair by the fire within. Crouching at the low window sill, I watch'd a Man enter the roome & don the *Hornes*. Alas, he wore a *Masque* that seem'd made of Ivy leafs, and this did obscure his face. But concluding that this must be *M. Herne*, I was about to ryse from my knees when another man enter'd, similarly costum'd with *Hornes* upon his Head & a Masque of ivie. There follow'd close behynd him a Man just the same. The first ty'd on his Horns taken from the chaire, whereat all three began a peculiar *Dance*, in which they did slap Hands & Shoulders, and clashe together their Antlers.

I was perturb'd by the syght, the dance appearing to me as a Pagan Ritual, or meant to caste some evil *Enchantment*. That one of the dancers was indeede *M. Herne*, I felt certain.

My Certaintie did not last, for creeping along the woodland laine to the next Cottage, I did see yet another man in Masque & *Hornes*, who jigg'd about the roome & made the women therein laugh and cheere. So my nyght pass'd, &

in each cottage o'ergrowne by the forest I perceiv'd *Horned Men*, with Leaves upon their cheeks, until Exasperaytion & Terror overcame me & I hurried home.

I did tell myself I shivr'd onlie at the Colde, it having seep'd by then into my bones. But trulie my *Protestant Soul* did recoil & shudder to witness such *Pagan Garb & Ungodlie Ritual*. I bethought myself, then, that M. Herne's *Nefarious Enchantmente* of evrie parishioner in Dulwiche was now compleat.

Next day, I took occasione to visit Capt. Ferver, & give him my best wishes for Recoverie from his unfortunate *Singeing* at the Snap Dragon bowl. Finding the Capt. in fyne fettle, and lifting a cup of Sack with his bandag'd hand, I did stay awhile, & dranke with him.

He bore me no Ill Wille, he said, for the *Mishap* with the Brandie that had burn'd him. This did surpryse me, for the Fault had been *M. Herne's*, but surmising that the brandy had muddl'd his Memorie, I spoke on other matters. Upon my asking in which House in Dulwyche I might fynde *M. Herne*, Capt. Ferver shrugg'd.

'I've not seene him before, though he be welcome, eh?' he said. He must have purceiv'd my agitation, for he proceeded to give a Lengthy Speeche, & did propose that in this guize as Lorde of Misrule, *M. Herne* brought to our Parishe a *Greate & Essential Relief* from the travails of daily labor, and from the Strict Rules which do beare down hard upon the life of Common Men.

I agreed that it was *M. Herne's* exhortations to Lawlessnesse that irk'd me moste, being a man who abideth by all

Laws of State & Churche. Knowing that Capt. Ferver is likewise a Good & Moral man, and a stickler for the Law, his replie did trouble me greatly. For he declar'd that it is the very *Chaos* of *Lawlessnesse* that doth *Benefitte* all men, be they rich in wealth or poore as mice. 'For the twelve days of Christmas Tide,' said he, 'the Order that kepes them in their roles, whether high or lowly, is done away with, & through revelry & mischief is much Resentment, Rancour & Envie thus *releas'd*.'

'What is releas'd,' I did argue, 'is devilry & a taste for Disorder.'

Capt. Ferver gave a sly smile. 'It is your own Embarrassmentes that you regrette, eh?' said he. 'Now, take another drinke with me & may you find Mirth and easy Joy that way.'

It gave me not content to realize that *M. Herne* had worked his *Perswasion* on the Capt. And so, with Heavie Hearte, I left him to his sack, to find mirth & joy alone.

It was to the Rev. Neice I next appeal'd. Finding him in the Church, attending to the messes of wax made by all the candles that burn'd there of layte, I did not wait to state my *Concernes*. As our Minister, Neice would surely know where I myght discover *M. Herne*, and confront him.

Neice, bent over his worke, took a moment to stand, & longer to give his answer. 'The Lord tells us, in his Booke, that we must show *Hospitalitie* to strangers, for thereby have some of us entertain'd Angels unawares.'

My face began to burne, & the heat spread in my body & limbs. Thus did I obtain proof that *M. Herne* was, if not the *Devil* himself, then one of his owne. For his Perswasive Enchantment had reach'd even Neice, & I had not the power to reverse it. I do not doubt that the flayme that seem'd to burn in me as I stood there was the *Devill's Presence*, clashing with my Soule which did reject it. And so I ran from the church as faste as my sore ankles permitted me, & was grateful for the colde nyght rain that did Cool my body & Freshen my thoughtes.

I was grateful withal for the Notion that came to me then: that one might *quench* Fyre with Cold Water. Upon returning to my house I plac'd outside pails to catch the Raine. As I listen'd to it, pattering on my roofe into the night, methought each Raindrop was a *Gift* from *God*, deliver'd to me direct, that I might use it in His Nayme.

EVE OF THE NEW YEARE

The Eve of the New Year was soone upon us, the days preceeding it having been blighted by many Discomfiting Schemes. These included much Mumming, Wassailing, & similar *Entertainments* so-call'd, that are no more than decorated formes of Begging. Many a pennie was I forc'd to hand to man, woman and childe who did knocke at my door demanding paymente for their paltrie Pantomime. The Guizers, being those fooles dress'd in *Antler'd Crownes & Leafy Masques*, prowl'd about & danc'd in any house that open'd the door to them. My neighbours, gawping and clapping at their Straynge Costume & Heathen Capering, pour'd coins into hands & ale into cups, & call'd toastes to our *Lord of Misrule*. The *True Lord & Christ's Birth* being quite forgotten, all now worshipp'd the Horns & wish'd to wear them withall.

Withe five dayes of Twelvetide remaining, my feare that my neighbours' Souls may never be return'd to Dutie & *Godliness*, nor *M. Herne* to whence he hail'd, be that Hell or an unfortunate village elsewhere, I was driven to acte with Courage. For the Eve of the New Yeare, all of Dulwich had been invyted by *M. Herne* to mete at M. Alleyn's Great House, and there to witness a grand displaye of *Fireworks*. Such Gunpowder Trickes being novell, and never before seene by the denizens of our Parish, anticipation was feverish. In the hours of darke preceeding, boys skitter'd about the streete waving Flayming Sticks, & smash'd burning gorse against the ground to make Flying Sparkes. Severall boys did Chayse & Taunt me as I hurry'd away from my house bearing in eache hand a pail of water. Such *Roguery* serv'd onlie to strengthen my Spiritte in its resolve to do *Good* that nyghte.

With ease did I discover the back layne to M. Alleyne's Manor House, it being bold moonshine. From there I crept into the grounds, and hid my pails behynde a Hen House that stood by the kitchen garden. The henne house, being in the shadowe of a high flint wall, did afforde me a clere view of the Lawne, where *M. Herne* & his helpers layd out the Fireworks. There was much giggling amongst them, & *Tomfoolery* with the poles upon which the fireworks must be fasten'd. I did byde my time, tho I grew cold, and began to wish I were warme in a straw bed like M. Alleyne's hens.

The moon shone bryte, and so many stars withal, it was a moste beautiful sky, with quite enough Celestial Lyghte for our enjoyment. I was gladde that I might prevent *M.*

Herne's earthlie fireworks from marring it. When, after more than an houre had pass'd, *M. Herne* & the companie retir'd to the house, no doubt to sup of more Brandied Ale, I slid from behynde the Hen House with a pail. Slowly, and with Caution, lest some one returne for a forgotten cap or lanthorn, I approach'd the Fireworks. Then one by one, in *God's Name*, did I dowse them with His Rain Water.

This being a True Relation of the events of Twelvetide at Dulwych, I confess that I yet cannot account for what happen'd in the houres that follow'd. I did join the Assemblie in the hall of the Manor House, and at the tyme agreed did followe them out to the Terrace that overlook'd M. Alleyn's lawns. And there did I watch as *M. Herne* strode from pole to pole, bringing a flame to the fuse of each *Firework*. And thus did I witnesse everie Fuse fizzing with *Lighte*, and *M. Herne* stepping back, his Antlers aglowe, & every Roquette then flying into the skye, there to burst into a *Thousand Sparkes* which did fall like ungodly fierie rain.

All about me scream'd and coo'd and clapt and call'd for more. M. Alleyn did clappe M. Herne on the back and throw his great armes around him in Congratulaytions at his Feate. I stood astonish'd, & waited for a firework that would not tayke light. But not a single one fail'd, & in my Shocke I did wonder if God had forsaken me, and had taken His rain-drops back before they could worke.

At the final *Roquette*, the cheer went on so longe that my eares did ring with it, yet I heard the voice of *M. Herne*, close by at my syde.

'You cannot beat me,' said he. 'I am in Every One here. I am in You.'

To which Suggestion my Soule took such *Offence* that I believe I did fall in a Fainte.

Thus did *M. Herne Defie Nature* & cause wet Gunpowder to burne, or cold water to vanish, such that Fireworks flew. And if this be consider'd *Witchcraft*, let him be Accus'd of suche.

TWELFTH NIGHT

& so, finally, dawn'd Twelfth Night. I had staid in my house full three dayes, so to kepe my Soul from *M. Herne*'s *Predations*, & as a Precaution against further exposure to the *Witchcrafte* that I knew now to be abroad in our Parish. Musing alone by my ever-dwindling fyre, the log pile being now diminish'd, I did rack my braines for a New Method by which I might quell this Christmastide's *Evil*. No man I knew had resisted *M. Herne*'s Charme. All were Enchanted, from M. Allene to the Rev. Neice.

It was on the evening before Twelfth Nyght that I had remember'd poor M. Pollen, abed from a Chill caught by falling into M. Alleyn's Ponde. With Trepidation did I leave my house in the darke & went to pay him a visitte.

I found M. Pollen yet shiv'ring under a heape of blankets, & tended to by his Mother and his Sister, the young Rachel, whom *M. Herne* had so frighted with his Misteltoe & *Forc'd Kisses*. Sneezing still & sweating from Fever, M. Pollen was myghtily glad to see me.

'I have miss'd it all,' he said, in despayre. 'And such Tales have I heard from Rachel, how sorely do I regrette it.'

Tho' his Skin had grown sallow, his Eyes shone bryte. I saw that *M. Herne's* Malice had not infected him. 'But you live,' said I, 'and your Hearte remains *Pure*, dear Pollen.'

This did not seem to cheere him. He went on, 'The worste of it is, that if I still suffer tomorrow, I will not see the great *Play* for Twelfth Nyghte, & will miss the *Bear*. I did so wishe to see him.'

I enquir'd what he meant.

'Rachel told me that the *Beast* promis'd by M. Allene for the play was to be a *Beare*, & that it would be Harry Hunks.'

I did aske who this *Harry Hunks* be, and why he would be playing the parte of a Bear here in Dulwiche, his being a Name I had not heretofore encounter'd.

'No, no,' moan'd Pollen, and sank back against his pillowes.

Rachel straightway brought a cup of Broth to him. ''Tis the *Bear* himself who is nam'd Harry Hunks,' said she, & smil'd, a little haughtie. 'Have you trulie never heard of him, Robert? He is a Hero of the *Beargarden*. Everyone loves Harry.' And still she smil'd as she fed Pollen his broth.

But I car'd not if she mock'd me. Already my Mynde ran ahead. Whilst, unlike the admirers of this Harry Hunks, I had no particular fondnesse for Bears, they were, each one, *God's Own Creatures*. Furthermore, the Mind of a Creature could not be infected by *Evil*, the way a man myghte be possess'd by the Devil. Harry Hunks could prouve to be my Beste & onlie *Ally* against *M. Herne*, & would give me my last Occasione to bring down his Reign of *Misrule* before it Wrecke the Souls of my neighbours and frends.

I bid Pollen Good Bye & Goode Health and did promise to relate all to him once *Twelfth Night* be over.

*

The Morning of Twelfth Nighte was dull, the cloudes reaching downe almost to the tree tops of the Great North Woode. Neverthelesse I strode along the layne with Purpose, the spring of *Victorie* in my steppe, and soone found the Stage mayde ready for the Play. I did recall that it was to be the Historie of *Herne the Hunter*, & truly an arrogant piece of *Self-Aggrandisement* on the parte of our *Lord of Misrule*. With bales & planks had been built a Platform, & hookes strung from branches on whych to hang many Lanthorns. More hay bayles made for Seats, tho already they were dampe & mouldering. Inspecting this scene, methought it hardlie resembl'd a *Theatre*. The bare trees about loom'd darke & bleak, and even the hollie near by lack'd for berrys. All was Dank & Chill.

I tooke enjoyment in the quiet Stillnesse of it for a moment, so pleasing in contrast with the *Noyse* that had Assaulted my ears for so many of the last Twelve Dayes. It was then I did notice that the Woode was not quite Silente, for there rumbl'd from somewhere close by a sounde not unlyke a *Snore*. Following this Sounde, I did wander through a Thicket of sodden birch trees, and beyond them behelde a *Wondrous Sighte*. Asleepe against a trunk sat *M. Burly*, wrapp'd in rugges, his mouthe hanging open & the rattling noise issuing therefrom. And beside him a great Cayge of wooden slats, in which lay the mightie furr'd bulk of a *Bear*.

In truth, I had not before encounter'd such an animal, and I approach'd with Curiositie. Steam arose from his muzzle, & the Brown Furre of his side rose and fell as he breath'd. A *Chain* about his Thicke Neck held him Faste to the frame of his prison. When I stepp'd closer, one of his eyes open'd, and did Look at me straight. In that Eye, its Gayze so *Clear & Honest*, I saw that I truly had an *Ally* in the beaste.

And the Beare, recognizing the sayme in Me, did stir and clamber to his feete. His Greate Paws resting on the wooden uprights of the Cage, he did looke at me long, while M. Burly slept on, & his message was of *Friendshippe & Goodwill* to me, the only Man hereabouts who was not yet under M. *Herne's* Enchantment. In that Bear did I perceive a *Saviour* for the Souls of the parish of Dullwych.

I thought to *Open* the cage right then, and did tayke in my hands the Chain & Locke that held it. But at the clank of the chaine, M. Burly gave a Grunt & woke from his slepe.

'Step back,' blurted he. 'It is a *Vicious Beast*.' He rubb'd his eyes and did appear Surpris'd to see that it was I who stoode before him. The Beare, perceiving that our Quiet *Connexion* was broken, turn'd away with a Groan, & I felt quite sorry, for his *Captivitie* and for the end of our silente Discourse.

'Looking forward to the Play, are you?' said M. Burly, & grinn'd. His nyght breath stanke of *Ale*. He pick'd the remains of a Venison Pastie from where it adher'd to his rug & threw it at the *Cayge*. The Bear tooke no notice. M. Burly's look was beady.

'Of course,' said I.

'Our *Lord of Misrule* & M. Allene do both say it will be most *Fantastical*. It is to be the tale of *Herne the Hunter*.' He haul'd himself upright & stamp'd his Feete for warmth. 'The Players will soone be here, for Rehearsal. Do you take a Parte, then?'

But I saw that he Mock'd me with his Question, so I did bid him Good Nyte, pausing only to examine the *Locke* upon the Bear's Prisonne before making my way home.

And so, I did pass that Day in considering the *Puritie* of the Animal Soule, and the *Corruptible Nature* of Man by contraste. As I will shew here, the Happenings of Twelfth Night, being the Nyght of the play, did serve to Demonstrayte the *Accuracie* of my Observation on this subject.

Arriving at the wood with a Swarme of villagers, some *Tottering* already from the endless downing of Spic'd Ale, I did gaspe with the rest. For the Stage was now litte by a *Hundred Lanthornes*, eache appearing to hover in the aire as if a Star in the Heavens. Our gentleman M. Alleyne did smile from the stage, Welcoming all in his booming actor's voyce. I loiter'd, to discover the position of the Beare, Harry Hunks, in his cayge, before joining the Throng, and did take occasione to sit upon the Hay Bayle chosen by the Maid Rachel, she being the person presente I deem'd leaste likely to suffer Possession by the *Devil*.

More hot Ale was brought, tho I dranke not of it, knowing of the *Brandie* therein. I notic'd that Rachel, tayking a Cup, did gulp it downe at once. The *Hubbub* about us growing, the crowde did erupt into Shouts & a thunderous Stamping of Feete upon the sudden syght of *M. Herne*, who seem'd to descend from the very Tree Toppes to land upon the stage. Then began the rolle of many Drummes, and the musique of Pipers hidden amydst the trees, yet moving closer round with eache beat. Such strange musique it was, its chords unfamiliar, whether new or anciente, & its Melodie moste *Uncanny*, & I did shiver, as did Rachel besyde me. I made to comfort her with a Warm Hande but felt her shrinke away.

As the Musick & Clamour reach'd a paineful pitch, from the stayge came a mightie *Blue Flashe* & a Cracke as of Lightning. This ending the *Din*, in sylence did the Crowde watch as smoke drifted away and upon the stage were arrang'd the Players. Their Costumes were those of *Huntsmen*, & with Capt. Ferver dress'd as a King in golden crowne & fur'd robe. Thus did the tale beginne, of the King & his Court who would go ahunting.

The players shouted above the Clappes & Whistles of the audience, who did seem to fynd even such a Dulle Tale great cause for *Merriment*. Missing from the stayge then was *M. Herne*, yet glancing about I did not spie him. Instead, M. Burly play'd the part of the King's Beste Huntsman, *Herne* so-call'd in the tale, & while the jokes prov'd *Bawdy* & the Speeches most overwrought, all did go tamely enough. Until the momente came in the tale when *Herne* is wounded by a *Stag*, & the Magician doth affixe to Herne's Head the stag's owne *Antlers*, that he be sav'd, though forever alter'd.

It was then that another Loude Bang was emitted, with muche Smoke & Sparkes of lyght, and the Lanthorns in the trees did chaynge their glowe from plain to a *Reddish Hue*, & in place of M. Burly on the stage, there stoode *M. Herne*, his Antler'd Headdresse glowing now red, and a Grinne on his face so *Demonick* that I did shudder on my sodden hay bale. He seem'd in that instant growne *Taller*, & his Voyce echo'd *Louder* even than that of M. Alleyn, whom I saw did watche in Admiration from besyde the stage. The players then lifted

M. Herne up High over their Heades, by some Uncommon Strength, & over the Pipes & Drummes and the whoops of the crowde did he crie, 'I am *Herne*, King of the Wood, the fineste hunter that ever did live. I am *Lord of Misrule*, I am God of *Chaos*, I am the Soul of all Earthlie Mischief. Followe, & I will lead!' And with these words did he begin to throw out Masques & Costumes to the audience, and all manner of Hunting Geare, that they myghte join him.

Thus did *M. Herne* invyte such a Frenzie as I never saw, men & women running & leaping on to the stage, and there dancing in a Greate Worshippe of their conceited Lord of all Trouble, & I did know with utmost *Certaintie* that their Soules were possess'd & *M. Herne* a Trickster who would call the *Devill* to Dulwiche.

Even the maide Rachel did rush to join them, & donning a Masque began to skippe and turne & sing with the reste. Containing myself no longer, I flung myself forward and push'd through the *Commotion* untill I reach'd *M. Herne* himself. Though he busy'd himself in greeting all who danced about him, & handing out to them more *Speares & Arrows*, I did pulle him clear of them. I shouted, as Loud as I was able, that he was but a *Charlatan*, that his intention was not to mayke our Twelvetide *Joyous* but to Infect good people with the *Devil's Canker*, & to Ruin morall men with *Debauche*.

Since few pay'd me any minde, I determin'd to make my Owne Spectacle. Grabbing holde of *M. Herne's* behorn'd Headdress, I did yank & twiste, meaning to Pull it from his Head & thus render him *Ordinarie* before all. But tugge as I might, I could not tear away the Antlers. Wincing, *M. Herne* did attempte to throw me off, but I tighten'd my grippe & yank'd as hard as if I would tug a *Mandrayke* from the Grounde. It was as if those Antlers were attach'd to his crowne, or did *Sproute Directly* from the bone of his Skull. *M. Herne* gave a pain'd Shoute and like a Stag did butte me away, so that I fell and *Tumbl'd* from the edge of his stayge.

I admitte I did find myselfe shaken, both by the Proofe that *M. Herne's* Horns may truly be *Intrinsick*, & by the unaccustom'd *Violence* with which I was thruste to the ground. The *Pandemonium* continuing around me, I shuffled, rather daz'd, further from the Stage, in search of a Momente's Quiet. It was then I recall'd that, not far from me, in the Darke beyond the lanthorns, lurk'd my Onlie Friend & Ally, *Harry Hunks*.

Tho' the everchanging lyghte caste by the Swinging Lanthornes did confuse the Wood, I soone found him. He stood in his Cayge, alerte & gazing at the stayge where all of Dulwyche frolick'd in their *Demonick Possession*, & he did looke quite Afraid. When I came neare, he Growl'd & strain'd at the chayne which held the Manacle at his necke.

If, as Rachel had said, *Everyone* loved Harry, he would prove the ideall *Dystraction* from *M. Herne*, & breake the Spell of self-serving Adoration caste by him. If All (excepting myself) did flocke to see the Sports of the *Beargarden*, then they would flocke to meet its faymouse Performer, leaving *M. Herne* to jig & blather alone. And the bear belonging to M. Allene, he would surely be Pleas'd to see how his new neighbours did *Appreciate* his Christmas Gifte.

I lean'd close to the Cage. The Bear roar'd & shooke his head. He wish'd for his *Naturall Freedom*, & I would give it to him.

The Locke on the cayge causing me some *Difficultie*, tho' it requir'd not a key but a Cunning Movement, I began to shayke it, hoping to throw loose the Essential Parte. This did upsette the Bear, & I redoubl'd my Effortes, shaking harder as the Beare roar'd & threw himselfe about within. From the Stage came the sound of muche Cheering & *Fire Crackers* being sette off. This did cause me to jump in Alarme, & my Harte to somersault. And so it muste have been for Harry Hunks, for at the third *Cracke* he did Lurch Sydeways, away from me. As he tip'd, the *Cage* tip'd with him, both crashing to the grounde. Amidst much Splintering of Woode, the Bear righted himself & began to *Lumber Forwarde*, dragging behynde him what Broken Timber still attach'd to the chaine at his neck.

I durst not follow. For the Beare headed strait towards the Stage, & straightway was M. Alleyn calling to *Bewayre*, though he back'd towardes the trees forthwith. From my shadowie spot I watched helplessly as Harry Hunks approach'd *M. Herne* & his Revellers, who were by now all full costum'd as Huntsmen & mayking a *Raucous Show* of pursuing *M. Herne*, who did prance like a deer. The Pipers halted their piping & call'd out withal. Heads turn'd on the stayge. A young woman, perhaps the maid Rachel, gave a Terrible *Screame*.

I set this out in my *True Relation* of the eventes of Twelvetide at Dulwiche, not to amuse the reader but because what did happen next represents a *Finall & Absolute Indictmente* of *M. Herne*, & in my opinion doth constitute Evidence of his use of *Witchcrafte*, *Deceit* & *Unnatural Powers*.

For as the people aboute him began to Scramble from the Bear, & some receiving in their panick a *Swipe* from his Mightie Paws, *M. Herne* remain'd Unmoving on the stage. Thus did I Observe him with Interest, as he pull'd from beneathe his costume a *Polish'd Horn* of some beaste unknowne to me, & did Blowe on it, long & loud. And tho' so *Little Sounde* did issue from it that none in their Dismay tooke notice, there straightway came a *Rumbling* from far within the Woode. This growing Louder, & nearer, at an *Unnaturall Payce,* while all aboute people did Screame & fall & run, it was onlie myself & *M. Herne* who did perceive, arriving through the black trees, a great *Horde of Riders* on horseback.

These Riders did *Flicker,* not in the Lanthorne Light, but in themselves. And they broughte with them a *Miste* that swirl'd about them & up thro' the branches, and this Fogge did have some *Magicke* in it, for it was as if it did Mute the *Cacophanie* of the bear's Roares & the people's Moanes, & did make everie thing *Slowe,* as if all mov'd underwater. And so, with a queer *Claritie* brought about by the slowing of Tyme, I watch'd as the first rider in this *Unearthly Troupe* did directe his Mount across the stage, & as he pass'd did *Lean & Pull Up M. Herne* to ride alongsyde him. Then on they went, the Hooves of the Horses mayking no sound though they Paw'd and Stamp'd, & their Whinnies and Snortes as quiet as if they rode past a mile away, & soone a *Hundred Horses* muste have pass'd over the stayge & on thro the wood, & not Touch'd nor Injur'd one person there.

But the Beare, abandoning his Frenzie, did sniffe the air, & as the Laste Horse swept away thro' the trees he follow'd, ambling fast despyte the Planks that dragg'd behind him. And soon, all that remayn'd was a *Bedraggl'd Heape* of men & women, all dress'd as huntsmen, & in the lanthorn lyght that now was Dull & Feint, they did one by one haule themselves up, & looke about them in *Confusion*, asking, 'Where is the Bear? Where is *M. Herne*?'

Shortlie was it surmis'd that the valliant *M. Herne* had Sav'd their Lives by somehow *Dystracting* the beaste, & they did reassure one another that he would soone return, with the Bear either *Kill'd* or in Submission to him, & all would be well on this most memorable Twelfth Nighte.

The *Injuries* done were these. M. Truelove receiv'd a *Wounde* to his back, & his shirt was much torne. M. Burly's head was *Crack'd*, & he carried home, not wayking again til Epiphanie. The maid Rachel receiv'd a *Scratche* to her wrist requiring much Staunching & is bandag'd still, but I am credibly inform'd by M. Pollen that her Spirittes have recover'd. Capt. Ferver lost a Toothe by his fall, which did toss from his head the King's *Crowne* he wore, he landing upon it.

Many Scratches, Bruises & other Minor Injurys were endur'd by everie person presente, excepting M. Allene, who had the *Goode Fortune* to remaine entirely unscath'd. I do recall the *Quizzical Look* he gave me, when he spy'd me standing on the spotte where had been the Beare's Cage. I do recall withal that he look'd at me a Long Time, yet without speaking, & turn'd away onlie when he was call'd to help lift the insensible M. Burly.

Thus did *M. Herne* imperill bothe the *Souls* and the very *Lives* of the parishioners of Dulwych, by invoking the *Abandonmente* of *Decorum*, inviting *Demons* amonge us, & by bringing into our midst an Animall capable of Great Harme. And thus did *M. Herne*, upon perceiving *Danger* to hymself, make his Exit, pursu'd by a Bear.

*

Though Harry Hunks have his freedom, I alas do not, impris-on'd as I now am in the cage of Lambeth Jayle, & weigh'd down by the *Blayme* unjustly heap'd upon me.

With this Accounte have I shewn beyond any doubt that it was *M. Herne* who did bring about *Injurie*, urge *Debauchery* & practise in publick *Vile Witchcraft*. And should he be founde, let it here be noted that I do requeste to be present at his Triall.

Whosoever should pass this documente to the Magistrate: I begge that you send my Best Regardes to poor M. Pollen & his sister Rachel, & do wish them bothe from me a belated Merrie Christmas.

Robert Burrman

THE RHYME OF THE DASHING HIGHWAYMEN

Tell us the name of your darling, your roguish gentleman?

O, I fell in love with Claude Duval,
The gallant highwayman.
Such chivalry and sweet romance;
He always asked a lady to dance,
And only took gold from a man.

O, I fell for Richard Ferguson,
The finest of all horsemen.
A cad and a wit,
Was our Galloping Dick,
But I loved him all the same.

O, I fell for Rufus Goodlove,
The amorous highwayman.
His name was his way!

For a roll in the hay
With him I'd commit any sin.

O, I fell in love with John Nevison,
The rogue they called Swift Nick.
From Kent he rode north 200 miles
To make the Lord Mayor his alibi,
For a theft I saw him commit!

O, I fell for William Davies,
The Golden Farmer of Surrey.
He'd eighteen hungry mouths to feed;
If only his wife had set him free,
I'd have had all that gold for me.

O, I fell for Humphrey Kynaston,
The wildest one of all.
He lived with his horse Beelzebub,
Up in a cave in Nesscliffe Rock,
And gave all his gold to the poor.

O, I fell in love with Oberon,
In his silks of colours so bright.
His name I did know
When he aimed with his bow;
Now his robin sings in the night.

And we all loved Jerry Abershawe,
The laughing highwayman,
Til he shot himself a constable;

Then poor old Jerry laughed no more.
How we wept to see him hanged!

Anon

5

GALLOWS GREEN
1691

Charm: No arrow flies so fast that I may not stop it with this song and with a glance.

A Monday afternoon in October sank towards twilight, and the furzy expanse of Thornton Heath purpled itself in gloom. Darker still stood the giant oaks along its northern bounds, great gateposts to the wood beyond where night shaded prematurely, pressed down by the low grey cloud that turned the leaves to browning shadows. Only a collier, black with soot from head to foot, would have roamed there at this fading hour, for he needed neither sun nor moon to find his path.

Here, at the southern reaches of the Great North Wood, the heath rolled, dour and defiant even on the brightest days, shunned by all for whom the crossing of it on the track from village to woodland route was not a grim necessity. Even the trodden path from Colliers' Water, where the charcoal burners sluiced their kilns, to the tavern, where they sluiced their gullets, took a wavering line around the heath's edge. This not only avoided the swarthy mass of springing moss and twisted gorse; it also spared the collier a clear view of the stocks, set on the green hard by the heath. These were the dread of their kind, though it was their own practice of over-pricing and under-packing their charcoal sacks that led each of them, in time, to a day spent trapped between those blackened beams. The colliers of Thornton Heath treated these spells in the stocks not as a humiliation, but as a sort of tax, for none of them was made an honest man by the punishment. One might as well have expected a sack of gold as a fair measure from a charcoal man, hereabouts.

Also close by the heath, but on the far side of the pond and its swarthy huddle of dwellings, loomed a structure much preferred by the colliers as a point of interest, and upon which the single, murky eye of the tavern gazed unblinking as they drank within. This was the gibbet that gave the village green its name. On this Monday afternoon in October, which by now had sunk past twilight so that five stars glimmered over the sullen heath, the gallows stood silent and empty as a thunderstruck oak. Only if we were to fumble at the base of this crooked tower would we find a sign of its fame and frequent use. For there were carved the initials of every victim of the noose, and as the colliers in the Heath Tavern told anyone who asked, upon a round of ale being paid for, every name dug into the scaffold was one borne by a highwayman.

The highwaymen of Thornton Heath, even as they were overshadowed by the gibbet, were much respected, and even admired, by those lower crooks, the colliers. One might even have said that certain of them were revered. For whilst the colliers were often alone deep in the wood, and were frowned upon for besmirching all they touched with their habitual soot, they were in no way outlaws. Rather, they were essential, albeit grimy, members of the small community at Gallows Green, and the villagers would not have got along so well in life without them.

The colliers' crimes were minor, and supplied fodder for grumbling, gossip, and the occasional eruption of vengeance meted out at the stocks. But the highwaymen shone with the glamour of the true outlaw. They stole not from the poor of Thornton Heath, but from those who, in opinions shared at the Heath Tavern, could afford it. They punished the arrogant, the greedy and the stubborn, with that most romantic of deaths: a pistol shot ringing out across the heath, a wisp of smoke spreading through the trees, and likely the lament of a lady, too late offering a string of salt-watered pearls to the widowmaker.

As the heath absorbed the last film of light, as dew into a rug, on that Monday evening in October, and the colliers asked for more ale so that their throats were now thoroughly wetted, they began to talk. Always their conversation creaked before finding its runners, for days and nights alone in the wood can rust a man's words, but find a track they did, and it was the same one that had occupied them now since midsummer.

Old Graves, a grandfather among the charcoal men, began. His wool cap was tugged down to his eyebrows. It was said not only that he had worn it now for over thirty years, but that it was hard as a burnt pie crust and would crumble to ash should he ever take it off. His bloodshot eyes squinted from a face as shrivelled as a peppercorn, and he scratched continuously at his neck as he spoke.

'Saw him again. Last week,' he said, and shook his head.

'Her.' It was Canter, a young collier, spry and not yet wizened by the elements, who spoke. 'Saw *her* again,' he repeated.

There was a snigger from Pullet, who sat beside him whittling a stick between his knees.

Old Graves glared at Canter. 'No woman could handle a bow like that,' he said. He shook his head again, and went on scratching.

'No man would don a costume like that,' said Canter, and smirked.

'No man has a pair of horns. Nor woman, neither.'

There came a halt in their talk, and they listened to the scrape of Pullet's knife on his stick, and the spitting of the fire.

'Red, this time,' said Old Graves. The corner of his mouth twitched, and he took a drink to hide it.

'Satin, was it? Or velvet.' Canter mimed a swish of skirts, and Old Graves could help himself no longer. He laughed, a sound between a cough and a caw that made Pullet abandon his whittling and look up.

'Too small,' he said.

'What's it you're carving?' asked Canter.

'Too small to be a man. Only up to here.' With his knife Pullet touched his breastbone. Then he added, 'Pretty.' He returned to his work.

'Pretty!' Canter snorted. 'Can't tell a man in a frock from a maiden, this one.'

The shaking of Old Graves's head grew vigorous. 'It's true,' he said. 'Face like a lady, I seen it. Soft-looking. Like the vicar's daughter, but finer, somehow. Delicate.'

Canter drank. 'A woman highwayman, with horns. In a red gown. With bow and arrows, to boot. You two agreed on that?'

A glance passed between Old Graves and Pullet, who sighed. 'Ask Elliot,' he murmured, cocking his head.

The other two leaned to peer out through the tavern's only window. On the track that led from the pond and across the heath to the wood, a lantern bobbed.

'Here he comes now.' Canter thumped Old Graves on the back.

'No,' said Pullet. 'That's him heading out.' He brushed the wood shavings from his lap. 'Told me she's called *Oberon*.'

'He,' said Canter. '*He's* called Oberon.'

'Oberon,' Old Graves echoed. 'There's something.' He began to pack his pipe. 'Pretty, though,' he said.

*

The name of Thornton Heath's latest highwayman of note was already well known to Carolina Pye. For weeks now, she had drifted about the vicarage, whispering *Oberon* to anything that might keep her secret: the stone cherub in the dark corner of the hallway; the portrait of Carlita Pye that forever daydreamed on the landing; the cook's cat.

She had whispered *Oberon* most often to her own reflection, attired in these moments in her mother's preserved wedding dress. This she had snuck, very late one night, from the chest in her father's chamber, and secreted in her own wardrobe. Alas, the fabric was not only a dull brown, but moth-eaten, despite the layers of paper and cloth in which it had been folded all these years. But if Carolina stood back from the mirror, screwed up her eyes and made believe the dress was a royal blue, she could conjure the image she desired.

The odour of the dress was musty, that of stale cloves and the dead wood of the chest it had lain in, so Carolina had brought to her room handfuls of leaves, a clump of dry moss and a sprig of hawthorn with its berries. If she crushed these between her palms and sniffed, she could bring to her mind the wood, and around the image in the mirror sprung dark trunks and the flutter of falling leaves. With a single candle, placed on the far side of the room, it could almost be moonlight, and Carolina gazed and implored, *Oberon*, *Oberon*, until the enchantment ebbed and her wicked face appeared once more in the glass.

Wicked, she knew she was, for Carolina had until now been a model vicar's daughter: obedient, kind and willing. These qualities she had brought to her recent courtship by Lowell Bearmont, of whom her father approved, and whose reputation in his own village of Dulwych, where he was a master at the college, was one of rectitude and good manners. Carolina had been content. The match would please her father; it would certainly please Lowell, whose round eyes fixed upon her every moment they were in each other's company.

So it had been humiliating, upon her visit with Lowell to Dulwych to see the college and his cosy lodgings there, to find herself feverish. She had not spoken of it, had not asked if they might take a pause in their perambulation of the endless college grounds, and by the time they were sipping tea in Lowell's parlour, the late September sun sinking already beneath the eaves, she had been overcome with faintness. She hoped that she had sunk back against the couch with grace, and that her mouth had not fallen open or her tea tipped upon the rug. But she had awoken to Lowell shaking her shoulders, shouting her name, and had burst into tears.

So, it had been her fault, unable as she had been to quell those tears or to find composure, that Lowell, concerned to the point of exasperation, had declared they would ride back to the vicarage. They had sat in silence in the coach, Lowell's eyes no longer upon her, and as they rattled up the hill, he called to the driver to make haste.

The coach turned on to the woodland road, the shortest route to Thornton Heath, and as the trees bent over them, dusk turned to night. Carolina leaned away from Lowell to gaze out at the trunks that seemed, in her fevered vision, to step closer as the coachman's lantern lit them, and at the ever-changing patterns of black and grey beyond. A fox sat by the road and looked straight up at her. The trees grew taller, thicker, casting night up from their branches. The road grew rougher. She glimpsed three deer, leaping away through the undergrowth, the spots on their flanks flashing, and she was about to turn to Lowell and tell him when there was a shout and the abrupt halt of the coach threw them both forward.

A horse whinnied. Footsteps approached, on Lowell's side. Carolina pressed a hand to her mouth, and felt her whole body turn hot with fear. Lowell's face was rigid as the door of the coach swung open. There stood a figure, not two feet away from them. She felt Lowell flinch at the sight of the bow drawn taut, and the arrow, fletched with black feathers, that was aimed right at him.

But the figure was curious. The archer wore a blue gown that trailed on the road. Spiking from the crown of the head were horns like velvet antlers. The hair was a knotty tumble, the colour indistinct in the weak lantern light, but the face – Carolina found herself rapt. She could not have said that it was a man's face, nor that of a woman. It was, above all, enchanting. The lips were pursed, the eyes sardonic. The thrust of the chin, the line from it to cheekbone and temple, made her feel she might weep again.

'Say my name,' said the beautiful mouth.

And while Lowell stuttered that he did not know, how could he, Carolina felt her own mouth form the word, *Oberon*. It felt as soft and sweet as a cherry rolled upon her lips. The juice of it wetted her tongue. She said it again.

The figure nodded but did not smile. 'Step down.'

Lowell was pulling a purse from his coat, holding it out, but Carolina pushed past him and jumped to the ground. Oberon let the bowstring slacken, staring all the while at Lowell, who quailed still in the coach.

Carolina felt she was floating. She was both there and not there, both dreaming and more awake than she had ever been. Oberon took one step towards her and kissed her. There was a scent of ivy flowers, of the air before a storm. She opened her eyes and saw that Oberon was holding a robin. She reached out her hand. The bird hopped on to her palm and nestled there, warm and thrumming.

Oberon drew the bow taut once more and aimed the arrow at Lowell.

'Take it,' Lowell cried, and threw his purse down on to the road.

Oberon laughed and nodded to Carolina, who reluctantly climbed back into the coach. And before she could catch another glimpse of their assailant the horse was moving, the wheels were rolling, and Lowell, his head in his hands, was making a terrible croaking sound.

On they drove, through the Great North Wood, until the trees receded and the stars spread above the vast black of the heath. The bird in Carolina's hands seemed to sleep. She did not look at Lowell until they were slowing alongside the vicarage, and he cleared his throat.

'We will not speak of this,' he said, his voice thin with shame. 'We will tell your father you were ill. This is true.' He glanced at the bird. 'Now, let us put that wild creature away from us before it scratches you.'

But Carolina would not let go of the robin. There was a struggle, then, as Lowell tried to prise open her fingers. The bird panicked and stabbed at his hands with its beak. Carolina felt its feet scrabbling and its wings lifting, so that when she did let go it bolted and flew back and forth inside the coach until Lowell threw up his hand and dashed the robin against the door. Its little body fell lifeless at his feet, and Carolina dropped on to her knees, gathering it up as her hot tears splashed upon its poor, broken head.

All this Carolina recalled as she lay on her bed in her mother's wedding dress, and wept. Since that night she had sent no word to Lowell, despite two letters she had received from him, begging her forgiveness for his cowardice, urging that they must reunite and write over that memory with happier ones. Her silence felt vengeful, a source of both pained pleasure and guilt. But lying there, a single robin feather pressed between her fingers, Carolina began to see that she might both wreak her vengeance upon Lowell, and at the same time make him her conduit to Oberon. For what other excuse did she have to pass through the wood, but to travel to Dulwych that she might comfort her heartsick love? She sat up and wiped her eyes.

If Lowell really would do anything for her, as he declared in his last letter, then all she need do was lure him. If her deceit convinced him of her regret, and her abiding affection, he would come at her bidding and drive her in his coach along any road she wished, at any time she desired. She would be wicked. And she would be happy.

*

Carolina Pye was not the only woman upon whose lips the name *Oberon* rolled sweet as a cherry. In the village of Gallows Green, and in the farmhouses, taverns and other remote dwellings that edged close to Thornton Heath, a caged robin had become a possession much prized. Where they were heard singing from windowsills, a passer-by could be sure that, within, a woman whispered to herself, *Oberon*, as she went about her work. And Carolina Pye was not the only woman who connived to travel with a male companion, across the heath and into the wood, in the hope of enchantment.

The gossip amongst the charcoal burners, upon their reunions at the Heath Tavern, continued apace. Oberon wore a green gown, or a silvered one. Oberon's bow was for show, and he carried a pistol beneath his skirts. His horns were real, and sensitive to touch. Oberon was a gypsy woman, hiding at the home of the queen of the gypsies, Margaret Finch. Oberon was Margaret Finch herself. The robins Oberon was said to give as gifts never sang, or they sang all night long. He never took money, or he took so much and was so successful that he must by now be the richest highwayman Thornton Heath had ever seen. She kissed only women, and never men. She bewitched travellers. She was a witch. Oberon would surely hang.

Wagers were placed as to when a brightly coloured gown would be seen fluttering from the gallows, for it was only a matter of time.

On this gloomy evening in early November it was Canter who began, rising from his stool by the tavern fire to declare, 'One month! If Oberon does not hang by the last day of the month, I'll pay for every drink taken in this house.'

Old Graves scratched his neck. 'No crime committed. Can't hang a man for handing out robins.'

'He is armed,' said Canter, stretching to mime a bow and arrow, and knocking Pullet's shoulder so that his whittling knife clattered to the floor. 'Only a matter of time.'

'No man's made hue and cry,' Old Graves replied, shaking his head. 'And who of us has seen him of late?'

'Her. Elliot's seen her,' said Pullet. Retrieving his knife he pointed it at Elliot Brown, who sat alone by the window, staring out. 'He's been watching.' He returned to his whittling beneath the tabletop.

'What's that you're carving?' asked Canter, but Old Graves nudged him.

'Not heard a word from Elliot these last weeks, have we?' Old Graves's reddened eyes narrowed and his crust of a cap sank lower, indicating a frown. 'Likely knows something.'

Elliot Brown, a slight man of middle age, had, like his fellow colliers at Gallows Green, worked his kiln in the wood since boyhood. To an outsider, he would have been indistinguishable amongst this clan: his skin and clothes were as stained with soot as the next charcoal man's. But unlike his fellows, Elliot Brown rarely threw off the reticence borne of days and nights alone in the wood once the ale at the Heath Tavern was flowing.

He drank, perhaps a little faster and deeper than the others, for he shared so little conversation with them. He rarely stayed late, despite the tavern being much the warmest and most convivial spot about Thornton Heath, but would leave just as another round was poured, while all eyes were turned to the barrel. Some thought him a miser, though he was not disliked. What distinguished Elliot Brown from the other colliers was that he did not consider his spells of solitude in the wood a chore.

Even in winter weather, and during the longest nights of the year, he was content to be alone with the trees. He did not talk to them, nor to himself, but his thoughts found shape when he knew that all around him stood only trunks, and he had favourites against which he leant or sat to doze. Never had Elliot Brown been moved to give his heart to man or woman, for none had seemed to offer him the solace that he easily found beneath the branches of a forgotten oak, or in the serene twists of a hornbeam.

Old Graves, Canter, Pullet and all the charcoal burners of Gallows Green were well used to Elliot's pensive presence.

But his sparse words had dwindled to nothing as autumn had set in, and while their suspicion that this new taciturnity hid a secret was correct, their divination of the nature of that secret was not. Elliot knew no more than the rest of them about Oberon. He had listened to the same rumours. He had heard a caged robin sing from the farmhouse window. He had, along with many who worked in the wood, glimpsed Oberon riding through the gloom. It is true to say that Elliot Brown's glimpses had been longer, and more numerous, but they had furnished him with no certainties about Oberon, except for one: he was besotted.

He had not identified the feeling. Rather, he found himself split between two compulsions. The first led him to neglect his work, forgetting to check the flow of smoke from his kiln and instead pacing about until, without thinking, he allowed his feet to carry him off, through the wood. He walked through dusk, into the night, listening for the tread of a hoof, watching for the shadow of an antler, the flash of a brightly coloured gown. The second compulsion led him to self-imprisonment, sitting in the Heath Tavern under the gaze of the colliers, so that shame would prevent him from making these wandering pursuits.

His obsession was both a joy and a curse. He felt already that it would ruin him, yet he could not relinquish it, for that strange face, that slight body, lived now in his mind and drove all else from his consideration. Elliot Brown whispered the name, *Oberon*, to himself a hundred times a day, a hundred times a night. His lips, so unused to regular speech, throbbed with it.

The heath he looked out upon, on this particular Friday evening in November, seemed a chasm between the green and the wood, and the pale road, just visible still, a narrow bridge across that might break at any moment. Oberon, surely, was amongst the trees, making a fool of the world, scorning fools such as Elliot. He wished he could laugh and shake his head at this nonsensical presence, and place a wager with Canter that made of Oberon a passing amusement.

Canter was approaching him now, pulling up a stool, clashing his tankard down against Elliot's. 'What's afoot, old friend?' he said. Dribbles of ale had smeared the soot on his chin and it showed red beneath the streaks. 'Got the latest on our favourite, have you?'

Elliot shrugged. 'No more than you,' he said, and returned his gaze to the window, though there was nothing to see beyond the glass.

Canter swigged, and belched. 'So, you haven't heard,' he said, and made to stand.

Elliot knew this trick, but still his heart clenched a moment. There had been much talk that evening, but he had not listened. He stared at Canter.

'Hue and cry's up,' Canter said, and pretended to look out of the window himself. Elliot caught his reflection, smirking. 'Won't be long now.' He sauntered back to join Old Graves and Pullet.

Elliot watched them, Old Graves waggling that wrinkled head of his, Pullet intent on his whittling, but all three grinned, the red of their mouths raw in their blackened faces. Compulsions jostled within him. His feet shifted with impatience. Without finishing his ale, he found himself walking towards the door, not turning to raise a hand goodbye, not looking, but hurrying out into the night.

He took his lantern from the tavern wall but left it cold. It was not long before he could make out the road across the heath, that lonely treeless bridge. To his right stood the gallows, blacker than the night, thirsty-looking.

He had heard no hue and cry. The last hanging of a highwayman had been in May, and a woman had been ridiculed for scattering blossom on the ground, as if at a wedding. But he could not risk disbelieving the weaselly Canter. For the men of Thornton Heath would pass on a hue and cry faster than the women their gossip, and their eagerness for a catch, a kill, to brighten the drear days until Christmastide, meant they would pass on a lie just as quick. Canter had made the first wager, but the true price for Oberon would be too high for Elliot to bear. This he acknowledged, in his sooty heart, as he set off fast along the heath road, then broke into a run.

As Elliot Brown reached the boundary of the wood, a horse and coach came hurtling towards him from between the trees. He stepped into the verge and, as it passed, he saw by the light swinging within the grimace on Lowell Bearmont's face as he peered out across the heath. Elliot did not wait to watch the coach's progress. Taking Lowell's grimace to be one of fear, which in turn gave Elliot hope, he quickened his pace and was soon amidst the trees, breathing the dank fungal scent of autumn.

*

On this Friday evening in November, Carolina Pye shivered against the side wall of the vicarage, wrapped in a cloak, a travelling bag at her feet. It had not taken her long to concoct a plan. Certainly, it was devious, and carried no small amount of risk, to herself and her honour. But there seemed no better way she could contrive to place herself in a coach, on a road through the wood, in darkness, and she did not hesitate.

She had forced herself to pack the bag as if she really would never return. She had wept real tears as she carried it down the darkened staircase, pausing only to ask her mother's portrait for forgiveness, imagining her father's face when he returned from his visit to Salisbury. Carolina did not distinguish between her pangs of dread and those of guilt, though the latter were strong indeed. Her scheme necessitated deception, but the explanations she might be forced to give because of it would cause her more pain and humiliation than she inflicted. It might prove worth it. And she might never return home, but instead live in some gypsy encampment, in blissful devotion to Oberon, their lives made all the more harmonious by the chorus of robins.

So, she dreamed, and shivered, and pushed away tears, until the rattle of the coach came on the lane, and then Lowell's footsteps, sprinting towards the vicarage. In the darkness he whispered, 'Carolina, Carolina,' over and over, until she hissed his name, and then his mouth covered hers and she endured it.

'I came as fast as I could,' he said, breathing into her face, clasping her tightly to him. 'My darling, I thought my heart would burst. Let us go, now, and on the way you must repeat to me all that you wrote in your letter, and all of the details behind it that you could not write, and we will be in Southwark before we know it.'

She permitted him to lead her along the lane.

'You are absolutely certain?' asked Lowell, when he looked at her in the light of the coach's lantern. 'You don't mind the danger? I don't mind it because I love you so, my sweet Carolina. And because now I know you love me.'

He leant to kiss her once more and she turned her cheek. 'Wait until we are in London, and we are free,' she said.

To make Lowell believe that the yearning she felt, and heard in her own voice, was for him, but to keep him at bay: this was the line she must tread. Silently she prayed it would not be for long, and that the freedom of London would never be theirs.

As the coach pulled away and turned towards the heath, Lowell let go her hands. 'Do not be afraid, this time,' he said. He delved inside his coat and fumbled near his heart. His eyes flashed with some meaning that Carolina refused to catch. Already her mind was intent on the wood beyond, her vision filling with black trunks, moon shadows, the crowding in of the trees on the forest road.

Elliot Brown threaded his way so swiftly through the obscure undergrowth, he might have been a spirit of the wood itself. He swept beneath low branch and around boggy hole, tripping on neither briar nor bramble, made nimble by sheer will.

He cut first up the slope that would bring him past the gypsy camp, where nothing stirred but a stealthy fox, its eyes staring insolently up at him from beside the damped fire. He climbed thence to a clearing not far from the road – a useful spot, he knew, to catch some small moonlight, should an arrow fletch need straightening, or a bowstring pulling taut.

The rustle there, ahead of him, might well have been a snuffling boar, or a badger scratching up worms, but Elliot's heart swung, magnetised, towards it. The darkest stretch of forest road lay just beyond. He strained his eyes for a flash of red, or blue, or gold, an impossible sign in the midnight dark, and plunged through the trees in pursuit. Already, the rattle of a coming coach, as tiny as a rolling acorn, grew nearer. Elliot Brown, the throb of his heart now matching that of his lips, prepared to make the first irrevocable gesture of his life. Never had he uttered more than a whisper, or a sigh, when alone at night in the Great North Wood. He begged his own throat to do as he bid. He bargained with the trees, promising a return to companionable silence if they would only forgive him this unnatural, selfish act. As he hurtled towards the road he took a great gulp of cold forest air, and with tears springing in his eyes, at the top of his rusty, unused voice he cried, 'Oberon. Oberon!'

Faster and faster still the coach drove, heading as Carolina hoped it might for the track that crossed directly from the green to the wood. The heath spread out either side of them as they lurched along, and she imagined this was what it would be like, to cross a stormy sea in the dead of night, water black and deep to right and left, and only the stars for compass.

As the wood loomed, blocking out the sky, she longed to whisper that name, *Oberon*, and the sheer ache of preventing it caused her to give a small cry.

'Fear not,' said Lowell, and drew her close. She felt his hand still clenched against his breast, under the rough wool of his coat. 'We will go at a gallop. And when we are out of the wood, then we will talk.' He thumped on the roof of the coach, and soon Carolina clung to the seat, and to Lowell, as they were thrown about.

'Please, not quite so fast,' she whimpered, not out of fear at the pace itself, but at the damage it did to their chances of an encounter there, deep in the heart of the wood. But Lowell's wide eyes had a look of such fierce determination, and did not glance at her for a moment but rather stared ahead, as if he saw straight past the coach, the driver and the horse, saw even beyond the road and into the future.

Perhaps it was this prescience that made Lowell gasp for no seeming reason at all, before they rounded a long bend, the coach leaning so that wheels lifted from the ground, only to shudder into a crazed zigzag. Carolina heard the horse skidding as the coach twisted this way and that behind it. She heard the horse's terrible shriek of pain.

Lowell's eyes gleamed, even as the coach began to drag along sideways. 'Stay down,' he said. 'Hide.' He pulled down the rug and flung it at her.

The coach lantern guttered out as they slowed to a stop. A sensation like that of pouring cream spread rapidly across Carolina's skin, right to her scalp, and she could resist no longer. '*Oberon*,' she whispered. Lowell did not hear her. His face was pressed against the glass of the small window.

In one swift movement Carolina pushed the door and slipped from the coach. The road, lit only by vague moonlight, seemed a thread of smoke amongst the trees. But she could make out a figure, hovering in the smoke, and by its stature, slight yet made tall by its noble horns, she knew that it was

Oberon. Lowell called her name, but Carolina heard only the throb of her own heartbeat, the light rasp of her feet upon the road. She heard her own whisper, *Oberon*, as she advanced.

The figure grew more distinct. She saw the bow drawn taut, the trailing gown. Though the weak moonlight denied the wood all colour, she was sure the gown was forest green, and the face above it, more beautiful than ever. Behind her, the panting of the horse and the scrabble of the coachman as he hurried to descend were muffled, as if she had left them far away. Voices murmured from the coach, but she cared as little as if it stood a mile hence. A few steps closer, and she would see Oberon clearly. Oberon would see her.

She began to walk forward, along the faint river of mist, and felt herself like a spirit, come to meet her fellow soul of the forest. Oberon did not stir, only held the bow stretched and perfectly still. The stillness itself excited her, its enigma filled with unspoken passion, a stillness in which a heart surely beat as hers did, the thud of it louder now and faster, until all at once Carolina realised that the thudding was of footsteps, running along the road behind Oberon. She did not stop walking. There were no footsteps that mattered, in this moment, not even Lowell's, which crunched behind her now until she could feel his agitated breath, hot on her ear.

'Carolina, get back,' he hissed.

His words lost their meaning as soon as she heard them. She sped up.

He kept pace. 'Get back.'

They were within a dozen yards of Oberon, whose serene stance contrasted so cruelly with Lowell's abject fear that Carolina wanted to laugh. She must get rid of him.

She turned, and saw that he held out in front of him a pistol. It was pointed at Oberon, who had shown no sign of alarm but still stood, watching them.

'I'll shoot,' Lowell shouted. But his cry was drowned out by a louder, more desperate one, and the footsteps that had thudded behind Oberon resolved themselves into a shape that loomed out of the dark. 'No,' shouted Lowell, 'get back!'

Carolina, furious at the dual invasion of her dream, clawed at the pistol in his hands. Lowell tried to twist her away. As they wrangled, the shot rang out.

The shock of it sent Carolina flying to the ground. She rolled over on the road, her ears singing, her heart breaking. But she looked up to see that Oberon still stood, and beside him, a figure writhed on the road just as she did. Oberon had let the bow slacken and was bending to attend to this creature, both unlucky but so very fortunate in Carolina's eyes. She saw Oberon stroke the brow and clasp the shoulders of her mirror image, and there in the scanty moonlight, she wished herself into that person. She would be held, and succoured, and stroked.

Carolina began to crawl forwards, staring as the figure on the ground slowed in his flinches, and grew still. Somewhere in the trees beyond the road, a robin let fall a ribbon of notes. As her lips made the sweet plum of the only name in the world, Oberon began to grow faint in the mist. She rose to her feet and staggered towards him, her steps as blundering and hopelessly slow as those in a nightmare, yet on she forced herself, as the robin sang higher, wilder, and the mist closed around her head.

*

Carolina wakes in a shaft of sunlight, as she always does these days. The glade is shrill with the morning song of robins. She cannot see them, but she knows their gleaming shadows flit here and there about her. Oberon must still be near; the pillow they share is warm, and there is a scent that lingers, of crushed moss and sun-warmed leaves.

She nestles into the dint left by her lover, and pictures Oberon waking to gaze at her as she slept, pressing a kiss upon her parted lips. Margaret Finch, the gypsy queen, will be along soon, with a honeymoon breakfast of bramble berries and borage tea. She will hold up Oberon's gowns in the dappling light and ask which it will be today: emerald, red or midnight blue? And as every morning, Oberon will choose instead to return to bed, sending Margaret Finch away on some invented errand, and the lovers will entwine there, in the web of robin song, until Carolina sleeps once more.

She never tires of this life, as consoling as a dream. Only in the evenings, when Oberon dresses and rides away, blowing kisses that land like moths on her cheeks, and she sits with Margaret Finch to read the cards, does a breath of melancholy cool her heart. She is never certain that Oberon will return. But the cards, in their flickering pool of candle light, show her the magician, the cups and the star, and always their message is one of love. Margaret Finch helps her to bathe and wash her hair, and from mysterious places beyond the glade she brings white and yellow flowers to freshen the lovers' bed. They remind Carolina of the embroidered blooms on the pillow she once had. She spreads her hair amongst them and lies in the dark, in the lullaby of birds, waiting once more for Oberon.

*

On the morning of Christmas Eve, Lowell Bearmont paid a visit to the vicarage. He bore a package as large as a hatbox. He was speckled with snow that melted as he entered the hallway and greeted Reverend Pye. Everywhere, candles were lit. To Lowell they suggested not festive cheer, but vigil.

He was permitted to enter Carolina's room alone. There she lay, her hair curling across the pillowcase embroidered with white and yellow flowers so that, in her white night-dress, she resembled a summer wood nymph. She would have resembled an angel, but for the expression on her face, which spoke unabashedly of pleasure, and a kind of pleasure that Carolina Pye, Lowell believed and fervently hoped, had never experienced. Her smile at him was sly, distracted.

Lowell placed the box at the end of the bed, and slowly lifted the lid. Then he dipped in his hand and brought out the robin. He had spent many weeks training the bird to take titbits of food, to come to his whistle, to perch on his reluctant finger. He had trained himself not to flinch when its beady eye turned upon him.

'For you, my darling,' he said, raising his hand gingerly before Carolina's gaze.

She sighed, 'Come back soon, dear love,' and turned her head coquettishly to receive a precious, imagined kiss.

*

At the Heath Tavern, Old Graves's head waggled, and his brow crumpled into a frown. 'You'll have no payout from me,' he said, glaring at Canter's outstretched palm. 'A shame, it is. Her up there in that blessed frock.'

Canter grinned. 'Man or woman, it makes no difference. I said Oberon would hang within the month.' He stood to address the room. 'Who will fill my cup? Old Graves weren't the only one bet against me.'

The charcoal burners, their sooty faces bent over their tankards, went on with their talk. Canter turned to Pullet, who whittled as ever between his knees. 'You were right. He was pretty enough,' he said. Pullet did not reply. With a sigh, Canter slumped into his chair, and made much of draining his last drop of ale. 'What's that you're carving, then?' he asked Pullet, but Old Graves nudged him.

'Leave him be,' he mumbled. 'Taken it hard.' He scratched his neck.

Canter scoffed. 'He no more knew Oberon than the rest of us.'

Old Graves looked pointedly at the stool where Elliot used to sit. 'Not Oberon. That one,' he said.

They sat for a while in silence, Old Graves slowly shaking his head, upon which was clamped a new knitted hat that, beneath its soot, still suggested its original colour of dun. His old hat, as foretold, had crumbled to a handful of ashen fragments when, standing before the grave of Elliot Brown, he had tugged it from his crown.

Pullet pushed back his stool and brushed the shavings from his lap. On to the table he placed a short length of wood, which was carved with the outline of a bare oak tree. 'He's no headstone. This is all I can do.'

Old Graves hauled himself to his feet. 'That's fine,' he said. 'Very fine.'

On this chill dusk in November, the three charcoal burners made their way by lantern light through the drizzle to the churchyard. To reach it, they walked along the village edge where it met the heath, but none gazed across that great, stilled sea with its undulations now cast in purple shadows. Their path took them, by necessity, past the gallows that gave the green its name, and it was here that all three raised their heads and paused a moment. Canter lifted the lantern and they watched its light play upon the gown that swayed there in the breeze, and shone a dark forest green.

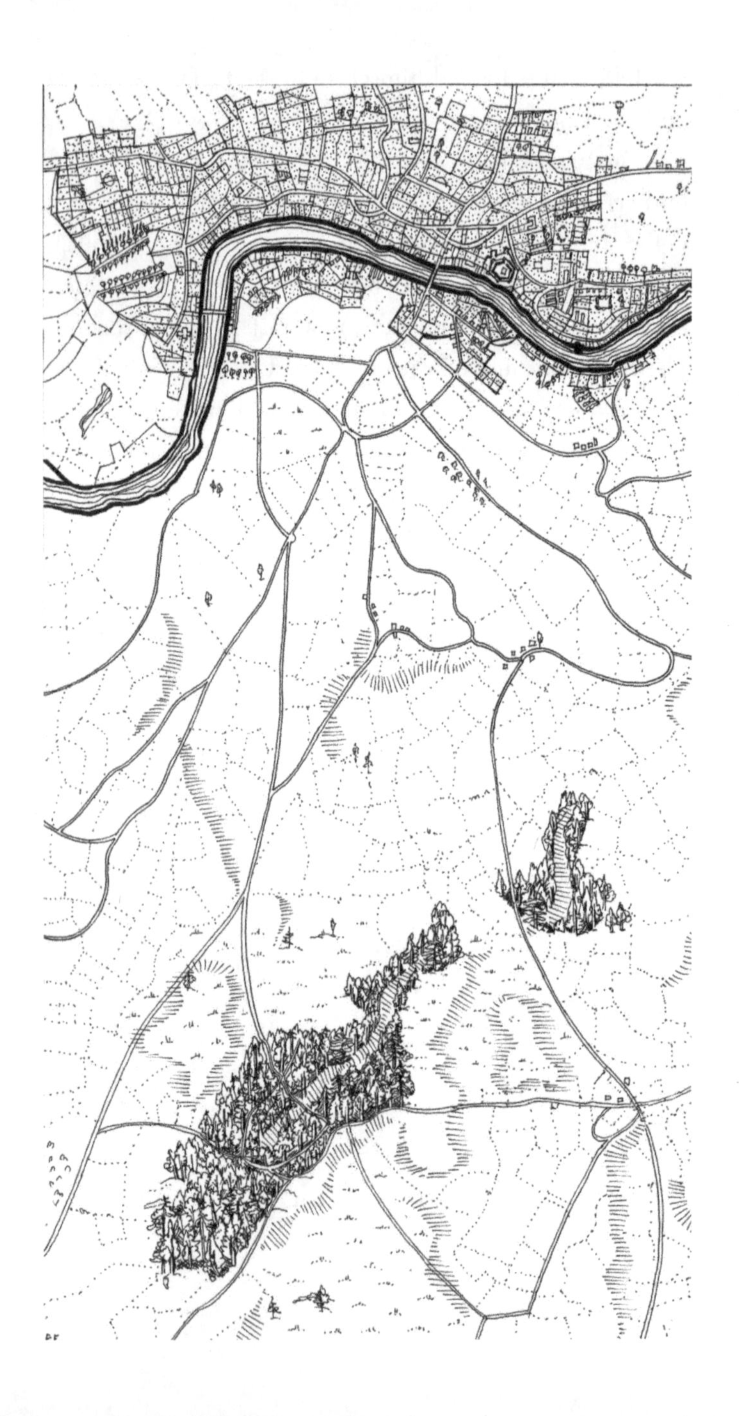

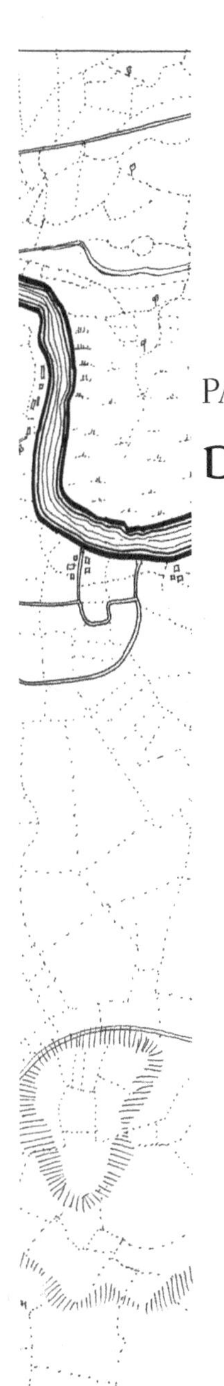

PART II

DISENCHANTMENT

HOW SWEET I ROAM'D

How sweet I roam'd from field to field,
    And tasted all the summer's pride,
Till I the prince of love beheld,
    Who in the sunny beams did glide!

He shew'd me lilies for my hair,
    And blushing roses for my brow;
He led me through his gardens fair,
    Where all his golden pleasures grow.

With sweet May dews my wings were wet,
    And Phoebus fir'd my vocal rage;
He caught me in his silken net,
    And shut me in his golden cage.

He loves to sit and hear me sing,
    Then, laughing, sports and plays with me;

Then stretches out my golden wing,
And mocks my loss of liberty.
William Blake

6

THE ERL-KING'S DAUGHTER
1760

Charm: Sprinkle a child's head with water as you sing this song, and never will she fall though battle may come.

'Now Phoebus sinketh in the west,
Welcome song and welcome jest,
Midnight shout and revelry,
Tipsy dance and jollity.'

As she sings, Ann Catley treads with bouncing step through the Great North Wood. She has not come far from the high road, and the Horns – just far enough to let the wood close in, so she might sing unheard, unseen by the Horns's dear denizens.With each phrase of her song she turns from tree to tree, imparting winks and winsome smiles. Her giggle, and her sideways elfin gaze, she saves for the alder tree where the woodland path divides. This is where she hopes to meet her friend.

'Braid your locks with rosy twine,
Dropping odours, dropping wine—'

She breaks into full-throated laughter. Two wood pigeons are blundering in the mass of green above her curly head. 'Oh yes, it's all for you, and aren't you handsome!' she coos. She pictures the trees' canopy as a soaring, gilded gallery, eager faces peering down and grinning with delight. A breeze comes rushing through the leaves and applause breaks out. A magpie caws his praise. But there's no sign of Erlekin, and it's for him she wishes to sing.

Ann Catley bows, long enough to pink her cheeks, and turns about the alder tree.

'Rigour now is gone to bed,
And advice, with scrup'lous head,
Strict age, and sour severity
With their grave saws in slumber lie.'

She waits, peering through the leafy shade, poised to start should Erlekin come ambling up, pretending he's not heard her. This has always been his way, to play at accidental rendezvous when, really, both know well he seeks her out. He even sneaks into the Horns and plays the part of coachman, mingling with the drivers there to snatch a word, a glance from her, and wink beneath his tricorne hat. But it's here beneath the alder tree that he has taught her strange old songs, older even than he is. He's been her natural tutor, long before her formal singing lessons; a sort of second father, though a wayward one. She wants to sing these bold new tunes and witness his surprise.

But no one comes. Ann Catley sighs, remembering that Erlekin had grimaced when she shared the news of her apprenticeship to William Bates, music master. He'd glared when she had told him of her plans to tread the stage, and sing for lords and ladies. She will not be deterred from this, and so, Ann Catley cocks her head, sways her hips, and gives the wood a smile that shows off her darling dimples. 'Oh, good fellows!' she cries, and leaps as if she had been goosed. 'And I but a girl of fifteen years!' Off she runs, towards the Horns, her father's inn and famous stopping place for coachmen weary of the woodland lanes.

The front door stands wide open and there her father, Berman Catley, leans, polishing a tankard. He beckons her and turns inside.

'Along she comes, Mr Bates,' Ann hears him call. Her tutor must be waiting. With a last deep breath of forest air and a coy shake of her curls, Ann steps into the dark.

A man sits close by William Bates. Before a soul in the room can speak he stands and bows, his head low before Ann. She puts out a hand, ladylike. With ceremony he takes it, and gazing up at her, he lavishes her fingertips with kisses. His lips are full, and deep, and wet. Ann endures the feel of it, and glances once at William with careful pride.

'Sir Francis Blake Delaval,' William smiles.

She has heard the name. An actor and, she thinks, a gentleman. He does not let go her hand but draws her near. His eyes have a compelling bulge to them. His cheeks and chin are round and pale, soft-looking. His lips stay wet, and when he speaks, tiny pearls of spittle fleck her gown.

'It is the greatest honour, Miss Catley, to know you,' he begins. 'Long have I yearned to hear this angel's voice that so enchants Mr Bates – and all who hear it.' He stops to raise his cup. 'To your future fame, and our enjoyment!' He might just as well be toasting his performance. Ann's father, proud behind the bar, claps approval.

'Good man, get the girl a drink,' Sir Francis snaps, and while Berman turns away, he pulls Ann down into his lap. William laughs. So, Ann laughs too. She suffers to be mauled about the waist and hips, for it's nothing but a game, and this man a friend. William's merry laughter tells her that. Still, she is released in time to take the cup her father brings, and all four drink, gleefully.

'Would you have me sing now, William? I've practised till I've got it good as Isabella had it.'

'No doubt of that,' her father says.

'Far sweeter, I'd wager,' Sir Francis booms close by her ear. 'For a lute! And I would serenade you, darling girl!'

'Go on, then,' her father interrupts. 'Perhaps stand over there, by the hearth, for the best effect.' He shifts his stool to let her pass. Sir Francis mimes a swoon, a broken heart, as she moves away, and William grins. Taking up the jug he fills their cups.

From where Ann stands, the open door shows green beyond, the wood a private, endless audience. Erlekin may lurk there yet. She clears her throat, and curtsies. '*Now Phoebus sinketh in the West*,' she sings. She sways and twinkles through the tune, as William has taught her. A dimple here, a deep glance there, a raised eyebrow, a flounce of skirt. It's not the style that Erlekin prefers, whose songs are rough or mournful. Her teacher nods encouragement, but Ann cannot ignore Sir Francis's look, rapt, adoring. His eyes are full of joy, a thing both dark and bright. His eyes are full of her.

'Brava! Brava!' Sir Francis roars, as she holds the final note. He slaps his thighs like thunderclaps. 'But Willy,' he says, turning to his friend and speaking loud, 'what of the *mise en scène*? She sings the part of Euphrosyne, and here, at our backs, the forest! Her very habitat. We might take a walk, together, and hear songs sweeter than the birds'.'

He beckons Ann. Her father has set his stool so she might not squeeze past and settle by Sir Francis. 'What say you, Euphrosyne? *I know each lane, and ev'ry alley green, Dingle, or bushy dell of this wild wood.*'

'But you know the play!' Ann gasps in mock-surprise, observing his delight.

'My dear, if I did not, I would be dashing home to learn it, that I might play alongside you one day. Come, to the forest.' He drains his cup.

'Be back by dusk, and stay close by my daughter,' Berman warns. 'The gypsies will be out. And worse.'

His look tells Ann he means her friend, for Erlekin to many is a bogeyman; at worst a murderous forest fiend, at best a sneaking thief. She leads the two men from the dingy pub.

All along the path Sir Francis chants, his baritone disturbing birds, which flit to left and right. '*Haste thee, nymph, and bring with thee, Jest and youthful jollity*. Miss Catley, you are the lady of the wood, a nymph true-born.'

She does not say that it is all too true. Ann Catley was a foundling child, left beneath this very alder tree for Berman to discover and take home. A babe of the wood indeed, and she's ashamed of it. Instead she smiles, the dimple smile, and sighs at all his pompous quotes. William starts to lag behind. They stray from the ride and its strip of sky to amble through the trees, in deep green light. No stage could hold this wood, Ann thinks. It has a scent so fresh, this time of year, it overwhelms. The blackbirds when they sing are downright bawdy.

Sir Francis seems to hear them too, despite his recitations, and turns to catch her hand. He draws himself up, his presence turning trees to theatre scenery, the mossy earth a soft-lit stage. He whispers now, his breath hot on her cheek:

'O nightingale that on yon blooming spray
Warblest at eve, when all the woods are still,
Thou with fresh hopes the Lover's heart doth fill,
While the jolly hours lead on propitious May.'

Her hand, in his, is on his heart. She feels the throb of it, too intimate, too quick. Ann blushes.

William snorts. 'No nightingales to be heard in here.'

'But you're wrong,' Sir Francis says. 'I have one, captured. And now she will sing for me.'

'I shan't sing until you set me free,' says Ann.

'Never.'

Her hand is growing hot. It's all for sport, this show of love; an actor's game. But something tells her not to disobey. The blackbirds are silent. She cannot find in her own heart the brazen nymph, the bold coquette that William Bates has taught her to portray. Her voice falters.

'Let her go, man,' William says, his laughter nervous.

Just then, the branches near them shake. Ann winces, knowing Erlekin, if it be him, will mock her company. Two heads appear. She knows those antic faces, gypsy boys from the encampment up the hill. Sir Francis jumps and looks askance. Her spirit rises.

'Good evening, little fellows,' she calls. She knows her grin is impudent. Her lover is wrong-footed. 'Fancy a song? I've one just for you. Come and sit.'

The gypsy boys are not afraid of gentlemen, especially ones that flinch at their approach. They greet only her, 'Miss Catley,' and loll against a sunlit beech, as lazy and at ease as fox cubs.

Ann's song, in this comfortable company, is as bold and blithe and libertine as ever. She swings her hips and flashes looks from boy to boy, and all the while Sir Francis prowls, a pale wolf in the shade.

*

Night, on the first full moon in May. The tree trunks are coal black, the leaves a shower of silver. White show the hawthorn boughs, ghosts massed along the rides where white mist gathers and snakes about the hooves of Olof's mount.

Sir Olof is riding towards his bride, a girl already wan and drawn with fear. She sits far off in a grey stone house, with Olof's grey mother at her side, one bony hand gripped at the girl's thin wrist. Golden shines their single candle light, so far off, too far to catch Sir Olof's eye.

Past the silent hawthorn ghosts he rides. The chill mist hangs. The forest is a fossil of itself. The air is skin-cool, still as a broken heart.

Midnight trunks give way to silver birches, wan and thin, and in the clearing, the moonlight glints on gold. Olof blinks and halts his steed. They are dancing, a ring of glimmering girls. Sweet notes of their music and their laughter chime in harmony. It is a sight he might talk of, all his life. A moonlit meeting in the wood, as he rode to meet his bride. A vision, perhaps, that foretells a happy wedding feast, a golden union.

*

At the private rooms that William keeps for teaching, Sir Francis lingers. He lies in wait as Ann rehearses scales and arpeggios, standing in the street below the window. William does not mention it, but his piano-playing feels louder and more urgent. The floorboards send the chords right through her feet. She glances out, from time to time, when William lets her rest, and sees that bluish coat Sir Francis wears, his tapping foot whether music plays or not. She sings her best regardless, and basks in William's praise. He promises the time is soon: the Drury Lane auditions for the roles in *Comus*. Ann will take a part, he's sure. Of all the roles, it is Euphrosyne she wants.

A morning's practice over, they wander out and feign surprise to find Sir Francis. He leads them to a public house, or to a club, and plays the merry host. Always, he toasts Ann's voice, her beguiling face, her way with gesture. She does not say that he has only watched her once, that day they ambled in the wood. No, Ann smiles flirtatiously and giggles at his endless flattery. For William always whispers, when she starts to stifle yawns, 'This man has influence. We both must court it.'

With this in mind, poor William complies as much as Ann does with Sir Francis's desires. Mostly, this means passing long and tipsy afternoons at games of cards. Ann does not play. Instead she takes the part of Moll, conspiring with each man in turn to throw the other. Sir Francis favours piquet, but will try his hand at any game on one condition: bets are placed.

Today the merry threesome take the window bench at Mr Long's establishment on Kemble Street. They've washed down partridge pie with ale and wine, and Ann is drowsy. She longs for the winding journey home, to breathe the wood's cool air once more, to seek out Erlekin in the alder's shade. Now every afternoon is spent in courting favour, she's no time for sweet idling. Sun pours through the bullseye glass, and while the men select their game and set their wager, she leans her head back in the warmth and dozes. The flick of cards against the wood, the chatter of the room behind, are soothing. Ann dreams of dancing in a grove of birches. She must have slept some time, for she is woken by Sir Francis's boozy breath as he enfolds her cheek in sticky palms.

'Ann Catley, dreaming nymph,' he booms. 'Lend me your luck.'

The sun has slipped behind the roofs of Kemble Street, and all is shadow.

'I should surely go home. My father waits,' she says. But it is Erlekin she thinks of, certain that he loiters now, where the two paths meet.

'But we come to the chase, Willy and I. My darling, use your wiles and put him off the scent.'

William is frowning. He does not look at Ann but stares intently at his cards. And so, she slides across and sits close by his challenger.

Ann nods as Sir Francis shares with her his hand, pointing to the Jack of Hearts, the Queen of Spades. 'Most wise. You'll surely win!' she says, though she's no idea what game they play.

'Cast your spell, my faerie queen,' he says, and the men begin their quiet duel. They play fast. Sir Francis, warmed by wine, pretends great horror, joy or puzzlement at each of William's hands. Several times he claims that all is lost, his reputation ruined, then grins and passes cards to Ann to lay upon the table.

William is ruffled. He wipes his sweaty chin and mops his brow.

'I don't doubt you'll take me for all I have,' Sir Francis moans. 'My sole comfort is knowing Ann will not forsake me. Will you, darling girl?'

'Never, poor Sir Francis,' she laughs.

William grunts. 'Well,' he says, 'it matters not, for you win.' He throws down his remaining cards, then pushes back his chair and stands. 'I'll fetch another jug.'

'Make it brandy,' Sir Francis calls. 'A splendid Armagnac, to toast my fortune!' He kisses Ann's cheek. Before she has time to gasp, he kisses her again, upon the lips.

The man has influence. She hears the words in William's voice even though he is not there.

'Euphrosyne?' Sir Francis is imploring. 'Forgive me my forwardness. But you of all must know how irresistible that cheek, those lips. I am bewitched. Truly.' He leans back in his chair and looks at her, takes her in from top to toe. 'And, Miss Catley, so will you be.' He grasps her wrists, and brings her palms to rest upon his heart. 'I will take you home, and you will be enchanted.'

Just then, there is the thunk of William's wine jug on the table, a second clap as Armagnac arrives. 'Fair and square,' he says, but there is something forced about his smile, something slightly bullish in the way he slaps Sir Francis on the back.

'How much did you lose?' asks Ann, playfully. 'I hope not much.'

'Oh, there was no losing.' Sir Francis eyes his friend. 'We all three won.'

William gives a tiny nod and pours out brandy. 'Winners all,' he says, and gives the largest glass to Ann.

*

Sir Olof, having drunk in this golden vision in the wood, prepares to take a circling path around the maidens, and ride on through the night. But then, one turns and beckons. She is fast beside him, reaching up a hand towards his own. Olof recoils.

'Come dance with me,' she says, her smile as full of secret promise as he hopes his wife's will be. Her fingers are beringed in gold. Her words ring like golden bells. All the glade, the maidens, music, leaves and moonlit ground, glitter bright.

'I must ride on,' Sir Olof says.

Now her hand offers him a pair of handsome boots. 'Fine buckskin, with gold spurs,' she says. 'Yours if you will dance with me.'

The boots are fine indeed, better than any pair he's worn. Better than any wedding gift he will receive.

'Forgive me, but I cannot dance. I must go on. I've many miles of forest ahead, and dark roads beyond.'

The boots vanish.

The music that charms the grove speeds up. The stately maids are whirling.

'Don't you know who I am?' the maiden asks, now at his other side. And in that moment, he does know.

'You are the Erl-king's daughter.'

She claps her hands and, like a fast-falling mist, a white shirt flutters from them. 'I'll give you this shirt, of silk blanched by moonbeams, if you will dance with me.'

Her smile suggests a dance of ecstasy, this night before he makes his marriage vows. The shirt would make the finest wedding suit, far finer than his own coarse linen.

Sir Olof looks away into the dazzled dark. 'I must depart. She waits for me,' he says.

The shirt vanishes.

*

The carriage jolts, its wheels splashing through potholes while the rain beats impatient fingers on the roof. William's talk is wild and fast. An invitation such as this is rare, he says, the Delavals have such a reputation, and the visit seals their favour with Sir Francis. She'll be a shoo-in for the part at Drury Lane, and as Euphrosyne her star will rise so fast and bright, a veritable comet. Still, he doesn't catch her eye but glares out at the whipping water. The countryside is smudged to brown and green, hills and fields that Ann has never seen before. She wears her finest gown, and feels self-conscious, a Cinderella going to the ball.

'You've been before?' she asks. William shakes his head. She wishes she could feel excited, but her teacher's agitation makes her nervous. They must both act the sophisticate at Seaton Hall, and neither has the breeding. Ann hums the tunes from *Comus*, and prods at William to find his voice and join her.

'We'll stop near Cambridge first,' he mutters.

'How much further after that?'

'Three days, in all.'

Dismay turns in her stomach. She looks down at the rose-pink dress, the new silk purse. 'But I'm dressed for dinner!' she says. 'And that won't come till Friday?' She tries to laugh, but really she would like to weep.

The coach wheels churn in mud. They hear the driver goad the horses, his cracking whip. Ann pictures Erlekin amid the dripping wood. *Call that a song?* he'd said, when he had heard her humming an air from *Comus*. So, she had not told him of this grand sojourn at Seaton Hall, and instead had listened, nodded, as he showed her how to take a robin's call and slow it down, picking out each note. *Don't forget the old songs, Ann,* he'd warned her. *The forest has the finest melodies.* He'll wait for her tomorrow, and when she doesn't come he'll slip into the Horns, his tricorne hat pulled down, and glare at all the spaces where she does not sit. While Ann will be on roads unknown, lurching through the wind and rain with William, at their driver's mercy.

*

As their coach pulls up to Seaton Hall, both William and Ann are green about the gills. She has not vomited, but neither has she eaten for the last two days. The journey was so long and dreary, but worse than that, each hour seemed infected with a kind of dread. She's had too much time to wonder how this trip was brokered, and suspects that game of cards in Kemble Street. Who really won?

William is sullen, has been sullen even when the sun broke through the clouds to show them soaring crags, great gleaming hills, a silver river swollen from the days of rain. Now, at the crunch of gravel underneath the wheels, he stirs and sighs. His eyes are bleary. The carriage air is stale. Above all, Ann would like to lie as still as stone, alone in her room above the Horns. Her father will be grumbling still. He made her teacher swear he would look after her. And William swore. So, all is well, or should be.

The coach driver has made no move, so Ann throws out the carriage door and gulps the mizzled air.

'Wait,' snaps William, but she has frozen at the sight of Seaton Hall. Such grandeur, such a serious face it has, it's hard to see Sir Francis living here. Brown stone, sweeping steps, and now, hurrying down them, a cavalcade of staff in black and white.

She cowers back inside the coach. 'I can't step out like this,' she says, 'I'm all mussed up.'

'You're pretty as a picture,' William says, and manages a smile.

Ann scowls. 'I want a bath, no doubt of that.' But still, excitement rises and she giggles as a footman leans to take her hand.

'Madame,' he says, 'this way,' and they are greeted by the rows of maids and butlers as they climb the regal steps.

The giant doors are standing wide. As Ann crosses the threshold a great din starts up. Trumpets, horns and drums blast out a clashing fanfare. Petals start to tumble from some unseen height and flutter down like scented snow. Several ladies dressed as forest nymphs are dancing down the endless hall towards her. They curtsey as they take her by the hand and lead her to a kind of throne, completely stuck with roses.

Ann feels the urge to weep again. But there is Sir Francis, grinning, in the guise of Comus. He looks quite gay, his crown bedecked with ribbons, his doublet and his cloak in clashing shades of flame and crimson. Above the fanfare, he bellows out Comus's lines:

'Can any mortal mixture of earth's mould
Breathe such divine enchanting ravishment?'

He helps Ann up on to the throne. William watches, rounded on by nymphs himself, and shakes his head in wonderment. 'Quite a show,' he calls out, but Sir Francis pays no heed. He looks only at Ann, who bows her head to receive a rosy crown.

Dizzy with the scent, the trumpet noise, the flowing petals, she whispers to Sir Francis, 'But I'm Euphrosyne, remember? Not the lady. My part is to persuade her all is well, not sit up here.' With a flutter in her stomach she recalls the story in the play. The frightened lady, trapped in an enchanted chair by Comus as he preys on her, with magic cup and weasel words. He plans seduction. Wanton sin. The lady risks her virtue.

'My dear Miss Catley, you may play whichever part your heart desires.' Sir Francis bends to kiss her feet.

She feels ridiculous, but under William's watchful eye she laughs and wriggles, playing the coquette. The throne begins to move. Pushed by the forest nymphs, it rolls on hidden wheels the whole length of the hall, Sir Francis leading the procession. There's nothing she can do but smile delightedly and wait for her release.

*

The music in the glade grows louder. The dancers move so fast that their circle seems a blurred band of golden light against the meagre birch trees.

The Erl-king's daughter sits behind Sir Olof on his horse. The hand that reaches round his shoulder holds a crag of solid gold. It is larger than a bullock's heart.

'I'll give you this, if you will dance with me.'

Her thighs are pressed around his own. Her breath is cool against his neck.

Such a mass of gold he's never seen. It would buy him and his wife a blessed life. A home, fine horses, meat and wine; silk and jewels and any gift his children ever asked for. His children!

'Give me the gold, but let me go. I must not dance,' Sir Olof says.

The music ringing in his ears becomes discordant. Where all chimed golden, notes begin to shriek in blue and black.

The Erl-king's daughter thrusts her fist between his shoulder blades. 'Take only this,' she shouts.

From the pain across his back spreads a shudder. He can barely hold the reins, nor kick his heels. Upon his jerking mount, Sir Olof hunches, and though he leaves behind the tortured tune, the glittering glade, the Erl-king's cruel daughter, the shudder grips him all the long ride home.

*

Ann's limbs are heavy with the weariness of three days on the road. To walk and nod, and smile and chew, is to do so underwater. Her ears are numbed by hours of rattling carriage wheels and sudden trumpet blasts. But there is no respite from her admirer's hospitality.

The dining hall is decked from top to bottom in great wreaths of ivy, honeysuckle, clematis and rose. In a window nook, a band of minstrels sits to strum and trill. A hundred candles float in bowls of water lilies, and food fit for an elfin horde is laid on whitest linen. Whole roasted birds, candied fruit, jellies bright as costume jewels, salads and vast piles of dainties Ann cannot identify. All stranger than a dream, more fanciful, yet here they sit, the three of them at one end of the heaving table.

Sir Francis heaps her plate with morsels, and pours more wine with every sip she takes. The minstrels croon. Ann struggles even to talk. The conversation seems to slide about, the voices thick and echoing. She nods often, and laughs when William does. It seems to be enough. Eventually, she hopes, she will be shown a room, a bed, and will fall gratefully to sleep.

But the night is long. Sir Francis revels in each dish, each drink, each chance to tell a tale as ludicrous as the one that now envelops them. His ribboned crown slides sideways. Ann droops, then hauls herself upright. She must be gracious, and enjoy herself.

In what feels like the small hours, Sir Francis says he'll show them both to bed. He claps his hands to summon nymphs, still costumed and obedient, and three of them lead William away.

'Goodnight, fair prince!' Sir Francis sings, and turns his demon grin on Ann. It's just the two of them, a greedy king and queen surrounded by half-eaten bounty. The blooming room swells and sways. On cue, the band of minstrels end their song, and vanish.

'My nightingale,' Sir Francis croons. He strokes Ann's burning cheek, then hesitates. His eyes are bright. 'I've just the balm for you. The sweet night air will freshen weary spirits. Come, and take a walk with me.' He licks his lips, already wet.

'It's very dark,' says Ann. 'Why don't we wait till morning?'

Sir Francis sighs, seemingly relenting. 'In truth, I have contrived a gift for you, which I long to share. But, if I must be disappointed …'

'Won't it be cold?' she asks. 'William says a chill would be a danger to my voice.'

Sir Francis stands, flicks off his crimson cloak and in one great swoop has wrapped it around Ann. 'There,' he says. 'Just a minute's walk? It's not far. And I promise you a bed fit for a lady.'

Ann thinks of pillows, cool white sheets; a blissful, silent rest. 'All right,' she says. 'A minute.'

Triumphant, he leads her to the velvet drapes that line one wall and swishes them aside. The tall doors rattle open. The air, it's true, is fresh as water. All beyond is black, but where the land meets sky, a retinue of stars that blaze with chilly light.

Ann is forced to take Sir Francis's arm, and step into the gaping night. They cross a colonnade, descend six steps, then walk on spongy grass. Her shoes sink in, and all around, the dizzy heavens tip this way and that. She smells damp moss, wet lawn, some other herbal perfumes that she doesn't know. Sir Francis guides her on. Though their walk is slow, his breath is heavy.

'Just a little further,' he mutters now and then. But all around is black on black, the house so far behind that she is not sure she could find her own way back. If it came to that.

At the sound of rushing water, Ann balks. 'Where are we?' she asks, as boldly as she dares. 'I think we should return, don't you?'

'We're here,' Sir Francis whispers, and she spies a faint flicker of candle flame not far ahead. The path feels muddy, but as the small light grows, Ann's heart is eased a little. There's shelter near, at least. She hears the clank of key in lock. She sees the slice of gentle light that widens as they push the door.

The room, so sudden after all that black, is a paragon of opulence. Rugs and furs, tapestries, silken drapes that hide, she sees, a gold four-poster bed. She gives a cry. 'What is it?'

The light gutters. Hastily, Sir Francis shuts the door against the night. He kneels before her. 'Starlight Castle. A fairy place for a fairy queen. And all of it, dear Ann, I built for you.'

She gazes at the patterned chaise, the candle sconce, the ornate table laid with wine and fruit in golden dishes. 'I don't believe you!' she laughs. 'You're teasing me.'

'Oh, no.' Sir Francis frowns. 'A week ago, this was a patch of meadow grass and daisies. But a queen deserves a castle. And though I lack the magic powers of Comus, I do not lack for zeal. Do I, Ann?' He draws her fingers close to those wet lips. 'Dance with me. We need no music.'

She lets him kiss, once, then steps away. The golden bed looms beside them. A pair of gold-heeled slippers, and a dress of silk, white as moonbeams, lie upon the counterpane. 'I should not accept such gifts,' she says. 'But do you mean me to sleep here? Not in the house?'

Sir Francis stands. 'Nobody need see us, or hear us, hidden as we are, with but the stars for company.' He is growing grandiose. 'Do not imagine I'm immune to those bewitching smiles, those saucy looks of yours. William might remain cold-blooded. But I am made of richer and more lusty stuff.' As he talks he sidles closer, while Ann steps back, and they slowly move around the room like this until they reach the table. 'Ann, you are wise in your own ways. Your angel eyes are knowing, your laugh designed to reel me in. And you have caught me. Your spell has worked. So now, my darling girl, it's your turn to give in.'

He grabs her round the waist. With nowhere else to go, she slips his hand and ducks beneath the tabletop.

'Ann, you need be coy no longer.' He bends and glowers down at her, the bulge of his eyes more prominent than ever. They are red-veined, and greedy.

'Did you tell William? That we were coming here?'

'He need not ever know you are my mistress.'

The key to Starlight Castle dangles from Sir Francis's neck. She'd like to snatch it, run and lock him in, but beyond is only miles of dark, a landscape she cannot even guess at. Ann smiles. 'Then grant me one more wish,' she says. 'Since this is Starlight Castle, let's admire the stars together.'

'Star-crossed lovers that we are.' Sir Francis beams and helps her up.

She suffers his kiss, his grin of victory, and calls on all that William has taught her. With dimples, blushes and dancing steps she steers him to the door. 'Let us share your cloak,' she says, and soon she's nestled at his chest, the crimson velvet round them both. The key is on a broad ribbon, knotted tight.

'Which is your favourite star?' she trills.

'Let me see.' She feels Sir Francis's fingers running up and down her sides, then resting on her ribs. 'This one,' he says, as his hand grasps at her left breast.

Ann twists about and flings her arms around his neck. 'You devil!' she laughs, and gazes with all the false lust she can muster into his swollen eyes. She leans up to kiss his mouth and, as she does, her fingers find the ribbon. She pulls his head down, lips pressed tight, and in one light flick has looped the ribbon up and round her own head.

Sir Francis's tongue is between her teeth. Ann bites.

At his yelp, she wriggles free and shoves him out towards the dark. She slams the door. She turns the key, then runs to lift each tapestry and check for other entrances. There's only stone. She is trapped, but so is he.

For some minutes he calls to her, praising her seducer's trick. She has stoked his fire, he says. He burns with love despite the chilly night. The stars all sing her praises, if only she will come and hear. His tone does not stay jocular. He pleads for a while; grows stern, then angry. His baritone roar vibrates the door between them as he rants.

'I would have married you, cruel Ann, and now I'll marry nobody. I'll waste away for want of you.'

A good thing too, thinks Ann, but tries to calm him. 'I sought only your guidance, your generous tutelage.'

'You wanted teaching? Ha! If you will not accept my gifts, then I curse you. May you never earn such gifts again. May you never leave that dreary wood, nor ever find true love, or fame. May your looks be mired, and all that look upon you shriek in horror.'

On he rages. Ann retreats and sits beneath the table, listening. Her mind runs to the morning, the look on William's face, the long and dreary journey back to London while he chides her. *The man has influence*. She thinks of Drury Lane, and the auditions she's been waiting for, the role of fair Euphrosyne. All their happy talk, of how she'll be the youngest ever to play the part, how she'll take the theatre world by storm and win a thousand hearts.

When finally her lover's howls dwindle and subside, Ann creeps once more towards the door. There she presses her ear to hear – what? His breathing? The silent night? She jumps when, instead, Sir Francis speaks directly to her.

'Ann. Ann. Do not be angry with me.' He pauses. When he speaks again, his voice is meek. 'It's William you should reproach. It was he, Ann, who lost at piquet. It was he who took my bold wager, and lost. He lost you, in that game, and I won. I've only tried to claim my prize.'

She hears him slump against the door. 'In truth, your voice is not so fine as Isabella's,' he says. And then he walks away.

*

At the grey stone house, Sir Olof's grey mother greets him. She is at the door, a candle in her hand. When he does not dismount, she comes to him and raises that small flame towards his face.

His mother gasps. 'But you are drawn and stricken. How you shake. You look as though the night has aged you all at once.'

At the window, he spies the pale face of his bride peering out.

'Douse the flame, Mother,' he says. 'Tell her it was a stranger who passed by.'

'But what has become of you?'

'Tell her I went hunting and did not return.'

'But it's night.' With one great sigh, his mother blows the candle out.

They stand in the moonlight, which bleaches the grey house white.

'The Erl-king's daughter has struck me,' Sir Olof says. 'And I must ride until this shudder subsides.'

When the moon has gone, and morning comes, Olof's grey mother sets to work. She lays down cloth and pours out wine, and piles sweet morsels on to plates. The fearful bride watches this. She sees how those bony fingers shake.

'Gold Mother,' she says, 'who was it that rode up to our door last night?'

'It was but a stranger.'

'But Gold Mother, why does not Sir Olof come?'

'He went hunting, Gold Daughter,' says Sir Olof's mother. But the silver in her eyes betrays her.

All day Sir Olof's wan bride weeps in her chamber. She turns the key three times in the lock and will not answer pleas. Flies drown in the cups of wine, and wasps feast on the morsels. All around the grey stone house, blackbirds sing and pigeons coo, making their own May marriages.

*

At the King's Arms in Seaton Sluice, Ann feels quite at home. The owner, a sprightly but serious man named Mr Milton, reminds her of her father. He's set a fire for her, despite the early hour, and there she dries her damp feet. She sips a thick and warming drink he called a 'brose', and ponders what the day will bring.

It was quite simple, in the end, to creep from Starlight Castle in the mawkish dawn, and follow the stream she'd heard the night before, away from Seaton Hall. She walked by it, through a strip of tangle wood, so like her own dear forest by the Horns that it raised her spirits. With its rushing voice, the stream led her to Seaton Sluice, a village. Most wonderful of all, it led her to her first glimpse of the sea. A great, grey, roiling mass of moody water; Ann thought that she should feel afraid. But the smell of it was so invigorating, and the size of it so awesome as to make Sir Francis seem no more important than a fly, that she lingered till the wind had chilled her. She would like to look again, before she goes.

How she will go, she is not quite sure. But it is not long before the front door creaks, and standing before Ann is a windswept man who wears a lumpen tricorne hat. She stares as Erlekin makes for the bar and thwacks the bell for service. She hears him ask for porridge, cream and brandy, and listens as he slurps and coughs, not turning once to look at her. When Mr Milton offers him more breakfast, he shakes his head. 'Be on my way now,' he says. 'Long road.'

Ann clears her throat. 'Sir, what brings you here? Are you not very far from home?' She cannot hide the smile that swells her voice.

Erlekin turns and smirks at her, taking in the rose gown, her muddied feet. 'Why, Ann Catley. I thought I'd find you up at Seaton Hall, playing the lady.'

She shakes her head. 'That's no place for you.'

'And you neither, by the look of it.'

Mr Milton stares, behind the bar.

Erlekin draws Ann away to huddle by the fire. 'You'll come back with me. To the Great North Wood.'

Ann blinks. Her face is burning. She could not wish for better fortune to arrive and save her from these straits. 'But how?' she asks, as he leads her past the innkeeper, and slaps a coin down on the tray. She would like to give her thanks to Mr Milton, for the fire and the brose, but he is glaring as they push the door and stand outside, buffeted by salty winds. A coach stands by the King's Arms, its livery familiar.

'Borrowed this,' says Erlekin, as casually as if he meant a handkerchief, and slips behind the inn towards the stables. While he hitches on a borrowed horse, Ann dawdles, gazing at the wondrous spitting sea. It's wider than the moors she passed with William, wider than her own dear wood, its rushing like the wind through frantic leaves.

Erlekin claps his hands at her. 'Get on up. You'll sit up front with me.'

Ann obeys.

The road takes them up the hill. To Ann's alarm they soon pass the gates to Seaton Hall. She grips the seat, to keep from bumping quite so much, and tries not to think of William, waking to find her gone and in disgrace. But her heart is sore with all she's lost. The thought of home is no relief. Her father will be furious.

The coach drives faster, rattling away from Seaton Hall, Sir Francis and the dream of singing Euphrosyne at Drury Lane.

'Fear you'll never sing for lord and ladies?'

She watches Erlekin, his gritted jaw, his expert hand that flicks the whip. 'I'd learned to sing the airs from *Comus*. I'd got it better than Isabella ever had it.'

On they ride, beneath a heavy sky. After half an hour or more, the coach takes a wild and sudden turn on to a lane, overhung with chestnut trees, and halts there beneath the garish blossoms.

'Come live with me, in the wood,' says Erlekin.

Ann feels a flutter in her stomach. She's never heeded forest gossip, tales of missing girls, of fallen branches, broken limbs, woodcutters laid low. Always she laughed and said no one man could be blamed for all the mischief in a wood. But now she quails.

'I'll teach you all the old songs that you've forgot. You'll learn a thing or two.' He reaches up and Ann flinches, but his hand lands on his misshapen hat and presses here and there. 'Too tight,' he mutters. When briefly he lifts the brim, Ann thinks she sees the shape of horns, made by his sticking hair. 'Old Berman wouldn't mind. The gypsies would make room for one who sings so well.'

Ann stares into her lap. 'We lose time on the road,' she says.

Erlekin looks at her, intent. 'I'll take you home. Where you belong.' The coach begins to rumble on. 'And while we make our way, let's have a song, that you might learn it.'

So, as they pass beneath the chestnut trees, Ann listens.

> 'The Erl-king rideth out ere dawn,
> Breaketh day, falleth rime,
> Bright day him came on.
> The Erl-king cometh home,
> When the wood it is leaf-green.
>
> 'Beneath the alder halteth he,
> Breaketh day, falleth rime,
> His bonny daughter there to see.
> The Erl-king cometh home,
> When the wood it is leaf-green.'

His voice rings with green and brown, with sunlit leaves and tangled ground. Ann sees her cherished alder tree, her foundling birthplace. She sees herself, a swaddled babe, laid down among the roots, and her father bending over her, to doff his tricorne hat.

She takes a breath, picks up the melody.

'The Erl-king cometh home,
When the wood it is leaf-green.'

GREEN GROW'TH THE HOLLY

Green grow'th the holly,
So doth the ivy;
Though winter blasts blow ne'er so high,
Green grow'th the holly.

Gay are the flowers,
Hedgerows and ploughlands;
The days grow longer in the sun,
Soft fall the showers.

Full gold the harvest,
Grain for thy labour;
With God must work for daily bread,
Else, man, thou starvest.

Fast fall the shed leaves,
Russet and yellow;
But resting-buds are snug and safe

Where swung the dead leaves.

Green grow'th the holly,
So doth the ivy;
The God of life can never die,
Hope! saith the holly.
Henry VIII, King of England

7

DENDROLOGIA 1797

Charm: I know songs unknown to any man or woman.
This song will bring you help, in sorrow or in strife.

JANUARY

Fruits in prime, and yet lasting:

Apples: Kentish Pepin, Russet Pepin, Golden Pepin, French Pepin, Kirton Pepin, Holland Pepin, John-Apple, Winter Queening, Marigold, Harvey Apple, Pome-water, Pome-roy, Golden Doucet, Apis, Reineting, Lones Pear-main, Winter Pear-main, &c.

Pears: Winter Musk (bakes well), Winter Norwich (excellently baked), Winter Bergamot, Winter Bon-chrestien, both Mural: Vergoules, the great Surrein, &c.

John Evelyn, *Kalendarium Hortense* (1706)

The wood is at its dankest, but still Samuel Matthews sits out, on a stump beside his cave. It is Saturday, and the weekend brings more visitors than usual. He has stolen the necessary bottles of beer, and bedded them in yew fronds lest they freeze.

Sure enough, here comes his friend and fellow gardener, Hodd, who pulls from his pocket a Norwich pear, then another, and another, handing each to Matthews. Hodd is soon shivering as they sit together, swigging their beer, watching the whitish smudge that is the sun beyond the bare branches.

'Master at Shelverdine told me,' says Hodd. 'It's coming. Ink on the Enclosure Act barely dry, he said, and commissioners carving up the forest. Selling this, leasing that, it'll be.'

Matthews is silent. He scratches at the scars that part his wavy hair, one above each temple.

'Time you got yourself a lodgement.' Hodd's teeth are chattering, and he stands to stomp his feet. 'How d'you bear it?'

The tree nearest Matthews's cave, opposite the opening, is a hornbeam. It has an elegant twist to its trunk, and the air of a dancer about to bend, one arm rising in a century-long flourish. Inside the cave, strung carefully where the air will always reach, are posies of hornbeam catkins tied up with string.

'I don't know,' says Matthews. It is his standard answer. 'Will you have supper with me? Might be others come along.'

Hodd wants a fire, and to roast the pears, if he's to stay, so they get one set and Hodd stands over it, waiting for heat. 'Got no family could take you in?' he asks.

'Here's a couple now,' says Matthews.

A few minutes later, a man and a woman appear on the path, and call greeting. They are delighted to have found the cave and its hermit.

'A friend told us,' they say, as all shake hands. 'We've wanted to meet you for so long. We came all the way from Deptford.' They smile and smile as Matthews pulls up logs for them to sit on, and dives into the cave for more bottles of beer.

As they wait for the pears to roast, Hodd tells the news again. 'Ink on the Enclosure Act barely dry,' he says, shaking his head.

'What will you do?' the man and woman ask Matthews.

As a parting gift, the woman hands him a neckerchief. It is obviously the man's, pulled crumpled from his pocket.

FEBRUARY

Set all sorts of Kernels and Stony Seeds, which Field-mice will certainly ruin before they sprout, unless prevented: Also sow Beans, Peas, Rounsevals, Corn-sallet, Marigold, Anny-seeds, Radish, Parseneps, Carrots, Onions, Garlick, &c. and plant Potatoes in your worst ground.

Rub Moss off your Trees after a soaking Rain, and scrape, and cleanse them of Cankers, &c. draining away the wet (if need require) from the too much moistned Roots, and earth up those Roots of your Fruit-trees, if any were uncovered. Continue to dig, and manure, if Weather permit. Cut off the Webs of Caterpillars, &c. from the tops of Twigs and Trees to burn. Gather Worms in the Evenings after Rain.

Samuel Matthews does not have to live off the wood's meagre winter offerings. Some have conjectured that he stews earthworms for his supper, but there is mockery in their meaning, not pity. When tourists visit him in the wood, it is most often bread and boiled mutton he serves them. Rustic enough to amuse; safe enough to eat.

The gentlemen of Sydenham and Norwood who employ him in their gardens do not pry. It is understood that Matthews lives alone in the wood and, since he is nimble and strong at the age of seventy-one, it must suit him. It is understood by some that he has always lived there; by others that before the wood was an asylum; by yet others that before the asylum, there was a wife, and children, hearth and home. The two scars that show through his hair might explain his peculiar preference for the company of trees; a treatment gone awry, or violence done, the horrors of the asylum marked upon him.

At Shelverdine, where Hodd tends to the small orchard and vegetable plot, the kitchen girls tease him. 'Off to see the prophet?' they call, when they catch him pocketing a carrot or a handful of beans. The kitchen girls have heard that Matthews the Hairyman, as they call him, can tell the future. He has all night to look at the stars and trace how they align, how they circle one another, collide and kiss goodbye. The sky is full of lovers, fortunes, life and death, and the Hairyman sees it all.

At Wells House, where Matthews works most often on Mrs Elverbrook's geometric borders, he is considered an enigma. For this man, who speaks so frequently to himself but rarely to others, has coaxed into glorious abundance Mrs Elverbrook's *Rosa mundi*, and his flourishing transplants of mignonette have filled the garden with such a scent as she has never known. The disparity between wiry, taciturn man and zealous blooms bewilders Mrs Elverbrook. Her brother, who is eccentric and frequents the local public houses, tells her that Old Matthews has permission for his hermitage from the Dulwich estate, and that he is simply an original. Mrs Elderbrook, entranced by those green fingers, suspects elfin blood. She imagines that each cicatrix upon his head once rooted a horn, sap-tinted and leafy.

MARCH

Flowers in prime, and yet lasting:

Anemonies, Spring Cyclamen, Winter Aconite, Crocus, Bellis, white and black Hellebore, single and double Hepatica, Leucoion, Chamae-iris of all colours, Dens Caninus, Violets, Fritillaria, Chelidonium small with double flowers, Hermodactyls, Tuberous Iris, Hyacinth Zeboin, Brumal, Oriental, &c. Junquills, great Chalic'd, Dutch Mezereon, Persian Iris, Auricula's, Narcissus with large tufts, common, double and single Primroses, Praecoce Tulips, Spanish Trumpets or Junquils, Violets, yellow Dutch Violets, Ornithogalum max. alb, Crown Imperial, Grape Flowers, Almonds and Peach Blossoms, Rubus Odoratus, Arbor Jude, &c.

Enclosures. Matthews considers himself, and is considered, the kind man of the wood. He offers pennies, beer, boiled mutton, words, to whoever might need them. The beneficiaries of his kindness linger. They pass the time in the presence of trees. Perhaps they notice their own enjoyment in this taste of a wild life, or perhaps he becomes an anecdote, a joke. In any case, he has brought them here. He has not frightened them away.

At the deepest part of his dugout is a ledge, cut last year, and laid out on it are acorns, beech mast, cob nuts, sweet chestnuts, horse chestnuts, and dried holly berries. Tied up in a square of muslin, hanging from a stick to keep it off the ground, are crumbled birch and alder catkins.

Enclosures. A word that straitens the mouth that speaks it, pressing the cheeks in tight to the teeth. The edges of Matthews's tongue ache after repeating it. He gets up from his stump by the cave and begins to walk, not heeding the path but in a straight line, west.

As he walks, the afternoon sun in his eyes, he names the spring flowers as he sees them. The timid yellow stars of celandine, a name that kisses the tongue. Soon after, a haze of violets, a name that leaves the patter of a raindrop on the mouth. Thimbleweed, the wood's own anemone, makes of its name a smile. On he wanders, towards a clearing crowded with wild daffodils. Crouching amongst them, he feels the breeze of their name across his lower lip.

There are many hundreds, perhaps thousands of seeds stowed in Matthews's cave. Enclosures of their own kind. Ones that might break out and run riot.

APRIL

Yet if the Weather prove benign, you may adventure about the middle of this Month, giving a Refreshment of Water not too cold: about four Gallons of heated Water, to twenty, will render it Blood-warm, which is the fittest Temper upon all Occasions throughout the Year: above all things, beware both of cold

Spring, Pump, or stagnant shaded Waters; that of the River is best, but of Rain incomparable. In heat of Summer, let the Water stand in the Sun till it grow tepid: Cold Applications, and all extreams, are pernicious.

Mrs Elderbrook takes up her position in the window seat. 'Aeration of the lawn,' Matthews said. There is no mention of this in the *Kalendarium Hortense*, a pristine copy of which she presses between her palms. But Matthews said that times have changed; it is a hundred years since that almanac was first printed.

Outside, on the lawn furthest from the house but within sight, Matthews is poking a cane into her beautiful grass and twisting. She winces, but holds fast. He bends, takes his hand from his pocket and pokes a finger into the hole. It is a blustery day of sudden showers. She supposes that his hands, left exposed, would get very cold. Matthews takes three steps and drives down the cane again.

His progress has not been methodical. Mrs Elderbrook cannot see the holes in the lawn from her window seat, but she knows that they are scattered unevenly, as irregular as blown petals.

She reads the almanac entry for April, and discovers that her dear plants are as averse to chill water as she is herself. She might be useful, then, and ask the cook to heat a few gallons. From the landing window she sees that Matthews is opening up a small cloth bundle and sifting through its contents.

Her garden has never been so splendid. Whatever his secrets, he must be allowed to keep them. Elfin blood, if green, is also vengeful.

Fruits in prime, and yet lasting:

Apples: Pepins, Deux-ans or John Apples, West-berry Apples, Russetting, Gilly-flower Apples, the Maligar, &c. Codling.

Pears: Great Kairville, Winter Bon-chrestien, Black Pear of Worcester, Surrein, Double Blossom Pear, &c.

Cherries, &c: The May-Cherry, Strawberries, &c.

Wells House is not the only garden Matthews tends to in the environs of the Great North Wood. Today he joins Hodd at Shelverdine, where they are to bring out the master's orange trees and transplant them. The orange trees lead cossetted lives, kept warm all winter in a grand conservatory.

Hodd takes up this subject as they begin loosening the roots of the first tree from the sides of its pot.

'They do better than you, eh?' he says. 'Found a lodgement yet?'

'Enclosures,' says Matthews.

'You heard the latest, then?' Hodd grasps the trunk of the orange tree and tests for weight. 'We'll want a pulley on this one.'

Matthews places his hands below Hodd's on the trunk and lifts. The tree rises a few inches. 'We'll do it,' he says. Hodd's eyes are bulging with the effort.

When they have settled the tree into its new, larger pot, Hodd squats, panting. 'You heard? There's to be new houses, up your way. Master's seen the plans. Great big mansions, he said.'

Matthews cracks his knuckles.

Hodd goes on. 'Wood round there's worth nothing, now, he said. Left to rack and ruin.'

A memory flits through Matthews's mind, gone before he can grasp it, of violence done to the wood. Branches torn, saplings trampled. Stars fighting in the sky. It does not seem to belong to him, caretaker of his patch of forest. It's true that the coppices have been neglected, and the oaks are few and far between. Blame the charcoal burners and the ship-builders for that.

'What is a wood worth?' he asks, as they begin packing manure around the orange tree.

'What is a wood for, if it's of no use?' says Hodd.

JUNE

Look now to your Aviary; for now the Birds grow sick of their Feathers; therefore assist them with Emulsions of the cooler Seeds bruised in their Water, as Melons, Cucumbers, &c. Also give them Succory, Beets, Groundsel, Chick-weed, fresh Gravel, and Earth, &c.

What is a wood for?

The orderly imitation of nature that is the style in the great gardens of Sydenham and Norwood provides one answer to that question. Nature there is an extension of the home. It is comfortable, sweetly scented, clean and tidy even in its profusion. The owners of the gardens where Matthews earns his crust do not stroll the woodland ways in the evening, as they stroll their box paths and espalier avenues.

June is humid. Matthews criss-crosses the clammy wood, a trowel pilfered from Wells House tucked into his belt. The moisture and warmth together have made the trees almost frantic in their foliage. Leaves bunch and frill, in shouting green. There are many seedlings, and, where the grown trees have not stretched to fill the sky, saplings. Here, Matthews digs.

The birds, busy with second broods, learn to follow him, watching with beady eyes the upturned earth. It is a double favour he does the wood. A magpie swoops alongside him as he shoulders his load back to the cave, and hops close by as Matthews moistens the roots and lays the saplings gently down behind a stand of holly.

Mrs Elverbrook fans herself, plumped in the shade beneath her pride and joy, a *Magnolia grandiflora* that grows by the side of the house. She cannot watch her gardener at his work from this position, but she has tired of spying. So, she does not see that, at the furthest edge of the sprawling grounds of Wells House, Matthews once again works with his trowel, digging directly into lawn and flower bed.

He plants the saplings wide, to give them space to thrive, but not so wide that they will not find each other, beneath the earth. Tender hornbeam, beech and oak, an ash, two alder and, by the fence, a modest grove of birch. He is sweating when he has finished, and he pours the last of the water pail over his bent head.

Flowers in prime, and yet lasting:

Amaranthus, Asphodel, Antirrhinum, Campanula, Clematis, Cyanus, Convolvulus, Sultana, Veronica purple and odoriferous; Digitalis, Eryngium Planum, Ind. Phaseolus, Geranium triste, and Creticum Gladiolus, Gentiana, Hesperis, Nigella, Hedysarum, Fraxinella, Lychnis Chalcedon, Jacea, white and double, Nasturt. Ind. Millefolium, Musk-rose, Flos Africanus, Thlaspi Creticum, Veronica mag. & parva, Volubilis, Balsam-apple, Holy-hoc, Corn-flower, Alke-kengi, Lupines, Scorpion-grass, Caryophyllata omn. gen, Stock Gilly-flower, Scabiosa, Mirab. Peru Spartum Hispan, Monthly Rose, Jasmine, Indian Tuberous Jacynth, Limonium, Linaria Cretica, Pansies, Prunella, Delphinium, Phalangium, Periploca Virgin, Flos Passionis, Flos Cardinalis, Yucca, Oranges, Amomum Plinii, Oleanders red and white, Agnus Castus, Arbutus, Olive, Ligustrum, Tilia, &c.

The Great North Wood has had many uses, not just for charcoal burners and shipbuilders. Farmers drive their pigs to feed on the beech mast. Its birds and beasts are hunted, for sport and for the pot. Gypsies have made their stopping places in its groves for so long, their name is now imprinted on the landscape at Gypsy Hill. Sap, fruit, flowers and leaves from its trees are stirred, mashed and fermented into wine. Berries, fronds, roots and seeds of its plants are steeped, pressed and ground into remedies. Boughs of rowan, holly and ivy bring luck, protection and cheer to the homes of those who keep their festive days. Mushrooms, from amethyst deceiver to shaggy parasol, make for rich mouthfuls and waking dreams. Lathes, barrows, looms, pegs, and more useful things than a man can count, are fashioned from its timber.

But the wood has a use, it has a worth, beyond these practical means of nourishment, inebriation, cure and custom. Matthews knows this. He feels it when he returns from the meticulous gardens where he works, when he walks the road that becomes a track, then a path that sinks between drifts of nettle and cow parsley, before leaping the sluggish stream and petering out amongst oak shade and bracken. It is the shedding, that happens then, of moral burden. It is the sudden evaporating of expectation, like morning mist. The straight lines of society's rules cannot extend into the wood. They are left at the road, and something else takes precedence in the mind at the sight, and scent, of trees.

Matthews also knows, though he does not understand why, that he is custodian of this particular truth.

He begins to steal more bottles of beer, and now food – cheese, bread, even meat – from the stores at the houses whose gardens he tends. The days are long, and he spends hours collecting bigger, stronger saplings, lugging them and piling them up in readiness. At Wells House, and elsewhere, he does not prune where he should. He ceases to tie and train the climbers. Any manure and compost meant for the exotic plants he hefts to those far-off spots where his saplings are now steadying themselves and reaching out, up, for their share of sky.

AUGUST

Now vindemiate, and take your Bees towards the expiration of this month; unless you see cause (by reason of the Weather or Season) to defer it till mid-September; But if your Stocks be very light and weak, begin the earlier.

Make your Summer Perry and Cider.

August brings more visitors to the wood. Matthews has time to sit with them, by the cave, and play his role of curious hermit. For Mrs Elderbrook has discovered the saplings, and her neglected roses, and has asked him, through clenched teeth, not to come back.

One afternoon, a dour man in a dark suit joins the little crowd around the dugout. Matthews has provided all with beer, but the tourists' merriment is tempered by this man's arrival. He does not join in the conversation, but sits, and listens, and watches. Matthews finds himself almost loquacious, telling what history of the wood he knows, surprising himself with lore and stories.

The visitors want to know about the gypsies. Are they his friends?

Before Matthews can answer, the dour man pipes up. 'Do they frequent this part of the wood? Or keep to their self-made midden over yonder?'

There is a snigger amidst the crowd.

'You might ask them yourself,' says Matthews.

'But do they bother you?' the man asks.

Matthews looks hard at the man, whose face is very white and strained. 'I'm a trouble to nobody,' he says. 'And nobody troubles me.'

'You got permission, didn't you,' the man goes on, 'for this?' He waves a hand at the dugout. 'The Dulwich estate looks after you?'

There is a murmur amongst the small crowd. 'What does it matter?' asks a youth, and glances at Matthews. Emboldened, the youth stands. 'Let him tell the stories he wants, not the ones that suit your fancy.'

In the silence that follows, the man gets up and walks away, his black suit oddly angular against the drooping branches.

The sun comes out and the atmosphere amongst the group brightens. 'Tell us about your childhood,' they implore. 'Tell us how you scared off the boar.'

But Matthews's eyelids flutter. His scars itch. He sees again the torn wood of that lost memory, flayed and aching, trees laid waste. Did he have some part in it? This time, the shadow remains. Stars fight in the sky.

SEPTEMBER

Fruits in prime, or yet lasting.

Apples: The Belle-bonne, the William, Summer Pearmain, Lording Apple, Pear-apple, Quince-apple, Red-greening Ribb'd, Bloody-pepin Harvey, Violet-apple, &c.

Pears: Hamdens Bergamon (first ripe), Summer Bon Chrestien, Norwich, Black Worcester (baking), Greenfield, Orange, Bergamot, the Queen Hedge-pear, Lewis-pear (to dry excellent), Frith-pear, Arundel-pear (also to bake), Brunswick-pear, Winter Poppering, Bings-pear, Bishops-pear (baking), Diego, Emperours-pear, Cluster-pear, Messire-Jean,

Rowling-pear, Balsam-pear, Bezy d'Hery, &c.

Peaches, &c: Malacoton, and some others, if the year prove backwards, Almonds, &c.

Quinces.

Little Blew-grape, Muscadine-grape, Frontiniac, Parsly, great Blew-grape, the Verjuice-grape excellent for sauce, &c. Berberries, &c.

Matthews follows the dour man in his black suit as he marches about the wood, compass in hand. He hears him counting steps, and watches as he marks trees with chalk. He learns that his name is Bermen. When Bermen has finished his work for the day, Matthews retraces his steps, and washes the chalk from the bark.

When Bermen returns, and discovers this act of sabotage, he begins again, this time cutting a large 'X' into each trunk with a knife.

Each cross-struck tree, connected by invisible steps, stands at the corner of a rectangle. There are six of these in all, sharing boundaries, sharing corner trees. Each rectangle is roughly a quarter of an acre.

Matthews explains this to Hodd, as they fill baskets with Brunswick and Balsam pears at the Shelverdine orchard. He has been permitted to help with the fruit harvests, under Hodd's eye.

'Plots,' says Hodd. 'Houses, like I said.' There are late wasps stumbling over the windfalls at their feet, drunk, yet methodical. 'You found a lodgement yet?'

What use is a wood? Matthews cannot articulate it. But it's there, in the shadow-memory he carries with him now, it's there in the stories he seems to conjure from thin air when his visitors come and sit, expectant, at his knee. They are not his stories, and yet they are.

'Did you ever hear a tale of Herne the Hunter?' he asks. 'Did you ever hear of ghosts or dead men, the Wild Hunt tearing up the wood?'

'You been up at the theatres?' says Hodd, and shakes his head as he moves to the next pear tree. 'Those won't be the last plots go up there. You'll see.'

The stories do not end happily. Wherever he has heard them, whenever it was he laid them down in store to bring out again, now, in his old age, they were not tales to comfort. Though he has never thought of himself as an outlaw, he feels a terrible kinship with these older denizens of the wood who haunt the tales. As if he heard the same song that they did, but is unable to sing it.

OCTOBER

Now is the time for Ablaqueation, and laying bare the Roots of old unthriving, or over-hasty blooming trees.

Moon now decreasing, gather winter fruit that remains, weather dry; take heed of bruising; lay them up clean lest they taint; Cut and prune Roses yearly, reducing them to a Standard not over tall.

Sweep and cleanse your Walks, and all other places, from Autumnal Leaves fallen, lest the Worms draw them into their holes, and foul your Gardens, &c.

There is no need to lay bare the roots of forest trees. And in October, they need the cover of fallen leaves and trodden earth, for hunters careen through the wood. The hunters do not cross the lines walked out from crossed tree to crossed tree by Bermen, for signs have been put up: PRIVATE PROPERTY.

Soon, these earmarked acres are comically busy, the creatures of the wood retreating beyond the signs where no hurtling horse or prowling huntsman can disturb their preparation for winter. Matthews joins them, surveying the trees within the bounds. Each tree is a standing song, a wordless incantation. If he cannot sing it, he can hear it, in his own hesitation, in the part of him that cannot say what use a wood might be.

When he first came to live in the wood, certain he would starve to death, it was a refuge from the familiarity of the built world, and from the invisible structures within which people live. Now the wood has become familiar, a home, yet it incites in him even now, especially now, a glorious feeling of transgression. To recognise this feeling is a strange joy. Standing under autumn rain, in the forbidden acres of wood marked PRIVATE PROPERTY, Matthews tips back his head and lets the water run into his eyes.

The next day, hungry for more of that glee, he leaves his cave early and hurries towards the same patch. It is raining again, the wood is loud with the flicks and slaps of water, but some of those slaps resolve themselves into deeper sounds, that vibrate through the forest floor. Not far beyond the first sign, men are gathered. Behind them, a hornbeam shakes with each hack of an axe to its trunk.

When he returns to his cave, Bermen is standing before the entrance hole, under a black umbrella. He hands Matthews a slip of paper.

'Notice,' he says. When Matthews does not look at the paper but lets it catch the raindrops that fall between them, he goes on. 'It's not only you. Those gypsies have received the same. You might go with them.'

Bermen's face is whiter than ever. His eyes look yellow within it. It is impossible to picture this man dancing, yelling, running amok. It is impossible to picture him closing his umbrella, tipping back his head and letting rainwater run into his eyes.

NOVEMBER

Flowers in prime, and yet lasting:

Anemonies, Meadow Saffron, Antirrhinum, Stock-gilly-flower, Bellis, Clematis, Pansies, some Carnations, double Violets, Veronica, Spanish and Indian Jasmine, Myrtles, Musk-rose, &c.

Unrest. The wood is not rebellious. It has had nothing to rebel against. But Matthews understands that to lose his cave, his minor life in the wood, will be a surrender. That if he cannot slide into the shape carved out for a man in the ordered world beyond, he will be cut to fit.

Drinking beer, alone, in his cave which is now damp with November rain, he considers all those men and women who have also been cut to fit. How many of them slide the other way sometimes, into the wood, where right angles and rules vanish?

With the third bottle of beer, he begins to feel possessive. If he belongs to the wood, the wood also belongs to him. More than it does to the gypsies, to Hodd, to all his visitors, and not just because he has lived here so long. To be the kind man of the wood has been easy, but also lazy. To be tormented by forgotten tales, by fighting stars: this bestows ownership.

He squirms out of the cave. The night air pours across his cheeks. His clothes feel itchy and tight. He leaves them in a pile and begins to walk, then to run, through the wood.

Matthews runs amok. He hops and whirls, swinging round trunks in the dark. He grinds his heels into rotting leaves and cold mud. His breath fills the windless silence, and gives the whole wood a thrumming rhythm. Here he wriggles between birch saplings, letting their slender trunks brush his shoulders. There he spirals into hanging ivy that twines through his hair.

His mouth is tense with rejected words. As he leaps and turns he spreads his lips wide and lets his breath turn to voice, a release of sound that is not joy, not anger. It is a cry with no right angles, no rules, but with many notes at once, a chord that contains the song of every tree he knows. He hears the echo, the trees' recognition.

DECEMBER

Fruit in prime, and yet lasting:

Apples: Rousseting, Leather-coat, Winter Reed, Chestnut Apple, Great-belly, the Go-no-further, or Cats-head, with some of the precedent month.

Pears: The Squib-pear, Spindle-pear, Doyonere, Virgin, Goscoyne-Bergomot, Scarlet-pear, Stopple-pear, white, red and French Wardens (to bake or roast), &c. the Deadman's pear, excellent, &c.

Hodd skirts the newly shorn acres on his way to Matthews's cave. There is cat-ice in the ruts and the ground is hard with frost. Clearing work has halted, for Christmas and, he supposes, because the roots are now trapped in the frozen earth. It is a sorry sight: felled trunks still in stacks, the heart-wood of the stumps showing like bone.

When he reaches the cave, he finds a sign, stolen and propped up: PRIVATE PROPERTY. Matthews is not inside. But there is a heap of kindling, dry enough, so he sets about making up a fire. He has brought wrinkled leather-coat apples, and they will roast nicely. While they eat them, he will persuade Matthews to come home with him, to share their Christmas food and drink, and remember the feel of a warm room, a real bed.

The apples have softened in their glowing pile, and there is still no sign of his friend. Hodd ducks into the cave again, hoping for bottles of beer. He fumbles, deeper, until at the furthest point his fingers find the ledge, with its last few shrivelled acorns, horse chestnuts, and dried holly berries. He brings them out into the light. They are no good to a hungry man.

He eats two of the apples, sucking at the cores, then lays the others gently inside the cave entrance. A magpie watches him, but he cannot wait to see that Matthews gets his supper. Dusk is falling. He pockets the acorns, chestnuts and berries. They are evidence, of something. He will call at the houses where his friend has worked, see if he's been by, perhaps for some Christmas alms.

JANUARY

Trench the Ground, and make it ready for the Spring: prepare also Soil, and use it where you have occasion: Dig Borders, &c.

Uncover as yet Roots of Trees, where Ablaqueation is requisite.

In over-wet, or hard weather cleanse, mend, sharpen and prepare Garden tools.

Mrs Elverbrook shudders, and offers the newspaper to her husband. They are right to suspect the gypsies; it wouldn't be the first time. She takes her tea to the window seat, trying to shake off the nasty images planted now in her mind.

The garden is sodden, and a magpie is digging in her lawn, tossing a worm in the air before pecking it up. 'Harmless', the article called him. But she had caught Matthews herself, sabotaging her garden with wild species, an act of sedition that had quite flustered her for days after. She had worried about that elfin blood. What might he have been capable of?

The bell rings downstairs, and the maid calls for her. There on the step is that other gardener, Hodd, a more steady type. He holds his cap in his hands. His face is creased with sorrow.

'Collecting, ma'am,' he says. 'That Matthews might have his burial in Dulwich.'

Mrs Elverbrook shudders again. Matthews slept under the earth even in life, she has heard. 'At the church?' she asks, then blushes at her own callousness.

*

Hodd has read the newspaper report. He has winced at the details it gave: the pile of clothes left outside the cave, the hooked stick, the pierced cheek and the broken jaw. He knows it was not the gypsies, who came to the dugout to pay their respects. He also knows what the report did not tell. That on Matthews's chest there was carved an 'X'. That the only knife found there was Matthews's own.

He dawdles amongst the black stumps in their marked-out plots, delaying his walk to the cave. There is no need to keep coming back, but the habit of visiting draws him. Perhaps it is better for his friend, not to see the uprooting to come in spring, the gouging of earth, the hammering down of foundations. The next plots to be cleared are already marked, the oak and beech trees cut with an 'X', the PRIVATE PROPERTY signs spreading further into the wood.

He feels in his pocket for the old acorns, the chestnuts and the berries. All are shrivelled up, dry and dull. Where the ground is muddy, he stoops and presses an acorn into the earth. On he goes, through the wood, pointlessly planting, as the remaining trees shake raindrops down, wetting his head.

A RIDDLE

I feak, I preen, I rouse,
I bate, I snite, I bowse.
I winnow, I warble, I tower,
I fur, I rake, I cower.
I teardrop, I glide,
I stoop, I dive.
I plume, I pluck,
I gorge on my luck.
What am I?

Anon

Answer: a hawk

8

HERNSER: HERON
1821

Charm: When witches sport in the sky, with this song I bewilder them and send them wandering home.

BERMOND GOES HERON-HAWKING

He sends her up, his hawk Queen Mab, his dark witch of the sky. So rare the vision, theirs to make, of the gracious heron turned frantic in flight.

It is as sweet to the heron-hawker's soul as any dream, to watch Hernser, vain daydreamer, Narcissus of the woodland ponds, tumbling Lethe-wards on awkward wings. His hawk Queen Mab, in her darkling majesty, calls the heron down, her cruel magic a kind of sublime—

The moment he longs for, when time stops, and two feathered bodies drop, queen hawk and king heron, agony and ecstasy.

Bermond's heart floods as he scrambles and leaps the

still stream to where Mab and Hernser turn in their throes, all panic wing and grasping claw on bloodied ground.

Mab's eye gleams. She arches, and at Hernser's elegant head merely nudges with that merciless beak, half-open.

Her nudge is a slice. Hernser, limp, reclines.

The hawker stoops, a bow to his Queen Mab, a nod to a heron's dying wish: admiring love.

THE HERON DREAMS

Up the hillside is a glade in the forest dim. There is a pond where, still in the reedy shallows, Hernser gazes often at the heron that glimmers on the water. So many blissful hours, all the same, spent in admiration of slender neck, upright leg, that wise and charismatic eye.

Leaving the near meadows, ringing he climbs until the pond, blemished moon of the wood, shines from her deep-delved earth.

Into cool water he wades. The wood sings of summer. Flies drone at the dog roses. Ripples ebb and Hernser bows, to the heron of the pond.

Instead, a man looks up at him. The slow wave of weeds is turned to ivy nodding in a breeze. The man wears a stag's crown, its branches shifting in the shadow-light.

They gaze at one another, two persecuted kings. At Hernser's breast, a stabbing ache, then sky, earth, and the dream breaks.

HERNE DREAMS

Always the hunt, the tireless headlong, hoof and heart at glorious judder, and the cry, the howl, the bright blaze of horn, the deepest shriek of the wolf interval, that heart song, that blood moon, red spilt over verdurous gloom, always the chase, the bottomless hunger, whip and bone that crack together, but this time I hear the cry, the terrible, warping scream of Hernser, the heron falling into me.

And now I am my namesake, not hunter but hunted, the claw of Queen Mab at my panting chest, and never till now did I know the fear that a hawk carries with her, as near to love as anything the heart can bear.

HERNE WAKES

Two tumblers, we rolled like lovers, in the endless fall, the all-too-brief fall, the jolt—

Herne jolts awake.

Where has he been?

Nowhere. Underground, overhead, lost in a shrinking wood.

But he dreamt! He fell from the sky and he knew who he was.

He is Herne.

Where has he been?

Hunting. Herne thinks: I had forgotten how. But Queen Mab has woken me.

He looks around, looks up, looks down. Does he dream still? That nightmare of relief turned to dread, the petals opening to reveal another bloom, another then another?

Herne shakes his head, pinches his knees, bites his cheek. He is, ever was, Herne. Where has he been?

He has been watching the wood, his wood, divided neatly into pieces and shared out like so much cake. He was not in his own head.

But here he is, refreshed. And this wood, his wood, is not a dream, Queen Mab does not fool him, but she has given him a nudge, a gentle reminder, because he has been forgetful lately.

And it is plain: if the wood is chopped up, shared out, reduced to crumbs, so will he be.

Herne stands, wipes the heron blood from his throat. I am the wood. It's me: bale-worker, ever-booming, frenzy-maker, horned one.

The wood never sleeps. I must not dream again.

ARBOR REVOCANDA

a mnemonic verse

Black is the thorn of prunus spinosa,
Potent the bark of alnus glutinosa,
White is the wood of tilia cordata,
Deadly the seeds of taxus baccata.
Populus tremula, betulus pendula,
Quiver so sweetly in spring breeze and shower.

For cramp, boil the bark of viburnum opulus,
For hearth fires that last, burn carpinus betulus,
Ward off plague with prunus padus,
Soothe any ache with frangula alnus.
Crataegus monogyna, sambucus nigra,
Clothe the May hedge in her soft white dress.

Brew up the fruit of sorbus torminalis,
Twist up a basket from salix viminalis,
Sour is the flesh of malus sylvestris,

Brittle the branch of salix fragilis.
Quercus robur, fraxinus excelsior,
Are the green-garbed giants of summer's rest.

Reverend George Joye

9

NULLIUS IN VERBA
1877

Charm: This song you must sing when the sick want healing.

FRIDAY, 18TH MAY

I write this sitting in a pool of electric light. It is the only such one in this house – in any of the houses on Sydenham Hill, I dare say – and it is in Hugo's study. Bold of me! But I did wait for Euphronie to retire, the maid too, and creeping here in secrecy has only augmented my excitement.

The electric lamp has not been switched on since the incident. As Euphronie put it, when a great light has gone out, none should shine in his house. But there is no more appropriate illumination for this writing than Hugo's incandescent bulb, and she will forgive me using it when I tell her of my plan.

It came to me yesterday, as I passed another lonely afternoon of so-called convalescence in the guest room at

Fairwood. The dizziness of the past few days had faded. The bruise on my head was far less tender. I felt well enough to be bored, but mine is not an idle mind, and my plan shall prove it. It was whilst sitting at the window, contemplating the woods beyond Hugo and Euphronie's rather staid garden, that the clever thought came to me.

From the house, one cannot quite see the plot Hugo had already purchased. It is further down the hill, towards Dulwich, the other side of the railway line. But I have seen it, of course, and I saw it then in my mind's eye. It is only a patch of useless woodland now, so grown with ground ivy, bracken, and other sprouting things, that on our visit Hugo and I could hardly beat our way through it. But while we stood there, bothered by flying insects and harangued by noisy birdsong, Hugo shared with me his vision, and it is this which has informed my plan.

In homage to Hugo, I will be the man to build the scientific school. I will bring his academy to life, and it will be grander even than he imagined. Its students will be tutored to the highest standard, and learn of all the latest advances in electric lighting, so that their work will make the bulb originally designed by Hugo, but now championed by me, the leading light – yes! – amongst all those lights currently baffling their slower inventors across the country. My academy will be lit inside and out. It will be an electric beacon where now only gloomy trees stand, themselves blocking out light.

And my plan will achieve many important things. First – though not really foremost – it will make up for Euphronie's loss, for I know she blames me. And furthermore, she will surely allow me to stay on at the house while I oversee the school's construction. I cannot face a return to Suffolk, which now seems so far away as to exist in a previous century. Secondly, it will allow me to become an expert such as Hugo was in theories of both electricity and light, and to make my name known in the same leading circles he used to frequent. Thirdly, this rise in status, knowledge, and surely fame, as I spread this new electric light across Norwood and beyond, will take me finally to the Royal Society, and there, to Fellowship. Put bluntly, this plan will serve us all: me, Euphronie, society, and the Royal Society. And even Hugo, if he be in the heaven he did not believe in. From there, he will see the Bergmann-Ship electric bulb – as it shall then be called, uniting his name and mine – illuminating first the wood, and then, the world.

I will have to convince Euphronie, of course, but once she is feeling better I am certain she will see the perfect sense in all of this. Her spirits are low, not surprisingly, but really, her bitterness over a few scratches and bruises has been disproportionate. It has been tiresome indeed to hear her moans from the adjacent chamber, and to see her lunch tray removed untouched despite so much bright coaxing from the maid. Suzy has no need to coax me. My appetite has returned doubled, and she seemed to think it quite improper when I asked for a second plate of eggs yesterday. She glared as if I had asked for golden ones! But now I must match my bodily strength to that of my mind, and begin my battle against bramble and creeper to properly survey the plot. This part of the plan, at least, does not require Euphronie's approval. In fact, completing it will almost certainly help to persuade her that it is the right thing to do, and I am the right man to do it.

Concerning bodily strength, I still marvel that I escaped from the incident so little damaged. While the bump on my head did protrude alarmingly at first, it has subsided so that I can touch the spot with only a slight wince. And the dizziness that made me sick to the stomach the first two days, and distressed my vision as much, is now so slight that, so long as I take measured movements and do not swing my head about as if dancing, I can forget it was ever with me. My stomach has settled – though I feel it grumbling now, so with my plan recorded, I will creep next to the kitchen to see what Suzy has squirrelled away in her larder. As for my vision, there is still the occasional blurred patch. I may, for instance, need to look sidelong at the larder shelves to be certain what lies there in the dark. But in this pool of electric light, every word I have written is as clear to me as if I looked through a magnifying glass. This only stirs my new sense of purpose. We must all have this light, and we must have it from the Bergmann-Ship bulb!

SATURDAY, 19TH MAY, MORNING

As I was about to leave Fairwood early and set out for the plot, I was confronted by Euphronie, leaning on her crutch at the top of the stairs.

'Should you not be resting, Mr Ship?' she said, and scowled at me. She resembled a sort of diffident witch, insisting as she does on wearing a black nightgown, so that she may be in mourning even as she languishes in bed. Her dark hair was in a messy tumble down her back. Perhaps this slovenliness is a habit of the French, but it offends an English gentleman.

I did not ask her, yet again, to call me Walter, nor correct her displeasing pronunciation of my name, which renders it *sheep*. 'I'm much better,' I told her. 'And you might be too if you would take some air.'

'I will not ever be better,' she said. 'Honestly, I wish you had never come here. But since you are so recovered, perhaps it is time for you to go home.'

It was not the right moment to tell Euphronie of my plan. But I could not resist hinting. 'All will be well,' I said, and smiled, though she did not much deserve my goodwill. 'I will make you feel much better myself.'

'Why did Suzy find the bulb switched on in Hugo's study this morning?' she asked. Her tone was quite icy.

Now that I recount this, I am quite proud of my quick remark. 'It is a good omen,' I said, and sped away down the hall. Though the crutch is excessive – she only sprained an ankle – she did not follow me.

Musing on this encounter, I concluded that, before introducing my plan to Euphronie, I had better try to win back her friendship. And the best way to do that would be to persuade her that her husband's sad demise was not my fault. Hugo was very dear to us both, and it is right that a widow should mourn (though perhaps not in a morbid nightgown), but to blame another who is suffering an equal loss is unseemly. It is also obstructive. So, I have delayed my urgent survey of the woodland plot, in order to spend some time considering how I will lay out my case to Euphronie, in such a way that she cannot possibly argue with it.

It is perfectly natural that I should come to stay at Fairwood in the first place, having exchanged letters with Hugo over several months. While mine were significantly longer than his, we all know that he was a busy man, whereas I had time to think and write as my interest in all things electrical grew – being all the more encouraged by this new correspondence. We were all three delighted, I am sure, when Hugo agreed to my request for a visit, to see his fascinating prototype bulb.

It is perfectly natural that, Fairwood being as close to the Crystal Palace as it is, and the wondrous Exhibition being in full flow, that I – a man so enamoured of all things worldly and scientific – would wish to see it. And Hugo, being a generous host and a man of science himself, was very kind to accompany me along with his wife. What a marvellous afternoon we had – Euphronie cannot possibly deny that – perusing the displays of wonders and inventions, walking amongst the soothing fountains in the gardens, discussing Hugo's work.

It was perfectly natural that, upon witnessing the hot air balloons rising from the terrace below the Crystal Palace to drift in all their majesty across the blue skies of Norwood, I should wish to pay the reasonable fee and take such a ride. In fact, in my excitement, I paid the ticket price for all three of us, and I distinctly remember Euphronie giggling, like the girl she is very far from being now, as we shook the balloonist's hand.

Indeed, it was Euphronie herself who told the balloonist that Fairwood stood only a mile or so away, and asked if we might look down on it from our floating eyrie. If it had not been for this comment, we would surely have sailed the same route as the other balloons, south of the Crystal Palace, and not, as it turned out, risked the winds on the north side of the geological ridge on which the palace stands.

Hugo enjoyed himself as much as I did, pointing out local landmarks as we rose beneath the swell of the great balloon, as serene and steady as the sun itself. As we soared higher in the clear blue air, we gazed across at London, shrunk to the size of a map, and St Paul's Cathedral a fat pin stuck in it. Euphronie did not stop asking the balloonist questions – about all his methods and materials and how he dealt with the dangers of travelling by air. I dare say her prattle was quite distracting, such that the danger we were in ourselves did not become apparent until Hugo interrupted his wife to ask if we were not travelling a little fast.

And it is perfectly natural that, fearing for his life, thinking of his bright future, a man might choose to jump into a sea of trees rather than risk being engulfed by the remains of a gas-filled balloon.

As it was, we know now that cowardice won out, and those of us who remained in the gondola were flung only a little way as we lurched down through the leafy canopy. Having lost consciousness myself, I could not run to Hugo's aid. And it is not Euphronie's fault, either, that she did not find her husband for some time, during which much blood had leaked from him.

In this way, I will absolve us both of the blame for Hugo's death. I will present him as a man braver than the rest of us, and not as one who paid too high a price for foolish panic. I also paid too high a price for the tickets.

SATURDAY, 19TH MAY, EVENING

I would have delivered the above absolution today, but since I have returned from my tour of the academy site, Euphronie has remained shut in her room. I noticed, however, that the bulb had been left switched on in Hugo's study, and so I made use of it again to write these words. Besides, her withdrawal permits me to attend to the far more important task of recording today's extraordinary events.

To begin with the necessary observations. The woodland plot is, as I remembered, quite overgrown, and what a satisfaction it will be to clear those looming trees and malicious brambles, gradually to reveal the ground that will be a foundation for learning. Still, the day being warm for May, I was able to turn the dense shade to my advantage and sit awhile, pondering my plan. While the ache in my head is now only mild, bright light still hurts my eyes somewhat, and the tree shadow was a welcome relief.

There is much work to be done – the clearing, then the construction. This I will leave to rougher hands and swarthier temperaments, while I concentrate on the details of laboratories and lighting. Perched there in the shadows, I pictured neat rows of benches, piled with the peculiar glass vessels, jars of powders and fine measuring instruments that are the scientist's tools. All of these will gleam beneath the electric bulbs, arranged so that not a single awkward shadow falls, thus ensuring the path to truth is brightly lit and sooner found.

I do not yet have a clear view myself of how best these students will advance the technology of the Bergmann-Ship bulb, but I can soon learn this. Hugo's study contains many books, including his own notes, and I will no doubt be the sole inheritor of these. (Excepting Euphronie, who will surely have no use for them. Had she provided an heir for Hugo, she might have passed on her husband's precious writings to him, but she did not, and that is not my fault either.)

While I dreamed my own bright future, there in the wood, something unexpected happened, that I now believe may be of even greater importance than the invention of electric light. As I jot down these words, I see that my own notebooks will one day line the shelves of an illustrious study, and that this page might be the most treasured one of all amongst those eager to learn of the greatest discovery of our time. So, I will write this carefully, such that my rationality and love of exacting scientific method may fill your mind as you learn, Dear Reader.

Nullius in verba! you may cry. And while this may be the motto of the Royal Society itself, you will be obliged, for now, to *take my word for it* with regards to what follows, until I ascertain a method of capturing my discovery for display by other means.

Deep in thought, on my damp tree stump, my gaze roamed as my mind did, though since there is not much to see in a forest I did not attend to the images that passed across my vision. Not, that is, until I perceived a small shimmer of movement to my left, low amongst the fallen leaves and ground ivy. Light conditions, as I have before noted, were poor, the trees being thoughtless obstructors of both direct and diffuse sunlight. (Even I admire the acuity of my observations!)

Yet I was still able to see, with my sidelong glance, several small figures in procession, making their way out from amongst the dark leaves. Let me be precise: when I say small, I mean four inches high (an estimate – at this time I did not carry a measuring stick with me). When I say several, I mean five, or possibly six. When I say figures, I mean human figures, their limbs and heads all in perfect proportion to ours, but shrunk down in size.

These tiny people were oddly costumed. Their colourful clothing and headgear was familiar to me, but I have not yet been able to determine why this is. Certainly, I have never witnessed a procession of tiny people before.

I did not dare move my head, for fear of scaring them away. So, I continued to watch from the corner of my eye as they began a kind of dumbshow. They danced and dashed about, seeming to address each other, though I could hear no small voices. (While my vision was somewhat affected following the incident, my hearing has remained sharp as a cat's.) I was unable to make out the meaning of their little play, though I did discern that one appeared as a woman, and the others as men, variously dressed in a cloak, a polychromatic suit, a white smock, and peculiar bright bloomers. The longer I watched, the more I felt the bubbles of recognition stir and attempt to break through to the surface of my mind. In desperation I turned my head to look straight on, and blinked to clear my vision. Alas, they must have moved as fast as startled wrens, for when I stared directly at the spot where they had danced, all had vanished.

Though I sat a long time, focusing on that ordinary bit of undergrowth, they did not return. I conclude that I must proceed with stealth on my next visit to the wood, and attempt a second observation. I do not doubt what I saw, but I must confirm the reason for that shock of familiarity when I inspected their strange costumes. And of course, I must find a way to provide evidence that will satisfy fellow men of science, and that is fit to present to the Royal Society. I no more believe in fairies than does any rational fellow, but it is of the utmost importance that I prove to them the existence of these little people. *Nullius in verba!*

But I see I have written quite enough for one evening, and my stomach demands again a recompense for the measly slices of ham served up by Suzy earlier. I shall approach the larder with caution. Last night, upon entering that dank and murky room, I saw looking down at me from a high shelf a scruffy black terrier. It must belong to Suzy, since I've not met such a dog in the house. Luckily it did not bark and alert her to my pilfering, but watched me as I backed out of the larder with a quarter cheese in my hands. A splendid feast that made too, and I could quite fancy another.

WEDNESDAY, 23RD MAY

Alas, I write this by the inferior light of an oil lamp. Several days ago, I came down to breakfast to find Euphronie dressed smartly (in black), her hair tidied into an imperious but quite fetching arrangement. Though she still leaned on her unnecessary crutch, she had a look of determination on her hard face. She rebuffed my attempts at friendly conversation, and since that moment has taken over Hugo's study. Suzy is often in there with her, flitting out now and then to return with fresh teapots and dishes of what smell like delicious little cakes, though I have not been able to discover any such in the kitchen. There is no sign of Suzy's terrier, only the hum of their voices behind the study door and, occasionally, laughter.

Frustrating as this was, I took it as a sign that Euphronie has given up her surly mourning and is quite recovered. Thus, my opportunity had arrived to present my case for absolution; though she is hardly behaving like someone weighed down with terrible guilt, I must be sure she no longer blames me either.

While I sat about, in the hall and the drawing room, waiting for her to emerge and hear my argument (they acted as if they did not hear my knocks on the study door, and I dared not enter unbidden), I had plenty of time to conduct what I think of as *inner research.* I brought to mind the vivid costumes of the little people I had seen in the wood, and roamed with them through my memory, searching for an explanation for that sense of recognition I had experienced.

I have scant enthusiasm for spectacles that involve outlandish dress. The theatre presents us with fictions which are themselves lies, and therefore the enemies of any steadfast man of science. Neither do I frequent frivolous masquerades or twee festivals. But I remembered that, as a child, I was several times herded along to a pantomime by my mother, who was fond of such things in her girlish way. Even then, I found the whole affair tawdry and noisy. I dreaded the shrieks and laughter of the boorish audience, and the exaggerated falseness of the characters on the stage frightened me. I was, after all, an observant and sensitive boy: qualities that have stood me in good stead as a scientific man.

Every pantomime – be it *Babes in the Wood* or *Herne the Hunter* – would resolve itself far too soon into the harlequinade, which the audience seemed to adore even though it was the same each time. The cast of characters transformed via a hasty costume change, and the familiar drama began: Harlequin pursued Columbine, while her father Pantaloon tried to stop him. Pierrot pined and Clown leapt about making trouble. None of it made any sense to me. I didn't find Clown amusing, though my mother would shake in her seat with laughter. Each time she nudged me, or asked if I was having fun, I felt more and more as if I disappointed her with my stubborn solemnity, but I could not pretend.

Now, though, I am glad indeed to have endured those tests of patience. For I have discovered in these memories the very costumes sported by the little people I observed in the wood! They appeared so vivid, so intricate, though I saw them from the corner of my eye, that there is no doubt: those homunculi were dressed as the cast of the harlequinade. There was Clown, in his silly bloomers; Pantaloon in his long cloak and unlikely hat; Harlequin chequered in red, yellow and black; Columbine, quite elegant really, in her pretty gown; and poor, pale Pierrot. Indeed, Harlequin even retained his horns, somewhat drooping, as had the actor in *Herne the Hunter* when he scrambled from one role to the next.

Whether they also enacted the harlequinade I cannot be sure, since I could not hear their speech. This I must investigate. But the realisation that my feeling of familiarity was quite correct excited me greatly. The little people could not possibly have been a figment – they were as real as any human on a stage!

I began, then, to pace the hallway of Fairwood, better to consider how I will present proof of their existence. As far as I am aware – and I like to think I stay abreast of important developments in the realm of science, connected as I am with luminaries such as Hugo – no such discovery has ever been made. In fact, the presence of diminutive people in our world has been dismissed as folklore – they are fairy stories for credulous children (unlike my own child self), entertaining fancies only. I paused in my perambulations to confront this obstacle to truth.

My evidence, presented to the Royal Society, would need to be irrefutable. There would be questions. Why did this miniature troupe live in a wood, and not somewhere more comfortable? Might we communicate with its members? Were there more of them? Was this most original harlequinade, in fact, just that – the living inspiration for the pantomime's most commonplace diversion? A notion, were it true, that would lend a certain validity to my claim. As my eyes widened in hope at this prospect, I saw that happy fate had led me to halt at that exact spot in the hall. For there, ranged in mahogany shelves that lined the depths of the hallway, stood the seventeen volumes of Larousse's *Grand dictionnaire universel*. No doubt Euphronie's imposition; and deemed unworthy of a place in Hugo's study beside the *Britannica*, but an encyclopaedia all the same, and, if deserving of the name one, that would furnish me with just such evidence.

My French is not what it might be, thanks to unsympathetic instruction in my youth by an overbearing *Suisse*, but I was able, upon flicking to 'Harlequin', to deduce that the name derived from the Old French, Hellequin, a certain leader in ancient myth of a demonic Wild Hunt that prowled through the night, chasing evil souls to hell. I was disappointed. While the archipelago of myth might overlap, so to speak, with fairyland, this was not the origin story I sought. Certainly, in English we would not say Hellequin anyway, but Woden or Herne. Nevertheless, I reassured myself, this feeble grasping at history's straws went some way to confirm that I was indeed the first among men to observe a sylvan harlequinade. No Frenchman had so much as posited that man first saw Harlequin in the wood!

As I stared down the dark hallway, deep in this satisfying thought, for a moment I believed I saw the terrier crouched in the shadows beyond the stairs. But the shape resolved itself into a heap of coal. It was just lying there, on the carpet. Suzy is a neglectful servant, but this seemed beyond careless. I was about to investigate further when the study door opened and there stood Euphronie, scowling as usual.

'Is there something you wish to say to me?' she asked.

Caught off guard, I slapped the volume shut and pointed to the coal. 'You may wish to instruct Suzy to clear that up,' I said, attempting a conspiratorial tone. I still wished to make a friend of Euphronie before divulging to her my plan.

She looked. 'Clear up what?' she said.

So, that was to be her attitude, I thought. Women can be so wilfully difficult. Wondering how I would ever present my case for absolution to this contrary person, I gazed past her into the study and spied, standing before the window on its tripod, Hugo's camera. He had demonstrated it to me on the rainy afternoon of my arrival at Fairwood, and produced a passable photograph of the magnolia tree that dominates their garden. A waste of a plate, really. But excitement swelled in my breast as I thought how my photographs would be anything but a waste. They would be a unique contribution to science!

'What is it?' Euphronie still stood in my way, frowning.

‘I wish to take the camera into the wood,’ I said, as calmly as I was able. ‘There are some subjects there of interest, and I intend to capture them.’

This seemed to pique her curiosity. ‘You are a *naturaliste* also?’ she smiled, pronouncing it with the French inflection. ‘I thought it was electricity that interested you.’

‘Very much,’ I said. ‘But it is not the wood itself I wish to photograph. Rather, something that resides there.’

Euphronie’s smile was most certainly false, but it did not fade. ‘Perhaps you have no squirrels in Suffolk?’ she said. ‘I assure you they are quite well understood here. I have written a study of their hibernation patterns myself.’ She turned just enough to point at the bookshelf where stood the row of leather-bound scientific journals I had admired on my last private evening at Hugo’s desk.

‘Not squirrels,’ I said, sternly. ‘I am quite familiar with those. No, I wish to capture images of something entirely new – something I know for certain you have never seen before.’

Euphronie laughed, but I waited patiently. A dose of sarcasm was a small price to pay for the use of the camera, and once I had my photographs all humiliation would be hers, not mine.

‘One thing I have never seen is your home,’ she said, still smiling. ‘I hope that you will go and photograph that.’ And with one backwards step, she shut the study door in my face.

Though I have tried to enter the study since then, and even made forays in the middle of the night, I have found it either occupied or locked. Euphronie’s claim that she had published an article on the behaviour of squirrels quite irked me, and as well as borrowing the camera I wanted to verify that her statement was a lie by reading those leather-bound journals. I also wish to learn the correct style and structure in which to present my own treatise, since I am so far restricted to a written account. My attempts to sketch the little people have not proved very successful. I do not possess a pen fine enough to properly render them with the same clarity with which I see them in life. To do this, I would have to draw them enlarged, as if they were full-sized human beings, and then how ridiculous I would look, showing sketches of pantomime characters to Society Fellows!

But all this has not much detracted from the thrill of waiting and watching for them in the wood. On my habitual tree stump, I have sat for many hours as the dapples of sunlight moved across the tangled ground, peering into shadows, my eyes and head quite soothed. The peace of the wood has surprised me. Now that the discomfort of spending all day quite still on a stump is utterly necessary, I experience the sun's warmth, the changing light, the prattling birds, and races between squirrels up and down the trunks, with an odd kind of pleasure. There is an uncommonly bold robin – I am sure it is the same one – that hops ever closer to me, circling round as if to view me from all angles. At first, I shooed him away lest he scare off the little people, but yesterday I shared with him a few crumbs of the pie I had purloined from Suzy's larder (no terrier this time – where is it?), and it was not long before he perched on my thumb and ate up the crumbs from my palm. He regarded me so intently, it was as if he read my thoughts. I wonder if he has seen the little people, and whether they are friend or foe to him.

So, this is how I have spent my time, for the last few days, and my many hours upon the stump have been rewarded. When the sun has dropped below the hill and dusk fills up the plot with greys and browns, so that I must turn my gaze sidelong to see things clearly, the miniature troupe arrives. They do not appear in the same spot, but always somewhere deeply shaded and never when I look directly there. This is their cunning way. Just as my mind drifts, to my future Fellowship, or to hopes of a better supper from the ever more recalcitrant Suzy, that is when I notice a small movement, as if dead leaves turned in the breeze. Then out they come, skipping or marching as if on to a stage, and begin their little show. I have been so amazed to see them each time, that I have not yet deciphered the story they tell, but I suppose it is the same one I endured as a child: Harlequin and Columbine defying her father in the pursuit of love, leaving Pierrot brokenhearted. Clown topples and rolls about. All are constantly moving, their tiny limbs swinging and gesturing, their tiny feet dancing. How much more marvellous they are to see in Lilliputian scale than full-sized in a torrid theatre!

They take no notice of me, and I suppose that my complete stillness disguises my presence well as they concentrate on their games. I do not think they will make a Gulliver of me. No, the difficulty is that, when I move my head, or so much as blink to improve my focus, they are away. Yesterday, when this happened, I lurched from the stump, legs stiff as tree trunks, and tore at the ivy leaves behind their chosen patch. But of course, I found nothing, not even Pantaloon's hat dropped in haste. They are too small and too light to leave footprints.

So far, then, I can make the following statements of fact:

These woodland-dwelling homunculi are roughly four inches high.
They are most active at dusk (possibly nocturnal, or crepuscular?).
They are skittish and easily frightened back into hiding.
Their movements are energetic, sprightly and deliberate, suggesting communication through gesture.
Their appearance is that of the members of the harlequinade, namely: a horned Harlequin, Columbine, Pantaloon, Pierrot and Clown.
They are skilled at hiding their pathways and their nest (site as yet undiscovered).
They make no sound detectable to the human ear, and leave no trace of scent.

What they eat and drink, I have yet to ascertain. Perhaps dew, the nectar of flowers or the fruit of the bramble when in season? But I begin to speculate.

The oil lamp burns low and my eyes and hand grow weary. I will write no more tonight, but rest in preparation for another day on my stump. Perhaps I already dream, or else my powers of observation were weak before this plunge into the intense collecting of evidence, but now I see, in the corner of the drawing room, a sleeping cat. Nobody has mentioned such a pet. It must be part of Suzy's menagerie, which seems to haunt this house.

THURSDAY, 31ST MAY

A breakthrough! Not with my work, alas – I am no closer to recording my sightings in a medium other than words – but in relations with Euphronie. Over the course of a week or so I barely saw the woman – I attending to my research all day, and she busying herself with whatever she does in Hugo's study all evening. My only conversations were brisk ones with Suzy who, upon delivering ever-shrinking suppers to me, asked each time when I would be leaving for Suffolk. I politely ignored this impertinence – it is not a servant's business – and have no doubt paid for it with hunger. Her offerings have deteriorated into stews of little more than gristle.

But my high spirits remained resilient, for my work in the wood has given me such a sense of purpose. It was this work that absorbed me, sitting on my stump a few days ago, when my reverie was interrupted by the crunch of approaching footsteps. Who should it be but Euphronie. Curiosity had got the better of her, no doubt. She stood beside me, observing my observation, for a while. It was a cloudy day, and I hoped the weak light would bring out the little people earlier than usual, for they seem – like me – to detest brightness.

'What are your intentions, Mr Ship?' she asked, when I did not stir. 'I would very much like to know.' She made my name sound more like *sheep* than ever.

I kept my eye on the shadiest places around me, though my heart beat a little faster. This, I knew, was my chance to gain some currency with her. While her own dabbling might have been restricted to noting that squirrels sleep in winter, Euphronie would be my most likely conduit to Hugo's friends in the scientific world, and this was a vital element of my new plan.

'Will you be sworn to secrecy, if I tell you what I have found?' I asked.

'Whom would I tell?' she said. I did not answer this. I knew I must proceed gently, as if coaxing a prickly hedgehog. So, I set out in measured tones exactly what I had seen from my stump in the wood. I shared my concern about proof – admitting that, for want of a camera, I had begun devising traps for the little people, even though this would risk damaging them or frightening them away permanently.

It was such a relief, and a joy, to be telling another person – even Euphronie – of all that had been obsessing me, that the very sound of my voice gave me courage. I told her of my desire to take my findings to the Royal Society, and of my great hope to be remembered as a contributor to scientific progress. I described to her how my days of watching had already sharpened my powers of observation despite the knock to my head during the incident, and I felt that, with the right introductions, a fine career lay ahead of me. Finally, I found myself declaring – my voice had grown louder as I went on – that this plot, their woodland habitat, must at all costs be protected from any interference or change. Hugo's academy would have to be built elsewhere, if it was to be built at all.

When eventually I paused for breath, I glanced up at her face and saw there a look of astonishment. This was not really surprising. I repeated my instruction that she keep my secret.

At that, a small smile grew on her lips. 'That was not quite what I meant, when I asked what your intentions might be, Mr Ship,' she said. 'But it is the most interesting story I have yet heard from you.' Her smile spread wider – she is a much prettier woman when she smiles – and so I returned it. 'And you are sure this is not some *mirage*, the result of your fall upon your head?'

'I will show the proof. And if you will lend me the camera, I will of course acknowledge your contribution when I present my photographs.'

'Three days,' she said. 'Tomorrow I travel to Canterbury, to visit my brother-in-law. You may have the use of the camera until I return, when I very much look forward to seeing what you have captured with it.'

'Three days may not be long enough,' I said. 'The little people do not keep regular hours. They might not appear at all during that time.'

Euphronie was already walking away from me, through the trees. 'Hugo's brother will return to Fairwood with me. He is coming to inspect the plot. I hope you will have something to show for yourself.' She turned to give me one last – and somewhat enigmatic – smile, and wandered off into the wood.

SUNDAY, 3RD JUNE

I will not dwell here on the frustrations of the last three days. It will suffice to say that, just as the little people never appear where I look directly, neither do they appear where a camera is directed. The apparatus I hauled from Hugo's study, after a lengthy altercation with Suzy, is cumbersome, and I have had only the most cursory lesson in its use. Once mounted on its tripod, the box cannot be moved without a great to-do of lifting and rearranging legs, such that I have not been able to get the cursed thing even into the correct position, let alone set the focus to attempt an exposure. To add to my increasing exasperation, the little people have been more active than before, coming out to dance and leap about several times each day.

On the third day of Euphronie's absence, and feeling a little mad with solitude and desperation, I cobbled together my last resort – a trap. I had already found the jar where Suzy hides those dainty cakes she is always baking for Euphronie, so I took several of these, along with a hatbox from the wardrobe in the guest room, and some thread from a sewing basket.

The weather had been quite sultry, the sky hung with thick grey cloud, and I dreaded the rain that would surely keep the little people tucked up dry in their nest, or burrow, or wherever they hide so effectively. But it could not be helped. At the woodland plot, I laid trails of cake crumbs hither and thither, each leading to the same point where I balanced the hatbox with one edge held up by a forked twig. To this I tied the thread, which I unravelled with me back to my stump. It was quite ingenious really, but my self-congratulation did not last long. There I sat, the hope in my heart eroded a little more by each bird or squirrel that pounced on the crumbs before I could worry them away. Even my loyal robin joined in the scrumping, stealing the crumbs nearest me, his look now more insolent than intent.

Such are the trials – and errors – of the aspiring scientist. I told myself that I was learning, and to learn, one must make mistakes. When fat drops began to fall between the trees, soaking me and what remained of my crumbs, washing away my last crumb of hope, I retreated to Fairwood with slow and heavy steps.

But how much more lively were my steps as I ascended the stairs to my bed tonight! My hope has been restored, and here is the reason why. When I arrived at the house on this sodden and sorrowful evening, it was to find the drawing room alight with merry chatter and the clinking of sherry glasses. There on the couch sat a glowing Euphronie, beside a man who so resembled Hugo that I stood still in shock, wondering if the incident, and the fortnight that followed it, had been nothing but a dream.

'And here he is!' Euphronie said when she saw me. 'I was just at this moment telling of your lucky escape, in the tragedy that took Hugo from us, with only an injury to your head.' She did not stir from the couch, but I saw the meaningful look she gave her companions, no doubt seeking their sympathy for my recent plight.

The man beside her rose, as did two more, who sat in the velveteen chairs nearest the hearth. 'Mr Walter Ship,' said Euphronie, and I forgave her pronunciation for she had at last uttered my Christian name. Bedraggled and dripping, I was forced to shake hands with each, and learned that they were Hugo's brother Stephen, and his friends, Dominic Ormandon and Jack Willoughby. They smirked a little at my damp attire, and stared at the muddy hatbox which I laid with as much decorum as I could on the floor. But Stephen poured a sherry for me, and Dominic gave up his seat that I should dry out by the warmth of the fire, and they soon returned to their jovial – and I must say fascinating – conversation.

How much I learned, sitting there amongst such educated and ambitious men. They talked of their research, their discoveries, and those of their colleagues, in the great quest for truth.

Dominic, a naturalist and, it would seem, a collaborator with Euphronie in this endeavour, described his theory about sensory perception in plants. This may sound outlandish, but his examples quite convinced me. To think that a tree knows when it is attacked quite sent shivers down my spine. Jack spoke of a new design he had created for the camera that would, if it worked, allow portability – the photographer could carry his equipment and forgo the tiresome tripod. How I wished he had a working prototype! In my excitement, I asked him many questions about how this camera would function, nodding as he gave me answers I did not understand. I became aware of the group's attention focusing on me, and after one particularly indecipherable reply from Jack, Stephen interrupted.

'You also have an enthusiasm for photography, Mr Sheep? What is your expertise?'

The fire had made me quite hot by this time. I went to take another sip of sherry and found my glass empty. 'Not photography, exactly,' I said. 'It is that I require a more amenable type of camera to collect my evidence – and the one Jack mentions would be just the thing.'

All eyes were upon me. I glanced at Euphronie, then, who gave a little nod of encouragement. She murmured something to Stephen, who rose to refill my glass. After a deep swig of the sweet sherry, I began. 'I have seen something in the wood – in fact, in the very plot bought by Hugo – that I believe to be unique. No man has ever made an accurate or irrefutable record of this phenomenon.' (I was pleased to have found that word, with its scientific tenor.)

'And what is it you have seen?' Stephen asked, leaning forward on the couch.

I hesitated. My moment had come, surrounded as I was with an audience of scientific men. I suppose it is only natural that, upon finding my peers, doubt should arise. We all understand the need for evidence to support hypotheses, and this I still lacked. I decided to begin with this confession, in the hope of gaining their sympathy.

'I have not been able to photograph the phenomenon,' I said. 'I wish I could deliver evidence to you now, and believe me, I have tried. But they are evasive.'

'Go on,' said Stephen.

I took a deep breath. 'I have seen little people. They come out of the undergrowth when the light is low enough, and they perform what appears to be the harlequinade.'

The room was silent. I looked to Euphronie again, for reassurance, but she kept her gaze firmly on Stephen – so like Hugo, it must have been perplexing for her also.

'The harlequinade. An element of the pantomime, I think?' asked Jack.

'Quite right,' I said.

'And these little people, are they dressed in pantomime costume?'

'Down to the last detail.' I noticed that Dominic had placed a hand across his face. My pronouncement must have come as a shock. As a naturalist, and *au fait* with the everyday life of the forest, this would have seemed a great and wondrous discovery to him.

'Well,' said Stephen, 'a unique observation indeed. And Hugo never saw these little actors, trespassing on his own land?' He turned to Euphronie, who smiled at him, surely pleased to see that he supported me along with the others.

'He never mentioned it,' I said. 'I have made many notes, about their behaviour. I hope to present them—'

'Why, of course,' Stephen cut in. 'And there will be just the occasion for it, in a few days' time, here at Fairwood.'

At this moment, Dominic fled from the room, coughing violently. I fear it was envy caught in his throat.

Stephen went on. 'Euphronie is to hold a salon here, in honour of Hugo and his work. We will all share our most recent findings. And you, Walter, should be among us.'

I was suffused with a warmth not derived from the fire, which had begun to elicit steam from my shirtsleeves. 'I would be delighted,' I said, with a new dignity. 'But I may still lack said proof – if this salon is to be so very soon?'

'No matter. We will enjoy your presentation greatly without photographs.'

Jack rose to pour the sherry once more, and a toast was made, with laughs of heartfelt joy all round.

And so, it is with deep happiness that I prepare my notes for this, my first step into the venerable world of science. My dream of Society Fellowship is so close, I have even dared imagine the suit I will wear when I enter that hallowed establishment, to be celebrated amongst the great names of our time. I posit that my next visit to the Crystal Palace will be as a lauded speaker, relating to a crowded hall my groundbreaking discoveries. For if Hugo's friends will take my word for it (*Nullius in verba*, indeed!), the general population will certainly be moved to do so. I see myself rising above the cynics. 'You claim to have seen fairies?' some cantankerous old gentleman will ask. 'Oh, no,' I will say, bestowing a kindly smile. 'These little people are as real as you or me.'

They are as real as the superb piece of brisket I have just eaten for my supper (it gives me immense satisfaction to think of Suzy being reprimanded for her previous neglect of my appetite). And they are as real as the terrier which I see now, sleeping under the window seat across the room, its black fur blending into the dark. He is a quite charming companion. I must ask Suzy his name.

SUNDAY, 10TH JUNE

I write this sitting in the summer house in my garden in Suffolk. Several days passed before I could bring myself to put pen to paper, and during that time, the sun beat relentlessly down as I paced the paths between overgrown lawns and untidy borders. It seems my gardener took a holiday during my absence, and all manner of insects have made their homes in the chaotic profusion, buzzing about and distracting me as I tried to gather my thoughts. But this affront pales in comparison with the one I suffered in Norwood, and which I have decided to address in this letter. It gives me no pleasure to write it, necessitating as it does such painful recollections.

Dear Euphronie,

I trust this epistle finds you full of remorse. Do not imagine that I write to absolve you, as had once been my desire. Rather, I wish to establish your error, and warn you that, while it is not forgiven, it will not stand in the way of my bid for recognition.

I was pleased, even grateful, that you welcomed me to Fairwood, and while your withdrawal from my company following the balloon incident was perhaps understandable, it was a relief to me when you showed an interest in my work. The loan of the camera – though futile – seemed to usher in a new friendship, and your introductions to Stephen and his friends to seal this supportive bond. I believed you respected my ambitions, and that having faced adversity together during the incident, we might now sally forth into new territories of scientific study.

I never did have the chance to tell you that, at first, I intended to oversee the construction of Hugo's academy myself. Had I done so, I might have won your affection and averted this most unbecoming development in your attitude towards me, your guest. It is one thing to rise above the rudeness and inadequacy of a servant (you would do well to replace Suzy with a girl more eager to please, and who does not keep animals in the house only to flatly deny any such thing upon being challenged). It is quite another thing to overcome the contempt of one's host.

On the afternoon of your 'salon', as you will remember, I was quite agitated with the anticipation of taking part and sharing my most unusual discovery. You reassured me that all would be well, and I sat, quite shaky with nervous excitement, through the speeches and presentations of all twelve eminent gentlemen you had invited for the occasion. I asked intelligent questions with the others. I played my part in serious discussion. In all, I felt I conducted myself quite as a new man of science should.

When my turn came to stand before your little audience, I spoke with clarity, honesty and humility. The silence in the drawing room told me that your gentlemen friends were quite awestruck. Or so I thought. Imagine my horror when, upon inviting you to stand beside me to receive my gratitude for the lodging and camera you provided, you made your own presentation, and with me as your evidence!

I am not a frog, to be vivisected for bloodthirsty entertainment. I am not, and will not be, the subject of hypothesis and experiment. And I was not the only man present who had never heard of this 'Charles Bonnet', whose studies of visual hallucinations you so energetically summarised for us. You said he was a Royal Society Fellow in his time, but I suspect he is a fiction, just as your interest in my own study was a fiction. I suspect the entire salon was set up as a base attempt to humiliate me and drive me from your house.

If indeed you have an interest in the natural sciences yourself – which I now very much doubt – you will agree that this is hardly a suitable method for disproving my experience and dismissing my findings. You may have succeeded in making Fairwood unwelcoming to me, but you have failed miserably to halt my further study. Now that I have a rival theory to challenge – this that you allege to have been proposed by Charles Bonnet – I will only redouble my efforts. If indeed he recorded hallucinations of little people, his accounts no doubt only served to inhibit the production of proofs such as mine. The homunculi I have seen are clearer to the eye, and to my mind, than anything visible in life.

The next letter I write will be to Stephen. I hid my dismay, earlier on that disappointing afternoon, when

Stephen opened the salon by announcing that he would be building Hugo's planned scientific school, as a memorial to his brother. I felt sure that, upon hearing about the little people, everyone there would agree that Hugo's plot should instead be preserved, so that I could provide my evidence and make a proper study, and so that my tiny friends should not lose their home.

Since, in your view, it is I who am the object of scientific interest, and not the woodland-dwelling homunculi I have now observed more than a dozen times, I believe you will do nothing to prevent the clearing of the trees yourself. I therefore warn you that I will do all in my power to thwart any such manoeuvres. If I am to defend the little people and their habitat alone, this I will do, and with zeal. One day, the Royal Society will thank me for it, and condemn you for your derision.

Yours, a true man of science ever,

Walter Ship

By the time I had drafted this letter, my writing a little jagged from the anger that shook my hand, dusk had fallen in my garden. I gazed out from the summer house, feeling quite spent. The clouds of insects only added to the grey-blue haze, the etiolated plants looming up through it like a miniature city skyline. As I stared, challenging myself to identify some of those plants by their outline alone (my mind is never idle), a movement in the corner of the summer house caught my eye.

There they were, the little people, tiptoeing along by the wall, gazing all about them. Except I could make out only four this time – Pantaloon, Columbine, Pierrot and Clown.

They seemed to be searching for their missing Harlequin. Up and down they rambled, while I looked on. I did not care how they had got here – except to wonder in which part of my luggage they must have travelled. I only delighted in their presence so far from Norwood. I hoped desperately that Harlequin had not been left behind, or somehow lost on the journey. Columbine looked quite sorrowful, as well she might.

I would build them a little home, I decided, since they must have abandoned their nest, and I would befriend them as a benefactor. They might willingly pose for photographs. They might even agree to meet other men. All this filled my heart with hope as my own maid, Amelia, came trotting down the path with a lantern to light my way to the house. I waved happily to her, and when I looked again into the dingy corner, the little people – as is their wont – had vanished. But I will find them, and they will be safe here, in Suffolk. Now, I will follow Amelia and partake of a finer supper than any served to me at Fairwood by Suzy. No doubt it was her terrier who had the best morsels all along.

THE BALLAD OF SCREAMING ALICE

When are you going to Sydenham Hill?
Willow, hornbeam, rowan and lime;
Remind one there I'm waiting still,
To know he'll be a true love of mine.

Tell him to steal me a palace of glass,
Willow, hornbeam, rowan and lime;
And on the hill's brow to make it fast,
Then he'll be a true love of mine.

Tell him to fill it with wonders unseen,
Willow, hornbeam, rowan and lime;
With jewels that sing and music that dreams,
Then he'll be a true love of mine.

Tell him to bring all of London to stare,
Willow, hornbeam, rowan and lime;

At sparks of flame that fly in the air,
Then he'll be a true love of mine.

Collected by A. L. Lloyd

10

OBEDIENT MAGIC
1936

Charm: No hall may blaze so bright that this song will not put it out.

'Watch this,' the man said to me, and he positioned himself against the wall so that, with the shadows cast by the streetlamp and the trees, he looked as if he had antlers sprouting from his head.

Then he offered me a cigarette. The flame from his lighter came at once and swept the horns away.

'Tell me, Crystal,' he said, as he went to loll against the tree. 'What is it like, to have a name that twinkles?'

I was proud of my name at that time. 'I'm named for the palace,' I said.

He seemed to hate this. He had never visited it, he told me. He had never actually been inside.

I didn't try to be cool. He brought out something childish in me, some kind of mischief. 'Let me take you on a tour,' I said. 'Or my father. He's the new general manager, you can look behind the scenes.' The man drew closer to me and blew a smoke ring that encircled my head. 'People call it fairyland,' I said. 'You'll be enchanted.'

I felt quite bold, working on him like that, gazing at him as if I couldn't care less whether he liked me, or whether he liked the palace.

We walked in the dark from streetlamp to streetlamp, and it began to rain, but I didn't hurry. We couldn't see the palace from there, the trees overhung the wall on that part of the hill. The man took my hand and I didn't mind, I liked the rough warmth of it and the thick pad below his thumb. I went on talking, in the rain. 'You won't have seen anything like it,' I said. 'Inside is like an endless garden, like a paradise. You can see anything, learn anything.'

'You don't remember what was here before,' the man said, not asking but stating. We were stepping around puddles now, little pools of lamplit gold, like molten glass.

'It's always been the palace, for me. Will you come and take a tour?'

'Watch this,' the man said. He reached up and swung himself on a low branch, until his legs flipped right over and he was sitting on the high wall, looking down at me. He was like an acrobat.

'We could go for a cup of tea,' I said. 'I'm quite wet.' I wouldn't show him I was impressed, he was like a boy showing off, and that would end in humiliation.

He grinned and then threw himself backwards. I heard the thump when he landed on the other side of the wall.

'You could come and meet us on Friday,' I called. 'At the low-level station.'

I don't know why I wanted to show him the palace, except that he didn't seem to care and that made the feeling sharper. It prickled me, but the sensation was one I wanted to keep. And I did keep it, all that evening while Daddy tried again to teach me to play chess and teased me for muddling knights and rooks, but I was distracted because Bunny would not stop barking at the rain.

'You'll have it by Christmas,' Daddy kept saying. 'You'll have it by Christmas, and we'll play all evening. I'll let you beat me.' He was so jolly, thinking of it all only a month away, and in the year he had made such improvements to his darling palace – had really saved it, he said.

I knew that after all this rain, the palace would be sparkling on Friday.

'You must be the only man in Norwood who hasn't been inside,' said Daddy as he shook the man's hand outside the station. The sun shone, and the palace shone, as if still sleek with rainwater, so it was hard to look at as we walked up through the sodden gardens. The man's name was Herne, he said, and I pretended I had known that. It took a long time to reach the palace while Daddy explained all the repairs he was making, how the fountains would shoot up hundreds of feet again one day soon and all the glory of his darling would be restored. It would be fairyland again.

'You are named for glory restored,' the man said to me, and I was pleased that he winked at me when Daddy's back was turned. The air was sweet for November, everything freshened, the few leaves on the trees and the wet ground giving a soaked scent, a distilled essence of water, earth, air.

Bunny raced, one moment elated, the next morose, her white fur browning and her little paws damp. The palace dazzled as if new, polished by the low sun, the great wonder and Daddy's pride, his joy. It looked bigger than ever.

Something I always loved to do, at the point halfway to the palace from the low-level station, was to turn my gaze back and forth, first to the palace rising up, the crystal mountain on the breast of the hill, and then away at the spreading plains, wooded here and rolling there, the wide and mysterious green and brown beyond. I made Daddy stop. 'Do this,' I said, turning my head, back and forth, so that Herne did the same and we swapped worlds, over and over. It gave me the same dizzy, lurching feeling it always had, and it made me nostalgic for the magic of everything when I was young, how even to turn my head back and forth, back and forth, was to cast a spell, and I could make reality dance. Palace; woods; palace; woods. It was like travelling through time on the spot.

It delighted me that Herne played this game too, but I wanted him to take Daddy seriously. Nothing made him so happy as seeing a person speechless with wonder at his palace. So I hung back, and played with Bunny, who liked to bark at the fish in the ponds and pretend she was a great monster to them.

I have heard Daddy's speeches so many times I could recite along with him. How the whole palace travelled from

Hyde Park to Sydenham Hill in 1854, after the Great Exhibition, and still they enlarged it further and filled it with yet more wonders. How her glory had waned of late, but Daddy had taken the job to turn her fortunes around, and just look what a fine sight awaited us! We traipsed through it all: the Pompeian Court, the Egyptian Court, the Alhambra Court, the Assyrian and Nineveh Court, the Byzantine and Romanesque Court, the Mediaeval Courts. All still swelled my heart, and the old breathlessness came upon me, listening as Daddy pointed out each sculpture, structure and specimen. But Herne lingered longest in the Industrial Courts, and in particular the one where all was formed of cast iron. It was the only one I found a little dismal, but I never said so.

Herne fingered the cool surfaces, and I watched the condensation prints of his fingertips spread and then fade away. I could not say why this filled me with melancholy, while Daddy went on with his explanations of Birmingham cast iron and Sheffield steel.

'Nearly one thousand tons of iron,' he said, 'and twenty-five acres of glass, make up this palace. And the original in Hyde Park – though lesser – was conceived by a gardener. Did you know that?'

I could tell that Herne did not like to hear this. He was stiffening, he did not stop any longer to catch my eye but followed Daddy in a trance. I suppose I forgot, how the soul might be overwhelmed by so many statues, by fountains and the living drapery of exotic plants, and by cabinets containing every splendid thing the world has made.

*

'Funny fellow,' Daddy sniffed, afterwards, while we waited for Herne to take one last look at the south transept. 'Funny friend for you to make, my dear.' But Bunny was straining at her leash, desperate to go dancing out on to the wet lawns again, and Daddy had to go to the offices then, and he didn't seem to mind that when we had said goodbye, Herne set off beside me.

The sun was very low, and the sky behind the palace a smudgy pink, and a little green above that, so that the glass looked like opal, my favourite stone after crystal. I didn't say this to Herne. I let him look at me, looking up at all that heavenly light. He could think what he liked, about me and all of it.

'Didn't you love it?' I asked him, as we wandered down towards the low-level station. But he seemed intent on the trees, which are just like any other trees except better kept. 'Didn't you?' I said.

He was eyeing me, that mischief look again, as if he would like to play a trick. Then he went bounding after Bunny who, free of the leash, kept dashing and barking, in love with the game and with being chased, and I had to follow them.

They were both much faster than me, though I ran with abandon, and let the waterlogged grass flick up at me and the bushes I pushed through catch at me. I ran all the way to the furthest lake before I found them. Bunny was leaping up, delirious, and there was Herne, sitting high on the shoulders of the tallest of the cement dinosaurs that wade and lounge all around the lake.

I laughed and called to him, and when he saw me he stood up, balancing, and stepped on to the dinosaur's head. He should have looked ridiculous, riding that great, inert monster, but somehow he looked grand, and so serious, as if all the trees and the spiky palms and the strange prehistoric ferns that grow there had thronged about the lake to hear him speak. Even Bunny stopped jumping in the air and settled, staring up at him.

'A thousand tons of steel!' he declared, spreading his arms. 'Twenty-five acres of glass.' He was looking, not at me, but down at the lake's surface. 'Every marvel of man's achievement! Fairyland.' I could see him too, down there, glaring up at the world from beneath the water. 'Spectacle! Glamour! Obedient magic! Come to the Crystal Palace, and be enchanted. For what could be more enthralling than things that men have made.' Then he lit a cigarette, and let the lighter flame burn, tall and trembling, for a very long time.

I picked up a stone and threw it, high, so that it fell into the lake with a long gulp. As the ripples obliterated that glaring Herne under the water, I threw another, and another, as if I could smash a window that would always mend itself. I didn't wait for the surface to settle again, and I didn't wait to hear what more Herne might say. I took Bunny and we snuck down a path that led away from the lake, not to the low-level station but out on to the comforting familiarity of Anerley Hill.

For a week, I sulked. I would call it that now. I walked round and round the garden at home, Bunny whining at my heels, suffused with a kind of dull anger that I thought I could excise by grinding my heels into dead leaves, and refusing to look at the sky.

A dull anger is a strange sort, it is a feeling like wearing a coat soaked through and heavy with water, but refusing to take it off. What is pride? I wondered as I stomped. Herne had too much of it. I believed I had just the perfect amount, for I was Crystal Buckman, named for the palace, for my darling father's ambitions, and I was doing all right, wasn't I? It should not matter that a curious man who was probably up to no good at all had made me feel like a ghost in a wet overcoat, and made the palace, my own fairyland, seem for a moment, a lonely moment by a rippling lake, like a bloated folly.

But it was not only the puzzle of pride and its consequences that weighed on me all that melancholic week. I had refused, upon meeting Herne, to even try to figure him out. The world had not demanded that I do so, and while it still did not, some stubborn part of me was now infuriated by the very slipperiness of him, and by my admiration for that. He truly seemed to be a free spirit, and to acknowledge this, to respect it, had felt noble. Pride, no doubt, had crept in there, too. I had been proud to act the unbothered free spirit myself, but I had made myself ludicrous.

Now, damp and angry in the garden, I wanted to feel free to laugh at him, and at myself, to turn heel and head inside and learn how to move a rook, or a knight, so that come Christmas, Daddy would not have to let me win at chess. Bunny huddled by the French doors. The glow from within was so soft and bright, so generous, I was screwed up by my inability to love it and all that it stood for. Daddy would be sitting by the fire, the newspaper in his lap and everything scented with woodsmoke and the comfort of evening, while I drooped out here in the gloom.

I decided I would walk it off, once and for all. Mondays were for beginning afresh, and there were a few hours left of this day. All the December festivities would fly into life tomorrow at the palace, and I could ready my heart to receive them with the love I had felt each year of my life so far.

I could not shake Daddy off when he insisted he accompany me and Bunny through the dark streets. I was not in a mood to talk to him, nor to hear about the pantomime rehearsals and the Welsh choir and the new skating-rink design that had filled his own day with happy chaos. He might have sensed this, for we walked quietly, even Bunny was quiet, and took our habitual route up the road to stroll the long side of the palace.

There were few people about, and the way felt dreary. I glanced at faces here and there as we passed under streetlamps. I watched the shadows of bare branches that crept along the wall. I was not looking for him.

We turned into the palace grounds. I heard Daddy's small sigh, a breath of happiness, and I envied him. So, I tugged Bunny along and I took a deep breath and I began my small, humiliating struggle to love it all once more. 'Tell me what there will be for Christmas Eve,' I said.

I let him talk without really listening, so that I heard only the merry calm in his voice, the restrained excitement, his own imagining of the crowds and their delight, the wonder that would seize so many and that he would organise and oversee, the modest conductor of Christmas. He slowed, gesturing down towards the lake where, frost obliging, people would skate.

'A tree, the tallest in Norway,' I heard him say. 'Carriages inlaid with furs. Lights in the shapes of fruits and flowers.' His voice petered out, and I pictured these things, as I knew he was doing, and I did manage to feel a small springing up of joy, to think of those electric flowers and shining fruits.

'Crystal,' Daddy said. 'Crystal.' He had stopped and was staring into the palace. There was a glow within the central transept.

We hurried inside, where smoke swirled, and we heard the sound that echoed around us, men calling and the hiss of water, and behind that, the faint flow of music from the rehearsal room, serene and strange. Bunny was struggling for the door, but I picked her up and followed Daddy.

Just as we saw the fire, and the sprays of water from the firemen's hose lit like scattering jewels above it, there was a great explosion of flame. Bunny howled and squirmed.

'The orchestra,' Daddy said, quite gently. 'Tell them now, and meet me outside,' and he walked towards the firemen.

I knew the music that rose as I ran to the rehearsal room. It was *A Tale of Old Japan*, I had heard it the year before, the night after my birthday, and then it had given me the sense that I sat and listened in an enchanted palace that floated somewhere above the earth, a cloud castle, detached and drifting away until Sydenham Hill was a distant dream. I had the same feeling, that I would push the rehearsal-room door and enter an unreal realm, that my voice would not sound, that I would be the ghost I had felt myself to be all that miserable week. But I heard myself shout, as the door banged shut behind me and the music dismantled itself note by note, 'The palace is on fire. The palace is blazing!'

*

It was said afterwards that a hundred thousand people came to Sydenham Hill that night. That even Winston Churchill joined the crowd, and shook his head, and pronounced the end of an era. That molten glass flowed down Anerley Hill, and that people poked it from the gutter and rolled it into balls. They said that the palace moaned as it burned, first as hot smoke rushed through the gigantic organ pipes, and then as her girders twisted and curled and fell. They called her Screaming Alice.

A thousand tons of iron. Twenty-five acres of glass. All the world's wonders of industry and art, moaning and screaming, lighting up the clouds. So you, Reader, will never be able to see what it was my father adored and Herne disdained. And if I was working on you now, if I cared at all whether you liked me or not, I would say that all of this, from that encounter beneath a streetlamp to the sound of each orchestra player ceasing to pour out their regulated notes, somehow damaged me. That would be the excuse I think you would like to hear; an explanation that would be, not nice, but credible, and pitiable. I would let you believe that I had gone mad, since even if you were horrified, the explanation would make it all safe.

But the mischief look in my eye is not madness, and I do not care at all if you like me. It is only out of pity for my poor old father that I have not told the rest of this story. For while the Crystal Palace melted and flowed away, and South London stood spellbound in its vitreous haze, I ran all the way down past the terraces and the fountains and the maze, and I pushed through the bushes and went on running, to the lake where the cement dinosaurs loomed in the dark.

I knew Herne by the orange glow of his lit cigarette, and the smoke he exhaled that encircled my head as I kissed him, and kissed him, until I had no breath. And there amidst the prehistoric ferns and spiky palms, I stripped off my clothes and stood before him until he did the same. Aeroplanes burred overhead, all sweeping towards the palace. Every person for miles around looked, and exclaimed, and hurried towards Sydenham Hill, so that there were only trees to bear witness when we fell together, on to the grass, and fell yet further into a kind of frenzy, in which I was not my old self, but neither was I something new.

We swapped worlds, in the undergrowth, where neither the vanishing palace above us nor the invisible woods below us could press themselves into our consciousness, but instead we incanted one another only. I was not under a spell. I felt that some spell had been broken. I was not feral. I would say now that I was honest, and that I had not known honesty before, and that it is not always sweet.

'Watch this,' Herne said, at a pause during that most free of nights, and he took my hand and pulled me upright so we could see the sky full of embers. I stepped back, and looked at his naked form in silhouette against the glow. Where he stood, beautiful before the bare trees all lit in shadow, it looked to me just as if he had antlers sprouting from his head.

TRUE LOVER'S KNOT

a canticle of moths

Brindled beauty, true lover's knot,
Black hairstreak, clay fan-foot.
Oh puss moth,
My sprawler, my anomalous.

Blotched emerald, burnished brass,
Flounced rustic, maiden's blush.
Oh gypsy moth,
My spectacle, my fern.

Water ermine, silky wave,
Marbled beauty, figure of eight.
Oh dew moth,
My confused, my rivulet.

Painted lady, merveille du jour,
Clouded silver, lunar thorn.

Oh ghost moth,
My streamer, my seraphim.

Dingy mocha, frosted green,
Beautiful gothic, copper underwing.
Oh fox moth,
My vestal, my brimstone.

Sallow kitten, mottled umber,
Tortoiseshell, wood tiger.
Oh leopard moth,
My grayling, my gem.

Tree-lichen beauty, delicate,
Star-wort, wormwood.
Oh heart moth,
My phoenix, my flame.

Dusty W. Small

11

NYMPHS
1968

Charm: Though a shy maiden shun me, if I sing this song, never will she leave me.

'I am a strong swimmer,' Carla says aloud. The pond is probably not very deep. But the dusk, and the silence of the surrounding wood, and the reason for standing at the water's edge, alone, make it seem like the deepest water in the world. A black hole plummets beneath the filigree layer of duckweed. A chill spreads up, flowing out into the warm air.

'For Mif,' she says, and summons to her swimsuited breast all the dread and fear that her friend is feeling right now; the uncertainty, and the tiny bit of hope, like a shard of one of Mif's crystals, broken off. What Carla is about to do might destroy that shard, or bury it in mud forever. But Mif needs to know. She said as much. And the police have been zero help, they have been infuriating and dismissive. Because, as Mif said, they are not mothers.

Carla is not a mother either, but she reminds herself that she knows how it feels to lose at least the beginnings of a child. She's hardly thought about it in the last ten years, if she's honest, but now she summons that too. She calls up all the darkest dramas, all the desperate moments of her and others' lives, and all the drownings she can muster: Ophelia, Virginia Woolf, Eustacia Vye in *Return of the Native*, which is the one that gives her the deepest pang. She longed to be Eustacia, once, to be wild, desired, fearless and passionate; all the things she has failed to be. Then she adds Shell to that list. Shell, Mif's frowning, tomboy daughter, is missing, lost out here in this unforgiving world. It works. The flood of grief pushes her two steps closer to the water's edge.

Her toes are in mud now. There will be mud in the bottom of the pond. She will have to dip into it with her feet. She will have to rake it with her hands, push right in, down to the bottom. It will be the bravest thing she's ever done, but it's the right thing to do, for Mif.

Mif does not like water, and Carla is a strong swimmer – Pisces to Mif's Gemini, water to Mif's air. Mif reminded her of this when she showed her the book on Shell's bed. *Nature is my Hobby*, such an innocent, wholesome title. Shell's *Magic Roundabout* bookmark was tucked into a section called 'Catching and Transporting Nymphs'. Carla had read with fascination, not understanding at all what a nymph was.

Because the nymphs of Odonata are aquatic for the whole of their lives, a search for them is relatively easy as it is always confined to such water areas as lakes, ponds, rivers, streams, canals and ditches. But although the nymphs of one species or another are likely to be present in these situations, it does not follow that a mere dip of the net will secure a specimen. Beneath the surface of the water all sorts of diverse conditions exist, and these are fully exploited by the various species to provide security and concealment.

*The nymphs of the broad-bodied Libellula (*Libellula depressa*), for example, are frequently found either buried in mud or hidden beneath debris at the bottom of ditches and ponds. Those of the Common Coenagrion (*Coenagrion puella*) and Demoiselle Agrion (*Agrion virgo*) prefer to live their lives in clumps of waterweed, while those of the Hairy Dragon-fly (*Brachytron pratense*) cling tightly to, and flatten themselves against, the submerged stems of reeds.*

When removed from the water, the weeds, mud or debris, some nymphs remain quite still for a short time and thereby escape detection, but if you wait patiently any nymphs present in the material will eventually betray themselves by moving.

She had just turned the page to scan the headings, 'Preservation of Nymphs', 'Preservation of Nymphal Skin', when Mif had closed the book on her hand.

'She headed for water. I know it. She's Scorpio – a water sign *and* an insect,' Mif said, softly, even more softly than she usually spoke. Mif's voice, with its trace of Australian accent, is like puffs of pale blue cotton wool, calm and soothing to Carla even as she explained a missing daughter.

Mif had combed Dulwich and Sydenham Wells parks, gone round and round the lakes. She had even walked all the way to Crystal Palace and climbed the fence around the fishing lake there. She had called the police. Twenty-four hours, they'd said. But Mif couldn't wait that long. Who could?

It was only when Mif had left for the police station – to stage a sit-in, she said, until they bloody do something – and Carla had returned to her own flat two floors down, that she had remembered. The Dewy Pond, in the wood behind their block. Even though the Bearmott estate was built right into the edge of the wood, Mif never went in there, because she said she sensed a malevolent spirit amongst the trees, watching. She wouldn't even know there was a pond.

So here Carla is, in the dusk, doing a policeman's job for him. Searching. Maybe finding.

Ophelia, Virginia, Eustacia, Shell. She lets out a little shriek as she steps into the water, immediately skids sideways, and falls with an undignified splash. The water is so cold. But her heart does not stop. Gasping, she rights herself. It is only waist-deep, but the bottom is thick with mud, thicker than she ever would have imagined. She is sinking.

'Mif,' she says. This works better than drownings as an invocation. She wades, sinking in, sweeping away the duckweed with her forearms. The mud at the bottom is up to her knees. She steps high and wobbles, keeps moving, until the water is just below her nipples. There is a kind of scrubby island in the middle of the pond. She longs to haul herself out on to it, but she clenches her teeth and begins a circuit.

She's getting used to the cold. She can still feel her feet, the mud is warmer than the water. She will keep wading, and when her breathing is a bit less like that of a panicked rabbit, then she will dip down with her hands.

A few steps on, her right foot comes down on something. Not stone, too soft, but not mud either. She jerks away, feeling her throat close up. 'Mif,' she mouths, and she forces her foot down again, a little to the side. More of the same. Images of crocodiles, sea monsters and water snakes flood through her mind. But she is in a pond, in London. And it is so, so cold. She takes in as much breath as she can and plunges down, then thrusts both hands into the mud. There is the soft thing. Her hands move along. A curve, a length, and then, unmistakably, fingers. Under the water, Carla cries out.

It takes several attempts, because her breath has gone and she is shaking, to get back down. She grasps the arm and pulls. She turns her face away as she drags up the body. She is aware of her own whimpers as she hauls it to the bank. It is someone else's scene, it is somewhere beyond her, this pond and the bedraggled woman heaving and tugging and finally getting back into the water so she can push and roll the muddy thing up, on to the earth.

Shaking all over, finally, she looks.

It is not Shell. Shell is ten years old. This is a woman. She has round breasts, rounded thighs, long hair that is full of mud. The mud is smeared all over her, a deep black-brown so she looks made of clay. But she is not. Carla pants beside her, amazed she got her out. Horrified at what this means. Something terrible. Death. But the body twitches, a knee rises slightly. There is a gurgle, a cough, and the woman sits up and draws an enormous breath. The eyes that open in the black-brown face are dark green. Carla backs away.

The woman doesn't cry, or wail. She must be in shock. Instead she pulls herself to the edge of the pond and sits with her legs dangling, splashing water up on to her arms and thighs, then on to her chest. She doesn't seem to mind the cold. Carla picks up her dry shirt and gingerly drapes it around the woman's shoulders. She isn't even shaking, though Carla's shudders have become more violent. She looks up with those dark green eyes, but her face is covered in mud and Carla can't tell what she is feeling.

'Are you all right?' she asks, though of course the woman is not all right. 'I'll take you home, we can clean you up. I live just over there.' She points through the trees to where her block stands, just beyond the wood. 'You can use warm water instead,' she adds hopefully, for the woman is still splashing herself, revealing skin with a greyish tinge. Carla holds out her dry shorts. 'See if you can get these on.' She will have to walk home in her swimsuit, but this is a crisis, it will be an act of heroism.

The shorts are bright blue, almost turquoise. The woman eyes them with curiosity, then stands and takes them from Carla. She pulls them on, over her broad thighs. They are far too small on her large frame. They resemble bikini bottoms.

'Sorry,' Carla says. 'It's not far, I promise.'

But the woman seems delighted with them. Carla helps her into the shirt and does up the buttons, her shivery fingers fumbling against the woman's skin. She is a head taller than Carla. It makes it tricky to feel protective over her, especially now that, in Carla's small clothes, she looks dressed for the kind of party Carla does not get invited to. The risqué kind, with acid-laced punch, and liberal amounts of pot, where by the end everyone is paired up, saliva-swapping on beanbags.

'Let's go,' she says. She holds out a hand to show the way, but the woman takes it in her own, for comfort Carla supposes, and they walk, an odd, muddy couple, through the dappling trees, towards Carla's flat. Unlike Mif, she has never felt as though anything was watching her in the wood, but for those few, long minutes, the self-conscious sensation is intense.

The woman is hesitant on the stairs, but Carla coaxes her up to the third floor. 'I'll run you a bath,' she says, as she unlocks her front door. 'You'll feel better.' Though so far, the woman seems better than she does. She looks strong, her long broad body flexing as she peels off the shirt and shorts in the bathroom. She sits in the running bath, turning the water silty, and gives Carla a toothy smile.

'What's your name?' Carla asks, vainly adding pink bath salts to the murk.

'Libellula,' the woman says.

'Gosh.' Carla dips her hands in the warm water to rinse off some mud, and wishes she were in the bath herself. She is still shivering. 'Can I call you Libby, then? Or Lula?'

'What you like.' She has a slight accent, Russian perhaps. Her voice is deep. 'Where is Effra?'

'I don't know any Effra,' Carla says, wondering if this might be the woman's assailant. She averts her eyes from the large round breasts, the dark nipples. Lula rakes her matted mane over one shoulder as she lies back in the bath, and plucks something black from one of the clods of mud. It looks like a tadpole, but before Carla can be sure, she pops it in her mouth and swallows.

'Okay. I'll leave you to it, then.'

'Okay,' Lula sings.

Should she call the police? Ask them to look for an 'Effra'? Mif said they're bloody useless, and she tends to agree. She'd be handing over a vulnerable woman to a bunch of incompetent men. And they might like the look of her. It wouldn't be sisterly. But is Lula vulnerable? Every fact of the situation screams that she is. Carla just rescued her from a pond, where she would presumably have drowned, and she was naked, and so presumably either put there by a man or driven to try and drown herself, by something a man has done. Just like Eustacia Vye.

On the other hand, Lula does not seem very upset. Memory loss is one possibility. Madness of some kind – trauma-induced, or just general madness? It's up to Carla to figure it out, before she goes calling any emergency services. Or should she call Mif, for advice?

In a horrible rush like bile to the throat, she remembers the actual crisis: Mif's lost daughter. She dials Mif's number; no answer. 'I'll be back in a minute,' she calls to Lula, then, uncertain if she should leave a woman with a recent history of near-drowning alone in a bath full of water, she pokes her head round the bathroom door. 'Will you be okay if I go out for a minute?'

Libellula's hair, now mostly free of mud, is spread out over her shoulders in a dark brown cascade.

'You can run fresh if you want,' Carla says, looking at the mud-coloured bathwater.

'Don't be crazy,' Lula says. 'This is great.'

Shock, Carla thinks. The woman is bound to act strangely. She should be calm, and kind, and help her through.

Two floors up she knocks on Mif's door. Nobody comes.

She leans there for a moment, picturing Mif's crumpled face earlier that day, and berates herself for having forgotten about Shell so entirely that she'd actually thought she could ask Mif for help. Mif must still be at her sit-in at the police station. She should be there for her, take along some tea, join in with some chanting. While she wouldn't normally, she would do it for Mif. But she can't do that and look after Lula.

She traipses back down the stairs. There are some new graffiti on the walls at the fourth floor. She wonders how they get in here, and why they bother if it's just to paint a flower, a butterfly. There are plenty outside.

Lula is lying on her sofa, naked and still quite wet by the looks of things. Carla pulls towels out of the sideboard, embarrassed now that she's stored them there, but Lula doesn't comment. She drapes them over Lula, and wonders if she should rub her dry, warm her up. It feels too intimate somehow, given Lula is smiling at her again.

'Do you want something to eat? Drink? Do you want to tell me – what happened?' she asks, nervous in the blaze of those green eyes. Lula's hair is dripping, soaking the sofa arm. There is a small pool of water on the floor. Carla mops it up.

'It's lovely here,' Lula says and wriggles, so the towels fall off her.

'It's okay if you don't remember. Or if you don't want to talk about it. Take your time.' Carla pats her broad hand. At least she looks less grey, now. She's almost got a glow.

'Don't be crazy,' Lula says again, grabbing Carla's hand and pulling her to sit on the sofa.

It's unnerving, being wedged in beside a large naked woman. But this is a crisis. She's doing her best.

'Really, it's lovely here.' Lula wraps her arms around Carla, who feels a little like a bug, caught. Give her whatever she needs. Human warmth.

It is nearly midnight when there is a knock at her door. Mif is beaming. 'Look what I've got,' she says, and Shell peeps round from behind her mother before running up to Carla.

'Oh, thank God.' Carla hugs Shell hard, and her eyes fill with tears as Mif smiles and smiles at her.

'Hey,' Mif soothes, and comes to join the hug. 'It's all right, Honey Bee. She's fine. We're all fine. Jimbo had her the whole time, that bastard. Playing at being a father when it suits him.'

Tears stream down Carla's face. 'I got in the pond to look for her, in the wood.' Her sobs are muffled against Mif's shoulder.

Mif pulls back to look at her. 'Seriously?' Carla is still wearing her swimsuit under her dressing gown, and Mif reaches out and pings a shoulder strap. 'You got in a pond, for us? I don't know what to say. You're the best friend in the world.'

Mif is beautiful even in her weariness. Those words, spoken in her soft voice, set Carla off again. Mif squeezes her tight, holding on even after Shell wriggles out from between them.

'Nobody in the whole universe would do that for me. Jimbo certainly wouldn't. Thank you.' Mif kisses her, right on the lips. 'Thank you.' Then she does it again.

'Mif,' Shell calls. 'Can we go home now.' She has never called her 'Mum' in the three years Carla has known them. Mif says it's good for her sense of independence.

'Shall we have a cup of tea, to celebrate?' Mif asks, looking over Carla's shoulder, into the flat. 'Or I've got that ouzo left?'

'Actually, there's someone here.' Carla sniffles and smiles, ready to tell her own story of the evening, but Mif frowns.

'Sorry, I didn't realise.' She lets go of Carla. 'We'll go home. I'm on the stall first thing, anyway.'

'I didn't mean that,' Carla says, 'it's not like that.'

But Mif is already at the stairwell. 'Another time,' she calls, and follows Shell away up the stairs.

Carla waits, in her doorway. Mif has never kissed her on the mouth, in gratitude or celebration, or anything else. Carla's admiration for Mif is not just about her beauty; she has reminded herself of that many times. Yes, Mif is tall and slender and golden where Carla is short and stocky and dark, but it's only because they're so different that Carla can't help noticing so much how Mif looks.

Still, that kiss was stirring, and surprising. Could she be part of the zeitgeist, after all? She pictures herself with Mif, wandering through a field of flowers and hippies, someone strumming a guitar under a tree, the sun bronzing their shoulders, their fingers entwined. *Free love*, Mif whispers in her ear, then kisses the lobe. But it's ridiculous. Carla is not sexually experimental. She's not even sexual, since Geoff. The summer of love and all this liberation that is supposedly in the air has made her feel inadequate, not free. She is not the adventurous type.

When she goes back to the living room, Lula has woken from her slumber and tossed away the sheet Carla had laid gently over her.

'I'll get you a nightshirt, or something,' Carla says, alarmed again by Lula's nakedness. She hadn't meant for Lula to follow her into the bedroom, but she does. Carla pulls out a crumpled T-shirt from the bottom drawer. It was one of Geoff's, and has a Grateful Dead graphic on it. She's never worn it, because it has two swirls on the front that hang right over her breasts, but she's glad she kept it now.

'This will fit you.' She holds it out. But Lula is looking at the bed. 'You can sleep in here,' she says, after a moment. 'You must need a good rest.' She hopes this in some way makes up for her failures, both as a nurse and as a host, in persuading Lula to eat anything or talk about her ordeal. But when she takes a pillow back to the couch to make herself a bed for the night, she finds that the seat cushions, the back and the arms are all soaking wet. Not just damp, as from wet skin, but dripping on to the floor, as if someone had poured water on to them deliberately. What was Lula up to, earlier, when she dozed off in the armchair?

'I hope you don't mind sharing,' she says, back in the bedroom. Lula is gazing at herself in the wardrobe mirror, twisting her long hair into a thick rope, pulling the yellow T-shirt so it stretches tight around her figure, like a minidress. She is a dramatic sight, rubenesque and disconcertingly confident, looking herself in the eye. Carla wonders if, rather than traumatised, she is actually deranged, and it would be dangerous to sleep beside her. She's out of her depth. She should have just called the police.

Lula catches her eye in the mirror and gives her that toothy smile. 'This is so great!' She laughs. 'You are so great. I feel really good.' She wiggles and looks at herself again.

What is that accent? Not quite Russian. Czech? Something Scandinavian, even? 'Tell me your name again,' Carla says.

'Libellula.' She rolls the 'l's off her tongue like pear drops.

'Libellula,' Carla repeats.

The effect is quite startling. Lula sashays round the bed to her, and gazes into her eyes. 'Say it again,' she says.

Carla hesitates, stymied by Lula's face and Lula's body, so close to hers. She takes a breath but before she can speak Lula kisses her, a long, firm press of her wide lips on to Carla's own. They are warm, and soft. The same muscle in her abdomen that beat like a drum when Mif did this, beats again.

'Did you see my friend, Mif, at the door earlier?' Carla asks, swallowing hard. Perhaps Lula thinks that kissing on the lips is an everyday expression of thanks around here.

'I don't care about Midge,' Lula says. 'I like you.'

It must be the moon. Is it a full moon? Carla wonders. Something in the stars. Mif would know. Has she reached her prime, just as the zeitgeist has infected all their brains, their hormones, their lips? It is not just her mouth that is humming, though. She recognises this feeling, from the first time she slept with Geoff, from the all-too-brief period when Felix came to her pottery classes and she had to watch his fantastically deft hands caressing clay for two hours at a time, while she breathed in the tangy scent he gave off.

'Okay,' Carla says. 'I guess I like you too.' Lula pulls her down on to the bed and squeezes her waist. 'Slowly,' Carla manages to say, but when they kiss again, it is not slow but urgent, almost aggressive. Don't overthink it, she tells herself. Just go with it. But she finds that her body, so underused of late, gives her no choice.

*

When Carla wakes to the uncurtained dawn, it is to a few moments of perfect peace. She cannot remember feeling this serene for a long time. It is followed by a plummet of dread, and then the full impact of horror. A half-drowned woman, in shock, in a state, and she has behaved like – well, how a man might behave. Not a woman. Not a feminist. It's almost as if she was drunk, yesterday, or worse. She can't bear to believe it. But there is Lula next to her, gazing at the ceiling, unperturbed.

Carla feels guilty little twitches of pleasure, memories in her skin. She should be scolding herself for taking advantage of someone unstable, but it didn't feel like that. She didn't seduce Lula, did she? Quite the reverse.

'This is lovely,' Lula says, rolling the 'l's around, and then rolling towards Carla. She is an amazing creature, Carla thinks, and wonders if that is something a man would think, too. But it's true. She feels, not tenderness, not the maternal instinct mixed with insecurity that she felt with Geoff, but a kind of awe. She kisses Lula's collarbone, her long wide neck, finding the slightly stagnant watery smell she had gulped in last night, and gives way to it again.

'What is it?' Lula asks when Carla offers her a piece of rye toast and peanut butter. Carla's mouth is full, she is ravenous. Lula shrugs and takes a bite from the slice in Carla's hand. 'So good,' she says, between chews, and they are both munching, in silence, when the phone rings.

'Did you find it?' Mif's voice asks, down the line. 'I didn't want to knock in case – you know.'

Carla feels herself blushing. 'I'm sorry,' she says. 'I had a lie-in, after yesterday. I was tired. I bet you were, too.'

Mif is silent for several long seconds. 'There's an invitation inside. Let me know if you can't make it.' She sighs. 'I'm so grateful, for what you did. You know what I'm like about water. And Shell's grateful too. We want to thank you properly. See you later?'

Outside the door of her flat is a rose plant in a green ceramic pot Mif made in her class. Its tiny blooms are pink. Guilt floods through her. She hadn't done nearly enough. Sure, she got in the pond, but she'd forgotten Shell completely the minute she'd found Lula.

The card tucked into the plant pot reads, in Shell's round writing, *Please come to our party tonight. Just bring yourself (and a friend if you want!)*. Mif has added the part in brackets.

'How do you feel about socialising?' she asks Lula, who has come up behind her and is tugging on her hair. 'Just a flat upstairs. Probably all girls.' She blushes again. 'If it's too much for you, I'll understand.' She is hoping Lula will say that it is, that they should shut the door and stay at home.

'Don't be crazy,' Lula says. 'That would be great.'

Carla finds herself wondering again. Is Lula some sort of extreme hedonist, who was giving herself an eccentric mudbath? Perhaps this is just what is going on around her, in these open-minded times, and she hasn't kept up. But what will Lula do in the presence of beautiful Mif, and her innocent, if boyish, daughter?

*

The door of Mif's flat stands ajar. Pale pink light and the sweet shouts of Aretha Franklin spill out into the hallway. It would have been so much easier if Lula had just come with her, now. But it's nearly eight o'clock, and Lula had insisted from beyond the bathroom door that she needed longer.

Without Lula there to glow intimidatingly beside her, Carla's outfit looks showy, attention-seeking. She tugs the swingy neckline of her dress up, and the clingy hem down, and enters, wine bottle clutched across her body.

Mif has draped pink napkins over the lamps. There is a mixing bowl of punch, with strawberries floating in it, on the coffee table. Shell comes pelting from the kitchen, laughter following her, and swiftly turns their collision into a hug.

'She's here!' Shell calls. Smiling faces emerge. Carla wishes they weren't all so familiar, these nice people her friend has invited and who will have to be introduced to the extraordinary Lula. Nice is not a word you could use about her. It would be like calling the Amazon River nice.

But here is Mif, a walking swirl of raspberry ripple, holding out her golden, jangling arms to Carla. 'We tie-dyed it,' she grins, between kissing Carla's cheeks. She twirls, and the white muslin kaftan with its cerise streaks blows out around her. Carla can see straight through it to Mif's knickers.

'My friend is coming,' Carla begins. 'She's a bit, well—'

'Welcome! Any friend of yours,' Mif trills. She is flushed; she gets drunk easily, Carla knows from their occasional dips into that ouzo bottle.

'She should be here soon. Sorry. And Mif, do you know an Effra around here? She asked—' says Carla, but Mif is drawing her to greet everyone, and in turn she clasps Lucy, who lives in the next block and teaches Shell how to identify birds, then Stef and Astrid, who run market stalls next to Mif's. Between them all, something fizzes: repressed laughter, some secret light. It cheers Carla up a bit. They might have their own surprises to share. Lula might not seem as unlikely, as shocking, as she actually is.

Mif shrieks as the music changes and begins to sway as she tries to ladle punch into a glass. 'Here's to you,' she gulps, once Carla has hold of her drink. 'Pond-diver extraordinaire. Best brave friend.'

'It's funny you should mention the pond,' Carla begins. 'A funny thing happened.'

Mif has a way of opening her face, inviting you into her pool of golden light, and she does it now. Carla smiles in response, takes a deep breath, ready to tell all. But Shell is tugging at the striated kaftan, practically winding herself into it, as if she were five years old again, not ten. She mumbles something into Mif's ribs, and they both turn to look.

There in the doorway stands Lula. 'It's okay?' she asks Carla, and Carla thinks she means the dress she is wearing, because it is what everyone in the room is staring at; because it is shimmering, sky blue, falling in waves to the floor, so that Lula resembles a goddess metamorphosing into a waterfall. Or vice versa.

Where on earth has it come from, Carla wonders, but she manages a nod. At which Lula breaks into that huge, toothy grin and steps forward, ushering in behind her two more women, as striking and luminous as she is. 'It's okay,' she says to them. Carla can feel Mif's eyes on her, asking. But she has no satisfactory explanation, for Lula, for the dress, for the two women with her, who seem to take up the whole room now they are rustling around it. She keeps expecting things to get knocked from shelves, snagged by all that gleam.

'It's okay!' says Mif brightly. 'Mercury is in retrograde. And I did say, any friend of yours. Could we?' she gestures.

'This is Libellula,' says Carla. That instant effect, like a magnet. Lula comes and curls an arm around Carla.

'Hello Midge,' she says, eyeing the kaftan with curiosity. 'Your dress is nice.' It sounds like an insult.

'And who's this?' Mif points now to the others.

Carla grabs her shoulder and whispers, 'I need to talk to you. They might be escapees, or refugees. They might be confused.'

Lula's arm tugs her back to crinkle against the pale blue of her hip. 'This is Demoiselle. This is Puella,' she says, rolling their 'l's just as she does her own.

The two women beam as if spotlit. Carla winces. Those names. They sound like stage names, and yet there's a flicker of recognition in her at the sound of them. And those frocks, like glamorous pantomime costumes almost, yet they look so beautiful and wear them so naturally. As flamboyant and ludicrous as Lula's; one a glossy panelled concoction of black and green stripes, the other a sheath of what must be shot silk, viridescent bronze. Where did they get them?

Shell is staring, with an expression of bemusement too mature for her young face. Carla fights back the urge to apologise again. But she doesn't need to, because everyone else – Mif and Lucy and Stef and Astrid – is welcoming these garish interlopers like old friends, enfolding them, finding them space on a sofa or stool to gleam in the clashing pink lamplight.

It is almost as though everyone but her was expecting them. Or are these women just bigger of heart than her, more accepting, altogether less timid? She has that feeling again, that she has missed something, that this weird zeitgeist has blown in and carried everyone else up with it, leaving her floundering below. She must keep up.

So she does. She slurps down the sweet punch, and helps Stef replenish the bowl with sloshes from each of the bottles they find in the kitchen. She sings along to Aretha, and then the Beatles, as if she gets this new music just as much as Astrid seems to, miming with aplomb. All the while, she tries not to glance too often at Lula and her miraculous companions. Nobody else is asking where they came from, who they are, so neither will she.

When Mif says it's time Shell went to bed, Carla volunteers to tuck her in. She's a little unsteady on her feet by now; the flat is so warm, filled with all these merry bodies.

'Is that who you met in the pond?' Shell asks, sleepily.

'Is that what she told you?' Carla sweeps Shell's hair back from her forehead and gives it a sticky kiss.

'No. It was a deduction,' says Shell and, for a fraction of a second, Carla thinks she said 'seduction'.

She stands outside the bedroom door, gathering herself. *Seduction*. It's this conscience, guilty, strait-laced, that is keeping her from letting go. She had rolled her eyes at it all: turn on, tune in, drop out. She has responsibilities. But Lula, resplendent, casting her spell on everyone here, doesn't seem to need her protection. She has actual friends. So come on, she tells herself. One night, at least. Stop worrying. Think of Eustacia Vye, that wild soul, hungry for a party, any party, and here is one being thrown in your honour.

Carla watches with curiosity as Lucy rolls a joint, not because she's never seen one before, but because this one is particularly large.

'To tide us over,' Lucy says, smoke streaming from her nostrils as she passes it to Mif. Both smile at Lula, and at Demoiselle, and Puella.

'Perfect,' says Puella.

'Boss,' says Demoiselle, and wriggles deeper into the sofa cushions between Stef and Astrid.

When it's her turn, Carla coughs, manages to laugh it off, tries again, and passes it on. She's got away with it, she thinks, but it's better than that. She actually feels good. She relaxes into Lula's warm side, squeezes her lovely round arm and rests her head against it.

'Have a drink,' says Lula, pushing a full cup of punch into her palm. 'It's great.' And Carla watches as she downs her own and begins serving more to everyone else. There's a sense of anticipation amongst them, that suppressed laughter that was there before but enhanced, somehow. She watches Mif, smiling at everyone, toasting her daughter, safe in bed next door. She watches Astrid, toasting their new friends, and Stef, toasting the punch itself. Everyone laughs.

'What's funny?' she asks.

'We add to it,' says Lula, and kisses her ear.

'Add what?'

'Magic.'

Which could mean anything. Or nothing. But she's not going to worry about it, here in this warm pink room with these mysteriously unfazed people. It seems to be a game, now, to empty the punchbowl, and it tastes so much better after a mouthful of smoke. Mif has put on the Doors, and as Jim Morrison exhorts them all to break on through to the other side, Mif comes swaying round to perch beside Carla. She looks at Carla for a long time, not smiling but not serious. Then she stands and announces, 'Let's go out. Into the woods.'

This is letting go, Carla thinks. Mif, who has been afraid of those woods since she's known her, is shaking off her own constraints, embracing the world. She watches the raspberry swirl of Mif's kaftan as it sends out little pink trails behind her. Her pulse shifts to match the music. In an effortless dance they all flow towards the door, out into the corridor, her hands held in other silken ones. Someone slams the flat door shut and they drift like thistledown to the ground floor, through the hall, and into the sweet, fragrant night.

This is what Carla remembers. The cunning tessellation of leaves, yellow and green, as they slid across the earth. Trees that leaned in when they heard her think of them, tuning their aerial limbs. Music that followed her, that she knew but could not sing, a sound like cinnamon, fur and smoke. The wood, tiny and endless, soft and echoing, laying down paths for them, leading them in. Lula, Puella and Demoiselle turned goddesses, shining impossibly in the dark, their shimmers pulling in cobweb strands of light from the far-off estate lamps. A fox, black velvet, sniffing at their hems. And everywhere, in every molecule of air, that presence that Mif had sensed and Carla had not believed in now thrummed, not malevolent but irresistible, the delightful orchestrator of the wood, of this, of Carla's heartbeat, of every cause and coincidence that had brought them here.

Lula, Puella and Demoiselle dancing, kicking up leaves, and the trees, some stern, some laughing, watching it all, the whole insignificant speck of a night, as Carla's feet with the others tickled the earth and felt it tickle them back. Lula lifting her up, swinging her round, so the air slid in ribbons through her hair and held it, twirled in time. And everywhere, in every molecule of air, that laughing presence, exulting at their exultation, triumphant at their joy.

A race, women streaming through the wood like deer, their skips turning to leaps, warmth through Carla's limbs like a rising chord as Lula, Puella and Demoiselle spun further away from her, spots of light bobbing between the trees.

Stars, circling and embracing, swimming into patterns that Mif would know, and should explain to her. Realising that Mif was not there, had not been with them in the woods at all. Gathering then around the Dewy Pond, leaning to find the stars' reflection in its black glass and seeing, lit by a spotlight of moon, a gleeful, beguiling face looking back at her, a reflected spirit, and in gratitude bending to stroke the magnificent horns that sprung from his head. Her fingers rippling the water, scattering stars, so that the horned head fragmented and there rose instead a woman, hair in coils and skin like weathered silk, who held out her majestic arms to Lula, Puella and Demoiselle and beckoned them home.

It had not mattered that she found herself alone, gazing at the sun rising over Sydenham, the trees no longer listening, the music drained away, because she had realised something. She had understood, it all made sense, and all she had to do was tell Mif.

*

Carla is staging her own sit-in, now, on the landing outside Mif's flat. Her friend has avoided her for nearly a week, but she will have to talk to her eventually. She can't just step over her.

It's been five hours. Carla taps at the door. 'I really need the loo,' she calls, deliberately pitiful.

Silence, again. But this time Carla hears the chain slide and the door opens.

Shell peers out at her. 'Mif needs cheering up,' she whispers, then skids back towards the sofa with her book.

Mif is on the balcony, scrubbing at the window with a white-and-pink-striped rag. She glares through the glass and scrubs harder. Even angry, Mif is somehow soft at the edges.

Carla takes a deep breath and throws her arms wide. She's practised her Aretha for this – Mif can't resist a bit of 'Respect' – but still she starts too high. By the time she has squeaked through two short lines, Shell has stuffed her fingers in her ears. But Mif is biting down on her lower lip, and she drops her rag.

Carla flings open the balcony door and takes her friend's soapy hand. 'I'm sorry, lovely Mif. Let it all out. Give me what for.'

Mif nudges a stool towards Carla. 'Tell me what you think happened,' she says.

They sit, looking out at the quiet, busy trees, at eye level with the watching canopy, and Carla tells the whole unbelievable story, from the pond to the party to the wood. 'And I had no idea about the punch. Honestly,' she says, when she has finished. 'That look you gave me. I thought you were in on it. You know, embracing the zeitgeist.'

'But you're the one who found the great truth, out in the wood, high as a kite,' says Mif, and the softened anger in her voice is worse than if she had shouted. 'I hope you're going to tell me it was worth it, bringing strangers into my flat, with Shell, strangers who lace people's drinks with acid. It was the only way I could think of, to get you all out.'

'Well, she's gone. They all have,' Carla says. 'And I'm sorry.'

Mif snorts. 'So, what was it, the great truth?'

'I thought you were there with us,' Carla repeats. 'I thought you'd seen it all too.'

Mif stretches her long golden arms in an arch, and lets one hand fall to rest on Carla's shoulder. 'You don't remember it, do you?' she says, with a sly little smile.

Carla glares out at the trees, now tight-lipped in their wisdom. She shakes her head. 'Lula left me a present, though.'

'Not that dress.'

Carla digs in her pocket and holds up a thin, crinkled envelope. 'The rest of the acid,' she says. 'I'm sure, if we took it together, I could remember, and you'd see too. It was really important, Mif. It really helped, with something.'

Mif pulls her hand away. 'You looked like you were under an enchantment.'

'Not a bad place to be. A gorgeous place, really.'

'But you don't mind she's gone? Lula?'

'I don't mind anything, except not having you as my friend.'

'Then we don't need this,' says Mif, as she snatches the envelope from Carla's hand and drops it into the bucket of bleach at her feet.

They both stare at it, as it shrivels up and sinks.

'But I do want to go into the woods with you,' says Mif. 'I want to see this Dewy Pond that grows hippie nymphs in its depths.'

'It's not funny.'

Mif tugs her up from her stool. 'Shell's been reading all about pond life. Let's take the fishing net.'

'Lula did leave the dress,' Carla says. 'It would suit you. Better than that tie-dye bloodbath.'

Mif pokes her toe into the pink and white rag by the bucket. 'It was see-through, wasn't it?'

'It was hideous. But Mif.' Carla takes her friend in her arms. 'You looked beautiful in it. Like a beautiful, clumsy lady butcher.'

She feels Mif relax against her, and lets the golden embrace soothe her.

'Thank you,' Mif says, into the top of her head. 'Such a two-sided, Gemini compliment. Now let's go.' And still holding Carla's hand, Mif runs through the flat, tugs Shell from the sofa, and the three of them go helter-skelter down the stairs and out into the soft, green air.

A STORM SONG IN THE ROUND

How many died in the Grote Mandrenke?
How many died in All Saints' Flood?
Hard Candlemas?
Culbin Sands?
Here comes the Big Wind
Here comes the Big Wind
Crash bang stop.

How many drowned in the Tay Bridge Disaster?
How many drowned in the Ochtertyre Storm?
Royal Charter?
Lacken Disaster?
Here comes the Great Wave
Here comes the Great Wave
Slip slap slop.

How many fled the Storm of November?
How many fled the October Gales?

Ulysses Storm?
North Sea Flood?
Here comes the Twister
Here comes the Twister
Snap crackle pop.

Anon

12

HURLECANE
1987

Charm: If I need guard a ship in a gale, this song will calm the wind and lull the waves.

Herne summons his voice from the earth. Drunk on fury, close to death, Herne will not be forgotten. This time, he will take what has been taken, wreck what has been wrecked. He wants more than fire.

Herne summons the sky.

His aim is careless.

*

It is 9 p.m., by Sol's reckoning, when he begins to sweat. He slows on the dark woodland path and pulls off the heavy jersey. It's a good one, left neatly folded by his camp only a fortnight ago, in time for the autumn chill. A strategic gift; not like the cans of tepid beer left in summer, or the box of washing powder left, he doesn't remember when, but he was never going to get running water. Ah, the luxury of turning a tap. The luxury of ice!

He should not feel this warm, in October, in the wood. But it is not a fever. It's the wind, warm as baby's breath.

He was walking for heat, to stoke his bones ready to wriggle into the sleeping bag and get a good few hours before the cold seeped up from the ground. A reliable method. Jersey on and march the paths, in the dark, which is easy now that he knows them and with the summer's growth dying back. Tonight, he turns up the slope instead and finds the bench in the clearing. The warm wind tickles his neck. It's like a leftover summer night, to be used up like a last ripe apple. Sol hasn't eaten an apple this year. People leave packets: biscuits, noodles, a jumbo bag of liquorice allsorts once. Beetles got into those, but what man can chew liquorice all day?

The trees shiver. Above the clearing, clouds are crowding the orange London sky. Watching them scud towards him gives Sol the sensation of falling backwards.

*

A few miles west, in Isleworth, Rachel Boermann is sneaking out late from the shared office at Syon Park. Her left ear is hot and a little sweaty from the pressure of the office telephone. It's the only place where Pete can call her in private, now that the phone in her shared house has gone missing. It's 8 a.m. where he's staying in Fiji, but that doesn't stop him asking what she's wearing, what she's wearing under that, if she might run a hand there and tell him how it feels, how his hand would feel if it were there, stroking.

Rachel glances at the butterfly house as she hurries past and sees that someone has left the guide lights along the path edges switched on. A waste. And she might be blamed, clocking out last. Her father still obsessively keeps tabs, on the house and the staff, claiming it's his right as the man who built it. *Attention to detail, it's the Boermann way*, he says, so obediently she heads inside.

The switch is under the ticket desk, but she can't resist ducking through the heavy rubber curtain, and into the familiar humid air. The path lights are dim, and the butterflies, tucked under branches and into crevices, are all but invisible.

Rachel leans over the handrail and lifts a ragged leaf of fishtail palm. A dark shape flaps up, brushing her fingers. It lands on her upper arm, dozy, and shows the glowing white spots on its midnight wings. *Hypolimnas bolina*: the blue moon butterfly. She tugs on her sleeve to dislodge it and send it back to its roost.

There are blue moons in Fiji. While she shuts off the lights and locks up, Rachel pictures Pete in the real tropical forest of Vanua Levu, sweating, grinning up into the green canopy. Pete calls her his 'beaut'. Pete's beaut. Her father says it makes her sound like a car, but she doesn't mind. It makes her sound more exciting than she is.

As she meanders towards the car park, her scarf whipping up into her face, she notices that the clouds, which had been pushing steadily away over Surrey, have turned about and are now racing back towards London. The air smells of seaside, of salt, and therefore of Pete.

*

In Peacehaven Caravan Park, Deep stumbles against the sink unit, and then grips the taps as his caravan tips back the other way. Perfectly normal, he tells himself again. The wind has been rattling the windows for hours, rattling all the loose-hanging mysteries on the underside of the caravan, but this is the English coast. It's supposed to get windy.

The bench seat lurches up to meet him and he sits with a bump. It is just like being back on the sea. He is glad this caravan has no sea view. Not that anyone else is suffering that sight. Every other caravan, in the identical cream-coloured rows, is empty. He has checked. Deep lifts a green chenille curtain to peer out for Sara on her way back down, but even the lamps along the tarmac strip are murky. Rubbing the glass doesn't help. They only scrubbed these windows yesterday, inside and out, in preparation. It turned the water in the bowl to brown scum. Deep jumps when a hand meets his on the other side of the plastic, and smiles as Sara's finger rubs a small square clean. 'Salt!' she shouts. Always one step ahead of him.

Sara opens the door and it slams shut before she can even get the jerrycan through the narrow gap. Deep is halfway to help her when the caravan lunges sideways again. He slips on the doormat-sized rug and crashes to the floor. The mat was meant to make things homely, not treacherous. As she opens the door again, there is a loud cracking sound from behind her, and Deep watches between her braced knees as a caravan further down the tarmac strip tips right over, free of its mooring.

'Perfectly normal,' he says, hauling himself upright.

Sara smiles at him. 'I can't leave you alone for a moment, can I? I'll do that window again in the morning. And the others.'

'We'll have to do them every day, at this rate,' says Deep.

'Every day until your brother comes. Look what I found.' Sara hands him a yellow apple. 'You call it a windfall.'

They bump together as the caravan rocks. Just like being back on the sea, where Deep's brother is right now, his boat tossing about not only in wind, but in deep, black water.

*

Sol, cocooned in jumper, anorak, sleeping bag and beanie hat, is vexed. Most evenings, he drops to sleep almost too easily. The whirrs and creaks and squawks of Sydenham Wood by night have become a lullaby; the roar and swoosh of cars on the road above as comforting as the hum of a refrigerator. But tonight, the trees are agitated. The ground beneath him seems to prickle with their alarm. Their heads flail and their shoulders shake. For the first time he realises that he has come to think of them as friends. An old ache arises: fearing for his loved ones, but unable to do anything for them.

'You'll be all right,' Sol mumbles. 'Look at you. Great big beasts, you are! You'll be fine, fine.'

The hornbeams nearest him groan in response.

Sol sits up in his hollow. In the light from the streetlamps beyond the railings, he can see dead leaves performing a crazy dance. More like a riot, a proper frenzy. He's never seen them blow up that high, from the ground. The trees are shaking their own leaves, a roaring crowd that clashes with the rioters. It's quite a sight. Down the slope, in the deep dark wood, something is tearing, screaming. The first crash of trunk against trunk shakes the earth.

*

Herne is all ears. From the wood to the sea, a sickening symphony.

The wind itself has no sound. It is the conductor of an orchestra hundreds of miles wide, its players possessed.

In Southsea, the waves fire pebbles up from the beach. Their lunatic tattoo beats along the front, beneath the wail of a hundred car alarms.

In Orpington, tile-hung house fronts play like ghostly pianos, flinging their keys into the air.

In Moorings Care Home on Canvey Island, the air-raid siren used for local flood warnings blares as Beryl sings her solo, undeterred. It is the song she used to sing to her twins in their Stepney bomb shelter. As she hits her quavering high note, all the lights go out.

At Knole House outside Sevenoaks, one hundred Tudor chimneys sing as the wind blows them like bottle tops.

Across Kent, Sussex, London, Berkshire, Oxfordshire, Buckinghamshire and Hertfordshire, the wind cracks the tops off trees and bends shrieks from their heartwood. The demented drum roll of snapping roots heralds the cymbal crash of each fall.

*

Rachel's alarm clock radio fades in and out, jumbling information. Her bedside light flickers. She wants to phone Pete to tell him she's all right, or phone her mum and tell her to stay away from the windows. But her housemates have denied all knowledge of the missing telephone. Half an hour ago, as she manoeuvred her single mattress up against her own window, she watched a garden shed fly through the air above the back fence. She wants to tell someone about that, too, but everyone else, having emptied a bottle of vodka between them, is asleep.

The radio crackle dissolves to nothing, and the bedside light dies. Rachel flicks the light switch by the door, knowing it's pointless, and remembers the switch at the butterfly house. She tries to recall what lies nearby, what might fly like a garden shed and split that arching glass roof. Wheelie bins? Café tables stacked out of sight? In the dark, nothing will come. Above all, she hopes her father will resist his protective instinct and stay away. His butterfly house is his darling; *my own Crystal Palace of wonders*, he calls it. And while its gleaming curvature may restrain nature, wrestle it into order, she hopes he will know when he's outgunned.

At Syon Park, all is dark too. Rain has swept through and droplets skirmish across the lawns like sea fret. In sympathy with the battles being lost nearby at Kew, at Richmond, at Gunnersbury Park, oaks and beeches have hurled themselves down, ruining treelines, opening up new vistas. A mother oak is falling now, slow, resigned. She gives up her root holds one by one. Nobody is there to commiserate, to bear witness, as her crown and then her trunk sweep down through the glass roof of the butterfly house. The splinter and tinkle of all that glass is nothing to her.

The wind dives in and begins to scour this unexplored space. A fishtail palm flails. A blue moon butterfly is thrown skyward, scrabbles amongst unfamiliar oak branches, then sails up, out, one of a thousand jewels flung. Butterflies flow in the eruption of humid air into cold. They somersault across lawns, crash together, twirl helter-skelter, their colours lost in the blackout.

*

Sara has made the caravan cosy with three new candles. She has stuck them in place with drips of wax, but Deep cannot take his eyes off them, waiting for one to tip, roll, and set all those acrylic cushions alight. He hides his nausea from Sara, unable to drink the sweet tea she has made for him. The cup is only gripped between his hands to stop it sloshing, should another lurch come. He has tucked the uneaten apple into his coat pocket. After the door flew open for the third time, they wedged it shut with a broom.

The roaring outside is like a turbine engine. Sara has her eye to the tiny patch of clean window, though even that is now misted with salt. 'Perhaps we should go,' she says.

'Go where?'

'The washing block? The shop at the gate?'

Both of these have been locked up since they arrived at Peacehaven.

'We can't break in.' Deep swallows another wave of nausea as the caravan lifts at one end and then rights itself.

'I could just go and take a look, you know—'

The rest of her words are drowned out by a thunderous crash, then another. Sara is shouting something but Deep can't make it out; his mind is being shaken by the terrible grinding smashes outside, and then his body is being shaken too. He sees Sara stagger towards the broom at the door just before he is lifted from the bench seat and slammed against the wall. Something snaps, a beastly tail lashes against the caravan and Deep rolls from wall to ceiling to floor to wall. A candle flies past his head. The toilet door swings open and green chemical goop spatters his legs. A mirror cracks and sends shards spinning. Round and round, upside down, Deep goes, caught in the nightmare current.

*

Herne is all eyes. From the wood to the sea, a demented dance.

The wind itself is no dancer. It choreographs a troupe, thousands – millions – strong, each member giving itself up to this extravaganza.

In Sheerness, summer clothes blown from their attic store frolic on telegraph wires above the streets.

In Broadstairs, a double bed moonwalks across the floor, as the chimney breast fills the room with its sooty breath.

In Ashford, a pear tree shakes itself into such a frenzy that one pear whizzes straight through the glass of a nearby window, landing in the lap of a nursing mother.

In Hyde Park, racing skiffs cavort on the Serpentine, only to lift off and fly into the embrace of waiting trees.

On Epsom high street, the ladies section of Mansfield's shoe shop has tripped out of the door and dozens of pairs of heels foxtrot across the paving stones.

Even as the stage lights gutter, the dance goes on.

*

After the streetlamps go out, there is nothing for Sol to watch. The orange London glow is no longer reflected in any clouds that scud overhead. Now, sound is amplified, and it is the sound of the wood destructing, trees giving in and throwing themselves down to die. It is not a healthy thing to listen to, alone in the night. He retreats deeper into his hollow, and sticks a leftover wine gum in each ear. He has never been plunged into dark this thick before. It is alarming not to be able to see the difference between eyes open, eyes shut, so he keeps them shut. Nothing to do but wait it out, wait for the light.

Something scurries over his feet and up his shin. Sol bats about and feels a soft body, the fluff of a whisking tail.

'Come in!' he laughs. 'One night only, mind.'

Squirrels have chewed through his precious Tupperware before, devouring whole packets of chocolate digestives before he found them. But the frantic creature has gone, off into the pitch-black. Sol lies back and tries to let the muffled roar lull him. In the dreams that follow, he will fly a plane through a jungle, be pursued by invisible sirens, and watch as cliffs crack and judder down into the sea.

*

Rachel is sleeping too, nestled in beside her snoring housemate, Darren. If Pete were here, he would not be huddled under a duvet. He'd be out there, whooping with delight, shouting, 'You beaut!', not at her, but at the crazy wind. He wouldn't be worrying about lost telephones. She pictures him waving his surfboard in the air, leaping into his rusty van to head for the coast, trees falling like spillikins across the empty road behind him.

When she falls asleep, her dreams are not unlike reality. Tattered butterflies litter the undergrowth of Syon Park, their iridescence smudged away, their bodies damp and cold. The next day, children tugged along by their forlorn parents will pick the butterflies up and ask how to make them work, how to throw them just right so they fly.

What she does not dream is the two that have escaped the park and are sheltering in a back garden on Epworth Road – a zebra longwing, and a blue moon. They have dodged the crab apples hurtling from the tree that has held its ground there, and, in the refuge of a brick-built barbecue stand, are feasting on fallen fruit. The yellowed apples are partly rotten, and the butterflies are getting drunk.

*

Herne is power-crazed. From the wood to the sea, energy crackles and fights.

The storm itself has no desire, no dominion. It is only the henchman in this affray.

At Capel-le-Ferne, live electric cables snake across the main road, sparking and snapping at car tyres as they pass.

In Orpington, the electricity substation puts on a firework display as it blows, sending flashes of red, green and blue into the sky.

Near Southfleet, staff at Castlebar Care Home finally coax the generator into life, then sprint from room to room as televisions explode, fish cook in their tanks, and electric blankets in beds begin to smoke.

On a hill above Clayton, a lovingly restored windmill turns its blades in the gale despite a chocked brakewheel. The mill fills with smoke and sparks fly up like comets against the dark.

In a Portakabin by Dover harbour, the fluorescent light flickers with distress. Beneath it, either side of a grey desk, sit Deep's brother, Roshan, and Carl, immigration officer. They are both weary, though Roshan more so. As Carl asks Roshan again where he plans to be staying, for an actual address, please, the door is flicked open by an immense wave of seawater. It fills the Portakabin and sucks both men back out with it. Carl manages to stand and flee from the next wave. He turns once, to look for Roshan, but there is only swarming, spitting water.

*

When Deep wakes, he is covered in detritus: bits of broken things he cannot identify, scraps of clothing, an acrylic cushion. He pats himself all over, tests his painful limbs, then begins to shout for Sara. He does not stop calling her name as he crawls around the dark space, feeling for a window, a door, something to tell him which way up they are. She doesn't answer. The apple she gave him is gone from his coat pocket.

He remembers the keyring torch he had attached to his belt loop, and tests the button. It works. It works! He dreads what he might see now, by its measly light, but though he shines it in every direction, opening cupboards and lifting cushions, there is no sign of his wife.

The caravan is upside down. The door has broken from its hinges. How he has survived this, Deep cannot begin to wonder. Still shouting for Sara, he climbs out and begins to stumble over the lumpy ground. The torch only shows him a few feet ahead. He works his way round the caravan, then begins to walk wider circles.

The wind is still roaring. Deep cannot see, with his keyring torch, that nearly two hundred caravans have broken their chains and rolled across the Peacehaven park, jumbling together like beer cans tossed down an embankment.

An hour later, Deep finally hears his own name, howled as if in mourning. He turns his torch upon Sara, crouched beside a flattened caravan, beating the ground with her bloodied fist.

*

Someone is shouting. Sol opens his eyes to see the trees flashing blue, on and off, taking up a new pose with each flare. It's like the strobe lights at Cosy's Cellar, the trees writhing to a silent beat. Sol pulls the wine gums from his ears and the shouting resolves itself.

'Mr Payne! Mr Payne.'

Well, that's his name. He's an institution round here, but everyone calls him Sol. As he struggles out of his sleeping bag he sees, in the sweep of blue light, that a trunk lies lengthways either side of him. They make it tricky to clamber from the hollow, so he stands and turns, waving his arms. Torchlights shine through the railings. Two policemen are on the pavement beyond.

'Hey, man,' Sol calls. 'I was sleeping.'

They stop waving their torches. One of them laughs. The other one swears. 'You want some help to get out of there, Mr Payne?'

'No, sir. I'll be just about fine.'

Their heads bend towards one another. Sol can't hear what they're saying. Then one yells, 'Sure we can't take you somewhere safe, out the way of them trees?'

Sol remembers the cells at the station, hard and grey and bleach-stinking. One night in there was more than enough. He turns back to look at the blue-lit wood. True, it doesn't look quite like it did yesterday, the trees are still dancing in frantic jumps, and he's got two hornbeams out cold in his camp. But it is home. He shakes his head. 'It's not raining,' he says, 'I'll be just about fine.'

A police radio crackles from a belt, and a siren sounds somewhere to the east. Car doors slam. It's a relief when all the lights retreat. Sol can see the beginnings of dawn now, creeping up the sky. 'Lord,' he says, as he settles back into his sleeping bag, 'thank you for this day.'

*

Herne is many things: bale-worker, frenzy-maker, trickster, trembler.

He is hunter, and lord of the hanged.

The storm itself has no calling. Life and death, freedom and captivity are all the same in its roving eye.

On the North Downs, between Bishopsbourne and Lower Hardres, a snow leopard drops its head against the gale. The air is full of new and disturbing scents: salt, seaweed, birds and insects, bitter smoke and freshly turned earth. It sniffs, awaiting the draw of something warm, something flesh. At Howletts Zoo, a few miles away, the fence of its enclosure lies crushed by a fallen beech.

On the coast at Shoreham, a seagull hangs, impaled on railings that stand guard on the seafront.

In a garden near Dartford, an Alsatian has managed to keep only two of her puppies inside their ragged kennel. Two are wedged between a struggling tree and the garden wall, mewling. Three more lie in the flower bed, cold. Their owner weeps under her kitchen table, too afraid to go out and help, or even look.

At Morghew Park near Tenterden, five wild boars have plunged out through torn fencing and are snuffling into the woods. They squeal and scramble when an ash tree crashes down behind them. They are twelve miles from the prowling snow leopard; far enough for now. Hundreds of thousands of acorns have skittered to the ground in the storm, and they gorge themselves, in readiness for freedom.

*

Rachel will have to walk. Her Ford Escort is imprisoned in the line of parked cars that have somehow jammed together during the night. One of them is trapped under a lime tree that leans at a 45-degree angle. The dawn streets feel unbearably mournful without their warm yellow lights. Traumatised, is how they look. Wrecked. She tries not to stop and gawp at every bent traffic light, every broken fence. Roof tiles and bikes and a thousand shredded rubbish bags litter the tarmac, their contents decorating front gardens and bushes. The wind is still whipping the smaller bits about. A baked-bean can scuttles down the street ahead of her, never quite making it to the gutter. The sound irritates her until she runs and kicks it under a hedge. After a while, exhausted by bearing witness to this wasteland, she pulls up her hood and walks with her eyes fixed on the pavement.

From the staff gate at Syon Park, she can already see the fallen oak, its branches akimbo where the curve of the butterfly house roof should be. She hurries towards the office, hoping someone else got there first.

She can hear the phone ringing as she struggles with the stiff lock, and when the door finally gives she hurls herself towards it.

'Pete?' she says.

'Am I through to Syon Park, London?' asks an imperious voice.

Rachel's heart sinks.

The man clears his throat. 'I think I may have something that belongs to you.' He sounds infuriatingly pleased with himself.

She presses the bell at number 42, Epworth Road, and is greeted by a smiling pensioner in gardening overalls. He leads her down a flowery hallway that smells of too many magnolia air fresheners, and out into the welcome cool of the garden.

'Yours, I believe?' He points, still smiling, to a brick-built barbecue. It has a piece of netting thrown over it, the kind people use to keep pesky birds off their raspberry canes.

Rachel glances back at him before crouching to look. The blue moon and the zebra longwing are wobbling across a heap of what looks like rotten crab apples, soft and yellow.

'You beaut,' she says.

'I beg your pardon?' The old man frowns.

Rachel stands. 'Can I use your telephone? It's a work call,' she adds, but he is already nodding, grinning, delighted to be of help.

*

Only one caravan at Peacehaven has remained steadfast on its hardstanding. Deep glares at it as they hobble past, he and his wife held tightly together, their arms around each other's waists. Sara is limping. When she was flung out of the door as their caravan began to tumble, she sprained her left ankle. Deep has fared worse, cuts and bruises beginning to ache all over, and in tender places. But he will not let go of her.

They approach the locked-up shop by the park entrance. Its mean windows are intact, though coated in salt and streaks of seaweed. Its felt roof has stayed on. He looks around for a suitable tool and can find only a fire extinguisher, which has rolled out from the storage area behind the shop.

'I don't care,' he says, when Sara gives him a look. 'It's not a day for rules.'

It takes both of them swinging the extinguisher at the lock before the door cracks open.

'Welcome home,' Deep says, as they fall inside.

The shop smells musty and damp. The bars of chocolate, the buckets and spades and firelighters and toilet rolls are all coated in a layer of sticky dust. The fridges are switched off, but Deep picks out two cans of Coca-Cola. He flicks the ring pulls on to the counter and hands one to Sara.

'What do we drink to?' she asks.

'Luck.'

'Bad luck?'

'Good luck.'

They sit on the gritty floor, holding hands, and swallow the sugary fizz in gulps.

'This won't do,' Sara says after a while.

'What?'

'For when your brother comes. He might arrive any minute. I can't clean up this mess, all this muck.' She runs a finger down the side of the counter, making a clear line through the dirt. 'And those windows.'

'Salt,' Deep nods, with mock-wisdom.

His wife smiles, and Deep's heart hurts, more than any other part of him.

*

Seventy-two oaks have fallen in Sydenham Wood. Sol has counted them. It is 11 a.m., by his reckoning. His stomach usually rumbles at 11 a.m.; he saves his biscuits for this time. But today he is not hungry.

He's not seen a soul. Even the squirrels are hiding out. He sits on the bench in the clearing and listens to the wood creaking, moaning, its open wounds still prodded by the wind.

He can't tell himself they're only trees. It's painful to look. It would be better to have that deep dark of the night. Everything is scarred, nothing is right. Under the bench, his foot nudges against something. A yellow apple is rolling in the dirt. There are no apple trees in this wood.

Sol picks it up, and stares at the sullen sky. 'Pleased with yourself?' he asks, and he hurls the apple as far as he can.

BUSHES AND BRIARS

Through bushes and through briars
I've lately made my way,
All for to hear the small birds sing
And the lambs to skip and play.
All for to hear the small birds sing
And the lambs to skip and play.

I overhead a female,
Her voice it rang so clear,
Long time have I been waiting for
The coming of my dear.
Long time have I been waiting for
The coming of my dear.

Sometimes I am uneasy
And troubled in my mind.
Sometimes I think I'll go to my love
And tell to him my mind.

But if I should go to my love,
My love he would say 'nay'.
If I show to him my boldness
He'd ne'er love me again.
If I show to him my boldness
He'd ne'er love me again.

Through bushes and through briars
I've lately made my way,
All for to hear the small birds sing
And the lambs to skip and play.
All for to hear the small birds sing
And the lambs to skip and to play.
Collected by Ralph Vaughan Williams

13

'ONE MORN I MISS'D HIM ON THE CUSTOM'D HILL'

2011

Charm: There is one song I will tell to no man, but only to her in whose arms I lie and who clasps me close.

'That's as good as saying you want to do it yourself,' says Richard. He is frowning at their fishbowl wine glasses as she sloshes in more Shiraz.

'Completely different! Saying you understand why people would want to, say, skydive, isn't the same as wanting to do it yourself. Is it?' Kate wanders down the kitchen, towards the oak table in front of the wide-open patio doors. He'll follow her. He loves a good debate, over the wine.

'This is hardly the same as jumping out of a plane,' he says, from his position by the sink. 'Sleeping with someone else doesn't come with a risk of death. You are death-averse, but not sex-averse.'

'It's upsides, downsides,' Kate says. 'Sleeping with someone else wouldn't mean risking death. But it would require risk-taking, and time. Organisation, deception, seduction. You imagine: first you figure out that 4 till 5 p.m. on a Thursday is the only option, because that way you still have time to wash and dry the sheets before your partner gets back from bridge class. But bridge is only once a month. So, you work back from there. You better start the flirtation at least a fortnight before, say.' She pauses to sip. 'Make sure you smell good that day, have a decent dress on, and so on.'

'Wow.'

'What?'

'Well I don't have to *imagine*, do I? You've done it for me. Thought it all through.'

'I'm making a joke, Richard.' She tries raising her eyebrows, Charlie Chaplin-style.

'Practicalities aren't funny. Practicalities are the part you deal with when you've already made up your mind to do something.'

'They're part of the process of deciding whether to do something. Upsides, downsides. Like skydiving.' She smirks, but Richard is just staring at her.

'So you've been weighing it up.' He doesn't even sound pleased with this gambit.

'It's a joke, for Christ's sake. What's got your goat?'

'A pre-prepared joke? You've thought it all through. Even the bridge class.'

'You don't play bridge.'

'No, I design bridges. It's your subconscious at work. And what is it you always say? Many a true word ...'

'I say that about other people, Richard, not myself.'

'And you're different from other people, are you? Above all that.' He has stopped drinking his wine, she notes.

'I guess my joke was just a shit one. Does that make you feel better?'

'It might have been funnier if you hadn't so clearly been imagining the practicalities of doing it with Tom.'

'Tom?' Kate laughs, loudly. 'Your mind. Not mine.'

'Who else would it be? Who else would be available to drag into your bed – our bed – between four and five on a Thursday, other than our own gardener?'

'Oh my God! I never even thought of that!' she says. This isn't true. She has thought of that. Several times. She's never entirely ruled it out, despite marriage, despite Richard's evident love. Previously evident love.

But Richard is looking horrified. She changes tack. 'It's you seeing him as a threat, now he's single. Not me.'

'Why do you think that is? He's hardly Quasimodo, is he?'

He's actually sneering. She can't resist. 'Do you find him attractive too? He might be open-minded.'

'Don't be disgusting. He's just an exhibitionist, flashing all that tanned flesh right where everyone can see him, coming into the house all sweaty.'

'Same-sex attraction isn't disgusting. And so what, if we can see him in our garden? You avert your eyes, do you, every time those Fitzgerald girls next door are sunning their pink parts out on the lawn? You draw the blind in your study and think harder about girder torques?' She snorts. An engineering joke. She does have a sense of humour. Where Richard's has gone is anyone's guess.

'You're pathetic,' he spits.

'I know I take a good look at them. I bet Tom does. Why wouldn't you?'

'We're not talking about the Fitzgeralds, or which one of them Tom might take a fancy to. We're talking about your adulterous leanings, and what you're actually saying, about this marriage. About me.' Really, he is beyond melodramatic.

'You would, though, wouldn't you? If one of them came round and wiggled her neat little bum at you and asked for it. Would you really say no?'

'I don't have to listen to this. I'm not going to listen to this.' Richard drains his wine glass, swipes his wallet off the counter and, sure enough, out he goes, through the patio doors, heading for the gate in the back fence.

'Say hi to Nik for me,' she calls merrily.

'Fuck off.'

She doesn't mind. She honestly doesn't. She's quite glad, when this happens, to have driven him from the house for a while. The relief of solitude. A relief she lets herself enjoy, these days. Because he always comes back. After a night on the lager with Nikesh. Or a boys' outing to the Green Man. Then a night on Nik's couch, to make his point. And when she comes in from teaching, or yoga, she'll be able to tell that he's back in the house, behind his closed study door. This being the final stage of the ritual. Before they reconvene in the kitchen, by the cupboard where they keep the wine, and begin again with a silent toast.

*

Richard closes the gate. Breathe in all the green oxygen, feel it wafting down from the trees, pooling in great glades of free goodness. Lung food, that's what oxygen is. Blood nourishment, pure and delicious. And an evening off without even having to tell Kate what he's doing, see that look of derision, as if his friends aren't worth as much as hers. Nik'll be about, he doesn't even need to check before he calls on him, that's true friendship. If they weren't such good friends, things might have been awkward after Nik's big announcement last week, but nothing's changed. They'll be propping up the bar at the Green Man in no time.

If something's up with Kate, better to figure it out over a beer and go back tomorrow. All that goading about the Fitzgerald girls, right when they were arguing about Tom. He'd thought for a moment that she must know, too. But it must simply have been a coincidence, because he's been sworn to secrecy, and he's not even hinted. There you go, true friendship in action right there.

But Kate will be pleased to see him, tomorrow, when he gets back. She always is. And then Laura, home from university on Saturday. A whole weekend of knowing exactly where their daughter is and what she's doing. He'll actually relax, in fact he's relaxing right now, just thinking about it. Ah, breathe in the beautiful green, tree breath and soil smell. The wind's so strong it's practically blowing the oxygen into his lungs. It's the kiss of life from Mother Nature herself. He'll go the long way round to Nik's, and make the most of this, being out in the wood. That way he won't pass the back of number 12, and Tom's caravan. He's not sure he can face Tom right now, and he might be out here too, taking the rich evening air.

Tom is a woods man, like him – well more than him really, almost a *woodsman*, if that's different. Kate's never appreciated the wood like them; instead she complains about the mud and the little heaps of tissues that accumulate at night under the rhododendron bushes. *Trust men*, she'd said, when he'd had to explain to her what they were. *Not bothering to clean up after themselves. And it's not very romantic, is it? Hardly lovers rolling together on a bank of moss. Ecstasy amid the birdsong.*

It wasn't like that when he and Kate did it outside that one time, either, but it was pretty hot all the same. Fresh air, it's the oxygen pepping up the blood. They were in a field, long grass that sloped down from an edge of woodland, and it was wet underfoot, even in the morning sun. Kate tripped, she was laughing as she rolled over and over, soaking her shorts and her T-shirt. 'Look at me!' she yelled at the bottom of the slope. And he did, and there was nothing more beautiful, then, than grass-stained, sodden, grinning Kate. He ran down to her – slid, practically. They didn't say a word. They didn't need to. Wet grass on his bare arse, wet Kate on top of him, lush, beautiful—

Something whacks the crown of his head and sends him hard to the ground. The branch lands on his back. Pinned, winded, out cold. Blood trickles from the gash, and from his nose, and pools in the shallow boats of dead beech leaves.

*

She'll enjoy the evening. She might even get a whole night. Glorious. A throne of pillows, a cool bed. No snoring. Best to make the most of it, while it lasts. Take the bottle of Shiraz into the bathroom. Right into the bath, in fact. Neroli oil. The radio, why not? Some soothing classical, perhaps, but she likes the attitude in this old kind of punk that's come on. It'll do.

Under the suds she pictures Richard and Nikesh, buying lager at the corner shop. Like a pair of teenagers. They probably don't even talk. Just grunt at each other, or the television. Or they might go to the Green Man. She sips at the warming wine. Grotesque place, now it's been done up. Does Tom ever go there? Would Richard actually repeat any of this to him? *You'll never guess what Kate said tonight!* Both laughing at the very idea he'd even consider sleeping with her.

No. Richard couldn't take the hit, admitting that. Male egos. Tricky business. So easy to pop them by accident, like overblown balloons. And therefore so tempting to pop them on purpose. For the bang. Though there's little more disheartening than a shred of coloured rubber where a balloon used to be. She smirks. There's an aphorism in there somewhere.

Sip of Shiraz. Her forehead is sweating. It's pleasant, the leaking out of toxins, to be directly replaced with red wine. Anyway, Richard will decide that even if it was a shit joke, that's all it was. He'll have to, in order to reinflate his little balloon.

What is Tom's ego like? There's not much sign of it. Though Richard did have a point about all that topless wheelbarrowing down to the bonfire heap. It does show the back muscles, the shoulder muscles, to great advantage. Especially when glistening with sweat. Glistening. She sounds like a Mills & Boon. But it is a hot June. And what harm in looking? Not much else you can do with Tom. Apart from what she has, obviously, imagined. But she's no idea where she'd start with that. He is taciturn: probably another high-frequency word in romance novels. He is with her, anyway. But Richard goes round to see him, in his saggy caravan in the garden at number 12. No doubt they sit there like two old men on a stoop, but without the bourbon and cigars. Without the good bits.

Tom talks to himself, she's noticed. Mumbling as he wires the clematis higher up their garden fence. Perhaps he's like that philosophical bin man of lore, quoting Kant as he sweeps the gutters. And she's seen him slip out through the back gate sometimes. Vanishing into the wood behind. What does he do in there? Take a piss, most likely. Avoid coming into the house. Even though they're all friends. They were all friends years ago when he and Lotte lived at number 4. Didn't turn their backs after he sold up and moved into the caravan. Took up gardening for a living. True, she and Richard have only done better since then. Revamped the conservatory. Extended the kitchen. But what difference should that make? He made a choice, became free.

Richard went out through that gate tonight. Through the wood to Nik's house, like an outlaw. Like Just William. Boys playing truant from real life. Still, it makes for this peaceful evening. And he'll be back. Like always. He'll have to come back, because Laura's coming on Saturday. Gorgeous, itinerant daughter, who dotes on her father. She can, because she doesn't see all the petty, furtive battles he directs. At least one of the women in his family adores him.

Will she apologise? She doesn't see what for. She just made a joke. She'll see.

*

Richard turns pale, at first, as one does after such a shock. He lies on his front, one cheek pressed against a tree root, the other showing its pallor in the sinking dusk. He does not look quite himself. The squirrel that comes creeping, sniffing along his thigh, does not recognise him, and turns to take a more welcoming path through the wood.

The ground is cool against his chest, but in the balmy June evening, now the wind has dropped, he is warm in his shirt. A purple hairstreak butterfly alights on his shoulder, flexing its indigo wings as it contemplates the carpet of pale green fabric. But it has no weight at all and of course he does not even twitch.

The blood from the back of his head no longer drips. The dark jam of it is picked at now and again by assiduous black flies, but Richard has never been ticklish. There he lies, still under his broken branch, the trees leaking oxygen from their blithe leaves above him. He is at one with nature, at home in her irresistible embrace.

*

Lie on the bed to cool off. Lovely fresh sheets. Changed them just in time to enjoy this whole bed to herself. Can't even touch the edges, if she lies in the middle. Good investment, Richard said. He was right. More space, even with two in it. That first few months they spent crammed into a single whenever they spent the night. Which was most nights. It required full entanglement. Being entwined. It didn't seem to matter, then. Would drive them both mad now. But they never have to do it. Never again.

Pub closing time about now. They'll be whingeing as usual about the lack of a kebab shop around here. Ha! A small triumph for health. Though what food Nikesh has mouldering at his place she dreads to think. They'll eat crap, pass out. Wake up with hangovers. Beer does that to you. Not Shiraz. She's immune, now. The bonus of getting older. An upside that compensates for about one per cent of the downsides.

Perhaps she'll make something delicious, for tomorrow, when he comes back. He'll be extra grateful with a hangover. She'll make aubergine parmigiana. *Deli-cho-so*, he always says. God, he must have said it hundreds of time, by now. Thousands? And it always makes her wince. But she knows he means it.

*

Richard has cooled down considerably with the fall of night. Shirtsleeves in June are one thing when you've got a few beers in you, but he didn't make it to the pub, and those two glasses of wine wore off hours ago. His jaw, against the tree root, has grown quite stiff. He'd struggle to get his teeth around a crisp, let alone one of the Scotch eggs in Nik's fridge. He keeps them lined up in the egg compartment, a joke Richard always enjoys.

But he is not thinking of Nik, or his fridge, now. He hasn't noticed the purplish colour that has risen to his upturned cheek, crept along the back of his neck. But why would he? Lying here, in nature, his mind is quite blank. He need not think of anything at all, nor even keep all those subconscious, automatic processes going, the background hum of life, so familiar we do not hear it. He doesn't hear the owl that hoots, further along the wooded slope, nor the mouse that scurries right over his calves in its hurry to be home. Neither does he hear the gate squeak at number 12, and Tom's footsteps as he lopes through the blackness of the night wood, along the path, heading for the Fitzgeralds' gate, the cellophane of a single red rose rustling in his hand.

*

'Tom!' she beams. 'There's coffee literally squirting out of its little thingy right this moment, let me get you some.'

As she thunders back down the hall to the kitchen, Tom's feet seeming to make no sound at all behind her, she calls, 'You were in my dream last night, you know.' Even as she says it, she realises he was not in her dream. He was in her argument with Richard. Who is not here.

Her cheeks are burning. She prods at the coffee machine with one hand and fans her face with the other. 'Perils of midlife. Crazy dreams and, well …' She fans harder. Tom is looking past her, through the patio doors. 'How do you do it?' she asks. 'You always seem so relaxed.'

'Flow,' he says.

'Oh?' God. Those brown eyes.

'Activities that create flow. You know, when you stop thinking about the rest of your life, the rest of the world, even time.'

There's only one activity she can think of that does that. Sex. And childbirth. Though that doesn't work for the time part. 'Well, perhaps you could tell me more about that, later.' She tries to keep her voice deep but it comes out like an attempt at an impression. Of whom? 'I'd love to hear.' Take another dip in those eyes.

'I'll be lining the pond today. Fitting the pump.'

The blush is getting worse. 'You're an angel. I'll be here. Grinding my way through that lot.' She points to the stack of exam papers on the kitchen table. *Grinding*. God. But he's already walking away, hitching his tool bag higher on his big, square shoulder.

Eight hours of marking, she estimates. Though a batch that size should take twelve. Criminal what they pay her, for a private boys' school. Criminal to be doing it on a beautiful day like this, with the place to herself. But she can sit here, with the view of the garden. She can take glimpses of Tom as little rewards, between essays on *Lord of the Flies*, and *Of Mice and Men*, the usual predictable male suspects. Why don't they ever change the syllabus? She will be a picture of sunlit virtue, when Richard opens the front door.

She peers down the garden over her reading glasses. The gate in the back fence is shut, like a secret. When Richard's spent the night chez Nikesh, he always uses the front door on his return. Feels more dignified, she suspects. Better than stealing back in the way he stormed out. Sets them back on the right track. Beginning again as calm grown-ups. And they do, however many times it happens. More often, recently. She's had time for more long baths.

Four minutes per manuscript. Get through fifty by lunch. See what number she's at when she hears the door. Then she'll make rolls for all three of them. Perhaps offer them both a beer. They'll both turn it down, for different reasons. But it means she can have one. A reward. For marking. For the cheer she will exude, despite the stupid overreaction to her joke last night.

She'll be doing it for Laura's sake, really. Clear the air so thoroughly before her daughter arrives tomorrow, that everything will appear perfect. Even Richard.

Sixty-five manglings of Golding and Steinbeck later, she slams down her pen. She's starving. Can't wait any longer for that stop-out. Get this show on the road, shove some ham into rolls, slap in some mustard. She leans at the patio doors for a moment, watching Tom, bare-backed, bending to roll up an offcut of pond-liner. It reminds her of one of her favourite paintings. Three men stripped to the waist, bending to varnish a floor or something. *Les raboteurs de parquet*, it's called. Just saying it in French sounds raunchy. But she finds she can't even enjoy this sight. Bloody Richard. And he's practically given her permission to enjoy it, by not coming home. Not that she needs permission.

'I've made sandwiches,' she calls. 'Come in whenever you're ready.'

Tom looks up and gives her a nod.

Plate of rolls, beer, bottle opener. She arranges them at the end of the counter and waits. Ten minutes later he's still working, moving rocks about by the dent that will eventually be a pond. She can't exactly summon him in like a forgetful kid. The beer bottle is sweating. It'll be warm. She swaps it for one from the fridge, then opens it and slugs, turning away from the garden so he won't see her. Why? Her house, her beer. Her brain, addled by sixty-five variations on boys getting things wrong, all in hideous handwriting.

Still, she takes the beer upstairs. Richard's study. Peek through the blind slats. Tom's still there, rearranging stones. She can see his lips moving. Concentration, is that what it is? This 'flow' thing? That or he's just a bit odd. He got looks. You can't have everything.

But it's not true. She knew him before the caravan, the gardening, and he was different. Less distant, if not exactly flirtatious, though there was the wife, Lotte, then. It comes of living alone now, perhaps, the habit of talking to himself. Forgets, in public. It's sweet. In a handsome man, anyway.

She plumps down into Richard's chair and spins around once, twice. Thousands of times, over the years, she must have had the fantasy. Living alone. In a space full of beautiful junk. Walls painted colours from Liberty patterns: peacock and peony and mustard – French, not English. One massive comfy chair, her legs flipped over the velvet arm. An elegant silver cat, nibbling daintily on a sugar mouse beside her … no, no, no. But it comes with the territory. She can't be the only one who does it, furnishes her fantasy nest every time she's ticked off with the full laundry basket, the sopping bathroom floor.

But she's ticked off now, and precisely because Richard *isn't* here. Contrary crosspatch. She should be enjoying this time. She thought she would, last night. But Richard is not sticking to the plan. In fact, she's cross because it's her best, wife-and-mother self that's in charge, right now. Her rising-above-it, bridge-building, family-glueing self, who made him ham rolls and planned aubergine parmigiana. Who will unite them before Laura gets home. Who has realised, now she's looking at Richard's diary, that it is Friday. Fish day. So, she can't do aubergine.

She can do better. She will go to the supermarket and buy a beautiful trout. Or squid. Richard loves squid, stewed with chorizo. *Erotic little tentacles*, he always says. She takes a long drink from the beer bottle. Nothing in his diary for today. A big 'L' taking up all of Saturday.

She'll go when she's finished the beer. Break from the godawful marking, all those boys making a mess of it, on their doomed island and on their doomed exam papers. Almost a guarantee that he'll be here, sitting right in this chair, when she gets back. Chastened. Grateful. He bloody better be.

She flips forward in his diary. 'Presents – start NOW' is written on 1st July. Then on the 15th, 'Presents – check??' Then on the 23rd, 'Paper. Card. Bottle.' July 25th is her birthday. Twenty-three years, and he still has to write it down. Probably transfers these instructions directly from one year's diary to the next.

Rise above it. Richard may build actual bridges, out in the world. But she builds the ones at home. By cooking squid.

She gets up and peers out through the blind. Tom is standing by the holly bush, chewing on a ham roll. He is glistening again.

*

Downhill from Richard, on the lower path, a group of volunteers in hi-vis vests are sawing at a dead hornbeam. 'A managed wood thrives, better than one left to its own devices,' their leader is explaining, screwing up his eyes against the sun that stabs down through the canopy. Richard's back, as purple as his neck now, is warmed in dapples by this sun. The blood on the back of his head has crusted over in the night, and stuck his thin hair to his scalp.

His hair was still long when he met Kate, and still mostly brown. The loss of it, baldness creeping across his pate, was an insult and a worry. Tom's hair, he had noticed more and more, stayed thick as a brush. He was sure Kate noticed too, and admired it, preferred it. But this no longer bothers him. He is immune to such insecurities, here in the wood. Nobody is looking at his head; not the volunteers fussing down on the main path, not the flies, which are concentrating on the congealed blood near the wound, circling, whirring, taking turns to feast. Richard is so stiff all over now, he wouldn't be able to bat them away if he wanted to.

He lets them go on, all through the afternoon, and why not? It's a beautiful day, to be lying amidst the trees, more carefree than he has ever been. He should have done this more often, before. He'd had time, especially once Laura was grown and had sprinted off into the world, not looking back, hardly ever coming back. The number of times he'd walked her through this little tangled strip of forest as a child, trying to instil the love of nature he thought essential, showing her the wood could be a haven – as long as she was only ever in it in daylight, and having told someone where she was going. He was so anxious that she should feel this, he hardly stopped to feel it himself. Always here, beyond the fence. He could see the waving treetops from his study. But he let himself be distracted, by work, by Kate, by Tom swaggering up and down the lawn on Kate's endless garden updates, by those Fitzgerald girls next door. He loved the wood, and he neglected it.

Well, not now. It is embracing him, forgiving him. It has one wooden arm slung across his back, companionable. He has not even brushed away the leaves that are scattered across his jeans now, green and yellow, bright in the sunlit air.

*

When she's parked back in the drive, with a boot full of marine delicacies and wines to match, she checks her eyes in the vanity mirror. Do with a tidy-up. She rummages for a cotton bud and dabs about. Wipes some fluff off a lipstick and smears it on with a finger. Who for? Richard. Of course, Richard. On the condition that he's in.

It's almost four. She didn't dawdle on purpose at the supermarket. But she can't walk past a tasting table. Or wine samples. She drove carefully. As she struggles into the kitchen with four bags in each hand, she sees that the counter, and the island, and quite a bit of the floor, are covered with more shopping bags. She smiles. Ah, Richard. That's where he's been. And without the car, too. Meant to surprise her. Make amends. And he has.

'Tom! You made me jump.'

He is lurking just inside the patio doors. 'It only came half an hour ago.' He nods at the bags. 'I just put the frozen stuff in your freezer. Wasn't sure about the rest.' He gestures at the rows of kitchen cupboards, sheepish.

'Isn't Richard …?' She turns to look back down the hall, and sees the order receipt by the microwave. Home delivery. Her cheeks are burning again.

'Sorry,' Tom says. 'I can give you a hand, now?'

'No, no. You get on. Or actually,' she bends to look at her watch, still holding her plastic bags. Hopefully her hair will fall over her cheeks. 'Beer o'clock? Or wine, maybe? You must be parched. I am.' He actually looks sorry for her. Unbearable. 'Come on. It'll keep.' Smile. Put bags down, gently. 'And I want to hear about this "flow" business.' Her laugh comes out wrong but she strides with purpose to the fridge. Cool, on her face. Blink a bit, while she's got the door open.

'Sorry, Kate. Got to get going.'

She could just climb into the fridge, close the door behind her. Eat all the cheese, doze off and freeze to death in her sleep.

*

The part of the wood where Richard lies is in shadow now. Tom has just cut down the slope instead, to catch the last bit of afternoon sunshine at the wood's edge before looping back up to number 12. The caravan is always shady in the evening. It's a shame, really, but on a warm day it's still pleasant to bring out two folding chairs and sit either side of the narrow door. Richard and Tom, shooting the breeze for an hour after work. They did it only a few days ago, when Tom had finished digging the hole for the pond. Richard took two bottles of beer from the kitchen and they smuggled them out through the back gate, then walked in silence through the wood to number 12. Richard has a kind of anxious respect, or is it envy, for Tom's ability to be silent when they are in the wood together. He doesn't feel the need to prattle, like Kate does, and Kate has passed him the habit, like some kind of noise virus.

That afternoon they sat in the folding chairs, and stared at the back of the house. The owner of number 12, Charles Dent, never returned from his city job before nine at night. They had the place to themselves. Halfway through the beers, Richard couldn't keep quiet any longer.

'So, it stayed a one-off?' he asked.

'Not exactly.'

Tom had told him the week before about sleeping with Megan Fitzgerald. Richard had made him swear he wouldn't do it again. When the parents found out, he'd warned, they wouldn't be inviting him round for a sherry. They'd tell Charles Dent some story, and Tom would be kicked out of the caravan. Most likely they'd do the same with the neighbours. He'd lose clients, his living.

'It was only sex,' Tom said.

'She's eighteen,' Richard had replied, as if that was all that needed to be said. He hadn't been a hundred per cent sure he wasn't jealous. He'd tried not to think about Megan Fitzgerald naked, aroused, manipulated into various sexual positions by Tom's strong hands. She hadn't made it easy for him either, sunbathing on the lawn with her sister next door, in bikinis so small they required binoculars to see them. Not that he'd actually done that.

When they took up their conversation again, back outside the caravan, he tried to push away those images, and be the sensible friend. 'You can't have a real relationship with an eighteen-year-old,' he said.

'I didn't have a real one with my wife. At least now there's sex.'

It sounded so brash, coming from Tom. His reserve had been broken, perhaps by a giggling, wriggling naked girl.

'It's not everything,' Richard said. But Tom was quiet again. Richard imagined he was thinking about it, the sex, not the lack of it with his ex-wife. Kate might not be a nymphomaniac, exactly, but she had this energy that still thrilled him, even after twenty-three years. It was too much, sometimes, but it was the one thing about her that stayed constant, glorious. Laura had it too, he could see that, even as he found it uncomfortable, the recognition of an attractive woman in his own daughter.

'Better get back,' he said, when his beer bottle was empty. 'Good luck.'

Tom nodded.

Lying in the wood alone now, Richard has found a way to be silent. He has no urge to prattle, and makes no comment as Tom passes on the lower path and then turns back, towards the Fitzgeralds' gate.

*

If you don't know where he is, why don't you just call him? her mother's voice snaps in her head. Because it's conceding. It weakens her position, shows she's worried. Still, she taps out a text. Terse. Informative. Got squid for supper. Deletes the 'got'. Adds kisses. Send. Richard's phone beeps, somewhere under the shopping bags. Typical.

She pokes about amongst the deliveries. All the stuff she asked him to order, for the weekend. Laura's favourite things, celebratory fizz. Why didn't he even get back in time for this? Let her do the unpacking, is that it? Indirect punishment. She pours out some of the white wine, Picpoul, which has warmed up but to hell with it. The last time he stayed away this long was, when? Not sure. He has done it, though. And what did they argue about that time? God knows. Chores, probably. Or money. Or whether to put in a sodding garden pond. Not that those things are ever what it's really about.

Out in the garden. Fresh air. Clear head. Fine, if he wants to take time out. Play the hermit. If that's what it takes to sort out his sorry male brain, refill the ego balloon. Whatever. But he shouldn't make her suffer with him. She's not the one who was offended, who can't take a joke. Her equilibrium wasn't even disturbed. That's what pissed him off most. That's why he's doing this. He takes everything way too seriously. It should be him talking to Tom about 'flow'. Whatever the hell it is.

She inspects the dent, the future pond. It looks too small, too shallow. Tom. God, he couldn't get out fast enough. Maybe it was the lipstick that did it. That and the flushing. What did she say? *Beer o'clock.* Sounds desperate, even to her. He's an enigma, that Tom. Mysterious. Perhaps that's what makes him attractive. But mystery is just pseudo-charisma. A trick by boring people to make themselves alluring. Was Tom boring, before? He's vague, in her memories. Hovering at the edge of parties. Nodding over dinner. What did he ever have to say for himself? Richard never shuts up. Probably Tom could never get a word in edgeways. What kind of friendship is that?

She listens. To her friends, to Richard. To her daughter. She's good at it. Because she's a woman? Or because she's her. But she hasn't heard something. She's missed something. What has Richard been carrying off with him to Nik's house, or to Tom's caravan? She considers the obvious options: illness, affair, debt. All three disaster scenarios flash through her head while she empties her glass.

You're being melodramatic, as usual, her mother snipes. She's right. It's easier to admit, now her mother is dead, and exists only as a bossy voice without the X-ray gaze.

The frozen squid has melted. Which is fine, because she's going to cook it. She'll whip through some more exam papers while it simmers. She's not waiting. She's busy. And it's a job best done with wine in hand.

She times herself. An average of 3.5 minutes per essay for the first six *Of Mice and Mens*. She's actually faster! And she's not listening out for the front door at all. It takes too much concentration. Stewed squid is best after two hours' cooking. He's got plenty of time.

Halfway through the ninth *Of Mice and Men*, it strikes her. Ask Nikesh. Check up, basically. But why shouldn't she? She's *the wife*. She didn't sign up to be Mrs Richard Berryman, and endure this yokel surname, for nothing. If she acted concerned, it wouldn't look like he was in trouble. No old nag, that Kate, just loves her husband. Is that what they'd say about her? The omniscient 'they'? It's true. It's why she stays married.

Not as much as I love you. That's what their first arguments were about. Teasing at the beginning. A game. But, many a true word. She stares down at the fat handwriting on the script in front of her.

It's what her mother used to say. When she was much younger, young enough for true heartbreak. 'In every relationship,' her mother said, as if it was obvious, this wisdom, 'there is the lover and there is the loved. It's never even.' And she'd pat Kate's shoulder. Cold comfort. At seventeen, she believed she'd always be the lover. The one with the bigger heart, the more swollen soul. The one who could be popped like an overblown balloon. Overblown. Is what this stupid argument has become. But the argument, for Richard, is never about the chores, or the money, really. For him, it's always about the underlying truth: that he is the lover, and she is the loved. It's uneven.

That's not even what 'overblown' actually means. And now she can't remember the proper definition. These essays are weakening her grip on the English language.

Love. That's why she'll call on Nik. The noblest reason. Who can argue with that?

*

The woodland volunteers have packed up and gone to the Green Man to refresh themselves with beer. The air in the wood is cool and thick, swirling in chilly eddies amongst the still trees. As the street lights ping from grey to dirty orange, a fox potters down the side of the Berrymans' house, leaves footprints in a long line through the dew of their lawn, and slips under the fence. It sniffs, a hundred familiar scents and one new one. Left along the fence, downhill a little, the smell intensifies.

The fox circles Richard twice, then sits by his shoulder and looks. This is the closest to a fox Richard has ever been.

It pokes its black nose into his ear, dots it along his cheek, and pauses at Richard's open mouth. A kiss from a fox, in the quiet dark of the wood. It makes a fantastical scene, but a brief one, that Richard misses. For the fox does not like what it smells. It backs away and, as if nothing has even taken place, trots off to slide under the fence at number 12, where Tom will have left a chicken bone, or a stale sandwich, beneath the caravan.

Richard's stomach is gurgling, too, though he doesn't feel hungry. At this time on a Friday night, he would usually be happily digesting a slab of halibut, or a bucket of mussels in white wine. Fish on Friday was a ritual instigated by Kate, and readily agreed to by him. Since he was in charge of roasting lumps of meat, it meant never having to cook on that last working day of the week, when wine tasted even sweeter than on every other day.

Tonight, his gut bacteria are disappointed, but they are busy, digesting, excreting, slowly filling Richard's empty belly with new gases. It is no more bothersome to him than the flies, though. And they, at least, have attracted other fantastic visitors. Two bats scoot back and forth above his head, taking turns to dip through the dark, snatching their insect supper. If only his head were angled better, he might have witnessed this, an air show of chaotic, perfect manoeuvres.

*

She takes the longer way, along the pavement, to Nik's. Too much like pursuit, going through the wood. Following Richard through the gate in the fence. Even if it is a day later. Is that all, a day? She stops for a moment, and breathes in the scent of the wisteria on the front wall of number 18. She'd like a wisteria. She should ask Tom. Only a day, but now she's on her way, she might as well complete the mission. Just leaving the house is probably enough. He'll be there when she gets home. Standing by the wine cupboard like nothing even happened. Bastard.

Nik's house is dark. The sun is low at the back, this time of day. In the garden? She peers through the gaps in the side gate. Only a strip of yellow lawn is visible. 'Nik?' she calls. 'Nikesh? It's Kate.'

Nothing for it. Next stop the Green Man. If Nik's there, say she's meeting a girlfriend. Unlikely, but he can hardly call her a liar. It's a steep uphill to the pub. Sweaty. Sticky. This is another reason why she never goes. Hard to arrive looking sleek. Though when does she ever look sleek, any more? Someone called her *gamine*, once. A very long time ago – in another era. She's held on to it, a bonbon that's gone mouldy but it's stuck to her hand and she can't let go.

There are young men standing at the front of the pub, smoking, baying, even though there's a garden out back. Dreadful place. All mock-antiques and contrived mismatching. Inside, she peers around, balking at the clashing patterns, the fake bookcases, until she spots Nikesh, on an overstuffed button sofa in the corner. Wave. He doesn't see. Buy a drink first. Keep up the pretence. My imaginary friend will be here any minute. Should she get two glasses, cement the illusion?

She sips too-warm Merlot, practically mulled, and turns towards Nik again. Wander by. Not over-friendly. Banter, that's what she should do. A language Nik understands.

'Hi!' she beams. Smile too big. God, she's basically baring her teeth at him.

'Evening. Kate.' There's another man on the sofa next to him. Not Richard. Not unlike Richard, though.

'So, good night last night?' she says, her voice as full of banter-ish implication as she can make it.

Nik glances at the man, then looks at her askance. 'Richard told you?' he asks.

'He didn't need to tell me.' She grins again.

'Oh. Right.' Nik puts down his drink. 'Well, it was a very good night indeed, actually. So, this is Neil. Neil, Kate. My neighbour.' The man raises his glass to her.

'And what did you get up to, last night? The two of you?' she asks Nik, ignoring the other man.

Nik's eyes widen. 'We tried out the new French place in Clapham, as it happens.'

'Really?' she says, with a drawn-out upswing she hopes indicates she's amused by their shenanigans. Is Nik blushing? Then she sees that the man's hand is on Nik's knee. Squeezing it.

'It was great,' Neil offers, and smiles at Nik. 'Really great.'

Oh, God. Swig of wine. Rearrange face. 'Wonderful!' she says, as the last drip of wine goes down the wrong way. She's going to cough. Choke to death, probably. 'I'll leave you to it,' she croaks and stumbles over a stool as she flees for the garden door. At least she can't hear them giggling behind her.

In the garden she coughs until her eyes water. Nik and Neil. Lovebirds. She had no idea. It's funny, really. It will be funny, when she tells Richard about it later. Except she can't tell him. Because that means admitting she was at the pub.

And then it dawns on her. If Nikesh was eating French food in Clapham last night, then Richard was not drinking lager chez Nikesh. And Richard definitely did not sleep on Nik's couch.

She leans on an aluminium tabletop, and her palms sink into a puddle of beer. Where is her husband?

*

Richard has never been in the wood at midnight on a Friday before, and it's a surprisingly lively spot. Music leaks from the Fitzgeralds' house, where the younger daughters are taking advantage of parental absence and entertaining a clutch of cologne-soaked youths from the boys' sixth-form. Two cats, from houses at opposite ends of the wood, meet in the middle to stalk and scrap, too transfixed by each other's infuriating scents to take any notice of Richard as they pass him. Just off the path that leads past the Berrymans' garden, but further along, near the public gate, two men lock together, long enough to exchange a murmur. One unbuckles his belt while the other drops to his knees in the dead leaves. He reaches for the standing man's cock and pulls it into his mouth, his hands gripping at denim, at the muscle beneath. Fifteen minutes later, another man waits in the same rhododendron patch, peering along the path until a shadow moves towards him, raising a hand.

When Nik had told Richard, only on Monday, Richard had immediately thought of the tissues and wet wipes in the corners of the wood, and the nocturnal couplings that produced them. He'd wondered if that's what Nik had been doing, all these years. Was it exciting, finding a stranger in the dark, or did longing just intensify until it overcame fear? But Nik was by then describing a man, who had a name, and who was meeting him at Clapham Junction on Thursday, for a proper date. Richard had smiled at this idea, of Nik at a restaurant, working his way through first-date questions with another man in a brand-new shirt. But he managed to make the smile convey happiness for his friend, rather than amusement. And he was genuinely happy for Nik, just a bit surprised. It made him rather proud, though, to be a confidant, and to be, it seemed, the only one.

The secret lives of his friends. He had examined his own life, for secrets, for excitement. What had he kept from Kate, over the years? The best he could come up with was that he'd never told her how the wood made him feel, how being there amongst the trees made something tight in his chest loosen, so that his eyes misted and his lungs let out a sigh. He'd never told her that living near a wood that was surrounded by fields rather than streets would have made him so much happier, because he knew she didn't want that.

And now he has a new secret: the simple fact of his lying here, quiet and unseen, while Friday night peters out around him. One of the cats, a tabby with a freshly torn ear, pauses on its way through the wood to sniff Richard's leg. There is a trace of mouse on his jeans, at the calf. The cat looks about, whiskers along Richard's shin, but senses this is none of its business and turns towards home.

*

Kate wakes with a start. Empty bed. Rain is flicking through the open window on to the sill. What bed is Richard in? The same one as the night before? Someone else's? Or a hotel bed, wrecked from sex, with someone else? Hell of a way to make a point.

She sits up, head thrumming. If he thought he had the moral high ground, being the lover not the loved, not getting the joke, he's fallen so far he's skulking somewhere on the ocean floor, right now.

Laura. She finds her watch on the floor by the bed. 10 a.m. She's got five hours. Which means Richard's got five hours too. To get home, to explain himself, to mollify her. To put everything back together before their darling is here.

All right, she'll email him. Desperate, yes. But she can send an angry one, now. Two nights have earned her the right. But in the kitchen her laptop is already open on the table, and she remembers. She did it last night. She'd even checked her own husband's Facebook page, like a forlorn teenager. Stared at photos from holidays a decade ago. Looking for clues. For love. Had she actually cried? There are tissues. Wine-stained ones.

Steel herself with coffee, before she checks what she wrote. Beside the machine the pot of squid is still out on the counter. Forgot to put it in the fridge. Richard's squid. Ruined by her.

Check inbox first, delay the cringe. There's a failure notice. Unable to deliver: inbox full. She could wring his neck. Making himself uncontactable like this. It's so careless. Rude. Not even a call. But she knows why. He never bothered to memorise their numbers, thanks to that bloody iPhone.

Pull self together. It's only been thirty-six hours. Which is nothing in the long haul of twenty-three years together, is it? Perhaps that's what she wrote last night. A way to forgive.

Richard,

Your daughter will be arriving at 3 p.m. on Saturday. It would be nice to welcome her home together, don't you think?

K

Phew. Except, there's a PS. Which starts, *My mother always used to say*. Oh, God. She scrolls down.

PS. My mother always used to say, in every relationship there's a lover, and a loved. I think you think the same as her, but it's not true. We are both lovers. We might not be Romeo and Juliet, but unlike them we're alive, so let's make the best of it. I love you.

Romeo and Juliet? How could she be so basic? So schoolboy? But he didn't get the email, thank the God of full inboxes. She had meant that PS to be meaningful, heartfelt. She did mean it, what she said. She's not just the loved. Must figure out a better way of putting it. Prepare something she can say, when he gets back. She's not got the energy, nor the will, now, to give him a hard time. Open arms. Forgiveness.

*

Richard's jeans and shirt are soaked, and still raindrops patter on the denim, on the darkened green cotton stuck with darker leaves. He did this once before. He came into the wood, not through the garden gate but by the steps, down over the railway tunnel, in rain that had already begun when he was on the street. It had raised that fragrance from the warm ground that seems impossible on a hot, dry day: a steam of nature's undergarments, a pungent kind of freshness that had made him gulp. Down at the bottom of the steps, he had hurried along the path through the wood to the small grassy clearing, and stood, letting the water hit and stream and drip. Then he lay down in the grass, and grinned up at the falling water, tasted it, felt it soak right through him, stitching him to the wet earth.

That feeling, being wet in the wet grass, *being* the wet grass. It had made him weep, for joy and for something stranger, a loss he could not name. When he'd got home, Kate had been bewildered by his soggy embrace, and by the earnestness with which he told her, *I love you.* He'd really meant it. He didn't always, but in that moment then, dripping on the hall floorboards, he did.

Was it, in fact, some kind of closeness to nature that had done it, produced the feeling that could only be expressed through weeping? He is even closer to nature this second time, lying in the rain. His upturned ear is filled with water. It puddles at the small of his back, and in his left palm. Pressed against the earth, his belly has turned a greenish colour, under his green shirt, and this colour is seeping outwards, so his veins show like creeper tendrils under his skin.

Richard, the Green Man. Nik would find it funny. Drink enough beer there, he'd say, it'll start to show, and he'd pat his mini-paunch. But Nik hasn't been through this patch of the wood, so he hasn't seen his friend. Richard is alone, greening in the rain, the earth softening to mud around his ribs so that he sinks, very slightly. Closer to nature.

*

She feels better fortified with a glass of the cook's prerogative as she stirs the chicken. Rain is still streaming down the conservatory windows, hammering on the skylight. But look on the bright side. The upside. She has food, wine. Laura on her way. Richard, no doubt, on his way. A house, with, imminently, her family inside it. A hot gardener. She will joke with Tom next time, about the shopping. How foolish she felt, arriving like that with even more bags. How forgetful. The perils of midlife, again. God, no, not that. The whole situation is a cliché, and a funny one. Soon to be funny, when they are all here.

Quick sweep of the house before they get here, check Laura's room has not silted up with drifting furniture again. From her daughter's room she looks out at the sodden garden. The trees beyond the back fence are drooping, dripping. She hasn't been in the wood for ages. Doesn't like it that much. But Richard does. They could stroll this afternoon, if the sky clears. A family walk. Like when Laura was little. Tom's pond dent is filling up. Another joke she can crack. Weather did the work for you! Ha bloody ha. Last time she was watching him from up here, she had a beer in her hand. She's left the bottle in Richard's study. Careless.

For some reason she pokes her head round the door this time before going in. His diary is open on July, where she left it. Three weeks of planning for her birthday, and it's not even a big number this year. Taking precautions against rage? Or making sure that she, Kate, his wife, has the best possible birthday present, the best possible birthday, every year. She shouldn't have offered Tom that beer. She shouldn't have asked about flow.

The doorbell rings. Only 2.30 p.m. Her heart leaps. 'Oh, shut up,' she says out loud, but she can't help it. Hope. He forgot his keys. He's brought flowers.

'Got a taxi!' Laura looks so pleased with herself, standing there in her too-short shorts on the doorstep.

'My girl. It's you!' she cries, and flings her arms around her laughing daughter.

The rain is still pouring from the sky, so that sitting in the conservatory is like being in an underwater bubble. Laura is doing her grown-up voice, draped on the wicker settee.

'So, what are the facts,' she says. 'It's been, what, not even two full days, yet. Nearly two days?' She lifts her beer.

Two *nights*, Kate wants to say. She hadn't meant to crack. But something about Laura being there, bounding through the house, her twanging sort of happiness, made her crumble. Just for a moment. She is composed, now. An officer reviewing the evidence. The junior officer.

'And this has happened before,' Laura says, carefully. Kate nods. 'And he always comes back.'

'Always.'

'And he has his wallet, just not his phone.'

'Yep.'

'And he was really mad? Mum?'

She's blinking. Blink faster. Try to breathe.

'It's obvious,' Laura declares, sitting up straight, twisting her lovely long tangle of hair in her fist. 'You had a fight a bit worse than usual. He did what he always does, but is just doing it a bit worse than usual. He's punishing you. And he's trying to be proportional. Proportionate. To his anger. Right?'

She nods. Her mouth won't stay straight. 'Right,' she says, but it comes out like a terrible moan.

'Mum, don't be silly. Men are stupid. They don't think things through.'

'I thought you thought your father was perfect?' She's almost offended.

Laura shakes her head and gives a resigned smile. 'Relationships are hard work,' she says.

Where has this tone of world-weary wisdom come from? Not from her, disguiser of all marital fissures. And she keeps her own mother's so-called wisdom, snarked directly into her mind, to herself. It would be sweet, but for the nightmare context.

'So, let's do the only sensible thing, and eat a ton of Brie, and get a bit drunk, and watch your favourite film, again.'

Oh, sweet daughter. Volunteering for a gazillionth viewing of *Far from the Madding Crowd*. 'Bagsy Gabriel Oak, this time,' she says.

'Sergeant Troy is mine, for all time, and you know it.' Laura takes her hand and pulls her up. 'To the telly, and don't spare the cheeses!' she yells, and they run, skidding down the hall, not looking at the closed, silent front door.

*

The rain that kept the Saturday dog walkers from the wood has turned to drizzle now. The paths are deep with mud, and everything drips, an irregular constant patter, a beat that never settles. Richard's green belly is bloated, pushing him up from the ground. He's never had a paunch before. He's managed to stay thin despite the desk work. But he's no longer burdened by comparisons: his mean shoulders against Tom's broad ones; his spindly thighs against Tom's rugby legs.

All his worries have washed away. And he really had been worried, by what Kate said on Thursday night. All their married lives, he'd been surprised by how easy it was to be faithful. There'd been no seven-year itch, no midlife crisis, no empty nest syndrome when Laura outgrew them. It had been enough, for him, and it had appeared to be enough for Kate, so he had finally let himself take it for granted. They were safe, and he wouldn't end up in a caravan in someone else's back garden. He'd let go of twenty years' worth of fear, that Kate would get bored with him, that being adored would stop being enough for her.

He did adore her. He'd just never been able to shake the feeling that it wasn't mutual; that she endured, rather than adored. So, of course it had rattled him, this so-called joke of hers. And it had been hard to believe she hadn't been thinking of Tom, when she said it.

But he never got the chance to figure it all out, with Nikesh, at the Green Man. And now Richard is the Green Man, hidden in the wood, as wet and dripping as the trees that lean over him, as quiet in his mind as every other dead thing that lies here with him, leaves and bird bones and last year's forgotten acorns. Left to his own devices, he would eventually become part of the wood, and there's a lot to be said for that. Stillness, green and brown, the slow, steady flow of oxygen.

*

By the time Bathsheba has married Sergeant Troy, they've finished the wine. On the sofa, Laura nudges her a bit too often, trying to coax out the quotes she usually cannot resist when she watches this film, the swooning sighs they've indulged in so many times that now they feel scheduled, expected.

'Tell me again,' Laura says, while they watch Troy walking out on his wife, 'about the time at that party when you said your name was Bathsheba.'

'Oh, but you've heard it before,' she says. She is busy puzzling. Which of Bathsheba Everdene's three suitors is Richard most like? He is not patient, sturdy Gabriel Oak. He is not Troy the irresistible cad. Is he jealous, humourless old Boldwood, then? Driven mad by her semi-imaginary lust for another? But Bathsheba doesn't love Boldwood. And who would, the miserable old git. Could she try to think of Richard as steadfast Gabriel Oak? Would that help? Make her believe he'll be back soon, he's just been out tending a flock on a hill, relieving some sheep of colic or whatever it is in that scene where he deflates them all like balloons. He'll be back soon, and this isn't the beginning of a deep, dark phase, starting with the letter 'D' and ending in internet dating. The Liberty-coloured flat and the single armchair made life. That she hasn't popped the balloon for the last time, and gone too far, ripped an unmendable hole.

But it's Sergeant Troy who leaves Bathsheba. Gorgeous, charismatic Troy, with his pant-wetting eyes. And he does it by pretending to be dead. Clothes on the seashore. A Reginald Perrin for his times. She snorts. Imagine. Richard leaving a heap of clothes in the wood behind the fence. He'd sneak round to Tom's caravan in his boxers. There to obtain advice on how to leave his wife.

'What?' Laura pokes her arm.

'I've got an idea,' she says. 'Get your shoes.'

The air is still damp outside, and they tack along the wet pavement, sidestepping slugs that gleam in the orange light from the streetlamps.

'Where are we going?' Laura asks when Kate stops outside number 12. The house is dark. Just the faint blip of the alarm-system box showing above the door.

'Remember Tom?' she whispers.

'Taciturn Tom?'

'That caravan of his is through there, in the back garden. If your father's been confiding in anyone, I reckon it's him. He'll know. Where he's gone.'

Laura shakes her head. 'I don't think this is a good idea, Mum. He'll be back tomorrow.'

'Tom left his wife.'

'So?'

'I think, maybe, Richard's been thinking about it. I want to know. If he said something.'

'Fuck,' says Laura. 'How d'you know he'll be in?'

'I don't.'

She leads Laura down the side passage, treading on several slugs in the dark. She can hear Laura's *eurgh, eurgh* behind her. 'Let me do the talking,' she hisses when they reach the garden. The caravan is right down by the back fence, a white lump like a giant loaf of bread. No lights on, that she can see. The trees in the wood hiss beyond the fence, warning her off. Be purposeful. Don't creep, in case someone's watching from next door, and takes them for well-dressed burglars.

How can Tom live in this box, with its poky windows and child-sized door? There are curtains drawn all the way around, but as she edges along the back by the fence she sees a chink of pinkish light. Aim for that. Just check he's there, before she has to bang on the door, alert the nosy neighbours.

'Mum, look! A bat!' Laura whispers behind her.

Her feet kick something over in the dark as she reaches the window. Wellington boots. She freezes.

But she can see a lamp, with a scarf thrown over it. The bed is pulled out, taking up half the space. And on the bed, Tom, entwined, with a girl. A Fitzgerald girl. Entangled. Naked. God, they are beautiful. Sleeping nymphs, the pair of them. His hand is splayed on her lovely belly and just the thumb is moving, slowly, back and forth. She remembers that weird comment Richard made, *never mind which Fitzgerald girl Tom fancies*. She jerks away.

'Home,' she mouths at Laura, pointing the way, in the dark. Before she weeps at her own foolishness, before she howls like a lost dog at the moon.

They get as far as the wisteria at number 18 before she lets it out. A wail, a howl, whatever it is turns into an ugly choking fit. She can't get air in, air out, at the same time.

'People will hear,' Laura whispers.

'I don't care,' she moans.

'What's the big deal?'

She looks up at the sky for help. Hysteria, under the wisteria. It's so unfunny she nearly laughs. 'Two secrets,' she sobs. 'Two whole secrets he's kept from me. How many others are there?'

'Only one way to find out. Mum?' Laura is tugging at her arm. She lets her daughter haul her along the pavement like a drunk.

'How?'

'He can't stay away forever, can he?' Laura sounds irritated. 'He hasn't even got his phone. Or his laptop? And when he comes home, he'll have to tell you. Whether you like what you hear or not.'

She wipes snot from her face with her wrist. 'I need a drink,' she says.

'So do I.' Laura drags her to the front door, and holds out her hand for the keys. 'We'll be ready for him,' she says.

*

The robin cocks his head at the sight of Tom, but stays put, on the branch that hangs directly over Richard. He has seen Tom at dawn before, taking slow steps on and off the paths, pausing under trees, long enough for the robin to get bored and fly off in search of a new curiosity. He has seen Tom even when he has been busy singing up the sun, and watched while Tom has shinned up a double-trunked beech and wedged himself there in the bird-loud canopy.

Today, Tom ignores him. He is looking at the fallen man. The robin looks too; flits to a different branch to get a new angle. Nothing much to see, but Tom keeps looking, staying very still. He stays so still that the robin gives up and flies for the nearest oak, to send a song high into the sky.

*

The bells are ringing, that glorious cacophony reserved for Sundays and weddings, and she must get up because they're ringing for her, it's her who is getting married today, and Gabriel Oak will be pacing up and down in the yard, impatient for the first time in his life, wanting to see her in her sweet, white dress, which she will have to borrow because she's forgotten to get one, but the Fitzgerald girl will have one, she'll have to squeeze into it, suck in her belly and run, because the bells are ringing louder now, summoning her, don't miss it, your own wedding, your own married life, he'll never forgive you, Richard, he's waiting but he's running out of patience …

She sits up in one movement. She didn't know she could do that. Doorbell. Richard. No keys. Her heart is jumping about, from the dream, but relief is flooding, now, better than wine. Just enjoy, for a moment. The relief. The grand homecoming.

She hears Laura's bedroom door open. Scramble out of bed. Make sure it's her he sees first, whatever mood he's in. Get her hands on him, around him, reunion. The pair of them, entwined. She races past Laura and down the stairs. Richard, you old fool. Richard, better than a whole flock of

Gabriel Oaks, a whole regiment of Sergeant Troys. Pause for a second, hand on the doorknob. Is she shaking? Laura has stopped halfway down the stairs. A respectful distance. Good daughter. Deep breath. Twist the knob. Smile.

There is a policeman on her doorstep. As if he knows how ridiculous he looks in that hat, like a boy playing at dressing up, he removes it and holds it in front of his belly. She glances over his shoulder. Where is my husband?

But there is only Tom, lurking at the end of the drive. He is wearing those wellington boots. The ones she tripped over. He is looking at her with his intense, brown eyes. But in this washed-out dawn light, they look entirely grey.

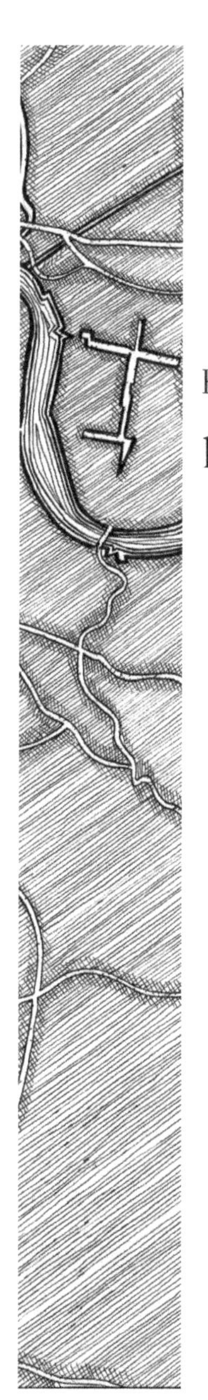

PART III

RE-ENCHANTMENT

STREETS OF THE GREAT NORTH WOOD

a skipping rhyme

Knock your head, find your feet,
Skip all the way on nimble feet down

Bluebell, Spring Hill, Woodbine, Peak Hill,
Allwood, Northwood, Forest Hill Road

Hillcrest, Laurel, Westwood, Hazel,
Larkbere, Highclere, Forrester Path

Willow, Bridgewood, Linden, Orchard,
Shrublands, Thicket, Sycamore Grove

Beeches, Ashurst, Chestnut, Hawthorn,
Maple, Laurel, Appletree Close

Mosslea, Ospringe, Meaford, Meadside,
Lakefield, Hartfield, Ravenscroft Road

Kingswood, Grassmount, Ringwold, Oak Grove,
Tredown, Snowdown, Evergreen Close

Acorn, Cypress, Elm Park, Tree View,
Fransfield, Pearcefield, Honor Oak Park

Woodcombe, Wood Vale, Mount Ash, Heathedge,
Oaksford, Haredon, Forestholme Close

Huntly, Buckleigh, Fox Hill, Reynard,
Copper, Sylvan, Turkey Oak Close

Crowland, Thorpewood, Hunter, Wychwood,
Braybrooke, Hambrook, Elder Oak Close

Ash, Fox, Heath, Limes,
Elm, Furze, Green, Pine,
Kings!

Traditional

14

HOOLIGANS
2042

Charm: Should one wish to blight me with runes carved on a root, this song will wreak his hate and set things right.

We drew the first on Wells Park Road. A big one, a fuck-off one, all along the yellow-brick high hard wall. Green spray paint, chalk highlights – by Laz.

We all gleamed in the night, and woke up webbed by snail trails.

It's a start, said Laz.

Here we come, we said.

We did Lapse Wood Walk next. Our knuckles racing green, a pocked garage door, a breeze-block wall, marked up, barking now with our raw joy noise.

Can they read it, though? one of us said, swigging under the hot dark.

They will, said Laz.

*

Sticky, high on our own fumes, we reeled down Fountain Drive, up Grange Lane, zigzagged Peckarman's Wood. Knives out, we gouged the fence. We had the sign by heart, we had it like an eyeball tattoo, like a brand. We were viral.

Hooligans! cried the voice at the PVC window, a yellow tear in the night. So we danced like beasts while his flash snapped us, made horns of our hands, made a razzle-dazzle unveiling of our new masterpiece for the furious cameras, ta-da!

Cut the ribbon! Ga Ga Ga!

We were the ravens flying the tower, we were Jack Frost on a bender, we were the greasy flood, our high-tide marks now high and low in dry paint, in deep cut, in blood, sap, mud, ash, rust, spit, fire.

On Crescent Wood Road, on Highwood Close, on Underhill Road, on Westwood Park, on Lammas Green, on Springfield Rise, we foxed and left our symbol stink.

Laz had us singing, back down in the tunnel, and pouring in Fresh to swell our flesh where all that sweat had rinsed us out.

We'll brew our own beer, she said. We'll get the gear, down here. She wiped her gorgeous, toothy mouth. What'll we call it?

We glugged and belched. Ga Ga Ga!

At dusk we rose, now that morning and afternoon are a long, cool doze. Laz unlocked the tunnel gate. Under the trees we pissed, and stretched, passed round the whetstone, sharpened up.

Private property next, Laz said. No damage, not yet.

She was serious. She was the wildest dog, she souped up our blood.

We're not hooligans, she said.

So we were children, for the golden hour. Mixing up Fresh with earth – remembering mud pies – in mud we dipped the tougher leaves, chestnut and oak, and pressed them round the moulds of our cheeks, our reeking foreheads.

The masks dry, we spruced up.

In our leaf cheeks, in our best charms, we prowled. The tunnel breathed cool calm behind us. The air burned dust above us. Down and along the strict back fences of Woodhall Drive we snouted.

With love, hissed Laz.

Our faces crunched. We hooked the fence posts and jumped.

Our hands, with the cans and brushes and blades, cast the spell. We spelled it out for them, in their own dead gardens, on their own dead wood, on private property: Ga Ga Ga.

Only one alarm sang. Only one light blinked. No disco for us, we were busy with our art, the new lines of meaning.

It's like Laz says: our aim is to enchant.

*

16th June:

1. Strip bed, sheets in freezer
2. Check Cool Pak chilled
3. Mum up, hydrated, meds
4. Iced tea → freezer
5. Sandwiches
6. Check restoration notices:
    (a) Petition
    (b) Timetable
    (c) Compensation offers???
7. Bleach, ant spray, citronella, DEET, windows
8. Order wipes, gel, earplugs, dry shampoo
9. Check energy – set A/C
10. Woods meet: 11 a.m.

But there was something else. It woke her in the night, it was so important she was sure she wouldn't forget, and now, with the fug of morning, so warm already, it has gone.

It's all about organisation. This is what the 'Beat the Heat' pages say, and Laura agrees. Plan, stay calm, be prepared, keep track. Don't run out. Don't run. Walk. She looks wearily at her creased tumble of sheets. It is early, there's time to try and remember.

She goes to push the window wider, a futile gesture, and there, emblazoned across the back fence, is some sort of graffito. A line more than four metres long in dark green, with arrowhead ends and crossbars at different angles. It looks like a hex.

There's a crash from downstairs. Her list is already doomed. Down she scuttles, *walk, don't run*, pulling her sweat-damp T-shirt over her thighs. 'All right? Mum?'

Her mother smiles from the swing-chair by the open patio doors, all innocence. 'Ga Ga Ga,' she says.

Laura spots the broken glass, in a puddle of water that's seeping fast between the parquet. The parched ground is sucking it in, swallowing it. *Hydrate, meds*. 'Did you at least get the pills down?' she snaps.

'Ga Ga Ga. That's what it says. Brian's put it on the LOOP.' Her mother swings the chair and scoops up her screen with both arthritic hands. 'Everybody on our road's got one.'

'Wouldn't want anyone feeling left out.' Laura drops the broken glass in the bin, turns on the tap, and sighs as it jerks and rattles. Alternate days already, and it's only June.

'Plenty of Fresh in the hall,' says her mother, without looking up from her screen.

'What about the petition? Has everyone signed that?'

No answer. It does her head in, her mother and all the other nonagenarian snoots on their road, revelling in impending disaster. They love being the centre of attention, the noble victims of a hare-brained scheme. Most of all, they are looking forward to saying 'I told you so', later, from their compensatory sheltered housing. To sign the petition, they seem to think, is to appear craven. Better to hold the moral high ground. Laura would prefer that they retain the actual ground, the house and the now pointless garden beneath their feet.

Restoration, they're calling it, as if the forest were being put back for a jubilant returning king, to hunt bouncing deer on his great white steed. It's a clever word, good for the PR, redolent of the ancient made good, the battered made beautiful. It does not conjure up wrecking balls and churned earth, diggers trailing bits of fireplace and drainpipe from their maws. It leaves out the dust, the mosquitoes, the godawful crickets, and that perky, inescapable slogan of summer: 'Beat the Heat'.

It also leaves out her father, whose grave, in the strip of woodland just beyond their back fence, is now the biggest bone of contention between Laura and her mother. 'I hardly think he'll mind,' her mother had said, when they got the notice. Everything is a joke now, it's her mother's modus vivendi, but Laura couldn't laugh. His skull is in there. Even if it's been splintered by tree roots, crunched into bits and rearranged by worms, it's still there.

'Brian says it's an ancient form of lettering. Like runes. Quite artistic really,' her mother says, swinging the chair so it squeaks.

'It's on private property.' Laura opens the freezer and counts iced-tea pouches. *Check the Cool Pak.*

'If you're looking for my paramour, I've already got him.'

Laura goes and pokes behind her mother's back, feeling for ice crystals in the rubbery Cool Pak cushion. 'Nobody else has a pet name for their assistive technology, Mum.'

'Brian calls his Catherine.'

'As in Hepburn?'

'Princess of Wales.'

Laura holds back a snort of derision.

While she works her way around the kitchen counters with the ant spray, her mother reads out snippets from the

LOOP. All the road's residents had seen the hex, as Laura chooses to think of it. There was one on the pavement at the end of their road on Monday, another on an old post box at the corner yesterday. They had sniffed disapprovingly and voted by virtual committee to get them removed. But now that it is their own fences, walls, even a hedge that has been defaced, they're getting worked up. This is not supposed to happen. *Keep calm, stay cool.* Especially if you're old.

Laura interrupts the stream of petty outrage. 'Anyone got the timetable updates?'

'It's not going to change, darling. Listen to this: Sally says they've actually painted it on to her lawn.'

She still doesn't see how it's going to work. 178,000 people all shunted and deposited elsewhere. They ought to just rewild the wild bits, surely, stick some more trees on all those remote islands and up those foreboding hills in the north. You don't have to be a cynic to think it's a mayoral PR stunt. *Doing our bit to beat the heat.*

She glances at the temperature monitor. Thirty-four degrees already. 'Want to go early? To the wood?'

But her mother is out in the garden with her screen, snapping the mark along their fence. She isn't even wearing a sun hat.

*

Back in the tunnel, by torchlight, we were psyched, we were pumped, buds about to burst. We twined gummy fingers, gazed eye to flaring eye, our hunters' souls were high as kites.

Sleep, soon, said Laz. Today we're doing daylight.

Our hands slackened. Thirst struck.

We scrabbled for cans of Fresh, drank with the single-mindedness of babies while she strode among us. She was our teenage witch, she was the ecstatic scratch for our nettle itch, and she knew everything.

We're not hooligans, said Laz. We're not ghosts, either. You are, all of you, summoners. What are you summoning?

Torchlight swept our masks. Our chins dripped mud.

Exactly, said Laz.

One or two of us nodded.

What will come to our call? This isn't a game. We're not trespassers. Well, we kind of are.

She jangled the key to the tunnel gate. One of us giggled.

Be bold! Summon it up, the thing, the wood, the lost, the feeling in there.

She thumped her gut.

Whatever it is, we need it back. What do we call?

A voice near her feet said, Ga Ga Ga.

That, said Laz, is the cry for a gentle battle. It is our enchanted mark. It's not a curse, it's not a mess, it's not a crime. Well, it kind of is.

She held the torch to her cheek and grinned, teeth of the wildest, glorious dog.

Ga Ga Ga!

We felt the beast energy in her throat.

And no, we did not sleep, we were on our feet, chanting at heartbeat, chanting so the dark turned to dance and the tunnel, the hill, the wood all grew with it. We were shaking it out, the thing, the lost feeling, we were summoning it up from the dried-out earth, a mouthful of wine from a corpse.

*

Along Crescent Wood Road, the geriatric procession begins. It is rather like a day at the races, or a regatta, the way they all insist on dressing up and then stepping out en masse, parasols twirling. Appearance ought to be the first worry out of the window when it's forty degrees outside, but her mother is wearing a long floral dress, a beaded floppy hat and has twined plastic clematis through the legs of her walking frame. She looks like a gone-over Flower Fairy.

'Brian likes this dress,' her mother says, and winks as the man himself hails them from his front gate.

Laura, struggling with the parasol, ice box, the bag of provisions and sprays and tissues and cushions, is sweating. There used to be a gate in their back fence that opened directly into the wood. But it was the one her father had used, the day he stomped off in a huff and met his death, and that had been that. A gate was the one idea her mother couldn't seem to find funny.

They perform this grand day out with verve, air kisses and shrieks at the same old greetings, compliments and profound glances, and carry with them towards the wood an atmosphere of refined gaiety. Her mother was not like this before. None of them were, that she knew. It is all slightly forced, but since their enjoyment seems genuine, Laura grits her teeth.

A huddle is gathering by the railings, some piss-taking and guffawing as a woman in a neon-yellow kaftan searches through her handbag.

'I'll do it!' Laura calls, she has the key clenched in her slippery palm, but no one pays any attention.

'Very Bloomsbury,' Brian is saying to her mother. 'Vanessa Bell in love.' She's heard this comment on the dress a dozen times.

Laura wrangles with the padlock on the tall, metal gate and stands aside to let the celebrants pass. Every time they do this, guilt mingles with relief. Privatising a public good, like a shrunken patch of forest in London, was exactly the kind of thing she protested against in her thirties and forties. Now, she is grateful – and reminds herself of this daily – that there is a safe place for her mother and the cronies of Peckarman's Wood, Woodhall Drive and College Road to keep relatively cool. She tries not to think about those who live back to back with other roads, eking out the energy ration. Thanks to the wood, she's got their air conditioning down to six hours a day.

Progress down the shallow steps is painfully slow. But the first waft of shady wood is always a pleasure. How it stays green while their gardens parch and yellow, she doesn't know. Deep roots? Secret springs? People used to visit these parts for healing waters. Perhaps that's what is keeping all these old people so spry.

Their gathering spot is at the bottom of the steps, by the old railway tunnel that was burrowed through the hill more than a century ago. All that earth acts like a heat sink, so that outside the tunnel mouth, the hill seems to blow a chill breath out between the trees. There is some commotion going on, down there, where they leave their garden chairs neatly stacked and the trestle tables folded. Laura tries to peer between the branches of hornbeam and beech, but she can't get a view. Raised voices, loud laughter; a rumble of confusion working its way back up the procession towards her.

'What is it?' she asks, but all necks are craning forwards, down towards the tunnel mouth. She dumps the bag and coolbox in the undergrowth and starts down, bellowing her beg-your-pardons and thank-yous, dodging round walking sticks and unsteady feet. At the bottom she angles her way between parasols, bright silks and muslin shirts, towards the centre of the fray. There is a girl she does not recognise, deep in conversation with her mother's friend, Sally. Behind her a motley gaggle of youths, looking nervously out across the crowd of residents. The huge metal panels that usually shut off the tunnel from the wood are wide open.

'Sally, who is this?' she asks, putting a protective arm around Sally's narrow shoulders.

'Ellie, was it?' Sally smiles at the girl.

'Erilaz.' The girl juts her chin at Laura. She is small, and grubby, and her hair is twined up from her head in two alarming, matted horns, but her round face is somehow radiant.

'You know you're trespassing. How did you get in here?'

'They've been using the tunnel to keep cool. Just like us, really,' says Sally, though there is a quaver of doubt in her voice.

'The tunnel should be closed off. There's a good reason for that. You shouldn't be in the wood at all.'

'The wood doesn't belong only to you,' the girl says, carefully.

'You're a resident, are you? What's your address?' Laura can feel her knees shaking a little. She swallows hard. It wouldn't be that surprising to find that some old fool on Peckarman's Wood had copied the key for a great-grand-daughter. But it's supposed to go to the committee, anything like that. The wood is a precious resource.

'We could let them stay, while we're here for the afternoon, couldn't we?' asks Sally.

'Hear, hear,' someone says behind her.

'I should call the police. Sally, I'll deal with this.'

'We were having a very interesting chat, weren't we?' Sally moves away from Laura's shielding embrace. 'It would be nice to carry on, I think. Don't you?'

Laura turns to scan the crowd. She spots her mother, with Brian, and he catches her eye.

'More the merrier!' he calls, and her mother grins. 'Let's get set up, chaps.' He waves the others towards the stacked chairs and tables and, with considerable alacrity, they are soon unfolding and dragging the furniture into their usual incongruous cabaret layout.

Laura can feel her pulse at her temples. Her back is clammy. 'You need to leave,' she says to the girl, and pulls her screen from her pocket. 'Start moving or I will call the police. And hand over the key.' She knows there is no signal down here, there never has been, but she can bluff. 'What's your name?'

'I'm Laz,' says the girl, as the gaggle of youths gathers closer around her. 'And you're missing something.' The others all nod.

Laura can smell them, mushroomy and uncivilised. Their murky clothes look slept in. She takes a step back.

'Are you afraid?' says Laz.

Laura wishes she would sneer more, be more openly offensive, so that she could let rip in return. 'Let me be clear,' she says. 'You're breaking the law. These people are residents. They have a right to be here, and they need to be here.'

'We're not stopping them.'

Laura laughs, knowing it is a disguise. She peers past the group at the dark tunnel opening. There are things piled in there: bags, empty bottles, cans of what look like paint. A prickle runs over her scalp. The fence, the hex, all the hubbub on the LOOP this morning.

'Stay right where you are,' she says, and backs away towards the path. *Walk, don't run.* If she can get to the top, get some signal, she can call the police before these hooligans realise what's happening, then nip back down here to keep an eye. They don't look that aggressive, but they might turn. The residents are sitting ducks.

When she reaches the bend that cuts off the view to the forest floor, she does run, stabbing at her screen, cursing the hill that blocks the nearest mast. Just before the gate a bar finally appears, but she can hardly speak for panting as the line beeps and the computer asks which service.

They've defaced private property, ruined fences, they've trespassed into gardens and now they're right down there, within feet of her own mother, yet she still hesitates for a second, two, three, before she whispers, 'Police.'

*

So, what's in there, they wanted to know.

There used to be bats, a guided tour. That legend, a ghost train haunting the tracks, the dead riding. There used to be beer cans, graffiti, God knows what else.

Not now.

The management company monitors—

We keep things neat and tidy—

Our proprietorship—

Nice to have our own wood, clean and quiet and safe—

We don't take it for granted, now that it's ours. Under our control.

Laz smiled through it all. We kept our nods bright, glassy, eager birds.

Are you anarchists, then, they wanted to know. Are you protesters? Do you think property is theft?

We liked the glints in their watery eyes.

We're looking for something, said Laz. We're bringing it back.

I hope you don't mean socialism, one of them quipped. That got a laugh.

We couldn't explain. The question in a strip of birch bark. The listening, straining tips of roots. Gossip amongst the dead crowns, peering down to where we are asking, searching.

We couldn't explain what we are asking. We were stumped.

So we took them in.

Bliss, said a woman.

Actual goosebumps, said another.

We let them adjust to cool air, to dark air, to the tunnel's wide-awake yawn.

Here be dragons, said a man. Not trolls, are you? Nobody laughed.

Candles on sticks, we got them all lit, we were dignified hosts in our rags. So they could see, in the churchy hush, what we meant.

This buried cathedral, defiant shrine. Roods of white ivy, hangings of moss. And every brick hammered into place by man now buckled, split or hurled to the floor by the head-strong roots, by the rootstrong glory, of trees.

The pattern of them. Wriggle and lurch, twine and circle, decades of work turning light into magic, an incantation of fractal growth that dismantles, that wins the gentle battle.

Not just trees, we whispered. We brought our flames closer.

Where brickwork gaped, where paving groaned gap-toothed, the wood's sweet secrets brimmed and burst. Mush-rooms, gamine as wallflowers, roguish as farts. Lone dancers, huddled squatters, the earnest, the deceitful, the foolish and the brave, all bubbled out from their soily webs, all alive in the dark. We loved them. We laughed at them. We gave them new names for they were as new as truth to us.

Wonderful, said a woman. And what have you been doing in here?

They were stirring. Nervy, excited. We heard their breath and their fiddling fingers. We knew their old skin prickled with the lost thing, the yearned for, the answer to the ques-tion that Laz would dig out.

Ga Ga Ga. She only whispered it.

They thrilled. Was that you, the paint on the walls?

Try it, she said. Ga Ga Ga.

It was on my lawn, someone said, indignant.

Laz was our wolf, she was top dog, she was on fire.

Are you annoyed? she said. Are you fucked off? I hope so.

We gathered, candles on sticks. With yellow flames we lit our beautiful witch.

Our sign, it's for summoning, said Laz.

Ga Ga Ga, we said.

We don't know what will come. But you came. Apart from that cranky one. Laz rolled her eyes.

That's my daughter, said a woman. She was standing close to Laz, dressed all in flowers. You're a lot more fun than she is, she said. Let's have it! Ga Ga Ga!

We felt the air pressure change. It was not what we expected.

The flower woman shuffled forward. We lit her too, flickering crone. She had that lure.

I know what's in these woods, she said.

It was like Laz had passed her the microphone.

And you're right. Whatever it is, it's pissed off.

You could have heard a toadstool spread its gills.

My husband's buried here, she said. She had a great big smile on her face. No, I don't mean him. I don't believe in bloody ghosts. But he loved the wood, and I wasn't that bothered. You know? And when I went too far one time, I'm prone to melodrama I know, but when I went too far, he came straight here, and whack. She swiped a gnarly hand through the nearest flame. I think the wood, or this thing, whatever it is you're after. I think it took him.

We didn't know what to do with her when she cried.

*

Trespass, damage, loitering, threat. She's used all the right words.

The operator pauses. 'Transferring you, Ms Berryman.' Click. Twenty seconds, thirty seconds. Laura paces, letting the sun sting her. The pavement is hot through her sandals.

The next voice is faint, laconic. 'We understand you're trespassing on designated land, Ms Berryman. Is that why you're calling us?'

'Not me. Not us. It's some kids, in our wood, you've got the address? And damage. They've painted—'

The voice interrupts. 'If you have entered the woodland area, you need to leave. The Great North Wood Restoration falls under the Act. All those entering are trespassers.'

'You haven't understood,' Laura says. 'We have keys, access rights. We are the actual management company. And they've broken in. There's graffiti.'

'Has anyone been hurt?'

Good question. 'Not yet.'

'Then leave the woodland area quickly and safely and I must warn you now that, under the Act, your presence in the wood does constitute trespass, and as such is an offence, and we will move to prevent further offences or arrest offenders if necessary.'

'But it's for health. The whole road has access so they can keep cool. They're old.' Laura is shouting. She can't help it. There is sweat in her eyes.

The operator sighs. 'Are you stating that you refuse to leave the woodland area?'

'We haven't done anything wrong.' But something is tapping, down the line. Her screen pings in her ear.

'I have issued a warning to your LOOP. This includes a copy of the Act, the timetable for your region and an outline of your rights. The warning is a statement under law. Failure to comply, et cetera. Thank you for your call.'

The line goes dead. Et cetera? She knows she's overheating. *Stay calm, keep cool.*

No. She'll take charge. That's not in the 'Beat the Heat' guidance, but neither is accepting invasion by young people with no respect for other people's property. Someone has to be responsible. For her mother, for the rest of them, down there.

Laura marches along Crescent Wood Road. Mad dogs and Englishmen, she thinks. It used to be a joke, harbinger of a bit of sunburn. Got to go red to go brown, they used to say, soaking it up. Even her knuckles are sweating. She has no parasol, but she has a plan; it will be a responsible sort of ambush, but all the same a wave of adrenaline like the first, long-ago drag of a cigarette washes through her.

The other end of the tunnel is buried in a scrappy dent of woodland, on the edge of the Hillcrest estate. On her way along Sydenham Hill and down Wells Park Road she passes three hexes, on walls and street signs, and each emboldens her. The patch she's heading for always used to be littered with fast-food wrappers, cans, even filthy bits of clothing. It's likely there will be cockroaches, which she still can't quite handle even after last summer's plague. But she also remembers that the tunnel gate at this end was so loosely chained that anyone could squeeze through. Not something she ever saw herself doing, but here she is. An ambush.

Down the steps away from the road, there's some shade now at least, but the gully in front of the tunnel is grown high with brambles. She stamps them down. This is how her father taught her to walk through high grass on holidays to the coast. In case of snakes. Silly, really; they were so rare back then.

The rusted chain on the tunnel gate has already been broken. Laura stands, listening. The tunnel murmurs and crackles. Further in, it could be swarming with cockroaches, rats, but she can't use her screen light, it'll give her away. *Don't run. Walk.* Responsibilities. As she begins to edge forwards, grateful for the draught of cooler air, she remembers her sheets left on the bed, that she didn't check her mother had taken her meds, that there have been timetable updates and the petition has stalled and there was something she forgot that she had to do, it was very important, but it wasn't on the list and, now, it is lost.

The tunnel feels much longer than the same route on the surface. With each step Laura tests the ground with her toes, nudging her feet between fallen debris, glad not to see what it is. She has never been so completely enveloped in blackness before, and she longs for the light of her screen, a glimpse of reality. She feels as small as a child, here in this cavern under the hill. Somewhere above her is perched their house. It has always been there, for her anyway. It's where her father was, in his study, swivelling round on his whizzy chair whenever, as a little girl, she did her secret knock at his door. *My Laura-saurus,* he called her, during her dinosaur phase. Then, *Laure-and-order,* when she wanted to be a policewoman. Thank God that passed. When she had gained entry to the study and commandeered the swivel chair, and he was whirling her around on it, he would sing, *You're so dizzy, your head is spinning,* his voice growing wilder and higher until she felt sick with laughing.

It must be the dark that is doing this. She should be focusing on what she will say, how this cunning ambush will work some magic trick and sort everything out. But with nothing to look at, and nothing to hear except her timid footsteps and her tiny breaths in this underground wilderness, her father is suddenly present, huge, and alive. His hands grubby from pencil work, his smell of stale cigarettes, and later, Trebor Extra Strong mints, the green shirts he always wore that never quite had all their buttons. That soft popping sound he made with his lips before he began explaining something to her, the nail of his little finger tracing the lines of a design on that huge whiteboard as he talked about invisible forces: tensile, compressive, shear.

Laura feels her skin tingle. It is cooler in the tunnel, but hardly cold.

She remembers him coming back in from the wood one day, so wet that she thought he had fallen in the pond. He had shaken his head, deliberately hard so that droplets of water flicked at her. *What happened, Daddy?* she asked him. She remembers he had a funny kind of smile, happy-sad. *Nothing at all*, he said. *I just lay in the grass.*

She had teased him, *silly Daddy*, *soggy Daddy*, and then run away screaming when he tried to give her a cold, wet hug.

She has stopped moving, she notices. There are voices echoing, further along, a glimmer of orange light, but she doesn't want to break this spell.

Through all these years of organising, tending, through her mother's grief, new life and old age, instead of her father, there has been an absence. And what is there to say to each other about an empty space? Now, she has his presence. A scent of damp earth, the crackle of his newspaper folded. She clears her throat and the small rumble echoes back. It is exactly like the sound he would make before he spoke.

Laura steps sideways until she finds the wall of the tunnel, though she can feel that it is all roots, not brick as she supposed. There she leans, with her eyes closed. She listens intently.

The sound comes through the bones of her skull, where her head rests against the roots. Tiny pops, scattered in time, each like the sound of a mouth opening, lips parting, the tongue readying, about to speak. With each pop, the expectation of her father's voice mounts, so clear and so familiar is the signal. It is wonderful, and unbearable, at once.

*

We got their chairs, brought them in, made a circle. There was wind by then, the trees hissing with it, hissing in our heads. The old ones sighed in the breeze. We were summoning.

Listen, said Laz.

I felt it too, once, someone said. So did I, said someone else. They were full of words, these codgers. They were interruption central, they were total spouts.

Go on, said Laz, and her torchlit eyes told us, *listen*.

So, we were all ears.

Tale upon tale, we got then, while the candles trickled and warped. The dumb, the weird, the never-ending, the scary, the sweet, the wild. We drank them up, we were Halloween ghosts, we were midnight feasters, we were under some sort of croaky spell.

Those old people had seen some serious shit.

Those old people had been in and out of this wood, they had webbed it like slow spiders, the paths were thick with their thoughts. They were at it before we were even born.

We all held bubbles in our throats. Our hair blew into our eyes. We tasted it – leather and bark and frogspawn and dew and all the old things – and we looked at Laz and we saw that she tasted it too. In their mouths, garnished with words, was the question to Laz's answer.

This knowing, this tingle, this burst of truth, turned the air around us green. We sniffed it up, fresher than Fresh, sweeter than cut grass, greener than life. And there we were, all sniffing, some eyes dripping, when the flower woman said, I know that smell. Oh, I know it so well.

It was the scent of the moon on water. The scent of a silver bell that chimes. The scent of the song of the cuckoo, lost in the wounds of forest time.

That's what he smelled like, the flower woman said. When he came in. When he actually made it home.

No, we thought. This scent is ours. It's the thing, it's the smell of the question and the answer. It didn't belong to her.

That green, ringing air that we all inhaled, that we swam in, it began to vibrate. It crackled faint and slow, then faster, louder. We glanced at Laz, in a green trance, we pleaded, don't let this spell break, we need it. But Erilaz, our conjuror, our drummer girl, our pied piper, she was on her feet, tinged green, she was turning in the green haze, and the beat she welcomed was footsteps, the crunch and snare of running feet, the cymbal hiss that tickles your soul and tells you oh, this is big, this is sweet, and down the tunnel came running the cranky one, the flower woman's daughter, and she shouted, as she broke our circle and broke it again, and carried straight on towards the wood, IT'S RAINING!

The flower woman stood. She high-fived Laz.

What's up, Laz asked.

Ga Ga Ga, she said.

We needed no more. We took the chant and made it as loud as the throat of a tunnel, as wide and as broad as the cry of a tunnel, we took it outside, into the manic shade, where our hair began to sparkle with rain, and our open mouths caught drops of it, gulps of it. We held the hands of our elderly friends, and what do you think we did? Slowly, raucously, we danced.

*

Laura stops running, some way down the wide path that stretches away from the tunnel mouth, and turns to watch. From the darkness they are emerging, an improbable crowd of self-consciously ragged youths and proudly glamorous pensioners. She glimpses her mother, her raised hand clasped in Laz's, a kind of crazed energy in her jerking movements as they start to sway together. Their chanting is ridiculous. But she feels embarrassed for them, not afraid. They are all trespassers, stumbling across each other's worlds, and they do not know it. The oldies are wildest, whooping and staggering, drunk on the rain. Ancient hooligans.

Laura keeps walking, past the sludgy hole that was a pond, and into the clearing. It is raining hard now, so that without the tree canopy for cover, her clothes are soon stuck to her skin. The water is not cold, but the feel of it, drenching and re-drenching, running off her fingertips and in between her toes, is bliss.

The clearing is a straggly patch of grass, dandelions and thistles, with a bench placed here and there, a haggard plastic bin. Will even this be filled in, planted with tottering saplings as the restoration project sweeps all human life from the wood? She pictures the new map: her mother's garden, the square of ground that was her house, their street and all the others for miles south and east and west, all dotted with curly-topped tree symbols. They will irrigate. Those trees will have their feet kept cool, they will have dust gently sponged from their ignorant leaves. All that nurture. All that tenderness.

Restoration. Soon, the only person still resident here will be her father, the fragments of him, dry, inert, then wetted, in the endless cycle of summer and winter.

Around her the leaves crackle. Laura breathes in.

I just lay in the grass, her father says. He is this scent of the wood wetted. That musky freshness – there's a word for it, he told her a dozen times. She's forgotten.

In the middle of the clearing, Laura lies down in the gleaming, drooping grass. She is heavy with water. The lumpy ground holds her up. The rain comes down to meet her. She opens her mouth and lets it fill.

Then she tips her head back to look at the trees upside down, pooling into the sky. There on a trunk is the hex. It has been cut into the bark, and the gouges filled with chalk which is now dripping, upwards, into the folds of the tree's roots.

It is a disfigurement and a summoning. It is stupid, but she is glad it's there, that she can trespass, in the company of hooligans and crones, that the wood accepts their mark.

Petrichor, her father says. How could you forget?

Laura wriggles in the grass. That's a made-up word, she replies.

Nothing wrong with that, he says.

Faint, beyond the rush of the rain, she catches the chant, rising and falling, tuneless and senseless, a human call: Ga Ga Ga.

CHANTALOUP, OR NAME YOUR WOLF

Odolf for the wealthy,
Hrolleif for the old.
Rollo for the famous,
Gunwolf for the bold.

Botolf for the messenger,
Weylyn for the son,
Convel for the warrior,
Fridolf for the peaceful one.

Raff is a red wolf,
Geri, Freki, greedy ones.
Ulrich is a she-wolf,
Skoll, the wolf that chased the sun.

All the little wolf cubs,
Canagan or Channon.

If you are an un-wolf,
Run, run, run!

Nilas Schwitzer

15

RESTORATION
2064

Charm: When I am made fast in chains, this song I sing to spring the fetters from my limbs.

So we'll begin at the beginning, right back, way back when the restoration started.
And go on until we come to the end. So you'll see how this whole thing got out of our hands.
Got out of everyone's. But it's Patrol like us who has to get their hams dirty.
Of course, we weren't there right back at the dozing, real dirty work.
We'd have done a better job.
But they were wet behind the years, weren't they? New jobs for youngers.
Even if it was knocking down your own house, your whole street.
We still find bits and bods, don't we? Door handles, air-con units, ceiling lights.

I found a teapot once, spout sticking out of the ground like a snake's head.

Funny how stuff won't stay still in there. Things move around, rise up, poke through.

Anyway, those youngers did the dozing, made a pest of a bad job, REFO got the planting done. That was back in 2046.

And bingo, we've got a forest.

You can imagine the security.

You don't need to, it's still there.

Wasn't supposed to be. They thought folk would get used to it, get bored, move away on the programmes and then they'd reduce Patrol.

But, started in '47, didn't we? Team Dee. And full-time ever since.

Mostly camera work, it was, after a while. Must be hardly a tree in there isn't wired up.

But before that, it was: perimeter walk, section foray. Always armed.

Tranks only. REFO wasn't trying to kill anyone.

But it was way worse than they expected.

Wasn't just the Turfers, breaking in, setting up camp, saying they had nowhere to go, didn't like the programme communities, calling the forest home.

It was Earthies too. Madus hattus, that lot. Said they were rewilding themselves, they wanted to be part of the forest.

Like they were tree spirits. Saw a few curious costumes on them, didn't we?

So we had a time of it, all these new bees on Patrol, pulling Earthies out of the forest almost every night, packing Turfers off to the programmes.

And all the media coverage, it gave youngers ideas. It was like a dare, for a while.
Go in and see how long you could last.
So the boss went one up. It was good for the PR, but it was also a chance to do what she'd really wanted from the start.
Every clown has a silver lining.
And REFO started introducing wolves.

It was 2049 by the time they got it set up.
Same year my daughter was born.
They were something, those beasts.
Beautiful things, strong and graceful, you know? I named my daughter Ulrika. It means wolf ruler.
But it was a worry. We thought, if it worked, we'd be out of a job.
Because who wants to go and live in a forest full of wolves?
The trees weren't that big yet, and the whole place was a mess, all tangled together.
You wouldn't have been able to run, not fast.
We hoped they'd be scared.
We were. Got upgraded to real guns, quad bikes, chain mail.
And put on a buddy system. Just in case.
Well. It did put some Turfers off. But the Earthies were mad for it.
The wilder the better, that was their view.
Didn't stop them taking in tarps, camping kit, bags of food, though, did it? Bending trees and building shelters.
Digging holes to hide in, like rats, when Patrol came through.
So, the wolves didn't help much at all.

And they weren't going to bother with bears, not after that commotion in Bristol.

Thing was, if you were on cameras, in that booth with all the screens, you'd be hoping for a glimpse of wolf.

The way their eyes glowed white, that look like they could see you, somehow, watching through the lens. It was magic.

But it was distracting.

That first few months, when we realised the Earthies weren't going home, we dreaded what we might find on our rounds.

Like we should've been guarding the people in there from the wolves. But it was vicer verser.

The boss, she loved the wolves like they were her kids. And fuck anyone who got in their way.

That's why we were scared.

That's why we're here, really, talking to you.

Anyway. You'd expect a few incidents. Got to make a few eggs and all that.

Team Bee pulled out a bloke with a couple of fingers hanging off. He'd been playing with a she-wolf, feeding her scraps.

Then there was that couple. She was covered in scratches, bite-marks. He couldn't walk. Teeth had gone right through a tendon in his knee. Said they'd be going straight back in soon as he was fixed up.

So, a few injuries. Quite a few, really.

But no deaths. Even when the wolves started breeding, multiplying.

I remember watching the cubs on cams, deep in where we couldn't get the quad bikes.

Just lovely, they were. Rolling about, playing like puppies.

So it could have gone worse, the wolf thing, but it could have gone better.

We kept our jobs. Just as many breaches as before, just as many Earthies playing at going back to the land, needing patching up when we found them.
And it had only been a year or so of the new normal, when the PR went bad.
It was one of our own team, Susmita, who pulled them out.
Tough as all boots, that Su was.
She'd found a couple with a baby, who reckoned they'd been in the forest two years and they were doing all right.
We'd never seen them before, not even on the cams.
But they also reckoned, once they'd come round from the tranks, that the mother'd had two kids in there.
Twins. And one had got left behind.
Ten-month-old girl, they said, all alone in the forest.
And that was it. All over the media. Remember? The Bearman Controversy.
'Baby at the mercy of wolves', total take-down on Susmita, the whole tranks method.
The father, he was out there like a wrecking bull, attacking everything and everything. REFO, the entire restoration project, the boss. It got massive.
The protest got so big, we were put on Patrol at Whitehall for a week.
But the boss was having none of it. She said, if it was true, about this baby, we'd have found her easily.
There was nothing REFO didn't have access to. Thermal imaging, motion detection, all that. She said the Bearmans were lying, that it was all a trick, a sneer campaign.
Right out and said it.
Someone on Team Bee said REFO paid the Bearmans to shut up, in the end.

And they did. But on the condition that Susmita lost her job. So, they made an escape-goat of Su. Said the father had made up the claims out of revenge, that Susmita had broken the rules and used restraint on the other kid and hurt them. It would never happen again, there'd be a review of practices, the usual stuff.

But the boss hoped that would scare people, too. Put them off.

And it did. For a while.

Lucky, too. Because that's when things started going properly wrong.

Any given night, a bunch of cameras would go. There were nearly eight thousand by then, fixed and remote control. Even where Patrol could still get through.

It was belting braces after the baby thing, boss couldn't take any risks.

But we were losing sometimes a hundred cameras in a night. Repair team couldn't keep up, so on top of Patrol they wanted drone cams.

Not much use when the leaves are on, but there's thermal, and the wolves were all chipped, too. So, they got them up, but they just couldn't get the feed straight.

Cams would blank for whole minutes. Drones would ignore the controls and fly out over the city.

If you looked at the drone stream, it was always full of black holes.

And guess what? They were the same spots where the cameras had blown.

Boss called it a blip. But honestly, we never did manage to properly fix it. Workarounds, that's all we had.

Plus targets. If you could catch an Earthie disabling a camera, you got a bonus.

When a black hole showed on the network, we'd get sent straight in there.

If we could cut through to the site, what would we find? Sod all. Wolf droppings maybe.

So, we did the odd deal. Persuade an Earthie to let themselves be marched out, confess to destroying REFO property, then slip them back through the fence with a sack of biscuits and vodka.

Bonus for us, results for the boss.

Everyone did it. Felt we deserved it, for the extra stress.

Extra duties.

Because it wasn't just the cams outing, and the drones going hop the wall.

Stuff was turning up that wasn't meant to be in there.

And we don't mean teapots, or old kitchen taps. Though there was plenty of that.

No. It was plants at first.

June of '52, when spring came, there were all these flowers.

Course, we didn't know any better, did we? We're Patrol, not scientists.

But we noticed because of the colours.

Never seen anything like it. But then I'd never been in a forest till this job, neither.

A patch up in one of the east sections, the whole thing was just purple. Like a carpet. Another bit further south, where it wasn't too overgrown, was covered in these little yellow ones, like stars.

So there was a lot of that kind of thing. Pink ones here, white ones there.
Sometimes a lovely smell, very soft.
But we thought it was just the forest bedding in.
The Earthies – we knew a few of them by then, what with the bonuses – they loved it. One place, they put up a kind of fence, from fallen branches, so the flowers wouldn't get trampled.
Gardening in a forest!
But the next year, there was way more. Vine-type things. Climbers.
We didn't know what they were. Flowers on them like orange trumpets, or big clumps of white foam.
Only in certain spots. But when you found them, they looked nice, just odd.
The next year it was saplings that didn't match what REFO had planted.
That was when we got put on training.
Us, learning about plants.
But the boss said, we knew the forest like the packs of our hams.
Which was true.
And she didn't want any science types poking around, saying she'd got the restoration wrong.
She certainly didn't want any science types bumping into Earthies and reporting it.
She'd had to accept them, by then. As long as they didn't damage anything, or rile the wolves, it was living let live.
So, we got an education.
Silvology. Sounds good, doesn't it?

The study of forests. And we were meant to identify the flowers, and the new trees, while we were on Patrol.
Take photos, take samples.
I used to sneak some home for Ulrika, sometimes. Show her something she wouldn't get on the school feed. There was one she especially liked called dog violets.
Latin name, *Viola riviniana*. Isn't that lovely?
Earthies would lead us to new plants when they came up, in exchange for stuff. Sweets, meds, waterproofs.
So our data was pretty good.
Team Dee, we were the experts. Silvologists supreme.
But apart from the extra work, it didn't change anything.
The boss sat on it. Our non-disclosures got updated.
Only way anyone out there got to know about it was when the odd Earthie got pulled. Which was their own doing, by then, if they'd had enough of the wild life.
The black holes were still a thing. So she couldn't keep track of wolf births, couldn't keep them all chipped.
REFO was on lockdown. Wouldn't let any new bees in, or ask for any help.
Boss was losing her grip. You make your bed, you line it.
That's why we're here, talking to you.
Anyway.
So, you can keep flowers secret, because they don't go anywhere on their own, do they?
But it was insects next.
2056, I recall. It was a retired naturalist in Camberwell reported that butterfly.
Nobody, including him, had seen a live one in twenty years.
That's what he said.

And it was a whopper.
Twice the size of the old kind.
Boss claimed it as a REFO success before we'd even spotted the same ones in the forest. Talking up rewilding, the whole biodiversity business.
Of course, the media didn't know the half of it. We were finding the crazy things everywhere in there.
Got home from a shift once with a bright orange one in my breast pocket. Ulrika was six by then, thought I was a magician.
Then it was, what? Stag beetles, bees, ladybirds, all the creepy-crawlies.
But big, you know? Had an incident in Battersea with a spider's nest, evacuated the block and everything.
You'd think it wouldn't have bothered us, seeing as we patrolled a forest full of wolves.
But we hardly saw them, and these bugs. They get in your clothes.
All right when it's a butterfly, isn't it. Not so keen on woodlice.
But, food chains and all that, you can guess what happened next.
I remember it. When we changed to earlies, July of '58, I heard my first dawn chorus.
Me too. It was like the whole world was singing.
Better than music.
Nothing like it.
REFO had tried with birds, back at the start, but they hadn't taken.
They'd had to fly them in. Imagine that. An aeroplane full of birds!

And now, we were busting all the projections.
It was starting to look suspicious. Kinds of birds that were long gone, suddenly nesting all over the place.
And then flying about. There were spotters all over London, couldn't believe their eyes. It was a craze that summer.
National news coverage.
And then it got properly weird. Because the starlings, they'd started making these shapes in the sky, like living clouds, like tornadoes, all sorts.
Then one evening, right above the north boundary of the forest, they flew up and made the shape of a stag's head.
Only lasted a few seconds.
But hundreds of people saw it, right up there near the city.
Some woman filmed it.
International news then, wasn't it?
We even had the media after us, asking questions. Was it military? they wanted to know. Were they robot starlings? Drones?
It went bat-shit gravy for a while.
Boss had us all towing the lime. 'Nature is a wonder,' we all said.
It wasn't a lie, was it?

And since then, what with everything that's been happening, well. Patrol's been as much about keeping the forest in as keeping the people out.
But nature finds a way. And what can we do if a stag turns up in a back garden in Peckham? Or a bloke finds an owl nesting on his balcony?
Not our remit.

There's a whole team for the deer now. And the boars. They can be a nuisance round the bins.

And people, mostly, they like it. My daughter was proud as punk when we got a frog infestation in the drains.

You might think, with all these creatures escaping from the wood – because that's where they were all coming from, as sure as regs are regs – that there must've been wolves getting out there too.

But we can tell you, not a single one breached the boundary. That we know of.

And yeah, we thought that was strange, at the time. They were very quiet too, by then. Less of the yowling.

You might have thought they were up to something.

But nobody commented. Too busy taking photos of giant moths, or badgers with litters of ten cubs all dancing about, or starlings making signs in the sky.

Because it was a sign.

And the wolf silence was too.

It was 2063, when the first footage showed up.

Came through a REFO camera. One that had been dead for years.

So how it came through to the control room, we still don't know.

You'll have seen it, because it's the most famous one. Of the girl, sitting in bright sunshine, a wolf either side of her.

It's iconic now, isn't it? The grey T-shirt, the mask made of leaves, the little headdress.

And the singing.

We still don't know who took the vid out of REFO.

Hand and heart neither of us was involved.

Boss doesn't know either. As soon as she found out about it, she deleted it from the server.

It was too late by then.

But, she did her best, spreading the word that it was a hoax.

Thought she'd got away with it.

We knew she was freaked out, though. Because all the old surveillance kit was back, plus new.

She'd given up on the drones and the cameras years ago. Now, it was all hands-on tech, 24-hour drone grid, wireless solar cams rolled out, with mics this time.

She didn't care any more what trees we drilled into, what nests got disturbed.

Didn't care either that the Earthies who'd stuck around in there actually protested.

Like they'd got rights! That was a laugh.

Course, it didn't work.

Everything that could go wrong, did. Drive overloads, data jams, blackouts. Drones freezing or being knocked out by hawks. That was a new thing.

It was worse than before.

So, a month of overtime for Patrol, doubling up on sections.

And even with all that, we didn't see a thing.

Just a starling murmuration in the shape of an oak leaf. And a new video, twenty-eight days after the first one.

You've seen that one too. And we're all used to it now, but the way the girl stared from behind her mask as she got closer to the lens, it was unnerving.

That look in her eyes. We thought it was triumph, didn't we?

Like she was victorious. She'd beaten the boss.
Who also saw it that way.
And between that one, and the girl becoming a kind of hero, it's hard to explain what happened.
You know as well as we do.
Apart from the mystery, how she was doing it, there was just a kind of feeling more than anything.
A bit like love. Some people call it that, don't they?
Everyone was enchanted.
Except the boss.
So, you can imagine. We had to round up the Earthies, question them, find this girl.
We got nothing out of them. All said they'd never seen her, there weren't any kids gone feral in there.
One of them thought she recognised the grey T-shirt, though, said she'd lost it a while back.
Other thing they said was, you'd never even know there were wolves in there unless you strayed into certain places. And those places were always changing.
If you did stray, you'd be up against a pack of hundreds, all standing their ground.
So it must be cubs they were protecting, the Earthies said, because they never saw any.
But of course, it was at the back of our mines, all of us.
That family that got pulled out back in 2050.
The father that said they'd left a tiny child in there.

So, you pretty much know the rest, if you've seen all the vids. It's been a job and a huff, trying to keep her followers out of the forest.

I wouldn't say we've succeeded, either.

But honestly, they've done no more harm than the Earthies, they're just a bit more loony.

Drifting about in there, heading the clouds, hoping for a glimpse.

They're waiting, really. They just don't know what for.

And my daughter, Ulrika, she was just as obsessed as all those other teenagers, poring over the vids, making her own headdress, painting leaves on her cheeks, singing those freaky songs.

You can get them online now, can't you? Print-your-own 3D antlers on a band.

It was harmless, until I caught her and a mate, planning how they'd get through the fence.

All Patrol live near the forest boundary, in case of short-notice calls.

She's only fourteen. They had their packs ready, even got hold of some tools.

He went eight-shit, didn't you? Grounded her.

Had to. But in the end, I realised I'd have to actually lock her up to stop her trying to get in. Four times, she tried and I caught her. It was that bad.

And you can't lock up a kid. It's illegal, for a start.

So I decided I'd risk it. Take her in safely, with me, for a wander round.

He put his job on the line for her.

I've only myself to blame. But it was strange, all the same, that night. Soon as we were on our way, Ulrika said she knew where Herndon was.

That's the name the youngers have given the girl.

She insisted we drive right round to the far-west section, and go in there. So we did. No harm, I thought.

Wasn't long, was it?

A few minutes, we'd been on foot, when I heard the growl. We had head torches, both of us, and they lit the wolves' eyes so they were blazing.

It must have been a sight.

But Ulrika walked forward, fearless, and called for Herndon. The growl rose to a rumble, so loud, and I was sure that the middle wolf was about to pounce.

And that's when he shot it.

You'd have done the same. One of your kids.

I would. That's why I'm here with him. He did the right thing. And that should have been the end of it. We should have gone home and I'd have sat down to write my resignation letter.

Because that was the first wolf, the only wolf, that's died in there. And our job, as far as the boss was concerned, was to protect them.

But Ulrika, she looked at me with this horror in her eyes. Like I was the wolf. And she ran away from me, towards the pack, and off with them into the forest.

There'd have been no point shooting more of them.

There were so many. Hundreds.

And she hasn't come back, has she?

So, this is the bind I'm in. There's Ulrika in the latest vid, her and Herndon hugged together like they've been friends all their lives.

But he's lost his REFO pass, and he's officially banned under pain of arrest.

And I want to know. What can I do? She might feel trapped. She might get sick.

We don't even know if Herndon can speak English. If she was raised by wolves, how could she?

I know it sounds like fantasy, that a baby got left in there and has lived with wild animals ever since.

But think about it. If she's pretending, it's even weirder. Why?

There's a ton of conspiracy theories about Herndon. But I haven't seen a single one that makes me feel all right about my daughter being in there, with her.

And there was that sign.

If you want to call it that.

So these flowers came up, in the paving cracks in his patio, overnight.

Tall purple things. I looked them up, like when we were in training. And do you know what they're called? Wolfsbane.

Turns out they're deadly poisonous, if they get in your blood.

And I wonder, are they meant for me?

We don't know.

So that's why we're here, talking to you.

We need your help.

We're desperate.

PAEAN

Rune-writer,
catcher, riddler,
bale-worker,
masked one.

Way-weary,
stormer, trickster,
frenzy-maker,
horned one.

Weather-maker,
roarer, screamer,
god of wishes,
high one.

At-rider,
quarreller, trembler,
sleep-bringer,

ancient one.

Spear-shaker,
pale and fleeting,
ever-booming,
beloved one.

Anon

16

HORN DANCE
2073

Charm: With this song I sing the names and natures of gods and elves. Through this song, men may learn them.

Rollo

Who is Rollo Bearman?
Poised in charcoal Kevlar, a small woman,
small like a bullet, a spring
tensed and secret in the small hours of the night.
She is beginning, breath and heart high.
She is doing her job that's all this is.
A foray.
A little light hunt.
A run and jump against the odds.
Rollo Bearman, a swatch of hard logic   hard-body
cut from her father's unflappable cloth and
slipped   through the access gate
in the western fence
of the Great North Wood.

Authorised.
Hopes pinned on her
like victory flags,
hope tussling with the wind
that warns:

Twelve hunters, empty-handed,
sent home tails between legs, begging
for a second go –
for mercy –
for compensation –

One felled by a bee sting, it was midwinter
One limping, ankle-twisted not fifty metres into the wood
One nimbly climbed a tree and there she lingered, her legs inexplicably numb, till noon
One whose inner compass spun, turned him in perfect circles, short-circuited
One who never came back, or so they say
Two who returned, ashen and torn, shook their heads and would not tell
One who lost faith
One who lost sight
Two pinioned by hornbeam heavies

And the last, part drowned man, part madman, telling a rococo tale of seduction by water, a goddess turned serpent, the best sex of his life no word of a lie.

Effra

With my aqueous eye, I spy
from my water-bed, opulent in festoon of weeds
and sliding silken mud,
our interloper, lucky thirteen,
as she rustles, synthetic, her own spyglass
gleaming from assured forehead, jogging
at a tiptoe bounce through the dark.
She makes her own maze path
between these distracted trees.
How easy to wait and see what fate
awaits this one, what sylvan conspiracy
will jigsaw the maze, booby trap
the lonely path, turn the way
south to the north, west to the east,
rally the slathering beasts to pounce.

Complacency is not in me,
Effra the wriggler, slitherer,
I'll follow her,
I've trounced one before, last time,
did my best serpent and goddess,
caught him between sex and death.
We are a vigilante forest now, keepers
of our unkempt daughter,
our stray singer: Herndon the herald.

Rollo

Who is Rollo Bearman?
She carries
In a pouch

In her heart
In its own private padded ventricle
Her father's promise bright bubbles in her blood:
Win this, for me, he said, *and I'll make you partner*.
Rollo will be
One equal half of
Bearman & Bearman Counterinsurgency Ltd.
No job too odd,
no odds too long.
Father and daughter, a crack team.

Rollo, running through the dark before dawn,
Night vision cartooning the trees,
Rollo alive in this ghost of a forest,
Heart and head high, lucky thirteen,
Her charm
not a stiff rabbit's foot,
not a silver bullet,
though for a chamber of those
she'd be grateful.
No,
her charm resides in her father's eye,
the all-seeing sequin glued to her frown line,
unspooling its signal across the night sky,
an impossible thread of flying spider web
whose precious vibrations arrive
a hundred miles hence,
enter her father's house by stealth,
and there spin on his crystal screen
the selfsame wood,
framed in his daughter's view.

Right-angled room, regulated temperature, precision lit.
Yet his skin prickles sweat.
His swivel chair creaks as he tips back and stares.
His wood. How it's grown,   blissfully unaware
of his absence these twenty years.
He would not go back.
What kind of imbecile would swap
this perfect house,
this cosy compensation,
for that feral chaos,
merciless nature and her feckless masters,
REFO weak in tooth and claw?

His wood.
He's invited it in through his plate-glass door,
and it struts and prances before Rollo's bouncing
camera,
flirtatious.
How seduced he was, wide-eyed youth of twenty years ago.
The wood itself made young,
fresh,   a new world for the taking.
In he had crept,
leading his wife by the hand, to play
at Babes in the Wood. How his heart had leapt
at the sheer   aliveness   of it all! Oh,
wood make me wild,
give me unfettered life,
and I'll give you—

Rollo   has paused to look at a pond,
like a child spotting tadpoles,   she looks   and looks.

Bearman recoils from the crystal screen, afraid
of what his daughter might see:
her reflection,
there in the wood where she
was born. She does not remember the removal,
forcible,
her mother and father limp in the arms
of REFO guards. She does not remember the refusal
of their plea, when they woke in the cell,
to go back,
to go further,
we are the mother and father
of two daughters. Two.
He hears
his wife's voice, the hell breaking loose
in her heart,
and in his, the shard of hatred
that the sight of their shaking heads inserted.

Compensation.
For a life, for justice, for a wife
who no longer loves
but only wails?
Enough, Mr Bearman, to buy a big house,
keep your family safe within four luxurious walls.
The warm, dry opposite
of a wood.
Was that why?
While his wife's heart-hell turned wild, grew,
strangled her alive,

his own scar tissue hardened
into right angles, straight lines?
Bearman reformed: keeper of the rule of law,
scourge of all boundary-breakers, of all fools
who think themselves free. All mischief-makers beware:
his is a man-made soul.

Rollo, nimble and quick,
dodges between the glowing trees,
treading where he dare not,
finding what he daren't find.

A conscious forest. What a thought!
We snigger into our crooks,
stuff damp moss in our mouths,
shudder our shouldered nests.
No nymphal twaddle to decorate our boughs
in these freshly enchanted days.
But animism never dies!
And so,
from bark crack, from ivied stump,
from split seed
we peer.
A nudge here, a wink there.
Whispers down the fractal lines.
An effortless conspiracy, really,
to take a hunter down:
a loosed branch,
a risen root,

a mirage of safe ground
          and there goes another.
Is it glee, in our applauding leaves?
Or a guileless breeze
that carries
only scent of earth, fungal spores,
up through the sleeping trees.

This one is quick,
light on her logical feet.
We watch
from mousehole, from berry eye,
from behind our old man's beard,
as she scuds towards our ward, our odd-child,
Herndon.
          Can a forest hesitate?
For this one is different. Murmur it.
There's her gait, for one,
the pitch of her breath,
a strand of red hair caught on a thorn
that bleeds a certain bitter scent.

There is nothing we forget.

Rollo

Into the heart of the forest   that fanciful poet's notion
     Rollo runs.
          Ears pricked, eyes wide, alert to the coming
                                        what?
     Threat,

assault,
the surprise that felled
an unlucky twelve
before her.
Dawn greys above the eastern ridge.   There'll be light to see
this overgrown fantasy gone wrong.
There's be light to see
her prey,
girl icon,
sacred Herndon,
thorn in REFO's side. And the insanity
of it all makes her smile,
briefly.
For here she is,
a small lone woman, armed only
with expertise and a brief to succeed where REFO has
admitted defeat,
jogging through the wood of their own making, this
jungle of
failed surveillance, of
slipped corporate grip on control   on reality,
she'd say. Because
she's played the videos, she's seen
the leafy mask, the crown of horns,
she's heard the voice that swoops,   gutters,   sings songs
that belong
to another more tangled world,
weird melodies that summon
to this awkward girl
a clan of crooning wolves.

They snout and nuzzle neck and palm,
where by rights,
they should bite.

Just a girl. A young, lone woman,
face hidden   her voice brazen, yes,
but surely no match for the powers of REFO, this girl
with unlikely, hairy friends.

Rollo pities her.
Rollo pities REFO, beholden
by their own protection order   to forbid any harm
to the wolves they planted themselves
and let grow   a swarm of tooth and claw.
Rollo has no gun.

Effra

Dawn, silvering liquid surfaces,
my transparent mirror shows me
the fairest forest, tapestry of
tendril, feather, paw print, quiet leaves.
Too quiet.
The trees' alarm ebbed and gone,
no cunning thrum
of plot to catch a thief.
I have swum as far as my channels will take me,
I have chased, incensed by the stranger's face
that stared into my pond,
all innocence.
Curled in a cave of willow root,

I knock and implore.
You have the might to stop her,
trip her, transfix her, fox her.
It's too late for my serpent trick.
Do as you did before!
But the willows hush and shake their heads.
Not this one, they whisper.
There's something about her.
Leaves in her eyes,
green in her blood.
There's nothing we forget.

Bearman

Sip of water. Nip of something stronger.
The decanter rattles in Bearman's clammy hand.
His work does not permit nerves. But
the wood
on his screen
rears and tips and swerves
as Rollo makes her way.
Unhindered, so far.
His daughter bold.

Not nerves.
The remit states:
bring the target out unharmed, make no mark, take
no animal life.
But he has put this task in his daughter's hands
and not told.
They work on the need-to-know. That's the job.

Do not disclose, there's no story,
no oxygen to the insurgent flame,
no glory, no fame,   the satisfaction only
of imposing the rules, the straight hard edge of law.

His daughter does not need to know   anything that might,
after all,
be irrelevant.
No drain to cognitive resource,
no baggage,
no personal cause.

No other daughter, lost in a wood full of wolves.

The brandy swashes cold and deep.

Rollo is trained not to scare.
Even wolves, those fairy-tale creeps, hold no fear
when the training kicks in. But there's been no way to prepare
for this target,
this Herndon, harmless outlaw.
No way to share his smallest, sharpest dread.

It's been said
that revenge is best served cold.   But revenge
in the form of a
fierce daughter,
unwitting soldier
in his own war?
It merits a stiff drink.
He could not have told.

What time is it, Mr Wolf?
The recorded howl begins low
from the speaker at Rollo's breastbone.
It hums through her chest
as it modulates,
becomes multitone.

And there,
there is the answer.
A wail through time
a snail-shine gleam
a silver moony beam of
shivering echo
sliding mercury
up the sensing hairs in her ears
bright threads in her blood.
Her father's words:
win this, for me.

Rollo presses earpiece, mic, into place, commands
signal to shrink the yawn of sky space
between here and there,
haunted wood and swivel chair.
'Dad. You ready?'

The thin, sure voice fills her head,
dousing the sparks of fear.
'Daughter.'

'I can hear wolves,' she whispers. 'But with an echo.'

His chair creaks.
His eyes close.
'There's a tunnel. That's where you'll have to go.'

He starts to reel off coordinates,
long-lost landmarks, memorised contour lines
but Rollo is listening on a frequency of
bones, of
cobweb chandeliered in dew, of
icicle drip and
starry midnight blue.

She lets peal a second artificial howl
and follows, downhill, the spiked silken trail
that will lead her, Orpheus, underground.

Light of dawn,
day begun,
hymn of the wood
daily sung,
Herndon wakes her velvet throat,
hatching full-fledged notes:
forest music,
melody of damp earth
chalk harmony
leaf-edge ornament
and Herndon's signature style of
wolf antiphony.
Through miles of

thicket, spinney, grove and covert
a fairy flight of morning-song
glazes the air,
ripples the pond

where Effra, goddess restored,
taints her realm with saltwater sobs,
sends up bitter bubbles that pop, sourly.
Poor Effra,
self-appointed guardian to
guileless Herndon,
making amends for the backfire
of that long-ago exile:
the rampaging hunter,
banished via backwater,
ejected from the wood, from enchantment,
from Effra's water-bed.
And now look.

We spy,
from fox hole, from pierced oak gall,
from white puffball eye,
this new hunter,
her black-cat prowl
sinking, with each silent step,
Effra's hopes.

She is close, now.
Through willow root, Effra begs.
Protect her,

Do as you did before!
But we sense there is more to this one.
Feel the spread of her toes, the spring
in her knees and her lifted elbows.
There is nothing we forget.
This one we know.

Rollo

Rollo, creeping through the Great North Wood,
heart and head high in the cloud of a memory:
her mother.
Who said she never should ever, darling
enter a tunnel
without knowing
how far away
the exit lay.
Rollo's gaze flicking upwards, her lips mouthing *sorry*,
her cheeks receive a sprinkled blessing of rain.

As the wood begins to patter and drip,
Rollo slip-slides down the tangle slope.
Do not think, she thinks,
that you should have been struck down by now.
Do not think, either, that the fact you're still here,
limber and clear,
means anything magical. Forest born, yes,
but trained and technical, that's all it is.

'There used to be a path,' her father says.
And sure enough, she finds

the line made by traffic human lupine
and Rollo follows it
and hears,
above the slow static of rainstruck leaves,
a voice, singing.
It does a wolf impression.
The expert wail and squall carries a smile,
somehow.
Rollo stalks,
wets dry lips.
The keening transforms, a rough kind of music,
tattered, torn from a wilder scale
than any she's heard before.
Even the videos viewed by millions have a tamer score,
Herndon, leaf-masked, horn-crowned, pouring baffling words
into tunes that hook the mind,
deep in a tender spot,
and reel it forth.
But this is it melody? makes Rollo feel
a thousand years old.

The tunnel mouth
is all ivy,
glossed and dripping,
a garlanded maw.
Rollo,
a small woman
in black Kevlar, stands
at its threshold and scans
for wolves.

In the gloom they loll, flopped
on their sides like languorous dogs.
wolfskin rugs

whose eyes follow her,

the late audience member, disrupting the solo show.
Her earpiece stutters. She whispers,
Not now.

Snouts rise and sniff.

On she goes.
Deeper,
the echo of song
purer, the melody
mocks her measured steps and then

She sees her.

Or someone is standing there,
leaf-masked, horn-crowned,
flooding the tunnel with rising sound that
tugs Rollo in
by the hairs on her skin.
Hood, says her head,
and she pulls it down. It's a tactic.
Meet mystery with honesty, show yourself
a lone woman.
It's just me and you.

The singing stops.

Ears prick.

'Well, this is weird,' the figure says. A female voice, young, smooth.

'Who are you?'

'Who are you?'

Their two echoes meld

and drift away.

In her ear, Rollo hears
her father's long intake of breath, the pop
of his lips.

'I'm Rollo Bearman,' she says. 'Are you Herndon?'

The woman steps closer. 'You're going to think this
is weird too.'

Her father is trying
to speak.

Not now.

Rollo pulls out her earpiece and says,

'Will you take off the mask?' She's aware
of the phalanx of eyes behind her, of the task
ahead if she gets any further, of
the sequin
that spies
from her bare forehead.

'Okay,' says the woman.

And she does.

She takes off the mask.

And Rollo

is looking into her own face.

With a weak finger
Bearman slides the lights down low,
beckons dusk into his carmine room,
better to see
what his daughter beams
from within the hill. Any moment surely
the signal will die,
the connection to her,
his bold daughter,
lost,
his wood
lost from view.

It's been REFO's curse,
every camera, drone and bug
scrambled, blown,
except the ones through which Herndon
using method unknown
has spoken.

Does he wish that he could not see?
He is riveted, the screen
magicking him in, so he floats into the tunnel, a fly
taking a ride, past
trickling walls, past
sprawling wolves, towards—

The figure emerges, clear
as a dream and he has lost his nerve.
Speak now, he urges his tongue
or forever—

Tell her to keep the mask on.

Tell her—

But Rollo has gone closer,

their voices a puzzle of

sound he cannot solve.

Bearman feels

a thousand years old

as he sees

the mask pulled away and standing

before his bold daughter,

the double

of herself.

This other daughter

is thinner,

her red hair longer.

She wears a headdress of horns.

Time unties itself wriggles free begins to speed.

Bearman, in his swivel chair

falls up through the branches,

twigs in his hair,

eyes full of leaves.

The wood shrinks, fragments,

a scatter of dew on a threadbare rug, it is

welling up,

seeping through,

a mossy patch spreading fast as green flames

as he falls

fights back against the wind.

Follow the horns, the feet running, rewound,
to that distant hunt, the cry, the howl,
the backwards shriek of the wolf interval,
for this is no dream of a namesake.
No. It was you
who brought down the axe,
who with tatters bound
the horns to that human head.
It was you,
your mischief, your magic,
    for charms are just words for desires that
    burn a hole in the fabric,
    let the horns poke through.
    It was you.

So
Bearman opens his eyes
and listens.

In the tunnel, silence.
Each daughter in her looking glass,
half herself,
half the other,
the forest-born seed split and antlered out,
mirrored sprouts of horn grown high, heads and hearts
now turned together.

His daughters touch hands, that
unselfconscious gesture of children.

And then

they are running,

past wolves, past ivy,

out of the tunnel,

a game, a chase between the trees,

whooping joy, whooping fear,

a wild song,

a strange song,

ending and beginning.

APPENDIX

'The Birth of Myth' – transcript of lecture delivered to classics students at Enleigh College by D. Ferraro

How is a myth born? Do we think that, out of boredom, or a bit of showing off, a guy – or girl – in a leopard-skin toga comes up with a particularly juicy bit of after-dinner entertainment by the fire, and it sticks? I doubt it.

Do we think that, for want of a proper scientific explanation for some natural phenomenon, or transcendent experience (drugs and booze are much older than you, ladies and gentlemen), a frightened peasant posits a higher power? Blame someone else for the hangover, eh. Well, perhaps.

Or is it more like a massing, bits and pieces of life, history, ideas, unknowns, flocking together until we see a picture, a resemblance, and we recognise it?

Take this image of a starling murmuration.[1] This photograph was taken in South London in 2058. What do you see?

1 Image restricted by copyright.

Come on, it's not hard, is it? Yes, to our human eyes, there's the very obvious shape of a stag's head. The starlings won't see it that way, but we do. We can't help ourselves.

Today, we're looking at the horned god, that stag's head in all our minds; indelible, innate, whatever nonsense you think of him, he's our example and I promise you that, once you know the murmuration is made up of individual starlings, it doesn't fall apart, or disappear. In fact, it's more marvellous than ever.

So: origins. There are a lot, let's just say, and we can't get right back, but we've got documents from the twelfth century that are quite sarcastic about certain leaders of the Wild Hunt.[2] Because that's what he was, in those days. King Herla is one singularly silly story about a visit to an elfin wedding that goes on for two hundred years, and includes an unfortunate goody bag for the guests.[3] We don't need the details here. They're not important. What's important is that, even in 1100-and-something, some people really didn't take that story seriously.

But Herla is one starling. His flock mates are quite similar – starlings being mostly sexually monomorphic. We get Odin, leader of the Wild Hunt; Hellekin, leader of the Wild Hunt; Herne, leader of the Wild Hunt; Ellerkonge, leader of the Wild Hunt; Erl-king, Herlequin, the whole *Familia Herlechini*, a kind of ancient, grisly mafia. And some get taken more seriously than others.

---

2 See Walter Map's *De nugis curialium*, tr. M. R. James, *Cymmrodorion Record Series* no. 9, 1923.

3 See *The True Annals of Fairy Land in the Reign of King Herla*, ed. William Canton, London: J. M. Dent; New York: E. P. Dutton, 1900.

Why a Wild Hunt in the first place? Any ideas? Well, yes, this Herne, Herla, Hellekin is a psychopomp, he's fear of death, out there in the storm, coming to get you, but he's not a bogeyman. Because he's a bit sexy too, isn't he? He's irresistible, he's fast and loud and dark and handsome, probably. If you've got to die, then what a way to go, whisked off on a thundering horse to the underworld by the man of your dreams. Or nightmares. The mafia used to be romanticised for the same reasons, eh.

So, they're the same, but different. Herne got the horns, for one. He's got a phallic head start on the others, and perhaps that's why his story went the way it did.[4] Because he wasn't cuckolded, but he was humiliated, wasn't he? It's there in the origin story when he loses, not a faithful spouse, but his skill. And he does sacrifice loyalty, when you think about it. But then, he demands it back. Perhaps that's the beginning of our ambivalence, right there, because who likes being told what to do? Perhaps that's the very first crack, the start of the psychological splitting, built right into the birth of Herne the Hunter?

Of course it is. But let's pretend you concluded that yourself.

As well as horns, Herne also gets a nemesis. What do we think of Bearman? A magician with a grudge. Is that an archetype, do you think? But Herne's been getting frisky with Bearman's daughter, or so the tales lead us to believe,[5] and we might sympathise with him – or at least the parents

---

4 See Chapter 1: Herne the Hunter.

5 See Chapter 2: Overheard in a Greenwood.

among us might. Herne is a threat Bearman wants to control. It's all about power, and that feels, I dare say, pretty natural when it comes to your offspring. The stakes are high: not just his daughter's chastity, but his own dignity.

We know how that goes. Power, control, wielded in anger, are soon out of his hands. But it means Herne has a context. He has an enemy, an opposite. If they had sat down and sorted it out over a jug of mead, Herne might be entirely forgotten by now, an amusing footnote in our mythic history.

Conversely, he is everywhere. He permeates both reality and the imagination, for we filter the former through the latter, and whatever takes up residence in your head shapes the perceptions that pop in to join it. We can see him in the name for a moth, or a mushroom. His template becomes an original; he seems to stand outside of, or before, culture as we know it. And when he does not fit into newer, flashier forms of enchantment, it's easy, from this vantage point, to see Herne as more fundamental, more essential.

The Shakespearian forest, with its fluttery fairies,[6] the Renaissance flirtation with nymphs, fauns, and deities of this, that and the other, is a good example.[7] It's not the omnipresent fantastical that's the problem. It's the rules. Herne, as a concept, can interact, but he can't have a compatible role. He's a bull in a china shop.

Tighten your societal rules, tighten them too far, and even small transgressions become not just disobedient, but devilish.[8]

---

6 See W. Shakespeare, *A Midsummer Night's Dream.*

7 See Chapter 3: Venery.

8 See Chapter 4: Lord of Misrule.

Ah, the Devil.[9] Another original; he was bound to come up. And a hellboy with horns, eh? A little bit sexy, gets all the best lines, suits, parties, songs, et cetera. What's the difference, then, between Herne and the Devil? Anyone got a succinct rundown?

Intention. Nicely put. If the Devil makes mischief, there is always malice in it. There can't not be, or he wouldn't be the Devil. But Herne – he might be a rebel with a cause, he might kiss the girls and make them cry, but his mischief has joy in it. Until it goes wrong, but we'll come to that.

Did you know that, in 1645, the Puritans in England succeeded in cancelling Christmas? I say succeeded, but there were rebellions, riots, folk got so angry they killed each other over it.[10] They needed their holiday, even if the 'holy' part of that word was less precious to them than a couple of weeks of getting wasted, gambling, carousing, doing everything that, for the rest of the tiresome year, was against the rules. Take away freedom to make mischief, and what do you get? All hell breaks loose.

That hairline crack, which is inside Herne and his myth, widens. He splits, becoming a hero to some, a villain to others. There aren't many opportunities to be a bit of both, when the world conflates mischief with wickedness. It's tricky to remain neither fully dark nor noon bright. Herne is dusky, dangerous and alluring, and where can he keep that up?

The forest is a good place to hang out. Here be outlaws, in the half-light. The highwaymen, those inappropriate

---

9 See R. Lowe Thompson, *The History of the Devil – the Horned God of the West – Magic and Worship*, London: Kegan Paul, Trench, Trubner & Co., Ltd, 1929.

10 See *Canterbury Christmas*, London: Humphrey Harward, 1647.

romantic heroes of their day, had plenty of chances to let off steam, to be dangerous, even lethal, yet adored.[11] So, it's no surprise to find a certain Oberon, especially when we recognise the resonances of that name, turning up to break hearts in ballads of the late 1600s.[12] Attention-seeking behaviour on the part of Herne, including some preposterous flourishes, but that's what happens, isn't it, when someone is ignored? They play up, lash out and, sure enough, get punished.

People who are ignored might start trying on different hats, to see what catches our eye. We've all known someone who cracks jokes, or tries to shock, becomes flamboyant or outrageous or downright unpleasant when things aren't going their way, the mood has shifted, the times have changed. They try to become someone else. There's that psychological splitting again.

All these starlings in that flock, each with their own unique markings, and yet, from here, we see only the stag's head. Art, history, myth, have zoomed in on every one of them at some point, led our eye to a bright beak here, a breast feather there. But the stag's head, there in the photograph, hovers over the Great North Wood. This is Herne's territory. He's embedded, entwined, here. Even as his own myth is sidelined, he's there in the stories of others, claiming their fame, preening at the edge of the flock. The famous singer Ann Catley,[13] and her disastrous connection with the

---

11 See Charles George Harper, *Half-hours with the Highwaymen: picturesque biographies and traditions of the 'knights of the road'*, London: Chapman & Hall, 1908.

12 See Chapter 5: Gallows Green.

13 See Anon, *The Life of Miss Ann Catley*, London, 1888.

aristocrat Sir Francis Blake Delaval, is a case in point.[14] We see a wild child in Ann Catley; up pops a wild progenitor.

What happens when a myth fades? Who knows how many we've lost entirely, back in those pesky mists of time. There's always those good old revivalists, though they do have a tendency to mangle what they dig up, eh. A myth can fade for lots of reasons. It might simply not be needed any longer by the human spirit. This isn't a theory I favour. The human spirit is unreliable and does not always look in the right places. We get distracted, beglamoured by the new, swayed by the promises of progress. There have been plenty of times when we've forgotten that we can believe many things at once, that things are not black and white, that if one thing is right it doesn't follow that another is wrong.

Progress. Is it the enemy of myth? It's certainly looked that way, sometimes, hasn't it? Progress is a slippery concept, though. It's all about context. At times, in our recent history, progress has been industrial, it has been built, scaled up, manufactured, homogenised. Progress has been steel and coal, in place of straw and wood. But it has also been scientific, empirical, analytic. We've had a good tidy-up, in our little human heads. We've declared ourselves enlightened, by which we really meant that our new religion was science. I'm being provocative – well spotted – but there's a connection. It's easy to believe that either one of those systems has all the answers, which means there are none to be found elsewhere. The magical is deemed merely mystical, and what image does the word 'mystic' conjure up? A silly one.

---

14 See Chapter 6: The Erl-king's Daughter.

When the world splits myth from science, you, like Herne, might lose a sense of who you are. If nobody thinks of you as 'real' in the same way that, say, tables and chairs are real, then where, in space and time, are you? Here comes progress, looking an awful lot like your old friend Bearman, and what is he up to now? Chopping up the wood, razing it for lovely new brick houses where everything is warm and dry and rooms have right angles.[15] You might well be disenchanted.[16] The enclosures were a literal snatching of common land, yes. But by doing away with those liberal spaces, declaring ownership, shrinking the wild, they did much the same to thought.

How does myth swerve mysticism and accommodate science? How can it fight back? Our starlings are strategic flyers. Intelligent birds, they can change tactics as the world demands. One of my personal favourites in this stag's-head murmuration is Harlequin – you can see the spots he shares with Hellekin, Herlequin, that old *Familia Herlechini*.[17] Juicy genes for a pantomime star, eh? But make yourself a syndrome, named after a doughty Royal Society member,[18] and who can argue with your reality, even as a hallucination? A small victory, since a laboratory never was built in the Great North Wood. Herne's territory, shrunk to fragments and slashed by more than one railway line, persisted.[19]

---

15 See Chapter 7: Dendrologia.

16 See *The Life of Samuel Matthews, the Norwood Hermit*, London: Harrild & Billing, 1803.

17 See Martin Rühlemann, *Etymologie des wortes harlequin und verwandter wörter*, Halle, a.S.: Buchdruckerei Hohmann, 1912.

18 See Charles Bonnet, *Essai Analytique sur les facultés de l'âme*, Copenhagen: Philibert, 1760.

19 See Chapter 9: Nullius in Verba.

We encounter Herne's hand once more in the great fire at the Crystal Palace;[20] a disaster, in the eyes of many, of mythic proportions.[21] The place sounds ghastly to me, full of milling Victorians eyeing each other while exotic animals languished in their grotty prisons. And yet neither this triumph, nor the much smaller one related in the diaries of Walter Ship, seems to have done anything to restore Herne the Hunter to the status he desired, deserved, and eventually regained. What is going on, in this battle of myth and reality? He beats Bearman, or Bergmann, or Buckman, here and there, at the progress game. He even tries the old gimmicky magic, invokes some nymphs, another preposterous flourish. When someone crosses the boundary – with the help of LSD, say – he might pop up.[22] But the wood does not grow. Herne is ever more obscure.

This is his crisis point, and every myth has one. It's that moment in the row when you've tried to be nice, you've tried seduction, sabotage, sedition, and now you're at your wits' end. You fly off the handle, you smash the prized casserole dish against the wall, accidentally wrecking your favourite painting in the process, and you storm out of the house, forgetting your keys.

Let's return to that crack, in Herne's very being. It's a crack that exists in all of us, or we may see it that way thanks to Herne. If we have room, literally and metaphorically, to be less than perfect, less than pious, if we have room to be naughty, risky, daring, reckless even, then things are looking good. We might

20 See Chapter 10: Obedient Magic.

21 See Alison Edwards and Keith Wyncoll, *The Crystal Palace is on Fire!*, London: Crystal Palace Foundation, 1986

22 See Chapter 11: Nymphs.

not take that opportunity, but knowing we can if we want to, need to, makes us feel free. Make noise, let rip, indulge; or simply laze, ignore, give up. Whatever you like. But if I say you can't, mustn't, whatever your choice, or you will be cast out, how do you feel? What if I take away your pub, or your dance hall, your park, your lounge, your toys? Tell you they are not safe, and neither are you, so that's it, no more?

If you've ever done this to a child, you'll know what happens. But adults can have tantrums; they're just more likely to cause serious harm. Squeeze any of you enough, and you'll either harm yourself, or others, or both. When that crack spreads, and the horned god splits off, no longer accommodated by the self, the world, then he's a force to be reckoned with.

I'm sure none of you remember the Great Storm of 1987, but it was one hell of a tantrum.[23] Just as stupid as a real one, because it was nature that suffered in the short term, especially the woods.[24] But it got our attention. I don't think many people had ever felt sorry for a tree, until the day after that storm, so that was a start, eh.

Nature. A topic we've hardly needed to touch on here, since Herne is of the Great North Wood, or we might say, is the Great North Wood, in some sense at least. Without it, where is he? What is he? Poor old nature has been a victim of human progress, a lot of the time. Power, control, warm dry right angles, have been at our fingertips in the Western world. But it's nice to have a bit of woodland on your doorstep, when

---

23 See Chapter 12: Hurlecane.

24 See C. Quine, 'Damage to trees and woodland in the storm of 15–16 October 1987', *Weather* 43(3), 1988.

you live in a city, isn't it? Something to boast about, especially at the start of the twenty-first century. Lots of learning opportunities for the kids, conservation projects for those so inclined, roll up your sleeves, get your hands dirty, count the last five frogs in your local pond and log it on a database. Stick a photo of a butterfly on social media. And when things start hotting up, a lovely spot for keeping cool. Nature as a resource: the name of the game.

It's not surprising that we don't see much of Herne during that period. Perhaps an idle kick at a passing human being now and then.[25] Nothing on the scale of the 1987 storm, but that must have been exhausting, even for a myth. It's hard not to infer shame, or even self-loathing, for the damage he caused, isn't it? We're only human. It takes a bit of time for us to hold our heads up high again, after a full-scale meltdown. And we had cleared up the mess for him, even if we did a bad job of it. But we were at peak progress by this time. The wonders of technology held us in their thrall. A nice bit of woodland was all very well, but not many of us really cared until we fell into the climate hole we'd been digging for ourselves, like nine billion idiots. Most of us were busy trying to keep cool, or warm, or dry, or irrigated. There were a few, though, weren't there, those tunnel-dwellers in the 2040s, who could sense something was missing.[26] But even they turned to the old myths, with their antique script and Celtic battle cries.[27]

---

25 See Chapter 13: 'One morn I miss'd him on the custom'd hill'.

26 See Chapter 14: Hooligans.

27 See John-Paul Patton, *The Poet's Ogam: A Living Magical Tradition*, Belfast: Lulu, 2011.

Myth is an opportunist. It's there waiting for us, and when we need it most, someone will finally notice it. And it seems obvious, from here, that if you restore the wood, you restore Herne,[28] but it took everyone by surprise. Boy, did it. Or I should say girl, because here came Herndon, the latest starling to join our flock.

Myth can become what we need it to be. The old need hadn't gone away: for freedom, for room to make mischief, let off steam, break a few rules or ditch them altogether. But with Herndon, we got a refresh. We could accept her. Does this mean the Herne of old was now old-fashioned? A bit of history we'd rather forget? Was Herne a reformed character, in the shape of Herndon, with nice shiny up-to-date values, or was this just a way of getting our attention, using our love of the new?

There are certainly new details, in this new myth. As well as some old ones – who doesn't love a child raised by wolves, eh? A bit of authenticity borrowed from Romulus and Remus,[29] a family secret, a reunion? But crucially, that crack at the centre of Herne has moved. Herndon, as delightfully loopy as she is, is already half of something. The crack is not at her centre, but at her edge. We might imagine she could feel it, that loss, the missing twin sister. Perhaps that's what drove her to sing, a kind of calling out. And we might interpret the myth by saying that her singing did summon Rollo,[30] that she succeeded in closing the crack, making a whole. But

---

28 See Chapter 15: Restoration.

29 See *The Roman Antiquities of Dionysius of Halicarnassus*, Loeb Classical Library, Cambridge, MA: Harvard University Press, 1937.

30 See Chapter 16: Horn Dance.

a whole that is made of a pair is still two things. It is a whole that may safely move apart and together again, but to be at its best, each half must know, and acknowledge, the other.

So, in Herndon, and Rollo, we have a new archetype. In their birth, there in the Great North Wood, the birth of a new myth that extends an old one. We still have our horned god, if you like, and it's true to say that Herndon and Rollo embody many ancient ideas, just given new outfits – a grey T-shirt and charcoal Kevlar, to be precise. We can be Rollo, and make room for Herndon, or vice versa. A Rollo can, when she is in the mood, embrace the storybook enchantment of friendly wolves, a forest den, the romance of songs sung for the world. A Herndon can, when life calls for it, enjoy the practical advantages of technology, to learn, to explore, to find the edges of her world and expand it.

Yes, myth is an opportunist. Myth can become what we need it to be. That murmuration can welcome hundreds, thousands more starlings into its midst, and still, from here, we will see a stag's head. We can zoom in, zoom out, the shape will persist, and inside our own heads, that shape will continue to influence how we see ourselves and our world. No one starling is progenitor of all the others. The one called Herndon is not daughter of them all. This photograph captures them in one moment, and if we had the video, we could watch that stag's head dissolve and re-form, dissolve and re-form, each time our mind's eye helping it on its way to meaning. They are mischievous birds, eh.

You can still watch the starlings above the Great North Wood. And there will never be a lecture on how the Herne myth dies, because it won't. That's my prediction for humankind, for as long as we last. So, go forth and be mischievous, do no harm if you can help it, make room for your wild Herndon and your serious Rollo, and remember, if you feel that crack start to widen and hurt, pay attention. Remember the myth. Remember your imagination shapes your reality. Enchantment is a state of mind, but that's another lecture, so you'll have to wait until next week. That's all, folks.

Now the high one's songs are sung.
Hail to those who sing them!

ACKNOWLEDGEMENTS

Thank you to my brilliant agent, Lucy Luck, my wonderful editor Allegra Le Fanu, and my fabulous managing editor, Lauren Whybrow, who have all been so generous with their ideas and enthusiasm for this book.

Thank you to SJ Forder, copy-editor supreme, for seeing both the wood and the trees.

Thank you to Marsha Swan, brave typesetter.

Thank you to Emily Faccini for her glorious maps.

Thank you to David Mann for his gorgeous cover design.

Thank you to Adam Marek for reading, listening, and talking about it all, so many times.

Thank you to Daniel Greenwood and Chris Schüler for sharing knowledge and maps of the wood with me.

Thank you to the Great North Wood, especially the fragments now known as Sydenham Hill and Dulwich Woods, for providing a beloved roost for my imagination.

Many other books informed this one, in different ways. Especially useful were: *Norwood and Dulwich: Past and Present* by Allan Galer; *The Crystal Palace is on Fire!* by Alison Edwards and Keith Wyncoll; *The Life of Samuel Matthews, the Norwood Hermit*; *The Life of Miss Ann Catley*; *Kalendarium Hortense* by John Evelyn; *Nature is my Hobby* by C. V. A. Adams; *Canterbury Christmas*; *Comus* libretto by John Dalton. With thanks also to William Blake, John Keats, Thomas Gray, Vaughan Williams and Thomas Hardy.

Also available by Zoe Gilbert

Folk

Longlisted for the 2019 International Dylan Thomas Prize

On the remote island of Neverness, the villagers' lives are entwined with nature: its enchantments, seductions and dangers. There is May, the young fiddler who seeks her musical spirit; Madden Lightfoot, who flies with red kites; and Verlyn Webbe, born with a wing for an arm. Over the course of a generation, their desires, gossip and heartbreak interweave to create a staggeringly original world, crackling with echoes of ancient folklore.

'That rare thing: genuinely unique' *Observer*

'*Folk* is a special book: immersive and dripping with life, each story a spell, an allegory, a dark, smoky poem divined from the landscape of our ancient kingdom … It reads like a dream that, once visited, is difficult to leave behind' Benjamin Myers, *Guardian*

'Will win you over ... Magical' *The Times*

'Absolutely stunning. I loved it' Madeline Miller

'An extraordinary debut novel, drawing on deep seams of myth and folklore – and strikingly contemporary, pushing at the edges of what we mean when we call a book a novel … A thing of strange and enduring beauty' Alex Preston, *Financial Times*

Order your copy:

By phone: +44 (0) 1256 302 699
By email: direct@macmillan.co.uk
Delivery is usually 3–5 working days.
Free postage and packaging for orders over £20.
Online: www.bloomsbury.com/bookshop
Prices and availability subject to change without notice.
bloomsbury.com/author/zoe-gilbert